Villa Fortuna

Cat Gardiner

Villa Fortuna

Copyright © 2015 by Cat Gardiner
Publisher: Vanity & Pride Press
ISBN-13: 978-1517552626
ISBN-10: 1517552621

This is a work of fiction. Names, characters, places, brands, media, and incidents are either the product of the author's imagination or are used fictitiously. Any resemblance to actual events, locales, organizations, businesses, or persons, living or dead, is entirely coincidental. In no way is the author's intent to demean, ridicule, or insult the Italian people or their expressive culture. In fact, it is the love of her family's heritage that strives to share its beauty with a touch of humor.

Cover Design and Format: JD Smith Design
Editor: Kristi Rawley

Acknowledgements

Mamma mia what a blessed gal I am to be surrounded by incredibly gifted women with generous hearts. To my BFF Sheryl, whose sisterly friendship gives me confidence to write what's in my heart. She is my rock and the word girl who makes my novels—and life—so much richer with her talent and love. I love you, girl! To Geri and Kristi, two lovely friends who have given so much to *Villa Fortuna* by editing, tweaking, and advising with their expertise and humor to deliver the best story I can. Special thanks go to my Facebook *famiglia* of friends, who have encouraged and fed me with brownies, smiles, and inspirational images for the muse. Thank you Maria Rizzo-Pagano for recipe contribution. To Bill, my *innamorato,* you make everyday *la dolce vita,* darling. To Pamela—my partner in crime and talented author—dear friend, you inspire me to be better. Your support and friendship I deeply cherish! Here's to looking forward to 2016 and God's blessing upon Vanity & Pride Press. Finally, a big hug of appreciation to you, dear reader, for all your continued support and excitement this past year of publishing! I couldn't do it without you.

Dedicated to

My Italian mamma and Italian-by-marriage papa
60 years of passionate communication
and wedded bliss

Author's Note

During the Great Depression, in 1932, the Great Rent Strike War began in a small section of the Bronx Borough of New York City. Activist protests took place rioting for rent reductions because the suffering economy left many unable to pay their rent, some just unwilling. Resistance against eviction increased by both violence and withholding of rents until finally in 1936, New York City organized its first tenant federation. This began rent control and low-income/low-rent housing. Eviction guidelines became much more stringent on the landlord.

Such was the situation my great-grandfather found himself on one winter night. Having built his family home in the Bronx in 1902, three generations lived within. When hard times came, he took in a tenant on the first floor of the two-story home. My family moved to the second floor. "An evil family, who tormented our lives," my father recalled. Thus, my great-grandfather, over a drink with a lady friend concocted a plan for eviction of the tenant family.

In order to remove a tenant, the owner needed to state that he was to take occupancy himself. But, my great-grandfather already lived in the house! What was a man to do? Chapter Three will tell you how my family's "Villa Fortuna" slipped from our hands in the blink of an eye.

So I guess I should thank my great-grandfather for the plot bunny that began it all.

~One~
Morte
(Death)

Flashbacks of her painful divorce from Frankie Puppino hovered behind Regina Clemente's deep blue eyes as she mindlessly stared down on the gridlocked traffic crowding 6th Avenue in Manhattan. Neither the dark mahogany paneling nor the discreet scent of the expensive Italian leather seating within her immediate surroundings could quell the anxiety she felt.

She didn't feel comfortable with lawyers, but today's unwelcome meeting was necessary. Her last *necessary* interaction with a lawyer had been the year prior. That meeting, with her divorce attorney, was when she'd finally kicked the cheating bastard she had once considered her beloved husband to the curb. She must have been delusional.

Admittedly, her sister Elizabeth had been right to caution her about marrying an Italian-American man, but the blanket warning felt like an insult to their father, rest his soul. *He* certainly had never been a cheater like most of them. Besides, trusting people had always been Gina's nature. Just as she had done with other jerks in the past, placing her faith and giving her heart to Frankie came too easily.

For three years and four days of marriage, she had naïvely given him the benefit of the doubt. She'd have to work on that, but some habits were hard to break.

Watching the bumper-to-bumper traffic eight-stories below, Gina shook her blonde head and silently admitted that she had been foolish to believe, repeatedly, his lame excuses. Especially after discovering him bopping her manicurist, Tina, in the stockroom of the Puppino family sausage shop. She chuckled wryly. *The family profession should have been the first heads up to his philandering nature. Like father, like son. Puppino, Sr.'s sausage had had a mistress for ten years!*

Only one month after the Tina-escapade, Gina discovered a used "sausage casing" floating in their apartment's toilet bowl. That was when she promptly telephoned her intelligent, well-connected, middle sister, who immediately called her own divorce lawyer. His services had been required six years earlier. He, very skillfully and very legally, butchered Frankie's sausage into little tiny pieces of Pupperoni. The Frankie nightmare was finally over; her Ex was now living in his grandfather's basement on Mulberry Street in the "other" Little Italy downtown. Happy to close that chapter in her life, she immediately changed her name back to Clemente.

Elizabeth had given her so much to be thankful for, particularly for generously paying the full cost of said butchering. Going above and beyond sisterly affection, for the past year Elizabeth had been sending a much-needed support check each month 'cause, Gawd knows, Frankie "the *cazzo*" had no intention of doing so.

But all that drama wasn't why Gina was at this high-class attorney's office today. This visit was due to another type of death, that of a distant great-aunt (otherwise known as a prozia), her father's Aunt Maria. She was the proselytizing one who frowned upon divorces (good Catholic that she was) and was the only member of their Italian-American family born in the Old Country.

Attempting to affect a calm poise, sitting with lady-like posture in the reception area of one of New York's top legal firms, Gina awaited Elizabeth's arrival. A little over a year had passed since they last saw each other and she wanted to make a good impression—one that announced, "Look at me, I landed on my two feet, and I'm doing fine on my own—I got my shit together after the jerk played me, and you don't need to send me money any more. The *cazzo* is finally paying me alimony!"

She had a new hairstyle and a new dress found on sale at Principessa Boutique, which coordinated very nicely with her imitation Versace watch.

"Your sister's flight must be delayed," the attractive legal assistant stated in Italian as she placed a glass of Lurisia spring water on the table beside her client.

Gina replied in fluent Italian. "Yes. Either that or she hit traffic. It's terrible out there. She was supposed to be on the red eye out of LA yesterday, but her job is very demanding."

"Yes, that's right. She's a physician."

"Not just any physician. Lizzy is a physician to the stars!"

"How exciting. Is she a cardiologist or a plastic surgeon?"

"Neither. She's a podiatrist."

Gina recognized the usual glazed-over look and requisite polite head nod whenever anyone heard "podiatrist" as if Elizabeth wasn't a "real" doctor.

"Oh, I see," was all the woman said.

Although extremely proud that Elizabeth had become the first—in fact the only—doctor ever, in the Clemente family, Gina changed the subject. "I hope we're not any trouble to Mr. Carpo. I'm sure he has other appointments following ours."

"It is no trouble at all. He has cleared his calendar for the afternoon. As it is Friday, Signor Carpo will be leaving early for the Jersey Shore with his family."

An easy smile, as pleasant as her characteristic demeanor, spread upon Gina's lips. "Your hairstyle is lovely."

The assistant ran her fingers through the bottom tendrils of her raven locks. "Thank you. I have a personal stylist in Rome, and given all the travel that Mr. Carpo and I do back and forth, he always accommodates me upon my arrival."

"Well, if you are ever in need and can't get to Italy, you should come to see me up on Arthur Avenue—in Belmont. I'm a hairdresser at Capelli Belli."

The woman tried not to look aghast at the pretty blonde before her, but honestly, no self-respecting Milanese woman of means would be caught dead visiting *that* section of the Bronx, let alone for a "big" haircut. Belmont was where many stereotypical New York City Italians had laid down roots. Their butchered accent and local dialect made her hair stand on end, an insult to the romance language and its native diction.

Thankfully, the elevator dinged behind them, interrupting their conversation.

Gina beamed bright when Elizabeth entered the lobby with that air of confident sophistication she always wore. Tall and absolutely gorgeous with cascading chestnut waves, she visually embodied Hollywood glamour right down to her very cool, and most likely, expensive leather sandals. Even that natural, black beauty mark on her cheek was perfectly situated. The colorful, pencil skirt with a lacy, yellow top ensemble made quite an entrance—as though summer sunshine and a sea of flowers suddenly had burst into the staid professional decor. No doubt, it was a designer label. With that high salary Elizabeth made, she would never buy off the rack. Her sister had a "wow" factor that drew every man, woman, and child directly to her—and the money to do it in style.

"Lizzy!"

Long, tanned legs crossed the parquet floor into the waiting room, where Gina nearly ran into Elizabeth's arms; they clung to each other in an affectionate embrace.

"I was so worried. You're so late."

Before kissing both cheeks, Elizabeth whispered into her sister's ear. "Please, please, it's Elizabeth in public, not Lizzy."

"Oops. I forgot. Sorry, *Lizzy*. Why are you so late?"

"Didn't you get my text?"

"No. I didn't think to look at my phone. I have it on mute. What happened?"

"Nothing important, just an emergency Cinderella bunionectomy before next month's wedding of a B-lister actress. Apparently, her diamond encrusted bridal stilettos were causing pain." Elizabeth rolled her dark eyes. "I'm so over these narcissistic people, Gina."

"Good. Move home and open a practice here."

"Not on your life. Neither heaven nor hell could make me move back to the Bronx."

It was bad enough she would be staying for two days at the apartment Gina shared with their younger sister. No, she would never return home for good. Thirteen years ago she left the Bronx for a new life: college, medical school, residency, and then finally her first professional position. She was an entirely different woman now, or at least trying to be. Fitting in and gaining respect in a male dominated professional environment was tough. Los Angeles wasn't what she expected, but she was determined to make something of herself for the sake of her family and their never-ending bad luck. And if, in the process, she could make a difference helping people to walk pain-free, so much the better.

A tender smile spread across Elizabeth's lips as she touched her older sister's fair locks. "I missed you so much, sis."

"I missed you, too."

She scanned Gina up and down with an appreciative eye. The change in her appearance was impressive—her sister looked more mature and put together than when she'd last seen her. Gone were the hot pink lipstick and the way-too-tight fashion disasters. Even her hair had toned down, no longer looking like a Mob wife from the *wrong* side of Arthur Avenue. Instead, she appeared her thirty years—naturally beautiful, more sophisticated, and with a head on her shoulders not teased a mile high.

"You look great, sis."

"Thanks. I feel awesome. I'm really happy since I dumped Frankie."

"I'm glad and so proud of you. You deserve better—better than those creeps from that neighborhood, and better than that cheesy beauty parlor you're working at, too. You and Nicki need to move out to the West Coast with me. Make a new start."

"No, I love my little section of the Bronx. It's home and I'll never leave. I'd go through cannoli withdrawal."

The sisters laughed as Elizabeth scanned the waiting room. "Where is Nicki?"

"Atlantic City."

"Didn't you tell her how important this is? A will only gets read once, and she's obviously in it."

"I told her, but you know how headstrong she is. She's trying to be a responsible adult by getting a job at Bally's for the summer."

"As what?"

"Anything she can find. After all, it's not like she has a ton of options with only twelve credits finished toward an Associate's Degree in Liberal Arts." She snorted. "Well, I suppose that's probably better than my degree in cosmetology."

"Big difference—you have a trade and a hard-won degree. Don't demean it. She won't make any money waiting tables, and she's certainly not qualified to be a croupier. Atlantic City is a passé, dying town, but Vegas on the other hand …"

Still speaking in Italian, the legal assistant interrupted their reunion.

"Mrs. Fairchild, I'm Antonia Donato. It is a pleasure to meet you."

"*Doctor* Fairchild," Gina interrupted.

"Of course. I'm sorry. Doctor Fairchild."

They shook hands and Elizabeth replied in English. "It's nice to meet you, Ms. Donato. I'm sorry to be so delayed."

"It is no problem at all. Did Mr. Fairchild accompany you?"

Elizabeth chortled. "There hasn't been a Mr. Fairchild since my second year of med school. It's just Regina and me today. Our younger sister, Nichole, is on a job interview. Is there someplace I can stash my suitcase?" Elizabeth looked toward the outer door where her rolling case had been abandoned when she'd entered.

"Mr. Carpo is ready to begin. I will place your luggage into the closet here and then, if you ladies will please follow me."

The two sisters clasped hands as they followed the legal assistant down a long hallway lined with paintings depicting the Italian countryside. Three sets of high heels clicked on the flooring until they finally entered a small conference room. A wide screen television hung against a wall beyond the round table where water bottles and three crystal rocks glasses were displayed. A small tray of powder dusted Italian cookies caused Gina's stomach to growl.

"Please have a seat and I will inform Mr. Carpo that you are ready for the reading of Mrs. Dixon's will. Can I get either of you a cappuccino or an espresso?"

"No, thank you," they said at the same time.

As soon as the door closed, the sisters promptly jumped into speculation. "I don't mean to sound so greedy and, of course, I am saddened by her passing, but what do you think Aunt Maria left us?" asked Gina.

"She didn't have much that I know of. It's probably a rosary or two. Maybe that statue of the Madonna she loved so much."

"Maybe it's those chapel veils she wore to church all the time. I know … maybe those holy cards of hers. She'd shuffle through them like a professional gambler, calling off each saint's name like she was playing pinochle."

"Who knows? I wouldn't be surprised if it was a country villa in Tuscany. It would be like her to have kept it hidden. Mamma always said that daddy's aunt had short arms, cheap woman that she was." Lizzy contracted her arms in close to her sides and wiggled her hands.

Gina burst out laughing. "Oh Gawd! Visions of T-rex! You're scaring me!" She promptly sobered then crossed herself as if blaspheming their dead great-aunt. An Italian *never* talked ill of the dead.

"Gina, it's pronounced God, G-o-d. There's no *A* or *W* in there. Please, control your accent. It makes us look like low class girls from the neighborhood."

"Stop being such a snob, Doc Hollywood. I *am* a girl from the neighborhood and proud of it! And, newsflash, you're a girl from the neighborhood, too."

Elizabeth gave her sister a smug look and a quick swipe of French manicured fingertips under her chin. They easily fell into their familiar playful banter.

"What I want to know—along with Mamma—is why Prozia didn't leave anything to her. She's Daddy's heir, the one that should inherit not us. Doesn't that strike you as odd?" asked Gina.

"Not really. I suppose she thought Mamma had enough religious articles in the house. You know they never got along—all the gossiping Mamma does. Anyway, maybe this is her way of attempting to bring the three of us back to the Church. She wasn't pleased with either of our divorces, and Nicki—well, *everyone* knows she's on a path to perdition."

The door to the conference room opened and in walked the gorgeous Mr. Carpo. Draped in expensive Italian suiting, exuding continental suave, he garnered the sisters' full attention immediately. One set of eyes riveted upon his hard bodied, trim form, and the other admired his Romanesque features—angular jaw, strong nose, and intense green eyes. The man was a forty-year old Roman god and Gina and Elizabeth instantly became worshipers at his altar of overworked, lonely women badly in need of a hot, uncomplicated booty call.

"*Buongiorno*, ladies." His sexy Italian accent washed over them like Frangelico liqueur.

Gina's jaw slacked.

"I'm-a so sorry for your loss. Your prozia was a wonderful, holy woman and her death saddens me greatly."

Elizabeth didn't hear a word he said, only *how* he said it, her dark eyes fixating on that subtle movement his tongue made when he licked his bottom lip after pronouncing the word "greatly." Suddenly sweltering, prickling heat climbed up Elizabeth's back; she cleared her throat then swallowed hard as Gina filled a glass with ice water then held it against the racing pulse in her neck.

"I appreciate your coming all the way into Manhattan as there are several documents that I need for you to sign, following Mrs. Dixon's Last Will and Testament video." He ran his hand through his wavy black hair and smiled politely, enjoying the attentive silent gaping of the two beauties seated before him, as they seemingly hung onto every word he spoke.

"Thank you, Mr. Carpo. I must confess that Regina and I are puzzled as to why we three sisters are the only ones to inherit from our aunt's estate. Especially me, since my falling out with Aunt Maria, when I was in med school, was deemed irreparable on her part. If she hadn't been such a devout Catholic, I near expected her to put the evil eye on me."

He laughed a deep sonorous sound that nearly burst Gina's ovaries.

"No, no, it is not like that at all, Dr. Fairchild. At the end, she was regretful for her harsh words to you. She later understood that the man you married was a no good non-Italiano, and she forgave you. You might say, her bequeath is her way of making amends. At ninety-two, she wanted to set things right. Shall we begin?"

Gina stammered, "Y-Yes…I'm ready. I was born ready."

Mr. Carpo depressed a button on his remote, which closed the blinds on the bright summer sun. Another button brought the flat screen to life. It wasn't just any flat screen. It was one of those super mack daddy, ultra, 4k high definition ones that Elizabeth desired. The looming image of her decrepit dear sweet great-aunt sitting in her bed, appeared as though she was about to get up, climb through the screen and smack her one with the back of her hand. *Maybe that TV isn't such a good idea after all.*

The dreamy lawyer sat beside Elizabeth, and she inhaled the scent of his BVulgari Man cologne. At least this was a heavenly way to begin what was sure to be a morbid video.

Maria Clemente Dixon took a breath from her oxygen mask, her light blue rosary beads wrapped around the fingers that held the apparatus to her mouth. She stopped, then primped her thin white hair one last time before addressing the camera. In her most pitiful voice, she spoke with her thick Italian accent.

"*O Madonna mia*, this is the end, but have faith, my nieces, that I will be reborn with our Lord … Death will find me … alive with a clear conscience that I did not go to the grave with unforgiveness on my soul. St. Dominic, St. Anthony, Santa Lucia, St. Michael and the Archangels will escort me home." She blessed herself, kissing her pinched fingers afterward, raising them up to heaven.

Gina and Elizabeth looked at each other and rolled their eyes. Their overly pious great-aunt had always been melodramatic.

"Regina, Elizabeth, and Nichole, you will do well to heed your prozia's warning about gossiping, judging people too harshly, holding grudges. This is your mother's way and should not be yours. Also, the three of you are failing to reach your God-given potential—especially as wives and mothers. Two of you have already disappointed Him in that department …" She put her hands together in prayer to make her begging point "… Do not let these things become patterns in your lives. Without a wife by his side, a man cannot be blessed and without a good man to love and care for, a woman will never be content."

Elizabeth grabbed the remote from the table and, to Mr. Carpo's surprise, she paused the video. Her aunt's wrinkled image stilled with hands steepled in prayer, her mouth contorted between syllables.

"Is this video going to continue to insult my sister and me? Because, I assure you, we don't say the rosary or wear chapel veils. Nothing is worth this amount of Italian guilt."

"*Mi Scuzi*, but what does the rosary have to do with Mrs. Dixon's bequeath?"

"Isn't that what she is leaving to all of us?"

He chuckled, "No, but a rosary is a good thing. Yes?"

"Yes, of course it is. I'm sorry. Please continue with Sister Maria's holy mission of redemption." She handed him the remote and settled back into her chair, readying herself for more judgmental disapprobation. From the corner of her eye, she saw Gina cross herself, again. *Sheesh*.

"Regina, my Regina, you are the kindest, sweetest, most *affabile* of my great nieces, but you are also the most *stupido*. You have bad luck with men and the Holy Father will not grant you annulments if you continue to choose poorly. You have so much potential, but you allow the wrong men into your life. You should have been a nun, but you did not have the calling. Had my nephew Thomas's wife fostered your holiness then it would have been so. But it was not God's will. So, I leave to you the sum of one thousand dollars to get your marriage to Mr. Puppino annulled so that at least you can marry in the Church when your true love comes along."

Maria sighed, closed her eyes and blessed herself a second time.

"Nichole, you are the most wild of my nieces, but unless you learn to keep your legs closed and say 'no' you will find yourself burning in hell as a *puttana*, but I want you to know that your prozia never ceased in her prayers on bended knee for your chastity."

She raised her hand in front of her face and pinched her fingers together, rocking it in front of her. "Even a good man will not buy the cow when he can get the milk for free. Remember that. I leave you one thousand dollars for new clothes that fit you as a lady and not a street-walker. There! I said it!"

After a moment, she took another deep breath from her oxygen mask then adjusted herself in the bed. The camera zoomed in on her wan face. Gina and Elizabeth both hedged backward as the image came so close that the little wiry black and grey chin hairs could be seen from where they sat across the room. Gone was the pitiful, dying voice when Aunt Maria proclaimed,

"And last but not least is you, Elizabeth. You are intelligent and beautiful but in your endeavor to achieve success and perfection, you look for hairs in an egg and in doing so you will never find your *innamorato*. Divorce was sinful, but that is what you get for marrying outside of the faith. In running from your culture, you have run from who you really are—born Italiano, always Italiano. There is no escaping it or the family. You are a Clemente, just as I have always been and just as your prozio Dixon became by marriage. *Capisce?* Take heed my niece that I have prayed to St. Rita for you for many years. I have faith that you will return home with a good man, an Italian man. I leave you my rosary."

Elizabeth leaned forward onto the table, her slender fingers wrapped around the remote again. Aunt Maria's face stilled with her hand raised, the rosary exposed with the little crucifix hung frozen in the air. "You said she didn't leave me a rosary."

"*Scuzi*, Dr. Fairchild, but I said she wasn't leaving *all* of you rosaries. Let us continue." His warm, strong hand folded around hers and he retrieved the remote as he winked at her.

Here we go—another womanizing Italian man.

"But that is not the extent of my whole estate, and this is the reason

I have called you here to witness my signature upon my Last Will and Testament. I bequeath to you, the only remaining Clemente heirs, three equal shares of a very special piece of property, passed down from my father Tommaso Clemente. Since I do not have children and your father has passed …"

She blessed herself again.

"… it is now yours as well as the financial means to maintain it and pay taxes. It is a historic building in Westchester County's Downtown Etonville—not far from St. John's Church." She crossed herself again as though every saintly reference demanded it. "Mr. Carpo will cover the details with you but its current real estate value is two million dollars."

Gina nearly dropped her water glass onto the table.

Mr. Carpo turned to see the gaping expression of disbelief upon Elizabeth's face. "See, more than a rosary."

Maria continued, "Many have made me offers of immense fortune, but what is an old lady to do with such money? My riches are in heaven. This building is your great-grandfather's legacy, our Clemente family's ancestry and now it is yours. Do not be fooled by those who will try everything in their power to obtain it from you or spread lies about its ownership. They are unfounded! Beware, especially of that De Luca woman. She was once a Russo!" Maria spit on the floor, her lip curled, and she muttered something in Italian. After raising her fist in the air, she coughed and grabbed the oxygen mask.

The handsome Mr. Carpo appeared on the video holding a clipboard. He held out his pen and the clipboard to Maria who signed the will. The video went to black.

With a click of the remote, the blinds opened and sun streamed into the conference room. The lawyer stood tall and smiled at the shocked women.

"Did my aunt just call that woman 'the devil's whore?'" asked Gina, her chin nearly dropping to her chest in shock.

"It is nothing to worry about."

"What's a Russo?" Elizabeth asked.

"Not a what, a who. Just a family. Old wounds of long ago, but nothing important. Now let me go over the stipulations of your inheritance." He placed a legal document requiring their signature before them on the table.

"She didn't say anything about a stipulation. What type of *stipulation?*" Elizabeth raised a sculptured eyebrow. Suddenly, the temptation of a two million dollar piece of real estate in the upper crust village of Etonville was losing its appeal.

"It is nothing. Only the smallest of details, really." He held up a copy of Maria's instructions. "One—You may not sell Villa Fortuna. Two— You must go to confession and repent-a your sins, and Three—You can take occupancy *after* attending Holy Mass at least once a month for three consecutive months. See, easy."

"And if we don't agree? I mean, I don't know about you, Liz-er-Elizabeth, but I haven't been to church since I got married. I think it would burn to the ground if I stepped in it, especially after that night when—"

"Regina, stay on point." Elizabeth cut off her sister before inevitably, she embarrassed herself. "Well, Mr. Carpo, what happens if we don't go to confession or to church? As my sister said, it's been some time for both of us."

"Then the property gets donated to St. John's and you will be ... how do you say? ... shit out of luck ... and *mucho stupido*. The train does not pass two times."

~**~

~Two~
Famiglia
(Family)

There were some fates worse than death, Elizabeth concluded. For her, returning home to the Belmont section of the Bronx certainly qualified. She had silently chastised herself for not staying in a chilled, moderately priced hotel in Manhattan for the short two-day visit, but by the time she reached the second flight of stairs leading to Gina and Nicki's apartment, she reconciled that she loved her sisters and would value this fortuitous time together—in spite of the oppressive heat. It was August in New York, after all. This sort of "make you sweat like a pig" weather was expected. She forced herself to ignore that the cheap pleather Payless sandals pinched her feet on each step upward to the apartment above Messina Pastry Shop.

Elizabeth gripped the old wooden banister that was sorely in need of painting and continued to climb, attempting not to exhibit her shortness of breath as she carried her suitcase. It had been entirely too long since she lived the life of a city dweller and the required day-to-day exercise that the lifestyle demanded. Obviously, spin classes had no effect on her overall cardiovascular fitness.

"How many floors?" she asked as a trickling stream of perspiration rolled into her cleavage.

"Four," Gina called down with an almost devilish tease.

"Can I still smell the baked goods up there? You know that's the only perk making this building worthwhile."

"Sure. Mr. Primo keeps me filled."

"With pastry?"

Gina snorted. "Of course. Sometimes I help him in the shop when his son doesn't show up for work after a binge. He's seventy, you know."

"The son?"

"No, silly. Mr. Primo. The only things he fills these days are cream puffs and éclairs."

"What about the son?"

"Toni is forty. He likes to drink." Gina looked over her shoulder, whispering loudly. "I don't mean to gossip, but just to give you a heads up—he's a cross-dresser, but not in the bakery. That's Toni with an *i* and the only thing he fills is an A-cup. Poor Mr. Primo doesn't know."

Another flight up, another trickle of sweat, another topic. "Have you seen your deadbeat ex-husband?"

"Nope. Frankie slept with his father's mistress a couple months ago and was banished downtown to live with his grandfather."

"He's a slime ball."

"He has hardening of the arteries."

Elizabeth clung to the banister, pausing to catch her breath. "I'll say. One artery in particular—the bulbourethral gland artery."

"The what?"

"That's the main artery that runs from the corpus spongio … never mind. It makes a penis erect."

"I'm not talking about Frankie! His *grandfather* has a *heart* condition!"

"Oh. His grandfather probably has an overactive hardening of that *other* artery, too. They're all alike—born to flirt, seduce, and cheat."

A step up caused Elizabeth to bite her lip, trying to hold back a wince as she silently vowed to save some money for better shoes. "Speaking of losers, are you dating anyone?"

"No. There's no one new in the neighborhood. I've known and dated most of these guys since we were kids. How about you?"

"I don't have the time—or the inclination these days."

"Well, here we are. Home-sweet-home."

The black door in need of a fresh coat of paint matched the tired, well-worn condition of the building, which must have been about seventy years old. A tacky floral wreath with a little Italian flag tucked within the fake foliage hung over the peephole. She was sure she had seen a similar one on the floor below.

Gingerly, Elizabeth touched the fading pink edge of one artificial carnation. "Nice wreath," she commented, sarcastically.

"Shut up. Mrs. Genovese in 3A made it for us as a housewarming gift when we moved in. She's a lonely widow and makes us a tray of ziti every Sunday." Gina again whispered loudly (a common practice when it came to Italians voicing ailments) before sharing, "She has cataracts."

The door opened into a sunlit living room, and Elizabeth walked toward the two large windows lacking either shades or curtains. Just beyond the rain-streaked glass, she could see the black iron fire escape and thought God help them if there was a blaze. The apartment felt barely cooled by a window air conditioner that appeared ancient. Little strips of colorful fabric danced inward from the vent's lukewarm emission.

A requisite crucifix hung behind the sofa amidst a collection of black and white photographs of the family. Already, the fallen-away Catholic felt uncomfortable, unconsciously worrying the edge of her blouse.

Elizabeth turned her back on the arrangement of wall decorations and with an appraising eye of subtle disapproval mixed with a heavy dose of Tinseltown snobbery, assessed the tiny apartment. She tried hard to conceal her shock, thinking, *this is what my money goes toward while I'm living on the balls of my ass?* The five hundred dollars a month she sent her sisters should be put to better use than this rundown apartment. "How much do you pay for this place?"

"Sixteen hundred a month."

Her eyes widened. The four rooms—one being the kitchen that contained a cast iron bathtub along one wall—took only eight steps to traverse. Thankfully, living in a coldwater flat no longer meant the lack of hot water. However, the thought of bathing beside the old refrigerator had little appeal, and Elizabeth hated that her sisters had been doing so for the last twelve months.

"You're kidding, right?" she asked with a slight downturn to her lips.

"What's wrong?"

"Gina, there's a bathtub in the kitchen."

"That's not for bathing, silly. It's for décor … and other uses."

"What other uses could there possibly be?"

"Well…um…our next door neighbor, Mr. Graciosa uses the tub to make his wine. His got ripped out years ago when it sprang a leak flooding out Mrs. Zeppo, the cat lady, in the apartment below him. He's the reason Toni drinks too much. His family recipe will knock you on your ass."

"Geez. What's with you and all these people—the tenants in this building? Do you know everyone's business, and do they know yours? Don't you have any privacy?"

Gina looked offended, in fact, for Gina, she almost looked downright angry. "These *tenants* are family to Nicki and me. Look, you took that job in LA after your residency ended, and Mamma hasn't been back to New York since she moved south to live with Aunt Lucy. She didn't even come home for Aunt Maria's funeral! I had to send her a friggin' photograph of Prozia in the casket. I'm on my own now after Frankie's cheating. Everyone in this building loves Nicki and me. They care for us, and we care for them since both you and Mamma abandoned us after Daddy died."

Elizabeth gazed back at the photographs, acknowledging in the recesses of her heart that Gina was correct. She had been absent and, with their mother now living in Naples, ostensibly her sisters had no one—no one other than the residents of this close-knit Italian and Albanian neighborhood. Sending them money hardly took the place of the other things they needed—namely, family.

"I'm sorry. I don't mean to be such a snob, or to disapprove your life-style or your home. It's just so very different from mine, but that doesn't mean that you can't be happy here until something better comes along. I just thought that the money … well, never mind." She smiled wistfully, recognizing that she had hurt her sister's feelings. Gina's response was to grab the handle of the counterfeit Louis Vuitton suitcase followed by an abrupt change of subject.

"Nicki still has a twin bed, so you can sleep in my room. If, of course, you haven't decided to leave already."

"I'm not going anywhere, besides we have plans tomorrow to visit this Villa Fortuna building." *And it could be just the thing you need to get you out of this overpriced slum.*

They entered Gina's tiny bedroom where a double bed, draped in their grandmother's crocheted coverlet, took up the entire room. In a bizarre contrast to the Old World heirloom, a colorful piece of expensive look-ing abstract art, painted in blues and greens, hung above the bed.

"Great painting."

"Thanks. One of the stylists at the beauty shop is an artist. I call her Picasso. She has a real eye for color."

Elizabeth edged her way to the side of the bed, examining the composition as though she were an art aficionado. It was pretense, of course. She only had prints in her overpriced rental but, in her humble opinion, they appeared sophisticated and classy. "Does she sell her work?" she asked as they shifted direction back to the living room.

"Nah. Dharma paints for the love of it. She's real avant-ee gard-ee: blue streaked hair, tattoos, and a nose ring."

"Then what the heck is she doing working at Capelli Belli? Unless, she's the one responsible for all those blue-haired old ladies I remember from the Italian-American Social Club."

"Ha. Ha. I'll have you know that we are a fancy salon now, catering to some of the wealthiest women in Belmont." Gina grinned proudly. "We even do crystal microdermabrasion and waxing. That makes us almost a spa, Lizzy!"

Elizabeth grimaced, unable to resist the natural proclivity to see all things through her medically-minded obsessiveness. "The waxing I can see. That's a necessity in Little Italy, especially on the chin. But do you have a plastic surgeon, aesthetician, or a registered nurse at the salon for the microdermabrasion? That procedure should be done in a doctor's office. There are health risks and protocols. If not done properly it could be unsanitary, even dangerous. You could be sued, Gina!"

"Get a hold of yourself. We're not talking chemical peels. Mrs. Drago uses the machine in the break room. It's perfectly safe and the room looks beautiful. She even plays Mantovani on the CD player! You should stop by and see the set up."

"Oh, Lord. Mantovani? As in 1950s Italian orchestral music?"

"Yeah. It's great stuff, so peaceful."

"Oh, Gina. We need to get you out of there."

The apartment door slammed before Gina could reply, but Elizabeth noticed how the smile of pride upon her sister's face quickly receded when the imprudent words of disapproval were flung. Damn, this reunion wasn't going as planned.

"Yo, Lizzy! Gina!" Nicki called out.

The sisters turned. One resisted laughing and the other resisted crying at the sight before them. What was Nicki's attempt at professional attire had gone dreadfully awry. The skirt was too short, too clingy, and a color of yellow-orange that defied all sensibilities. The sheer white blouse was too low cut and appeared painfully tight. The matching jacket was too snug, its button straining as her breasts spilled above it. Yes, Prozia was correct. Nicki, with her jet black, mile-high hair, and mascara-clumped lashes did look like a streetwalker—on crack!

Elizabeth barely had time to sigh, let alone proclaim the necessary "oh my God" that the costume required. Instead, she bit her tongue; having already insulted (albeit unintentionally) one sister, she was not about to do the same to her other. Lord knows, that wild Nicki wouldn't take it as graciously as "should have been a nun" Gina, and would most likely give her kick in the gut with those freaky, platform stiletto shoes she was teetering on. All three sisters hugged at the narrow doorway threshold.

"I'm so happy you came home, Lizzy! You look awesome—very cool and very rich!"

"Well, she makes the big bucks now. Podiatrist to the stars!"

How could she tell her sisters that she wore knock offs? They were so proud of her, but the truth was that her salary barely was keeping the roof over her head after she paid her student loans and sent them their monthly check. The only indulgence she allowed herself was the membership fee at the fitness club, and that was because she was trying so hard to fit into the Los Angeles scene with all its über-fit, sculptured residents. She had an image to uphold, but how could she tell her beloved sisters that the lower a physician worked on the body, the lower the income potential? Neurosurgery paid the most, feet paid the least, and she, not only worked for a cheapskate, but was a lowly junior Associate to boot! It didn't take a brain surgeon to do the math—she was having a tough time making ends meet while trying to keep up appearances in the City of not-so Angels.

"Oh hardly stars, more like wanna-be's." *Like me.* "How did it go, Nicki? Did you get a job in AC?"

Five-foot-three and full of sass, Nicki made a raspberry sound with her lips and turned her back on her older sisters, strutting into the kitchen. "Yeah, I got offered a *job* when I was getting into my car in the parking lot, but I said no—even if the kind of job the creep wanted could probably have gotten me fifty smackas, tax-free."

"And an arrest for prostitution, not to mention herpes labialis," Elizabeth added.

Nicki reached into the refrigerator; its annoying hum filled the kitchen as she removed a can of Pepsi. With a pop to the top she said, "You know you really suck when the only job offer you get in Atlantic City is for a blow job. Had I not had my business suit on, I might have taken the asshole up on his offer for the gas money home.

"Speaking of money … what did Aunt Maria leave me? It betta be cash, 'cause I ain't usin' no rosary no matter if it was blessed by the Pope." With one hand impudently installed upon her hip, she took a long gulp of soda from the can clasped in her other.

Gina and Elizabeth broke into a fit of laughter at that last statement, and Elizabeth was happy to see that, for once, Gina hadn't felt the need to bless herself.

"She left you a thousand bucks to replace your 'business suit' with something a little more ladylike," Gina said, waving her hand in the direction of the straining jacket button.

"Figures, and who's going to oversee my purchases? You, Gina? Or Miss Hollywood here?"

"The dreamy, Roman god, Mr. Carpo, Prozia's attorney. Everything regarding our inheritances needs to be overseen and managed by him. It's a criteria." Gina nearly swooned at the thought.

"Where's the fun in that?"

"Oh, trust me, Sis. When you see him, you won't object in the least. The man is hotter than Mount Vesuvius. Lawd knows he almost made me erupt!"

"There's more. She also left us a building in Etonville. Gina and I are meeting Mr. Carpo up there tomorrow so that he can introduce us to the tenants and decide what to do with the empty storefront."

"A building? I thought Prozia had short arms, but she gave us a building? What the hell are we going to do with a building? Can we sell it—take the cash and go to Cancún on vacation? I need a real tan, none of this radiation crap."

Elizabeth slid the kitchen chair across the vinyl press and peel floor tiles. A mismatched one under the table caught the leg, and she tugged. Her thoughts drifted for a few seconds from the tempting plate of rainbow cookies in the center of the Formica table when she wondered if the flooring tiles were the asbestos type from the 1980s. She made a mental note to inquire about both her sisters' health. There could very well be mold in the apartment too. Refocused from her obsessing, she responded to her younger sister's split-second bid for instant gratification.

"No. We're not allowed to sell it. Trust me. This is a really good thing, Nicki. It's an investment in your future. If managed correctly, we may be able to get you two out of here and into a lucrative business up in Westchester County. With a yearly income already guaranteed by the two tenants, you may not have to consider dropping to your knees ever again."

Nicki laughed. "Say it, Lizzy."

"Say what?"

With exaggerated enunciation and a bodacious lip movement, Nicki said, "Bloww ... job ..."

"I'm not going to say that. It's vulgar."

"What about blow outs!" Gina blurted.

"Huh? What do you mean?"

"A hair salon! I've always wanted my own shop. Maybe we can open one up in the storefront. We could all work together and continue to live here."

"No. That's not possible. The point is to move you *out* of here and up near this Villa Fortuna place in the wealthy suburbs. That is why Prozia bequeathed it to us. I'm sure of it. Besides, I'm not leaving LA." Elizabeth looked around the kitchen, her glare settling on the discolored water stain on the ceiling. "This place is a health risk."

"It is not!" Gina folded her arms across her chest, and as best as Nicki could, she did as well. "I'm not leaving *here, Elizabeth*. I told you. I love everything about Belmont. I love the people and their freaky quirks. I love the festivals and how the Avenue comes alive with culture and faith, not to mention music. I love the freshly made food just beyond my doorstep where I only need to walk ten steps to the butcher or the fish store. The Italian retail market is reason alone to stay in Little Italy."

She waved her arms just as their mother did whenever she became passionate about her argument. "Mr. Andretti tips his fedora hat to me and Mrs. Dardani tries to teach me Albanian every time I come into her café. And yes, I even love it when Vinnie the Turtle whistles at me every time I walk by his father's pizzeria."

"Vinnie Balducci still lives in Belmont? Wow, what a loser. You didn't date him, too, did you?"

"Stop it! Don't forget, he was once your boyfriend, too!"

"I was ten, Gina."

"Whatever. You're from Belmont, too, and I'm not a loser because I stayed."

"I may be *from* here, but the key point being that I didn't *remain* here and don't pretend that you don't know why."

"I understand why you ran, and I understand why you're embarrassed by the neighborhood and the silly stereotype. Lawd knows those stupid reality TV shows about the boys from Belmont and Jersey Shore didn't help how people see Italian-Americans, but your family is here and we love you—and *we're* not losers," Gina stated plainly.

Elizabeth looked away, noticing the kitchen blessing plaque above the stove and then sighed, instantly feeling, once again, like a total judgmental idiot. "You're not a loser ... I'm sorry."

"Lizzy, I may not have a man around these days, but I'm happy here and I'm not moving, even if I am what people think I am."

"Yeah, what she said," Nicki declared, moving over to stand next to Gina, reinforcing their sisterly solidarity.

Elizabeth frowned, rubbing her temples. She couldn't help the rising thought that maybe, just maybe, she was a little jealous. Sure, they had different lives, but who was the happier—who was really the richer and felt the most accepted and comfortable in their surroundings? In the end, it wasn't about money or material possessions, not even about a professional career track. Was it?

She sighed, defeated by her "*stupido*" sister's intelligent argument and her own slowly emerging self-awareness. "Well, since you are both adamant, let's at least consider your idea of opening a salon in Etonville. What would you call it?"

Gina's defensive posturing turned on a dime and she clapped her hands, laughing with glee. "Oh Gawd! I've thought about this foreva, but maybe we can all put our heads together and come up with something ... something ... Italian!"

Lizzy looked to heaven and crossed herself. It was going to be a long two days, getting her sisters on their feet and headed in the *right* direction.

_~**~_

Doctor Michael Garin of Manhattan Aesthetic Associates (MAA) was known among the affluent strata of New York City as *the* cosmetic surgeon for everything from simple Botox or Radiesse injections to laser fillers and surgery-free facelifts. Following in his father's footsteps, he had built quite an esteemed reputation for himself in the advancement of body sculpting. So much so that the 4,106 friends of the "MAA Body Fan Club" on Facebook reverently referred to him as "Michelangelo." It was an abhorrent nickname on a social networking site he privately despised but acknowledged with a cool ambivalence since its creation this past year by one of his obsessed patients.

Bright blue eyes stared blankly at the sculpture on the 60th Street and Park Avenue mall beyond his office window. It was two in the afternoon and he was killing time between appointments. Actually, that's a lie. He was gathering strength and nerve, awaiting his next patient's arrival. She was a plastic addict, a Barbie Doll wanna-be, and he didn't quite know how to proceed because she was also his best friend's sister. Tenting his index fingers against his lips, he surveyed all his potential responses to her, banishing each one as they popped into his mind.

But you were a C-cup three months ago. I won't do it, not again. No, that wouldn't be effective.

You know that catwoman person? Well, you're headed in that direction and going to ruin my reputation in the process. I'm a dog person. That would be a mean, below-the-belt comment, though very tempting.

Blair, your lips will end up looking like your labia. No, that may be the look she's going for. He'd already tailored *those* lips to her specifications. Come to think of it, he almost backed out of that surgery, too. He shuddered at the remembrance of her labiaplasty.

You're beautiful enough. I refuse to make any more changes. No, she might take it as an invitation for dinner, or worse—sex. Surgical alteration of *that* area, with her under anesthesia, was the closest he'd ever go to laying his fingers to her flesh and, for the record and his own sensibilities, he had double gloved. Yet still, he was the one who had to live every day with the disturbing image burned onto his brain.

Mike shuddered again.

Every scenario he played in his mind seemed to draw the same expected, repeated conclusion—her manicured fingers flirtatiously running down his white lab coat with a coo of "I just have to have your hands on me." The recollection of her tug to his necktie, attempting to pull him onto her suddenly reclining form, made his flesh crawl and he resisted the compulsion to depress the antibacterial pump at the corner of his desk.

This was always the hard part of what he did—denying a patient their right to pay for surgical enhancement. At times such as this, he wished himself to be a greedy man or, more importantly, an atheist. His religiosity and conscience battled with a career in which he spent his days altering God's perfect creations with the slice of a scalpel all for vanity purposes.

"Doctor Garin, your grandmother is here to see you," Gwen, his assistant, announced over the speakerphone.

He gazed up to the ceiling thinking that this day couldn't get much worse. It seemed that finding his peaceful center before Blair Channing's appointment was not to be had. "Thanks. You can send her in."

He sat back in his chair, readying himself for the mini-tornado about to blow into his office.

In other Italian families, his grandmother would be referred to as his "nonna" maybe even "nonnina" because of her slight five-foot-two inches, but Stella was no sweet, lovable nonna. There was nothing remotely nonna-esque about the dictatorial, full-of-spit-and-vinegar redheaded hellion.

Stella Russo De Luca, his mother's mother, burst into his sanctuary with her usual dramatic flair, slamming the door against the wall and nearly toppling the bronze Rodin replica statue of two hands from its pedestal. She stood at the office threshold with nude-colored fingernails clutching slender hips, seemingly clawing the fabric of the white Oscar de la Renta suit she wore. Her short hair had been re-touched recently, as well as her Botox injection, which was obvious when perfectly arched eyebrows remained stationary as she employed her usual expressionless expression.

Once again, Mike wondered why she still allowed her salon aesthetician to inject her illegally when he could do it without the common side effect.

Having made her grand entrance, the haughty whirlwind nearly sucked the air from the room when, with chin raised, she spoke through puckered lips, "They've arrived!"

He sighed and rubbed a hand across his brow. "Who has arrived?"

"Those damned Clemente women! That's who! The will has been read. How dare they stake claim to my ancestral home."

"No, it is *their* ancestral home and has been for something like eight decades."

"As my eldest grandson, it is also your building!"

His six-feet, two-inch tall frame walked around the desk, then affectionately kissed his diminutive grandmother's cheek cautioning, "Calm yourself, or you'll have a coronary."

"I assure you, Michael, I will not be dropping dead before Villa Fortuna has been signed back over to a Russo heir."

"I hope you're right. Apart from the fact that I'd miss you, it's a great building and a great location. Once I turn it into luxury condos, it'll be the perfect investment. I've had my eye on it for some time."

Stella took a seat facing his sleek steel desk, and removed a compact from her handbag, dabbing repugnant summer perspiration from her cheeks. "I have been engaged in this battle for Villa Fortuna for 20 years, and I am not going to give up the fight now that the witch is dead." She closed the powder case with an abrupt snap. "I intend on ramping up my efforts."

From his private bar, Mike poured them both sparkling waters, carefully squeezing a lemon into her rocks glass. He made sure to wipe the granite counter of any splattered droplets of citrus before handing the drink to her. "She wasn't a witch. She was a nice old lady. Stubborn, with chin hair, but nice. Can you honestly blame Mrs. Dixon for not wanting to part with Villa Fortuna?"

"She *was* a witch, not even a real Italian, just a superstitious Sicilian. You know how those overly pious types are. They attend daily Mass as they pray for you to get struck by lightning, putting the evil eye on you with each Hail Mary!"

"It's not nice to speak ill of the dead or the rosary."

"She's not dead. I'm sure she's haunting Villa Fortuna!"

"Well, that is one way to get rid of the Clemente sisters." He smiled sardonically. "What do you know of them? Are there other heirs who will be contesting the will? Do you think they're willing to sell?"

Sitting in the charcoal leather armchair beside her, Mike leaned back, enjoying the refreshing San Pellegrino. It took everything he had to hold back the laughter when his eighty-year-old grandmother donned her trendy black-rimmed, retro seventies eyewear then removed an iPad from her Gucci handbag. With the swipe of a manicured finger she proceeded to list "the facts" as though she were a federal agent. Come to think of it, she resembled Cousin Joey, a detective with the NYPD.

"There are no other heirs, only three great-nieces, typical low-class Sicilians from Belmont, all single and trashy. The father, Thomas, dead since 2013. I have been assured that his death was no accident. Apparently, Cosa Nostra ran him down in the middle of Arthur Avenue for embezzling from a made man."

Mike raised an eyebrow, speculating on the veracity of his grandmother's information. He was fully aware of her proclivity to bend the truth to suit her convictions, and even admitted that if anyone knew the mob, she did. He thanked God that his mother had the keen resolve to turn her back on *that* part of her family history when she married his father.

"And how did you come by this information? Joey?"

She pffted. "All I ask from him is a little information and his insolent, smart-ass reply is that 'he's straight.' No, your sanctimonious cousin is a dead end. I get my information from another source."

Now that was a statement he wouldn't pursue, quickly surmising that it may be that greasy Famizi character, who kick-started this whole thing. "And the Clemente mother?"

"She resides in Naples. I assume, hiding from The Family."

"Naples, Italy?"

Stella raised the eyeglasses, to give him a look that basically implied, "You've got to be joking?" only lacking the emphatic eyebrow movement.

"No, Michael. Naples, *Florida*. As if *that* family could make claim to being Neapolitan. They'd be kicked out of Campania on their Arthur Avenue asses the minute their dirty Sicilian feet touched soil." She pffted again, and he shook his head.

"Frankly, I don't give a crap if they were from Mars. Will they sell?"

"Doubtful. This is a step up to easy street for them. Perhaps they'll be shunned. You know their 'type' will never fit into Etonville. In fact, I'll see to it that they *are* shunned."

She paused assessing her debonair grandson up and down—from his black, wavy hair, light stubble beard, to his size twelve Ferragamo shoes.

"Of course, there is another way to reclaim ownership of the building."

Familiar with that devious look of hers, he abruptly stood, heading back around to his desk chair, effectively putting space between them. "Oh, no… forget it. Don't even *think* about it!"

"But why not, Michael? Marry, divorce, and then buy the *puttana* out of her share of Villa Fortuna. It is your duty to your *famiglia*."

Mike glanced at the photograph of his father, Vincent, on the wall behind his grandmother's crimson head. It had been taken the day MAA opened in 1974 when plastic surgery meant reconstruction, and implants were silicone. Procedures such as microsurgery and liposuction were barely beyond the pioneer stages and certainly not with the intention of defying age. Following eight years of residency, fellowship and additional training, Mike had already "done his duty" at his father's insistence when he joined the family practice, but by then, plastic surgery had become cosmetic surgery and his father had expectations. That was four years ago and after the first three, the world-renowned Vincent Garin decided to retire to Switzerland with the step-monster. Now the heir-apparent was stuck in a field that had quickly devolved and continued to move in a direction opposite of what he wanted. Body sculpting rich, narcissistic socialites wasn't the reason he chose to become a plastic surgeon.

"Did you hear me, Michael? Do your duty. I don't care which one you marry, just pick one, and be done with it. You're almost thirty-four for Christ sake. It's time you married and had children. Not a Clemente's child, of course. It would pollute your gene pool and my father would roll over in his grave."

He ran his hand through his hair. "That's not going to happen. I won't be dating any of these women as a means of laying my hands on a piece of real estate. As much as I desire the building, in the scheme of things it's not all that important to me. It's also unethical and deceitful and, like Joey, you know it goes against my grain."

He paced before the expansive window. "Besides, I don't get involved with women who have connections to the mob. You know that."

Stella rolled her eyes. "Oh, please, don't be such a saint. You know very well that your own blood traces back to the Mancini Syndicate. And it's not like you're having great success with your dating endeavors. Your little sister Amelia tells me all about this latest dalliance of yours into the virtual world of online dating." Another swipe of her finger on the iPad brought up his profile on eDating. "My daughter, Theresa, rest in peace, would come back from the dead if she knew you were resorting to such measures on the internet!"

"I disagree. I happen to think my mother would be happy that I was going in search for Mrs. Right."

Stella raised the tablet so he could look at his pearly white, smiling image on the screen. "Seven figures a year, a body like David with a face like Cary Grant and you resort to selling yourself like a used Mercedes in need of an overdue tune up. You should be ashamed." She bit the side of her index finger in one of those occasional Italian moments of expression, though she was careful not to get lipstick on her knuckle.

"Yes, well, my sister gossips too much, as do you, and I'm not ashamed. It's damn hard to find an intelligent, professional, and beautiful woman who makes me laugh. I'm not above thinking outside the box to find that special one."

It hadn't been more than fifteen minutes since his grandmother's arrival and already he was having chest pains. Well, not actual chest pains, but definitely *agita*, which felt more like a stabbing filet knife to his gut. She did that to him, consistently. Lord knows, he loved her dearly, but she could be very trying … most of the time. He downed the remaining sparkling water wishing it were a double Mezzaluna vodka.

"Perfect! Marrying a Clemente is about as outside the box as you can get!" she said.

"No and that's my final answer. I'll do it my way, not yours, and if taking out a personal ad or joining an online dating site to find someone suitable is the answer, then so be it."

"You're just too picky. You look for hairs in an egg. There are plenty of attractive women at the Metropolitan Italian-American Center."

"Several of whom are mob connected, and a few of whom also have chin hair. Look, I appreciate your concern, Grandmother, but my dating habits have nothing to do with the building or my investment. That *is* the topic of our conversation, is it not? Securing ownership isn't an affair of the heart. It's a business transaction and money talks." He turned, giving her his million-watt smile. "You of all people know that."

She sighed in resignation, and slid her iPad back into the Gucci as Mike finally took his seat with the desk between them as though a metaphoric line had been drawn in the sand.

"Where's Ann today?" he calmly asked, changing the subject.

"My Antoinette, the poor dear. She's had a dental appointment, and you just know how she hates that. I'm on my way to pick her up in the town car to take her for a pedicure followed by dinner at the Bistro Chat Noir on 66th. She does so love French food. Would you care to join us?"

"No thanks. I have a full afternoon of patients before I hit the gym tonight."

"Hmm. Will you at least consider my idea, Michael? About the Clemente sisters?"

"Again, no, but I might make a suggestion to you. Stop into Villa Fortuna and introduce yourself. Let them know that you have a private investor who is willing to pay a lot of money for their real estate and see what happens. Pretend to be a nice old lady if need be."

"I'm not old."

"No, you're not old, but try at least to be the sweet nonna I know you've always wanted to be … and don't call them trashy Sicilians."

"Ha! You're too nice."

"Tell them that your anonymous buyer is prepared to make them an offer they can't refuse."

"Now you're talking my language. My father the Don would have been so proud."

He chuckled. "Don't remind me."

"Well, since you won't join us for dinner tonight, will you at least come up to Etonville and visit at Hillside Manor tomorrow? It's very lonely now that my bridge club is on summer hiatus."

"On one condition."

She removed her eyeglasses, staring him down, her mouth set in an anticipatory purse.

"Join Mia and me at St. John's for Saturday evening Mass. It'll do you good."

"Bah! That's the witch's church. No thank you."

"But you haven't been back to see the memorial plaque to Grandfather after completion of the narthex's construction. It was your donation that made it possible."

"In case you haven't noticed, Michael. I've been busy. Between this Villa Fortuna issue and Ann's digestive issues, attending church is last on my priorities."

He rolled his eyes and shook his head. It was useless. She was as tenacious as Blair Channing, both eager to take knife to flesh.

"Doctor Garin, Ms. Channing is here for her two thirty appointment," Gwen announced through the speakerphone.

"Thanks. Put her in exam room number three, and I'll be there in five minutes."

"But Doctor Garin, there's no exam table in number three."

"Exactly."

~**~

Tri-Color Rainbow Cookies

3 sticks salted butter
6 eggs
¾ cup sugar
1 tbsp pure almond extract
1 tsp vegetable oil
1 cup flour
1 tsp baking powder
2 cups Hershey's chocolate morsels
Apricot Jelly or Preserves
Red food coloring
Green food coloring
3 aluminum baking pans – 11 ¾ x 9 ¼ x 1 ½
Baking parchment paper

Set eggs and butter out at room temperature for two-three hours, until butter is soft. Cream butter, pour in sugar, veg. oil and mix. Add eggs one and a time as you continue to mix. Add extract, flour and baking powder. Mix until well blended, scraping sides of bowl.

Separate batter equally into three small bowls. Using food coloring color one bowl's contents green, another red (be sure to use enough red or cake will be pink upon baking.) Third bowl leave uncolored.

Preheat oven 350°F. Spray cooking pans with Original Pam, then pour batter, spreading red to cover the bottom of one pan, green cover the bottom of one pan, white, the bottom of the last.

Bake 11-13 minutes, until set. Do not brown.

After cooling, remove red cake from pan onto parchment paper and smear a very thin layer of jelly, careful not go to the edges. Place green cake on top and repeat jelly, finally adding white cake. Wrap tri-colored cake in parchment and/or plastic wrap, then transfer to refrigerator, placing a cookie sheet on top, evenly weighted by a food cans to compress cake. Let sit a few hours.

Remove wrapping. Microwave one cup Hershey's morsels to cover top of cake evenly. Refrigerate until chocolate hardens. Flip cake, microwave another cup of chocolate, repeat application on bottom, and refrigerate to harden chocolate. Cut in rectangular pieces with sharp knife.

~ Taken from Gardiner family recipe

~Three~
Mafioso
(Mafia)

Stella rarely ventured downtown to Manhattan's Little Italy, but today she had no choice before picking up Ann for dinner. Although born in the ever-diminishing ghetto of Italian ethnicity, she and her mamma had left for greener pastures several years after her father's tragic death in 1936. She was just a child then and Mamma had secured a position in midtown at Macy's Department Store. At that time, during the war, a shop girl position was highly sought-after especially for single mothers. Mamma had never breathed a word about her deceased husband's stature as the head of the Mancini Syndicate, instead bending the truth that her husband had died fighting in the Pacific. She took great care in concealing—and hiding from—their connections to Mafioso, but no one could ever truly escape.

The Russo females were happy living just the two of them on 29th Street in a coldwater flat within the flower district. As a child, it had seemed like *la dolce vita* until her mother married a *cazzo* GI, returned from the war, who turned out to be a wife-beating drunk. The only good things that came from that unholy union were his money and the re-establishment of those connections that the Russo women, previously, had run from on Mulberry Street.

Now, almost six decades later, sitting in the back seat of the luxury limousine as the MetLife building towered before her, Stella smiled wryly at the memory of her most memorable trip to the old Little Italy neighborhood. Because of the wife beater, she had turned to "the family" that her mother reviled, visiting the man who replaced her father as Don to the syndicate.

She was twelve and, back then, it wasn't considered too young an age for a lecher like her stepfather to lust over the possibilities, but she was having none of it. Stella Russo would never be the victim, and she'd die protecting her mamma from remaining one.

Thanks to that trip downtown, three months later the *cazzo* swam with the fishes and she and Mamma inherited his family's estate in Westchester County. The days of living hand to mouth and bathing in cold water in the kitchen had ended. They had moved up in the world—a completely different world where her mother's dream of a house to call her own had come true. Life was truly good, but those early experiences taught Stella never to bite the hand that fed her. She was eternally grateful for the protection of the Mancini syndicate for "taking care of their own."

The Lincoln stopped at a red light, and she lowered the glass between her and her long-time driver, Angelo. "Famizi instructed us to pick him up at The Mulberry Tavern," she said.

"That's the old Mare Chiaro Bar, isn't it?"

"Yes. His grandfather owned the joint in its heyday during Prohibition. It was a social club back then."

"Does the grandson still run the place?"

"No. He's a wannabe Mafioso associate."

"Oh, one of those. So he's nothing more than a stool pigeon."

Stella sniggered. "Something like that, just another greasy private investigator."

Before increasing the air conditioning, she depressed a button and raised the glass, separating the front from the rear seats, as well as effectively dividing the established social stations.

Summer in New York City was her bane of existence. Every year, she promised herself that, by the next time the temperature inevitably rose to these levels, she would be living abroad like her successful son-in-law and that *puttana* wife of his. Sweltering heat and oppressive humidity made even this woman of substance feel grimy and low class—two things that, long ago, Stella had left behind. She was no longer that poverty-stricken, filthy urchin selling flowers on the sidewalk to help pay the rent.

Hopefully, this would be the last year she expended recovering her father's rightful property to his family. Although she had many connected friends who could have done the job quickly, this endeavor to restore his patrimony was her responsibility to accomplish. She would give to her three grandchildren a piece of her roots, which began as the immigrant dream of her father.

Within only thirty minutes, the black limo pulled up at the curb beside The Mulberry Tavern where, as expected, Ralph Famizi stood by the establishment's door, a cigarette pinched between the tips of his thumb and index finger. *Smelly, filthy, disgusting habit.* She shuddered and, if it weren't for the 95-degree weather, she would have exited the car to speak with him, but she rationalized that enduring his stench accompanied the information he would impart.

He waved an envelope that had been tucked under his armpit, and she cracked the side window open just low enough to command, "Put that cigarette out and get in, Famizi, and try not to breathe when you speak."

Overtly, she gave his cheap suit the once over when he settled into the white leather seat across from her. She knew that stereotypes like him were a reality not just fabricated characters in movies. Some middle-aged wannabees and low-level connected men loved the idea of living in the alternate universe embodied during the 1950s, 60s, and 70s. The glorified glamour of the Rat Pack and *The Godfather* combined with the allure of rubbing elbows with modern day equivalents of mob bosses such as Gambino and Bonnano kept them socially stagnant, separated from real life. They spoke in underworld lingo or "mobspeak" as though it was a real language. Conversations between these types consistently contained butchered slang phrases like "fuhgeddaboutit," "whatsamatta," and "yuhgata problem witdat." She despised men such as Famizi, but they served a purpose. Their greed and aspirations to be mobsters made them indispensable; their love of the "the family" made them comical; and Famizi was downright hilarious in her opinion. She would have showed it, if either her heart or her facial features remembered how to laugh.

That emotion vanished 23 years earlier when she buried her beloved youngest daughter, Theresa, devoted mother to Michael and Amelia, rest her young soul. Stella stifled the thought, refusing to allow herself the pain that came with it. God was cruel to give Theresa a good marriage to a nice physician of Italian descent and two beautiful babies – only to wrest her away.

"What news do you have for me?" she demanded of Famizi, handing him an envelope of crisp one hundred dollar bills.

"Carpo is taking them to visit Villa Fortuna tomorrow," he said in thick Brooklynese. "The brunette sista is a knockout."

"Hmm, trash."

"Yeah, trash but she's got a pair of—"

"What else do you have for me?"

Famizi handed her the brown envelope aged by the passage of time. "I think you're gonna love dis. I found it in an old suitcase stashed in da basement."

She opened the clasp then slid out a folded *New York Sun* newspaper carelessly stained with evidence of eighty-year-old glass rings. Dated January 30, 1936, the front page read "Mob Boss Run Down."

"Dats an interestin piece of family history you got there. Bona-fide confirmation that the story my old man told you years ago was handed down from his own father, who overheard the entire Villa Fortuna transaction. The one and only witness to Clemente's thievery of Villa Fortuna. See, pops wasn't shittin ya, rest his soul. It says in that there paper, that your old man's death was an accident, but I don't think so. That Clemente was bad news." His manicured finger pointed to a corner of the page. "See there."

Two words were written in pencil: *La Bocca* (The Mouth)

"Eh? Whaditellya?"

Stella had never seen this article before, never even knew that her father's death had been covered in the newspaper, or that his obituary was even noted. This certainly *was* interesting, and yes, it seemed as though Gino Famizi had a juicy story to tell when he told his son, who told his son – the man facing her—about Villa Fortuna—the house of good fortune.

"Is that all?" she coldly asked, suddenly feeling a chill in her bones.

"Yeah, that's all I gotz, but I'll stay in touch after I stake out the sistas for a week or so. You want photographs? I can email 'em."

"Only if something incriminating crosses your path. I'll need leverage, something blackmailable."

"You got it, Mrs. D."

She leaned over and opened the door, dismissing her informant. "Thank you, Ralph. May I keep this newspaper?"

"Yeah, sure. You can put it in a family album for posteritability."

What was the use of correcting his improper word usage?

He left, and Stella tapped on the glass, signaling for Angelo to drive on to get Ann. The poor dear was probably chewing her nails in anxiety by now.

Carefully, she opened the antique paper and began to read. *If only I knew the whole story, the real story.*

~**~

Winter -1936 - Downtown Manhattan
Little Italy, NYC

Gino Famizi, owner and bartender at Mare Chiaro Bar on Mulberry Street, attempted to appear busy dunking a used whiskey glass into the water-filled sink. He then began wiping the glass dry with a not-so-clean dishrag, listening with one ear to his two regular patrons at the far end of the counter.

They weren't just any customers. These men were two of the most feared gangsters in this small, tightly controlled section of Lower Manhattan.

Although the rest of the nation was spiraling into what the newspapers were calling a "depression," these two well-respected Mafioso were in here every night of the week, spending dough and gambling. They openly commiserated over whiskey or vino, no topic off limits—family, business, their enemies, or even their mistresses. The latter topic was a frequent discussion between the men, and the bartender knew each *puttana*…as well as their fathers, brothers and uncles.

In fact, aside from the local beauty parlor, Gino's bar—or rather—the "members-only social club" was *the* place for gossip—even about the mob bosses themselves who patronized it, the very same mobsters Gino paid to protect it.

With each needless swipe of the cloth around the rim, the long-dried glass in his hands squeaked. He surreptitiously observed the patrons and the typical fearsome look upon the face of Vito "Scarface" Russo. The man's nose was as hooked as the downturn to his lips, and the prominent jagged scar across his cheek alone would send greenhorn waiters running in fear. Word on the street was that the older mobster sitting beside him, Tommaso Clemente (known in the neighborhood as Tommy the Mouth) gave Russo that very wound fifteen years ago during a turf war. But that rumor was probably started by Clemente himself. Such was his method. He came by his mob name the logical way; he ran his mouth like a Thomson Machine Gun: non-stop. The man was a bull shitter with a gift of gab, which only seemed to have strengthened his power in Little Italy—smart advertising in Gino's opinion. The bigger the lie, the faster the rumor spread, the greater the fear, and the more power he could wield on his side of Prince Street.

The barkeep and Clemente continued to listen carefully to Russo's latest gripe, his lips, at times, drawn into a thin line. His thick Neapolitan accent further distorted his drunken grumbling. The mobster's head was turned in such a manner that his black Fedora covered his piercing blue eyes. All Gino could see was that distinct nose and the threatening mouth, which grew more menacing as Russo fell deeper into his cups.

But no matter how inebriated, the two mobsters appeared impeccable. No one would ever dare mistake them for working stiff immigrants struggling to feed their families in this bad economy. Hand tailored, double-breasted suits, flashy ties, gold pocket watches, and (although Gino couldn't see them) silk socks and two-toned oxfords were their usual attire. During the day, both men walked their turf, strutting like peacocks among the pushcart vendors and organ grinders, as the commoners paid homage, worshipping them in fear with hearty salutations of "*Buongiorno, Signor Russo!" and "Buonasara, Signor Clemente!*"

Thirty blocks comprised this Little Italy neighborhood—fifteen were managed by Clemente and fifteen controlled by Russo as head of the Mancini Crime Syndicate. Half of the community was Neapolitan and the other half Sicilian and never shall the two get along. Yet, these men seemed to defy that precedence, or perhaps it was more a matter of each keeping their enemy close. The scar certainly gave credence to the claim that Clemente and Russo were long-time enemies and competitors, but one never knew for sure. On the exterior, they appeared to be the best of friends in spite of the age difference, co-existing in what mob families called "The American Way."

Clemente's slurred Sicilian dialect boomed when he slammed his empty glass on the bar, causing Gino to run over with a jug of wine. "Throw him out on his ass!"

"I'll kill 'em," Russo stated, also sliding his glass toward the bartender.

"You can't whack him then move your mistress into his apartment. Think straight, Vito. The coppas'll be all over you!"

"He won't take the cabbage I offered."

"Then he's a rat fink, but you still can't clip him, even if he's all the way up in Etonville."

Gino poured quickly, and then moved back to the far end of the bar, continuing to wash the remaining glasses—and eavesdropping.

Not another patron was in sight when Russo abruptly stood, pushing back the barstool. He paced, removing his hat and ringing the brim in fisted hands, obviously losing his cool.

"Villa Fortuna is my building!" Scarface's Neapolitan dialect was as cutting as his finger across his neck in implication. "Damn Socialists and that damn rent strike. A landlord can't even kick a deadbeat out on his ass. Well, I can do whatever I want and I want him dead! That's the Russo way of eviction!"

"No, no, no. You're going about this all wrong, my friend. You are a businessman. Sit down."

Russo slid the stool out, mumbling in drunken slurs. "I'm gonna kill the housing authority. Slice-a his neck.*"

"Silence!" Thin lips smirked and Scarface's eyes lit in drunken enthusiasm.

"I'm listening. What's-a your plan?"

The bartender took a step closer, making sure he didn't miss a single word. Not that he'd tell anyone, but it was the job of a bartender to remain in the know.

"There are ways to work around the new eviction laws. I did some askin' around. The way to evict a first floor tenant is to say that the owner needs to move into the building into that particular apartment. It's all on the up and up. Trust me."

"You forget, I *already* have an apartment on the third floor." Vito slugged back his wine.

"You do?"

"Yeah. My other mistress is living there. I wanna keep 'em all in the same-a building."

Now it was Clemente's eyes that gleamed, but with a different kind of enthusiasm—one of opportunity. "Ah … well, then I'll pretend to be the owner who needs to move into the building. You sign over the deed to Villa Fortuna to me. I'll evict-a your tenant, and then I'll sign the deed back over to you. Then you move your other mistress into his apartment. *Capisce?*"

Russo motioned to Gino for a refill, and of course, he was eager to pour, again coming quickly with the big jug of family recipe. The wiseguy was obviously mulling over the option, but suddenly looked down into Clemente's face with mistrust narrowing his eyes. Yeah, he'd be a fool to trust that man. Everyone knew that The Mouth was all lip service and a chiseler and swindler of the worst kind.

"What you say, is true?" Russo asked as he toyed with his diamond pinky ring.

Clemente nodded, but Gino had seen that type of nod before. It was one given to his cousin before the coppers found him sleeping with the fishes at the bottom of the East River.

"I swear on my sista's eyes."

Clemente didn't have a sister, at least not one that Gino knew of. Russo probably knew for sure, but was most likely too drunk to remember. As was evident when he said,

"*Bene*, I'll have my lawyer draw up the papers and tomorrow I'll meet you here to transfer Villa Fortuna to you." Russo towered over his "friend," his lips tight, his pupils growing as dark as his suit. "If you so much as cross me, Clemente, I'll kill you and curse your descendants until Villa Fortuna is mine again. However long it takes, even from my grave, the evil eye—the *malocchio*— will follow your family."

… eight days later

The social club had been quiet for days. Fifteen blocks of Neapolitans were in mourning and no one was coming in for a game of cards or a drink even if Mare Chiaro had the best family recipe in Little Italy. For three days straight, a line of the bereaved (and maybe not-so bereaved) had wrapped around Lazzari Funeral Home on Prince Street. In the bitter cold, they awaited their turn to kiss the cheek of the dead in respect. They stood in the snow, waiting to give condolences to the deceased's wife and infant daughter. The wailing in the streets at all hours was finally winding down, and Gino was thankful that life—and business—would return to his side of the neighborhood.

A week-old *New York Sun* newspaper spread out at the far end of the bar declared in bold letters: "Mob Boss Run Down." The front page story claimed that Vito Scarface Russo's death was an accidental hit and run but Gino knew otherwise. He was right here that snowy night to witness the signing of the deed to this Villa Fortuna place. Russo asked one last time for assurance that this scheme would work and, once again, Gino observed that particular head nod from Clemente as Russo signed over his property to The Mouth.

There was no doubt in the bartender's mind that it was backstabbing Sicilian thugs that ran Russo over when he crossed Kenmare Street in broad daylight. Now Scarface Russo was a cold corpse, and Clemente's faction had gotten away with murder.

At first, Gino assumed that a vendetta would be declared immediately—Russo's camp against Clemente, Neapolitan against Sicilian. But the coroner officially ruled it an accident in his report, neglecting to mention the single bullet hole in the victim's chest. But Gino knew everything from his side of the bar, including that the coroner was a close relation to Clemente's mistress and the investigating detective was on the take.

He would never tell a soul.

Well … maybe just his young son, who loved when his father regaled him with fascinating stories of the important men that patronized his papa's bar.

Still, he couldn't deny that he hated both the Sicilians and the Neapolitans. He shrugged, feeling ambivalent about Russo's murder, but Gino would never speak ill of the dead in case they somehow came back to earth—superstitious Southern Italians believing in the bad luck of the evil eye. How could the *malocchio* be for real?—After all, Tommy "The Mouth" Clemente now owned Villa Fortuna free and clear and that was damn lucky in this Venetian's opinion.

~**~

~Four~
Destino
(Destiny)

The impressive three-story, classic Tudor structure of Villa Fortuna dominated the view the Clemente sisters studied as they stood opposite the building, on the main thoroughfare in Etonville, ten miles north from Belmont in the Bronx. Elizabeth loved this quaint village, which had maintained its country club cachet throughout the years. She could visualize herself living here, ensconced in an opulent colonial mansion after achieving success in LA as *the* foot and ankle surgeon: repairing children's clubfeet, healing diabetic wounds or, in her grandest professional fantasy, acting as *the* official NFL podiatrist. If this village was good enough for New York's elite families, then it would be good enough for her sisters. Well, once they'd gotten their act together.

Enviously dubbed "Snobsville" by everyone who was not a resident, some buildings on Main Street dated from the Revolutionary War attesting to the rich Anglo-American history of the exclusive hamlet situated along the Bronx River. On the sidewalks across and behind them, blue-blood inhabitants shopped beside the nouveau riche, dotted by couplets of yuppie mothers pushing identical top-of-the-line strollers. Amazingly, everyone looked the same—each sedately manicured to an established ideal—all bland— like white bread. Even the cars parked at the curb all resembled one another: Mercedes Benz, BMW, and an occasional Audi blending in varying shades of silver grey. Mr. Carpo's sleek, red Maserati, like Nicki's belly ring, stood out like a sore thumb.

Mr. Carpo held his clipboard, checking off something Elizabeth surmised was another of Prozia's expectations.

"So you see ..." he said in that dreamy accent of his, "Villa Fortuna is an impressive building. Prime real estate in the center of town." He nodded his head to indicate the direction as he continued, "And within walking distance to St. John's church on Grant Street."

"Look *Guido*, I won't be going to church. Not now. Not eva," Nicki stated with stubborn conviction, her finger wagging in his face just like their mother had often done.

"Then-a you can kiss your dreams good-bye. I bet Father O'Malley will be very happy to hear that. He has had his eye on this building for years to make into a youth center."

He raised an eyebrow, and Elizabeth wholeheartedly approved of his tactics in dealing with her smart mouthed sister.

"You see, although Etonville already has a beauty parlor ..." He turned his head again, to point out its location, "... a little competition is a good thing. It is the way of capitalism, but I think yours is the better location."

"It's not too close?" Gina asked, already feeling dashed by the idea of rivaling with a hoity-toity salon with an established clientele. "I mean, this Halo Salon is an upscale spa, probably with nail techs and massage therapists, maybe even eye brow threading! We can't compete with that."

"Do not worry, Miss Clemente. You will find your niche. You and your sisters will be a breath of fresh air to this stuffy village. The residents here need some diversity, a touch of culture, so to speak."

"Hmm ... diversity ... culture," Gina repeated, her mind working furiously. *Espresso ... cannoli ... Dean Martin. Yeah, culture. I can't do hair extensions, but culture I can do.*

"Excuse me, Mr. Carpo, but didn't our aunt caution us about someone attempting to remove us from the building? Do we have something to be fearful of? I mean she did let something slip about its suspect ownership," Elizabeth said.

He sighed. "Mrs. De Luca. Yes. She is a semi-retired local realtor who has made many claims that this building was stolen from her father during the 1930s. It is nothing for you to trouble yourself with. She is just a bitter woman who loves to make others miserable. The title is clear and that is all you need to know."

"Stolen?"

"Do not worry. Vito Russo legitimately signed the deed over to Mrs. Dixon's father, Tommaso Clemente, your great-grandfather, and then Russo died two days later. We can never be sure of the intent of such a transaction, but it is all legal and that is what matters."

"Geez, that's bad luck," Gina said.

"That depends on whose perspective. It is lucky he gave it to your great-grandfather before his tragic death. The house of good fortune has belonged to your family for eighty years, and you are free to do what you like with it—except sell it." He looked down at Nicki with her bare midriff and hip-hugging short shorts. "After you go shopping for new clothing and make a visit to church."

Gina couldn't keep from glancing over her shoulder at the would-be competitive salon. In the scant ten minutes they had stood on the main street discussing the building and this trouble-making Russo De Luca woman, she had counted three men, sixteen women, and two escorted children, enter the salon. By her quick tabulation of the services she was sure they offered, those patrons alone could easily net over four thousand dollars in a town such as this. How the heck were they going to compete with a place like that? All she knew was to cut, style, and blow. Angelina's Beauty School under the "el" (elevated subway) didn't prepare her for *this clientele.*

"Lizzy, we're going to need the big guns. I'm gonna call Picasso and see if she wants to work for us. We're going to need a colorist."

Elizabeth shrugged. "Whatever you think is best. I trust you implicitly. This is your world, and I'm only here to help you get settled—and to go to church. Come tomorrow afternoon, I'm on a flight back to LA to forget all the promises I'm about to make in the confessional."

"Very good, Elizabeth. You would like to go to St. John's now? Afterward, we can look at the empty storefront and start the planning stages for the beauty parlor."

"Sounds like a plan. Are you sure this whole 'confession' thing is non-negotiable? I'm happy to bribe you with a cappuccino and we can call it even." She beamed up at his handsome face, trying to win him over with a smile she thought would unhinge him. Elizabeth may not have desired to date or marry an Italian, especially one with this much continental charm, but that didn't mean that she was naïve about how to manipulate one.

He took her hand and kissed it, his soft lips dispensing a definite tingling with the first and second gentle deposit. "How about a romantic dinner? I know the perfect, secluded restaurant down on Lexington Avenue."

Suddenly feeling self-conscious, especially having heard Nicki's unladylike snort beside her, she withdrew her hand from his. "I don't think your wife would approve, Mr. Carpo, but my offer for a cappuccino still holds."

"Please, Elizabeth, call me Salvatore."

She shook her head with a humored smirk, and he sighed audibly in resignation.

"Very well, let us go to see Father O'Malley," he said with a wink and a smile.

~**~

The Clemente sisters entered the one-hundred year-old stone church, each unconsciously enacting the long-ingrained ritual of dipping three fingers into the holy water font upon the wall and blessing themselves, followed by a kiss to their fingers. Simultaneously, Elizabeth and Nicki were both surprised that they hadn't burst into flames upon hand to forehead contact, though only the latter giggled aloud at the thought.

The traditional narthex of St. John's Catholic Church was welcoming in its peaceful, pious silence punctuated only by the occasional cough or creak of a wooden pew in the nave just beyond the open doors.

The two sisters held back, resisting entrance into the nave. Entry meant atonement and neither wanted to kneel in the old confessional box. Elizabeth, in particular, was embarrassed even to *think* the damning requisite words "it's been x-number of years since my last confession." Twelve to be precise, but whose fault was that? She had been busy carving out a pathway to her future—a one-way ticket out of Little Italy. Surely even God understood *that*.

Nicki elbowed her in the ribs as she noticed they stood directly before a large, bronze plaque embedded into the wall, which read, "In memory of Louis De Luca, donated by Stella Russo De Luca."

"It's her," she whispered. "That old battleaxe Carpo spoke about. She must be a money bags."

To one side, below a three-foot statue of the Madonna, artificial candlewicks flickered within glass pillars, some flashing intermittently in need of new batteries. Gina immediately drew near, removing a dollar bill from her back pocket and slid it into the donation box, followed by a press to the candle's respective red button. Old World tradition officially collided with modern, safe efficiency when the lamp lit.

"*Andiamo.* Come. I texted Father O'Malley. He awaits you in the church," Mr. Carpo said in an appropriately low tone.

"The priest has a smart phone? Sheesh, that's a new one. Does he have that new make your confession over the phone app? 'Cause you know if he does, I'm all over that!" Nicki proclaimed. "There ain't no way I'm going behind the curtain. Last time I did that, that ancient priest on Arthur Avenue started some exorcism ritual from his side of the screen."

Elizabeth laughed then whispered, "Good old, Father Rocco. I loved coming to church because I knew he would be there, greeting us with a smile and blessing us. He was so cute, so kind, especially to you in trying to tame your wild ways."

"It didn't work," Nicki snorted.

"I remember that day of your last confession. I was home on spring break. You have to admit, you made Father drop his prayer book three times. Wasn't that the confession when Mamma pulled you into church by your ear after she discovered you and Ronnie Greco getting it on in the basement?"

"Yeah. Her timing sucked. You should have seen the look on her face and mine the minute he dropped his linen. That guy was hung like a big, thick salami swinging from the deli ceiling." She kissed her pinched fingers. "*Magnifico!*"

"Shh," Elizabeth warned, glancing over her shoulder at Gina. "Don't talk sausage. It might remind her of Frankie."

"I just don't understand the point of confession. It's not like I didn't go right back after church to get a mouthful," Nicki added.

Elizabeth shook her head. "You are terrible."

"That's not what Ronnie Greco said."

The sisters entered the marble-pillared nave, expecting the antique arched roof to cave and the ground to tremble beneath their feet. Upon their entrance, their eyes were drawn to the few worshipers in prayerful repose, kneeling before the crucifix that was hanging on the wall behind the altar. Elizabeth had to admit it was a magnificent church, and she felt a familiar sense of tranquility. It tugged somewhere deep down within her soul, and she could understand how so many found solace from their problems by visiting here. Several women, silently reciting the rosary, sat in a cluster beside the statue of St. Patrick toward the rear of the church. Even the illuminated red light above the antique confessional felt like an odd balm to Elizabeth's overall disharmony, and for just a moment, she allowed herself to wonder why she had ever stopped coming to church. Why had it always felt like a duty or worse, an abhorrence?

Then she recalled. It was her ex-husband and his family who had rooted her disenchantment. In fact, it was *their* repugnance of not only her faith, but also her Italian-American ethnicity that propelled her to run from both, fostering her discomfort and the embarrassment of her upbringing. They made it so much more appealing to reinvent herself as someone other than who she was raised to be. Elizabeth Fairchild, the wife of a soon-to-be cardiologist, sounded so much more Connecticut, elegant, and WASPy than Lizzy Clemente: Italian-American, Sicilian Catholic from the Bronx. She was All-American now. There was no hyphen of prejudicial distinction and nothing to stereotype with jokes about the Mafia.

Now, standing at the entrance of her cultural and familial foundation, the awkward feeling had suddenly dissipated. She strangely felt at home, inhaling the permeated scent of incense within the structure. Reacting as only one who had been brought up deeply entrenched in her faith would, she instinctively walked to a pew, genuflected, blessed herself, then slid down the bench to accommodate Gina and Nicki as they followed suit.

The Parish's pastor, Father O'Malley exited the sacristy to the left of the altar, his shock of red hair advertising his Irish ancestry. He waved and smiled at Carpo as though an old friend, and approached him, standing in the aisle beside the sisters.

"Welcome!" He said breaking the reverent silence in the church, prompting several head turns from the prayerful.

"*Buongiorno,*" Carpo returned in hushed tones. "Father, these are the Clemente sisters. Mrs. Dixon's great-nieces of whom I spoke with you. They are the new owners of Villa Fortuna."

"Ah, yes. Villa Fortuna, the hoped-for location of St. John's Youth Center that has long been an object of our prayers. If only the church could have been as lucky as you ladies."

Upon greeting each of them with a handshake and a pleasant hello, he glanced toward the confessional booth where the other parish priest continued to give the sacrament. There was a long line of the penitent awaiting their turn, some looking fearful, others as though they surely were sinless and just going through the motions. Either way, they were all the same in Elizabeth's opinion, no different from her and her sisters— doing their duty, fulfilling an obligation, and most likely would be going back to whatever the church edicts would consider "their sinful ways" the next day.

"I am afraid that there isn't enough time to hear your confessions today," Father O'Malley said apologetically.

"*Mi Scuzi*, but you assured me that you could give the ladies their sacrament. It is important so that we can carry out the stipulations to Mrs. Dixon's Last Will and Testament."

"Yes, I understand." His eyes narrowed with disapproval after settling on Nicki's bare midriff and belly ring.

Elizabeth watched as Carpo raised his eyebrow to what she viewed as another obstruction to this requirement of the inheritance.

"Can we come back another time? Tomorrow perhaps?" she asked, not sure whether he was telling the truth. Father Rocco would have immediately offered, "Let's hear your sins in the empty confessional."

"We only give reconciliation on Saturday, and Mass will be commencing in thirty minutes. I'm sorry, ladies, perhaps next week."

"Well, could you make an exception? Today *is* Saturday and confessions *are* taking place already. It's just that I leave tomorrow to return home to LA," Elizabeth stated calmly, already feeling that this whole deal was starting to stink.

The clergyman entwined his fingers over his chubby midsection. "I am terribly sorry, but the line is already too long. Perhaps you can go in your parish back home."

"I understand," Gina said, giving him the usual pass that she gave every man.

The white collar caused her to seamlessly slip into that "church lady" mode they had witnessed their mother do for years. Mamma truly believed that if one sucked up to a priest, she would gain heavenly favor.

"It's because you would like to give us a special blessing, right, Father? Maybe even visit Villa Fortuna with us so that you could bless the building for our good fortune?" She beamed that perfect, innocent smile of hers and he smiled back.

Right then Elizabeth realized there was quite a scheming side to her sister she had yet to discern, particularly when Father O'Malley's smile acquiesced contrition.

"Of course, Miss Clemente. I will be delighted. I will make the arrangements with Salvatore for next week."

Gina slyly winked at Elizabeth and nodded proudly. "You won't forget the holy water?"

He fidgeted, shifting weight from one foot to the other. "I will bring the holy water."

No, Prozia was wrong. Gina would have made a terrible nun. Apparently, divorce had taught her a thing or two about manipulating a man—even one wearing a white collar. Elizabeth was so proud.

At the end of the sisters' pew, the velvet curtain to the confessional was suddenly pulled back and the light above went green as the next person stood in anticipation of their reconciliation. As though time slowed in a delicious torment, one supremely perfect specimen of raw masculinity stepped out of the box, and Elizabeth ceased listening to the conversation between Gina and Father O'Malley. In fact, she altogether forgot that she was sitting in church when her thoughts instantly turned naughty.

Oh to be in that confessional and hear what wicked things that gorgeous guy did! Oh to be the co-star of that naughtiness and the subject of those confessions! *Mamma mia.*

She picked up a parish bulletin forgotten on the pew beside her and began furiously fanning herself as she admired the tall, gorgeous Adonis. He wore a tailored, light blue dress shirt and black—no—navy trousers. His wavy, dark hair, and fine physique caused a visceral reaction in her, and she sat spellbound, unable to look away—a hot flush growing from chest to cheeks. Elizabeth outright stared and couldn't help admiring every nuance of how he walked, his broad, muscular chest, even the concentrating crinkle to his forehead.

He looked over to where they sat and she could swear that the corner of his beautiful lips slightly lifted. Their vision locked for a milli-second until he looked away toward his destination: more battery operated candles beside the altar, on the opposite side of the church.

Suddenly, church—this church—had become an appealing prospect. Three consecutive months of Mass? Yeah, she could do that—*here*—on Saturday evenings, maybe followed by dinner and some dancing—between the sheets.

Nicki elbowed her again before she reminded herself that, come tomorrow afternoon, she'd be flying high on a different kind of body.

Elizabeth watched as Mr. Hot Bod removed a handkerchief from his pocket and pressed the button to light a candle.

"Do you see him? He saw us. I think he looked at my boobs," Nicki said, sitting up straight and pulling her shoulders back.

"Oh, I saw him, alright." Unconsciously, Elizabeth brushed the hair away from her neck and licked her top lip, mesmerized by the perfect shape of his tight backside in those navy—yes, definitely navy—slacks, when he knelt in prayer before the statue of St. Joseph.

"Good Gawd. I gotta get me some of that."

Elizabeth slowly nodded, lost in a daydream. "Yeah … me too."

"Shit, he even makes prayin' look sexy."

Another slow head nod. "Yeah … I know."

Both sisters stared until the guy's brief prayer and subsequent blessing of himself ended. He walked to a slender blonde sitting a few pews behind the candles, gracing her with a dazzling smile, brighter than the stained glass window beside him.

Elizabeth guessed that the woman was as perfect as he was. "Figures," she whispered.

"Yeah. I'm all for takin' that bitch out."

An unladylike chortle at Nicki's statement escaped Elizabeth's lips. For once, she heartily agreed with her sister's crass manner of stating things plainly and truthfully.

_~**~_

Mike slid into the pew beside his sister, Amelia, known only to a select few as Mia. At twenty-four, she was still shy and had yet to find her comfort zone. In private, she was a ball of fire, loved to joke, loved to laugh, and was quite expressive; in public it was a very different matter. Failing to see herself for the beauty she is, insecurities held her back, and try as Mike did, nothing succeeded in releasing his sister from her shell.

They were close siblings in spite of the age difference, and many times he had acted in the role of father where their own had lacked sympathy or the attention she required. It was sad, Mike inwardly lamented, that his father had ceased acting as a parent following their mother's death when Mia was just a baby. Vincent's disaffection was compounded further, barely three years later by his surprisingly quick marriage to the twenty-five year old MAA receptionist at the time, Candy Shugga. The mercenary woman never stopped, from that day till this one, orchestrating friction and disagreement between father and son.

Today, church felt like a soothing unction, a necessary mercy in preparation for the upcoming evening's visit with their grandmother. Although attentive to Mia, she was excessively proficient in beating a horse dead when insistent on something she wanted. Mike anticipated that what lay ahead over dinner would be a prolonged assault plan to achieve her desired demands. He hoped church would mentally prepare and spiritually fortify him to dissuade her schemes against the new owners of Villa Fortuna.

Gazing at the altar, he sat readying himself for Mass, attempting to purge his heart and mind of the anger he still harbored against his father, the anxiety he felt about Stella, and the ever-increasing disharmony he faced about his career. Not to mention the paramount annoyance: he had been forced to shake hands with someone on the confessional line and had forgotten his pocket-sized antibacterial bottle in the Lexus.

"What are you thinking about?" Mia whispered.

He continued to look forward, whispering back. "Grandmother."

"That deserves a rosary."

"More like an exorcism."

"You are so bad."

"I know, but she's killin' me with this Villa Fortuna vendetta. She actually suggested that I marry one of the new owners."

Mia sniggered. "Well, it would be easier than online dating."

"Very funny, and you're to blame here."

"Me? What did I do?"

"You showed her my eDating profile. She called me a used Mercedes."

He glanced sideways at the innocently stoic expression on his sister's face, her blue eyes lit with humor.

"I only showed her how many women have favorited you. You should be proud. Last I looked it was up to 1,035. Certainly, you're a Jaguar at the very least."

"Yeah, well, stop gossiping about my dating life."

He closed his eyes, once again attempting to rid himself of the subject but in doing so, he immediately recalled the image of a pair of magnificent looking breasts. The brunette woman sitting behind him was knockout gorgeous, and his mind's eye couldn't help its natural migration to her chest, as only a hormonal male and connoisseur of shapely breasts would. No plastic surgeon, even one nicknamed Michelangelo, could have sculpted such a pair as those. Only the God of creation could form such perfection. That silky pink blouse she wore fit as it should on naturally gifted D-cups graced with full curves and enticing nipples blessedly pebbled from the chill in the nave.

Good Lord, he almost groaned aloud. He was nearly aroused by the thought, and he silently chastised himself for thinking such things, let alone for objectifying someone in such a way—and in church no less! He began a meditational recitation of the rosary, praying that each Hail Mary would deliver his thoughts far from the woman's tempting assets, even though he wished for nothing more than to remain focused on them, and not from a clinical perspective. Instead, his instant obsession turned to her lustrous, cascading waves, that black beauty mark on her cheek, and the warmth of her expressive eyes. He thought he imagined a quirk to her plump, pink lips when their vision locked, but was regretfully sure that he might be mistaken. It was only a heavenly second before forcing himself to look away, afraid of staring, or worse—his eyes gravitating back down to her alluring chest. Self-restraint was his motto in all things, and by God, it would serve him well today.

Above in the choir loft, the organ played and Mike smiled thinking that although he rarely attended Mass at St. John's, there just may be a reason to come here every Saturday evening instead of the church closest to the Garin family condominium on Sutton Place.

Of course, he thought with conviction, his desire to see her again wasn't to gape at her figure, but instead to behold her enticing "fine eyes." In addition to the fact that in that fleeting milli-second, he felt something he'd never felt before—a lightning bolt to his heart.

✳✳

~Five~
Casa
(Home)

"You'll call when you land?" Gina implored as the three girls approached the winding lines for airport security.

"Of course. I want to hear all about your meeting later today with Dharma and whether she'll be joining the salon. We have a lot of work to do before your grand opening in December."

"Yo, Lizzy, if you see Jared Leto make sure you give him my numba." Nicki ordered, passing over the extended handle of the rolling carryon. She was more choked up than she had expected and was trying to make light of Elizabeth leaving them yet again. The weekend of sisterly bonding had turned out to be exactly what was needed and, surprisingly, she wished to God her sister would come home for keeps.

Elizabeth's laughter didn't mask her sarcastic dare, "Of course I will, and if either of you see that hottie at St. John's, make sure you say hello for me."

"What if he's an Italian, Lizzy?" Gina teased.

"Well, first ask if he knows what *strufoli* is. If he answers 'no', then feel free to tell him that I dream of fondling his amazing backside."

"I have to admit, he certainly gives Mr. Carpo a run for his money in the looks department," Gina confirmed. "He was hot."

"I agree. That guy was so good on the eyes that if I lived in New York I *might* have considered saying hello—in spite of his obvious devout dedication."

Nicki snorted. "If altar boys looked like him, I might even hang out at church."

Gina touched Lizzy's arm, surprised that she would have pursued an introduction after repeatedly claiming no interest in dating. "You really would have said hello? Really? Well maybe if I run into your altar boy next time I'm in Etonville—"

"Don't you dare!" Elizabeth blurted. "You know I am not looking for any entanglements, particularly a long distance one. I need to concentrate on building my professional reputation, start performing surgeries that truly matter. I need to stay focused."

"Sister hug," she ordered, holding out her arms as they came toward her again. Gina sniffled and Nicki uncharacteristically giggled as Elizabeth, feeling almost maternal, admitted, "I'll miss you. I love you both, and I hope you know that you can accomplish whatever you set your minds to. Remember Mr. Carpo is here to help with anything you need and I'll be back for Christmas. Don't hesitate to call or text me whenever you want. Okay?"

Gina swiped at the tear rolling down her cheek. "Promise me you will come back for the holidays."

"I'm sure I'll be able to get the time off. I do have some vacation coming to me."

"I want your word," Gina insisted.

"You have my word. I'll be here, and we'll have a grand opening the likes of which Etonville has never seen. Your salon will be such a success that no one'll be able to take Villa Fortuna from us."

Elizabeth turned away, heart heavy, almost regretful. Inheriting the building was one thing, but kick starting this future for her sisters was a commitment that might require her to reside in New York full time. The associated guilt that battled with the beckoning of the distant boarding gate made her a bit nauseous. Minutes later, lined up for the TSA body scan, a glance over her shoulder showed Gina and Nicki tightly holding onto each other. The eldest cried, as the youngest, hand clutching hip, looked ten shades of Sicilian pissed off.

One last glance backward as she neared the walk-in scanner, conjured the sad realization that LA wasn't her home; it was just the place where she'd lived for the last sixteen months. Three thousand miles of separation suddenly felt far lonelier than it had before.

~**~

Sunday mornings in Mike Garin's Sutton Place corner of the world were ritualistically spent with espresso, the *Wall Street Journal*, and sweeping views of the East River as Mozart drifted out onto the grand terrace 22 stories above FDR Drive. Comfortable in workout shorts and an old Harvard T-shirt, he hardly noticed the already increasing August heat as he sat at the breakfast table in the gardened section of the terrace. A slight breeze crossed his cheek, and he closed his eyes for a moment, thinking how perfect this private patio space was—even if the rest of the penthouse was a reminder of the pretentious lifestyle his father had shared here with his step-monster. This residence had become their (*not* his) overdone palace, and he had long hoped that Mia would have been ready to move by now so he could place it on the market.

Unconsciously, his head shook recalling the arrival of Candy "Sugar," obviously a contrived name his susceptible father felt to be an invitation instead of the tip off to her true intentions: her successful search for a sugar daddy. It was clear from the onset that her gregarious personality and flirty ways drew him to her. It certainly wasn't the Garin family's need for a nurturing mother figure for then three-year old, Mia. The young woman clearly hated that role. Within one month, she had installed the second of nineteen successive nannies in their home and every remnant of his mother's classic décor had been replaced with garish, trendy adornment.

Mike was thankful for small favors when his father and Candy moved to Europe, thereby separating Mia from the woman's cautiously concealed, jealous comments to his sister who was expected to inherit over twenty million dollars upon their father's death.

Unable to ignore the persistent need to reinvent himself, actually, to stay true to himself, Mike hoped that moving might usher in changes for both Mia and him. Switzerland may have separated him from his father, but he was still tied to him in a way that affected him daily. He was expected to continue practicing medicine measured by his father's successful credo: slice, dice, make money.

Inside the condo, he heard conversation. The deep baritone and distinct inflection of his cousin, Joey Falco, carried through the open slider. He must have just come off the midnight tour or surveillance because otherwise he'd never travel uptown, let alone be awake and functioning, this early on a Sunday morning.

Mike looked up when Joey's head peeked out onto the deck. The creased tan sport jacket over a rumpled white T-shirt, and blue jeans made it obvious that a night of detective work with the Intelligence Division of NYPD had just ended. His chin was scruffier than usual; his dark brown hair in disarray, and the bags under his blue eyes gave testimony that he was bone tired and in need of a double espresso. Although he loved eating, sleeping, and breathing his career as one of New York's Finest, the thrill of anti-organized crime investigation was kicking his ass.

Mike beamed. "Hey, what brings you up this way?"

Joey sat opposite his cousin and pulled Mike's coffee cup to him. He took a drink.

Although repulsed by his chronic fear of germs, Mike refrained from outwardly grimacing when Joey's lips touched the rim. "If you'd like, I could make you one."

"Nah, I'll just drink some of yours. I'm gonna crash in about five minutes. A full cup of this diesel fuel you drink would have me wired for sound."

Mike slid the red demitasse cup back in front of him, the porcelain saucer scraping against the wrought iron tabletop. As discreetly as possible, he wiped clean the edge of the cup with his index finger. "Are you planning on crashing here?"

"I hope that's all right. I'd rather not go home," Joey said, something in his voice tipping Mike off that all was not happy in his world with the "hot barmaid from McSorleys" who moved in three months ago.

"That doesn't sound good. Is it Sam?"

"Yeah. She's naggin' the hell out of me. The sex is hot but, I gotta tell ya', there ain't no way in hell I'm gonna learn to put down the toilet seat—in *my* place. That habit is long ingrained right down to my DNA, man."

Mike smirked. "Don't say I didn't warn you. You asked her to move in a little prematurely and now you're paying for it."

Joey reached over to the red cup, but Mike grabbed his fingers, squeezing them firmly, intercepting the mission before they could grasp the circumference. "Are you sure you don't want me to make you a cup? It's no problem, really."

"Nah. It's all right. You know how I love to bust your balls about your germaphobic tendencies."

"I'm not a germaphobe. I'll admit to being orderly and a little OCD about certain things but, as a physician, I'm understandably cautious about cleanliness and germs, especially yours. Who knows where your lips were this morning?" Mike grinned, slapping his cousin's hand as it reached for the cup, again.

"So what's up with you and this online dating thing Gran tells me about? Have you met anyone you need me to run a trace on—wrangle a subpoena for medical records, toxicology screening? You can't be too sure of the types you meet on the internet." He wisecracked. "Some have all kinds of germs and diseases. There are some crazy babes out there, as apparent on that Facebook page of yours."

"It's not *my* Facebook page, and I have a better chance of meeting a *clean*, cultured, upstanding woman on eDating than you do down at some sleazy after-hours bar."

"You know what I'm sayin'. I'm happy to check out some of these women you've matched with."

"It was my understanding that you've refused to engage in *family* detective work."

"You mean that Clemente thing? I told Stella that I won't run mob family info back to her. If word got out that I'm leaking names to the daughter of a former boss of the Mancini Crime Syndicate, I'd be steeped in shit—outta the force and outta my pension as quick as you can say *pazzo*. I'm not that crazy."

Mike swigged the last sip of espresso and rested the cup down with a clink. "But you'll tell me, right?"

Joey snorted. "Of course, but first, did you know that Gran's father was called 'Scarface?'"

"Well if that doesn't scream mobster I don't know what does."

"Yeah. That whole Clemente family is mob, too. They trace back to Tommy 'The Mouth' Clemente, a vicious son of a bitch during the days of Prohibition and the Depression. Don't tell Stella, but I did some digging into old police reports down at the 5th Precinct archives. There was speculation that The Mouth had Stella's father whacked in 1936, run over in broad daylight, a .45 caliber bullet was lodged in him. A couple of years later the investigating detective on the case was sent to prison for racketeering. The whole thing stinks."

"So somehow, Villa Fortuna transferred to the Clemente family by default?"

"Something like that, but the details are sketchy, which I suppose is the reason that her obsession with this building has passed all reason and logic."

"Tell me about it. At least she isn't attempting to force you into marrying one of these women," Mike groaned.

"You can thank my mother for that. Like your mom, she had the common sense to steer clear of the family history, not to mention my mother's skirts must be hiding a pair of church bell-sized balls because she's got no problem going head-to-head with Gran. I made the right decision choosing the path I did. Why do you think I joined the Intelligence Division?"

"Oh, I *know* why. It was the only way you could legally carry a concealed weapon in New York City. Not to mention that it makes you feel machismo."

Joey grinned. "Well, true as that is, it was really meant to separate myself further from our notorious mobster lineage. No different from you becoming a doctor. Only you get to fondle tits and ass all day while I'm sitting in an unmarked police van, listening to Luigi Santucci screw his mistress above a social club on Mulberry Street. What better way to show my loyalty than with a detective unit committed to anti-organized crime?"

"Is that really true? Mobsters all have mistresses?"

"Every single one of them. Doesn't matter if they're fat, old, or twisted in the head. They're getting laid 24/7, and you gotta see some of these chics." Joey whistled, tracing the shape of a woman's curves with his hands. "Va-va-voom! Hot, young, and stacked. It's the only time I wish I *was* a wiseguy in the mob."

Mike rose from his seat, picking up his cup and saucer for a refill. "I'd settle for just getting laid once a month—with the right girl, of course." He grinned mischievously.

"You're a friggin' babe-magnet. You can have any girl, round the clock."

"Not the *right* girl."

"Such a good Catholic boy," Joey teased. "I didn't know you visited the religiosity cafeteria line."

Mike shrugged, thinking of the brunette he noticed in church the evening before. "Not just for anyone, but someone special could certainly tempt me to indulge."

"That kind of girl is a good girl, and what the hell do you want one of those for? The sinners are much more fun."

"Says who? Billy Joel? No, good girls are the best kind." Mike waggled his eyebrows.

"Considering your germaphobia, I don't think the church would frown on you using a rubber."

Mike blushed.

"What about Rusty's sister?" Joey asked.

"Follow me to the kitchen and I'll tell you why Blair, as 'hot and stacked' as I've *made* her, isn't the woman for me—and the best excuse for using a condom."

The cousins vacated the private sanctuary of the terrace and headed toward the condo's kitchen through a spacious Louis XV styled, formal living room, marble entryway, and the ostentatious never-used dining room that sat 12 comfortably. At an expansive and rather unheard of 5,000 square feet located in the luxury Sutton Towers, the Garin home was valued at $19 million in the current New York City real estate market. Stella couldn't wait to get her hands on the listing whenever Mike was ready to give her the go ahead.

Although a far cry from Joey's two-bedroom apartment down in Alphabet City, he was unfazed by the environs, having spent so much of his youth in the condo. But it didn't suit Mike, and it was a mere matter of time before he would find himself some mod, Euro-styled penthouse down in TriBeCa.

After thoroughly washing his demitasse cup, Mike stood at the Nespresso machine to make two fresh cups—one for him, one for Joey.

Still wearing an oversized sleep T-shirt, Mia sat with bare legs dangling from the stool at the granite breakfast bar. With long locks pulled into a messy ponytail, her shyness and insecurity were concealed behind the computer screen as she surfed the internet from her laptop. With one hand shoveling granola cereal into her mouth, the other communicated with online friends. The small flat screen television above the countertop silently broadcast some muted Sunday weekly news program. Between mouthfuls, she crunched, "Dad emailed. He's reminding you to wire his quarterly distribution from the practice."

Mike ignored her.

"And Candy wants you to ship her the Frank Benson painting in the guest room."

"Over my dead body. Dad purchased that at Sotheby's for Mom when you were born."

"I hate her," Mia stated dropping her spoon into the bowl.

He turned then leaned on the counter's edge, smiling wistfully. "I know. Forget about them today."

"Yeah, Mia. Just hit the delete button and claim it went to junk mail," Joey advised.

With a dramatic pointed finger, she pressed the mouse, "Gone!" and went back to surfing the net, promptly announcing, "You guys gotta read this comment on MAA's Fan Club Facebook page. It's from a new friend Double D-Lighted."

Joey laughed, removing his sport coat, revealing the requisite shoulder holster and pistol tucked under his arm. "Obviously, another happy customer! You lucky dawg."

"Hardly. I'm afraid to ask what it says."

"This man's hands on my breasts worked magic."

A guffaw preceded Joey's slap to Mike's back. "Like I said, you lucky dawg."

"See what I mean about this Facebook crap! Can you delete that, Mia? It totally implies that I'm some sort of predator—like I fondle my patients for the thrill of it."

"Oh, I don't think it implies that at all, Bro. If anything, by the number of likes her comment is getting, everyone agrees. It may go viral at this rate and you'll most likely see an increase in new patients."

"What? Are you kidding? I sound like a lothario!" He ran his hand through his hair and paced as the espresso machine behind him gave up its aromatic brew with a hiss.

"What's a lothario?" Joey asked. "Is that anything like: My doctor screws me at every visit?"

Mike pivoted, his eyes boring into his cousin's good-humored ones for a long second. "What it means is that obsessed women like this D-Lighted chic are going to be the death of me! What it means is that my reputation is being destroyed for the important work I hope to be able to focus on in the future."

"I wouldn't say that. Your reputation is doing just fine according to your Facebook friends. This one here wrote that you made her nipples so erect she could lick them herself," Mia choked through her laughter.

"Get outta here! She did not!" He yelled, running to the laptop, forgetting all about the espresso. He leaned over his sister's shoulder, wrapping his arm around her to scroll down the timeline of the fan club's page, each post making him more agitated by the moment. Sexual innuendo after innuendo was made with only minor veiled references to his actual *skill* as a cosmetic surgeon. Anyone reading this would have little idea that he was actually a physician! He broke out into a sweat, flushing in exasperation and mortification at each post he read.

"I sound like you—a total manwhore! Even I can't believe I've done this! I did not tickle Mrs. Conrad's inner thigh! She's sixty-two for Christ sake! Why would she write that?" He scrolled down a little further then suddenly stepped back, aghast. Again, running his hand through his hair, his palm now adhered to his crown. "Holy Shit! Shit! Shit! Blair must have taken that photo yesterday after her appointment!"

Joey came to stand beside him and all three gaped at the image on the screen.

"That's me looking out my office window onto Park Avenue. She's posted a close up of my butt for God's sake!"

"I don't know what you're so pissed off for," Joey stated. "If I had an ass that tight, I'd brandish it all over the internet, too. Only I'd be naked!"

"Hey, check out one of the butt comments. 'Michelangelo's bum is so finely sculptured it should be bronzed like the Rodin in his office.'"

"I think I'm gonna be sick."

Mia laughed when Mike plopped down into the desk chair in the corner of the kitchen. He sat cradling his head in his hands, bemoaning his ruined reputation.

"It's no big deal, Mike, really. Nothing to get agita over. Do you want me to report the image? I can you know, but your face isn't exposed. So, in a way, you're safe," she offered clearly concerned at the groans coming from her brother.

"Try to ignore it, man." Joey said, completely unfazed by the posts that his cousin felt were an absolute violation of privacy. In a detective's line of work, this was nothing. Mike should see some of the things that show up on video surveillance. Salacious stuff that most men dream about, but most women would commit suicide over if they knew it was being viewed back at the office on continuous loop. "I gotta get some sleep," he pronounced as he strode from the kitchen.

Mike and Mia's eyes met when upon reaching the dining room, Joey let loose a howl of laughter. "Lickable nipples! Bah, ha, ha! That, I'd love to see! Bah, ha, ha!"

"What are you going to do about this?" Mia asked.

"There's nothing I can do. Is there?" He abruptly stood, walked to the Nespresso, and then downed his lukewarm caffeine.

"I could kill dad for this. This is not what I bargained for. Mia, I have to move on and I have to move out, not only from this over-done showplace, but also from my so-called career as a body sculptor. I love you, but you have to give some thought about selling this place. It's time for you and me to make some changes in our lives. With the money you'll make from the sale, you can invest it and give some serious thought about your future."

Surprisingly, she didn't look nervous or upset. Instead, she twisted her lips, obviously considering his idea.

"It means that much to you?"

"It does."

"You're that unhappy?"

"I am."

"Then I'll tell you what. If you find a girl by the end of the year, I'll be amenable to putting the place on the market in the spring."

Mike beamed. "Deal."

~**~

Two weeks later, with her heart hammering in her chest, Elizabeth tentatively stepped into St. Clement Catholic Church located on Sunset Boulevard. Filled with light, its white plaster walls and bleached oak pews immediately welcomed her with a different kind of peaceful solemnity than she felt at St. John's in Etonville. In a word: joyful. Through the glass panes separating the narthex from the nave, she noted the few worshipers kneeling within, some praying the rosary, none awaiting confession. The blue-colored stained glass appeared modern in contrast to the traditional marble altar and awning above it. In fact, the church itself was a comfortable blend of Old World and modern—just like its parishioners.

She dipped three fingers into the holy water font and blessed herself just as a young priest dressed in the standard black plants, shirt, and white collar approached. His smile caught her off guard. Apart from Father Rocco back in Belmont, no priest she had ever known greeted worshipers upon entrance into the church.

"Are you Elizabeth Clemente," he asked.

"Yes, how did you know?"

"I can see the fear in your eyes." He chuckled and extended his hand. "I'm Father Mintern. I was just praying that you'd keep our appointment for confession."

"It's nice to meet you, Father. When I telephoned, I wasn't aware that priests wrote things like confessions on their calendars." She shifted her weight, fidgeting at the thought that she was minutes from the dreaded confession.

"Of course. Apart from the Mass, it is one of the most important sacraments you can make in your faith walk. It shouldn't be done on the fly."

On the fly? Wow. He must be about 30.

"Follow me; we'll talk in my office."

"No booth?"

He searched her face. "No booth. Just a good ole heart-to-heart followed by absolution from my easy chair."

"You know, I think I like St. Clement church already."

"That's good to hear."

They walked down a hallway, which ran parallel to the nave, and her palms grew sweaty at the thought of purging twelve years of sins. Did she even know what to say? Did she even remember half of the things that were considered sinful? Well, she'd just have to wing this unusual, untraditional, experience. Somehow she knew that Father Mintern and his easy manner would allow a few mistakes in the recitation of the requisite prayers.

His office looked like any other business workplace, until he lit a candle on the coffee table and kissed a purple stole before placing it around his neck. Taking a seat in what looked like an EZ-Boy recliner he motioned for her to sit across from him.

"Now don't be nervous. God is all ears. So whenever you want to begin ..."

"Bless me Father for I have sinned ... um ... do I have to say that prayer? I don't really remember it."

Father smiled. "Why don't you just tell me what's on your mind?"

Her eyes settled upon a print of Rembrandt's Prodigal Son behind him.

"You mean like a therapy session?"

"It is therapeutic to cleanse your soul. So, yeah."

"Hmm, well, up until two weeks ago, I hadn't stepped into a Catholic church since my father's funeral two years ago, and before that almost a decade. I've been divorced, and sexually active using contraception—although not in a while—and um …"

She twisted her fingers on her lap and looked away from Father Mintern. "… embarrassed of my family and culture, rarely going back home to New York."

"And why is that?"

"It's complicated." A hard swallow of the knot forming in her throat precipitated a moment of silence.

"I've been hurt by a few people: one, had professed himself a good Italian-Catholic who wanted to marry me and raise a family and he ended up being a liar and a cheater, like many other Italian men of my acquaintance. Another saw my religion and ethnicity as a scourge upon his family. I overheard him call my mother a crass, uneducated guinea from Little Italy. I divorced him since we weren't, obviously, married in the church."

"So you have issues with your upbringing? I see that a lot out here in LA. It's not as uncommon as you think. People run from their roots."

"Really? I feel like the only one. Two weeks ago I returned home for the reading of a will and stayed with my sisters in the old neighborhood, and it was difficult. Their whole world is Little Italy, as though they are living in a vacuum. Yet, I simultaneously feel an immense amount of guilt having left them, the Church, everything."

She sighed deeply, feeling partly unburdened by her admission, but unwilling to shed all her history. She wasn't completely ready to discuss *everything*.

Father Mintern tented his fingers at his chin. "Elizabeth, what do you want? What is your heart telling you?"

She pursed her lips, pausing, and by God couldn't stop the tear that rolled down her cheek. No wonder why she dreaded this confession so much. Facing pain wasn't something she did – running from it was.

The priest held out a box of Kleenex.

Pulling the tissue out, she admitted with a small voice. "I want to be happy, Father, and I'm not."

"I suspect that what you really want, but are afraid to admit is that you *do* want to go home. You love and miss your sisters, and the traditions you grew up with have made you who you are. Elizabeth, your faith is embedded in your soul. You can come home whenever you want. The door is always open."

"But I have a life here, a career path, a plan. No, I'll never move back to New York."

"A rabbi friend of mine once told me 'Man plans, God laughs.' I say: Let go … let God. Why don't we pray together?"

~**~

~Six~
Affari
(Business)

The Wednesday before Thanksgiving, Elizabeth stood just outside an examination room of West Hollywood Podiatry Center (WHPC) wearing a white lab coat and an inward frown. She watched the departure of her new pediatric patient as he hobbled in leg braces toward reception, supported by small crutches alongside his mother. After two years, the family had switched doctors, seeking a more aggressive treatment plan, and they had asked specifically for her! The Andrews family was a new referral from a patient who came to her for relief from painful hammertoes. Although saddened by the six-year-old's deformity, she was confident in her ability to help him.

"Happy Thanksgiving. I'll see you in the New Year, Mrs. Andrews. Bye, Brandon. You're doing great; keep up the therapy until then."

Poor little guy, she thought, reflecting on the conversation the boy had initiated about all the normal childhood pursuits he longed to enjoy. Few were options without a particular surgical procedure she had trained for and successfully accomplished during her extensive forefoot and rearfoot residency.

Brandon stopped midway and turned. "Doctor Fairchild, are you going to help me be a policeman like my dad?"

She walked to him, squatting to be level with the boy then glanced up to his teary-eyed mother, who was biting her lip to keep from crying. Heartfelt compassion aching within her chest, Elizabeth took hold of her young patient's hand.

"I'm going to try my hardest, Brandon. Don't you worry about a thing because as soon as I'm back after the holidays, we're going to work on fixing that foot of yours. Until then, have a merry Christmas, sweetie. I'm sure Santa is very proud of you."

His chin rose, eyes shining at his new doctor, who, with a reassuring smile smoothed the hair on his forehead as she reluctantly released his small hand and stood. Mrs. Andrews mouthed "thank you."

Elizabeth's composure nearly faltered as she turned away, walking directly back to the exam room. Determined, she grabbed the small laptop where Brandon Andrew's x-ray remained illuminated upon the screen. Yeah, she could do this surgery and if it appeased her boss, he could observe, even assist if he felt uneasy about her ability. Unfortunately, they seemed to be still in the "Bench Test" phase of their relationship, which annoyed her having been with the practice as the junior associate for sixteen months now. She'd never outright call him a jerk, but that's what he was. Intuitively, she knew he held her back out of jealousy. Old-school Dr. Alfred Greenwald and the two other partners were grandfathered into the ever-evolving podiatric requirements, but she had gone the gamut in surgical training.

Peeking her head into his ultra modern, minimalist office, she clutched the laptop under her arm. "Al, do you have a minute? I want to show you a couple of x-rays from a case that just presented."

"Sure, have a seat. Let's see what you have."

"A six-year-old boy with relatively stable spastic equinous, but possible undiagnosed cerebral palsy. For the last two years, the family's current podiatrist has been treating conservatively with therapy: stretching, strength enhancing, and motor skill development coupled with bracing. None of which are helping. I believe he has myostatic contracture. I've referred the family to a pediatric neurologist for CP evaluation, but the patient is a prime candidate at his age for Achilles tendon lengthening of his right foot."

Al nodded as he pressed the mouse to advance the images and review the clinical notes. His prolonged silence caused Elizabeth to shift uneasily in her chair. She hated this, hated that she required his approval on everything. Oftentimes, she wondered if it was because she was the only female physician in the practice. Certainly, she was the youngest but, more to the point, she was the one with the growing patient list. This latter fact was becoming a bone of contention to some of the senior associates.

"And what would be your plan for the tendon lengthening?" he finally asked, raising a quizzical brow.

Removing the small notebook from her lab coat pocket, Elizabeth drew a schematic, explaining her plan and delineating the patient's expected recovery and outcome. Al's initial response was to nod silently, and she knew that never bode well. His lips were set in their usual downturn.

"I admire your confidence, Elizabeth. Your diagnostic skills are one of the reasons I hired you, your training evident. You are correct in your evaluation and based on your chart notes, I would concur with your assessment. Although surgery would have its greatest results from age twelve and up with less chance of recurrence, given this patient's history he could benefit with both bracing and tendon lengthening."

She beamed. How could she not? This was the pat on the back she had been waiting for. "I'd like to look at scheduling surgery after I return from New York."

"Whoa. You're getting ahead of yourself, here. While I value your eagerness and willingness to help this Andrews patient, this isn't the type of procedure that we want to handle here at West Hollywood. I'd like for you to refer it out to Children's Hospital's neuro-orthopedic department."

Stunned, her voice raised slightly, her long suppressed, outspoken Clemente fervor attempting to surface. She wanted to shout to the unfeeling oaf on the opposite side of the desk, "That *'Andrews patient'* has a first name and a future."

"But I can do this, Al. I trained to do this, and have done so on numerous occasions over my three-year residency. It's why you hired me, isn't it? It's one of the reasons I'm going to the surgical reconstruction conference in Manhattan in a couple of weeks."

"I hired you for a myriad of reasons." He looked her up and down, causing her fingers to grasp onto the open button of her lab coat protectively.

"We clicked on a patient and physician level, and I gave Brandon and his mother my word," she stated.

"Well then, there's your first mistake. You never make promises you can't keep, particularly when it comes to surgery."

He closed the laptop and slid it across his glass desk in her direction. "I'm sorry, Elizabeth. We do cosmetic surgery here and we operate a cash business with that in mind. I thought you understood that. Children's Hospital will be able to assist this patient."

She rose from the chair and grabbed the laptop, holding it close against her midsection. "I can't tell you how disappointed I am. As disappointed as I'm sure Mrs. Andrews will be when I tell her that we're going to give her a run around, just like she received from their last physician."

"We're not giving her a run around. We're giving her a referral to a practice that'll help her son. I understand you being upset, but truth is, you're only a junior associate here and this is over your head."

"Then assist the case with me. We'll scrub together. You can oversee everything and I can finally prove myself to you."

"You know I don't have the training or hospital privileges to do rear foot surgeries. My answer is no."

Wrong answer, her mind groaned, her indignation displayed by the hand clenching her hip in anger. She felt like Nicki, but restrained her ire and resorting to colorful expletives.

She took a deep breath choosing her words carefully. "Al, I feel … well, I feel as though you are holding me back from getting cases toward my board certification, and I'm not sure why. I am experienced, and I can help Brandon Andrews and all the other patients that you've taken from me. I sincerely hope we can further discuss this matter after my trip."

The sixty-year-old jerk chuckled: big mistake number two.

"About that … December is a busy time for vanity reconstruction. The film industry takes a hiatus and many of their people plan on the month of non-weight bearing over the holidays. I need every Associate at the ready."

Stammering, her arm straightened to a rigid position as she balled her fist at her side, her face growing red. "But you promised in August, approving my three week vacation. I've already purchased my ticket to leave on the fourth."

"You'll have to return it. You're needed here."

"It's non-refundable, and you yourself just said, you never make a promise you can't keep. I gave my word—my promise—to my sisters. *They* need me, too."

Again, he raised an eyebrow. "I'm sure your sisters would understand, or perhaps, you need to reconsider your future with West Hollywood." He pointed to the stack of resumes piled neatly at the corner of his desk. "There are a lot of other young physicians who are chomping at my heels for a position here. The decision is yours."

"Yes. The decision is mine." Elizabeth stormed from his office heading directly to her own space on the opposite side of the clinic, quickly contemplating the nature of the requirements Dr. Greenwald would deem important in his next new hire.

She shut the door of what resembled a suffocating closet, collapsing into her recycled desk chair. More bad luck. All her family ever had was bad luck. Close to crying, she fought the response, swallowing her frustration and willing herself to see the positive. *I'm going to turn this into good luck: a new beginning for Gina and Nicki, maybe a new employer for me. Someone kind, someone who cares more for people than for making a quick buck.* Al had played his last hand—he was messing with the future of her sisters.

Her heartbeat thundered and she felt anxious, wanting to blow her top. "I can't believe this. It's one thing not to support me, but it's a whole other matter to keep me from supporting my family, especially after giving me his word."

Unaware of what possessed her, in the absolute privacy of her small, staid office distinguished only by a framed piece of modern quilt art, she pulled her handbag from the lower desk drawer. With trembling hands, she dug to the very bottom, fingers finally grasping the small pouch she had carelessly tossed in there three months prior. Neither attendance at Mass nor the very difficult "confession" had prompted its retrieval from the bottomless pit. Clutched within her palm, a sensation of calm spread through her as she pulled out Great-Aunt Maria's rosary beads. Just fingering the worn, supple leather of the pouch provided the strength to help make her decision.

Long minutes passed in thought, concluding with a spontaneous prayer and recognition of the solace and hope she was experiencing. She called Carpo from her mobile to inquire about Gina and Nicki's progress at the salon and to inform him when she would be arriving home.

~**~

With a smile upon his face, Salvatore Carpo hung up the telephone. With only three weeks remaining until the grand opening, everything was coming together for Pal•Hair•Mo Salon and the Clemente sisters.

Just this morning, he felt satisfied as he reviewed the stipulations of Mrs. Dixon's will, checking off the progress that his young clients had made over the last three months. Frankly, he was surprised by the eldest's tenacity when offered the opportunity for her lifelong dream to come to fruition. He was also taken aback by Gina's bizarre, almost Savant-like ability with numbers. Who could have guessed what various talents were hidden behind a lovely, amiable, but rather bubble headed exterior such as Gina's? Nichole had also come as a surprise. The youngest of the Clemente sisters, unabashedly, wore her Sicilian passion and quick-temper as openly as her bare midriff. He wondered, now that winter was upon them, what her manner of dress would be, given that she had yet to conform to her prozia's last wish. That, however, wasn't the cause of his surprise. That petite *vivace* woman could swing a hammer and wield a nail gun better than any construction laborer he'd ever seen. Back in Italy, her ability to get the job done in under a week— no ifs, ands or buts—would be highly prized by every unwelcome Americano living in Tuscany. Because of Nicki, the beauty parlor's opening was right on schedule.

As Elizabeth's telephone call confirmed, she, too, was on schedule. Her anticipated arrival back to New York from LA on December 4th brought the prospect of a much-desired personal distraction and appealing mission. Over the months, he had kept in touch with her to ensure completion of her confession and religious service attendance, and found himself even more attracted to her then initially. There was something about the doctor that made all the women who had come and gone in his bed pale in comparison. Perhaps it was the challenge she presented.

With a sly smirk, he leaned back in his desk chair and twirled the pen in his hand, allowing his thoughts to focus upon the middle sister's sun-kissed, shapely legs. Imagining his hand smoothing lotion up her calf, he shifted in his seat, already delightfully uncomfortable.

He kissed his pinched fingers in exquisite appreciation of the image, as though she were a plate of delicious lasagna. *Mamma mia*, this was going to be a wonderful Christmas and, no doubt, Dr. Fairchild would be affected not only by the holiday sights and sounds of the city, but surely by his own easy Romano charm. A little vino, a few kisses under the stars, and with his suave banter, she would be his next lover.

His smile broadened when he surmised that an intellectual such as she was most likely well-read. He would need to discuss *Dante's Inferno* or maybe that *Thirty Shades of Red*. Books always worked, not that he read them, but debating literature was a surefire way to spark conversation, which usually ended up in a luxury suite at the Waldorf Astoria once discussion turned to sins of the flesh and the softness of Italian silk ties. Elizabeth would be a hard-won prize but one worth pursuing and pleasing. He'd have to call upon every skill of seduction he had honed over the years. Perhaps once her impenetrable exterior was cracked, she would make the perfect mistress—not too clingy, but definitely unconstrained enough to give into that hot-blooded passion hidden below.

~**~

Dharma, known to her friends as Picasso, stood in the cold between Gina and Nicki in front of her new place of employment. They watched a couple of beefy construction guys, utilizing pulleys and planks, raise the bright red and yellow store sign above the newspaper-covered window. All three friends nodded with an awesome sense of satisfaction at the work they had collectively accomplished since August. Dharma especially observed how Gina's wide grin projected a sense of pride at having named the salon in honor of her sisters' Sicilian roots: Pal•Hair•Mo. Its colors and the salon's décor were politely pilfered from the state flag of Sicily. With images of Medusa and the Trinacria throughout, Gina thought the inspiration was perfect. She had toyed with the idea of taking a photograph to send to their sister in LA, but quickly reversed the idea, figuring that some things should be left to discovery *after* they came to full fruition.

Overjoyed for her long time friend, Dharma smiled, thinking that Gina's talent could finally be exposed to a larger community with an affluent clientele. She hoped that they would accept her and Nicki who, like herself, were a very different breed from those who lived in Etonville.

"Is your sister going to be happy with the salon name? It is kinda weird, but definitely kitschy and memorable. A little piece of Italy in this uptight Wasp world," she said with a slight whistling lisp in her speech due to her tongue piercing. She continued to look up at the colorful sign, admiring the shaft of wheat underlining the name. That was her idea.

Nicki snorted. "Sure as shit, Lizzy is gonna be pissed. Hope you'll be here on the day she arrives to see it. You gotta check out those lips of hers. She sucks 'em in before she blows like a volcano. It's so funny."

"Is she going to be okay with the décor you chose?" Dharma shifted uncomfortably suddenly worried about this high-class physician to the stars and her possible reprobation of the artwork lining the salon's interior.

"Maybe," Gina said. "But she said this was my world and my dream and that I should do what I thought best. The three-legged mythological Trinacria from the flag was a natural choice. It represents who we are. Three legs: three sisters, Medusa: hair. If Medusa is good enough for Versace's logo then it's good enough for Clemente's PalHairMo. I love the idea that when a client mentions our salon, it'll sound like they're visiting Palermo, a place where the people are warm and welcoming—where everyone is family!" She nearly clapped at the thought.

"Don't worry, Picasso," Nicki assured. "Lizzy'll be cool once she calms down and stops rolling her eyes. Apparently, after she married that snobby dickwad during med school, she started pretending that her ancestors came over on the friggin' Mayflower. One slice of pizza from Arthur Avenue and she'll be back thinking that 1492 *Santa Maria* boat was the bomb."

Gina chuckled. "You surprise me, Nicki. I didn't think you even knew who Christopher Columbus was."

"What'a you think I am, an idiot?"

Dharma glanced over her leather-clad shoulder, taking in the local denizens. This village needed something more than an Italian salon with a gorgon mascot. It needed a total attitude adjustment, and she hoped that her blue hair, tattoos, and piercings wouldn't negatively impact Gina's dream before the doors even opened. She noted the posh clientele exiting from Halo across the street.

"Is your appointment today, Gina?"

"I nearly forgot!" She glanced at her phone. "I have a three o'clock with their top stylist in thirty minutes. I need to see what the competition has to offer before we put together our salon menu and price list."

"Will you tell her who you are?"

"Not on your life! I booked my appointment under the name 'Carpo.' If she knows who I am, she might shave off my hair. I'm sure they can't be too happy at our crashing their monopoly on the Etonville beauty business. They've been the only salon in a six-mile radius, but not any longer."

"Yeah, we're gonna kick their asses all over this place."

"I hope so, Nicki. I want to make Lizzy proud of us, and more importantly, I want her to come home permanently. She's not happy and she's not herself. I hardly recognize who she's become."

~**~

~Seven~
Diavoli e Angeli
(Devils & Angels)

Buoying her nerve, Gina entered Halo Salon with a cheerful demeanor and a determined outlook. The heavy glass door opened into a wholly lackluster beige environment bombarded by the invasion of the bubble gum pink faux rabbit jacket, furry white earmuffs, and matching Après boots she wore. Certain her choice of attire was the cause of the multiple head turns, she politely ignored the disapproving expressions on the women in the reception area. Responding with a genuine smile, all eyes in unison abruptly redirected back to the iPhones clutched within their manicured fingers. Yes, this village needed change, just as Mr. Carpo had expressed.

The famous Halo was one of those hair salons where its claim to fame in Westchester County was customer service, and that was what Gina expected when she entered. With eager anticipation, she stood at the counter waiting … and waiting … for the receptionist to hang up the telephone or even to acknowledge her presence with a welcoming expression, a friendly wave or simply, eye contact. None came.

She made good use of the delay to calculate the chair to client ratio and the number of assistants working beside each stylist, doing the grunt work of sweeping and restocking supplies. The place was a busy hive, each beautician attending their client as patrons sat in reception, thumbing through crisp copies of *Travel & Leisure* or *Marie Claire* magazines. Apart from earsplitting club music reverberating in her chest cavity, there was very little extraneous noise in the beauty parlor; no one conversed, not even the hairdressers with their clients.

If this is a "spa environ" surely Mantovani's Orchestra would be better suited for relaxation than this loud music! PalHairMo will definitely play better stuff!

Helping herself to a salon menu from the counter, she flipped through the four pages of available services, her eyes widening at the starting cost of a simple wash, cut, and blow dry—a whopping $150. She shoved the leaflet into her handbag and again, with a keen eye for detail gazed around the salon. Modern and spacious, each stylist's station was a separate partitioned cubicle offering a fully secluded sanctuary. The establishment clearly focused on an individual's desire for privacy to enhance their spa experience, but as superficially soothing and personal as was the intention, it felt wrong to Gina. The space lacked any warmth or feeling of community. There was nothing fun or exciting about the environment and considering these clients each spent a good deal of time here during their appointment, it seemed such a shame.

Within the floor-to-ceiling array of beige tones that varied all the way from off-white to pale latte, even the granite countertops felt as bland as the town. If her patronage on this day hadn't been to scope out the competition, she would never come here, even if she had the excess money.

Capelli Belli was nothing like this and neither will PalHairMo be!

Perfectly precise displays of expensive product lined every station, cubicle, and wall unit, adorning every tabletop and horizontal shelf. Noting the brands, and that most patrons left with a small shopping bag bearing the salon's circular halo logo, she mentally calculated the outrageous prices of the outgoing shampoo, conditioner, sprays and gels, multiplying by the average number of patrons on any given day. The owner was reaping a goldmine of overpriced product. Well, her salon would prove that it could still be successful without her clientele spending a ridiculous amount of extra money for their hair care!

The young female receptionist finally hung up the phone, tapped upon her keyboard, then pointed to the iPad on the counter. "Sign in, please."

"Hi, I'm Regina Carpo. I'm a new client and have a three o'clock with Vanessa for a cut and style."

"Sign in on the iPad and have a seat."

No smile, no warmth, or even a simple "please." Apparently, there was no angel at the Gates of Halo— just a disinterested twenty-year old who couldn't give a crap; Gina was frustrated. She wondered if the owner knew how impersonal the salon felt and how this employee represented it so poorly. Lord knows, as a new client, she didn't feel welcome at all.

"Oh, and would you like a sparkling water?" the girl added.

"Do you have any juice or iced tea?"

"No, just water and coffee. If you want coffee, the pot is over there." The girl barely nodded in the direction.

Gina straightened her shoulders before sitting on the plush sofa between two women who surreptitiously eyed her pinkness up and down as though she was wearing some sort of contagious disease.

Welcome to Halo!

Sardonically finding humor in the entire scene, she inwardly chuckled, and began compiling another list of all the practices she would institute at PalHairMo, specifically noting what her salon would *not* have – partitions being the first taboo and a tired looking coffee pot, the close second. At these prices, the owner should at least splurge for a Keurig with free pods and something a little more posh than an ugly straw basket holding hard peppermint candy. Even Mrs. Drago at Capelli Belli knew that! First thing she was going to do when she left here was to call Carpo and have him order a fancy barista cappuccino maker. One of those super imported ones like Mrs. Dardani has at her café on Arthur Avenue would do fine.

She watched a good-looking guy wearing tan slacks and a light blue dress shirt exit the back room and approach the receptionist. Gina fidgeted with the furry earmuffs she held, wondering if his appraisal was of herself or one of the hoity-toity women flanking her. One was probably his client. He offered an easy smile, and she smiled back just in case it was directed to her. Mesmerized by his ginger ponytail and sparkling eyes, she couldn't help staring. Confident that he was not an Italian, she unconsciously breathed a sigh of relief after reminding herself of her *cazzo* cheating ex-husband, her sister's vehement objections, and her prozia's criticism about how she always chose "the wrong type of men." Not that she'd be pursuing anything with the redheaded eye candy now speaking with Miss Congeniality behind the desk. Wrong type could also mean gay. Perhaps he was gay. He did have a ponytail.

Scoping out the pink bunny sitting on the sofa in the reception area, Russell "Rusty" Channing, owner of Halo, enjoyed the visceral reaction that stirred in his loins. She reminded him of an innocent-looking

Vargas 1940s pin up. For a moment he mused how he'd love to see her painted—or in the flesh—wearing nothing but those furry boots and the earmuffs she held in her wedding band-less hand. Better yet!—a Playboy bunny suit with erect nipples ears. Naughtily, he imagined her lying in a lush green field with nothing but that pink coat, awaiting a wolf to come and devour her.

Rusty shook his head, snapping himself from the satisfying daydream. His day had already been maxed out with a series of monumental screw-ups; the last thing he needed was to be caught leering with a hard on for a client. Bad enough that the Keurig had broken first thing this morning and then the salon ran out of their signature specialty chocolate during the lunch hour rush. The new full-color ad in the local paper didn't run, and worst of all, this temporary receptionist that his sister Blair had sent over from her boutique down the street was incompetent. Frustrated and feeling overwhelmed, the gorgeous breath of fresh air that blew in wearing that faux fur coat was just what he needed to find his smile and restore his equilibrium.

He leaned over the reception desk, turning Emma's computer screen to face him. "Vanessa is still tied up with her client so I'll be taking her next appointment slot."

"But … you? Mr. Channing, I was told that you don't take new clients."

"I'll be making an exception to that rule with Ms. Carpo." He looked the new client up and down, his brow knitting. "Why didn't you take her coat?"

"Ew. I'm not touching that pink thing. I have a good mind to call PETA."

Normally easy going, he sobered, standing to his full six-foot height, enjoying how she leaned back from him on the opposite side of the counter. "It's imitation fur, Emma, and if you disrespectfully speak about any of Halo's clients again, you'll find yourself out of a job. Do I make myself clear?"

"Yes, Mr. Channing. S-Sorry."

Damn that felt good. He loved flexing his "boss" muscle, and when he approached the flaxen-haired beauty waiting in reception, he unconsciously flexed his other idle muscle in response to the alluring image she presented.

"Ms. Carpo, I'm Rusty Channing. Welcome to Halo." He held out his hand for a shake, delighting at the feel of her fingers wrapping around his when she stood. Soft ... like her bunny fur and the rosy flush to her cheeks.

She giggled and that affected him, too. Innocently demure ... as though an impish tease lurked below that sweet smile.

"Hi. It's great to meet you. You're the owner aren't you?"

He blushed, already getting signals that she liked what she saw, too. "I am, but please call me Rusty. I hope it's okay but I'll be ..." he coughed, then tried to suppress a smile. "... servicing you today. Vanessa is tied up with a foil highlight, and I'd hate to have you waiting too long before getting you into the chair."

"You want to *do* me?" Her glossy pink painted fingernails rose splayed to her chest.

A little twist to his lips accompanied a head nod. "I do."

"I'm so flattered. Usually *big* owners of impressive salons like this don't get much hands-on."

"That's true, but I'm happy to use my hands on you and that beautiful head of hair of yours." He touched her shoulder, adding, "May I take off your coat?"

This was getting fun, and he reveled in this bunny hopping innuendo, hoping it wouldn't turn her off—or worse, end with a sexual harassment lawsuit.

"Oh, yes, please. It's getting hot in here. Stripping off is a great idea. I mean ... taking off my coat is."

She turned just as he dropped the downy cocoon from her shoulders, his fingertips brushing against the back of the form-fitting white sweater she wore. He breathed in, enjoying her strawberry scent, nearly swooning like a horny teenager at the thought of tasting her berries. *Good Lord, stop it man! She's a client! And you're not a pervert!*

Rusty led her to the first cubicle at the front of the salon with a view of Main Street. The station was very quiet and that was just fine with Gina. She was going to slyly pick her competition's brain with a flirtatious smile, maybe even some of Nicki's *puttana* tactics. There was always confession at church on Saturday to wipe all the naughty innuendo away as though it never happened. She was on a business mission and surely God would understand.

After sitting in the fine leather chair, her eyes locked with the owner's in the oval mirror before them. He had stopped her heart when their hands met, but she pushed down her attraction forcing herself to stay "on point" as Lizzy often cautioned. Her enthusiasm always got the best of her. "Is your salon always this busy on a weekday?"

He spoke low in reply, seemingly not to violate the prevailing silent atmosphere. "Usually. I've had to hire a few additional stylists over the last six months, so that means that business is growing. How did you find out about Halo?"

"I um … a friend told me. She had good things to say. Then I read the reviews on Yelp and Google. And Vanessa came highly recommended."

"She's the salon manager. I'm really fortunate to have her, but today she was slammed with clients, and well … I've had to put out a few fires."

"Well, then that's my gain—you having to fill my slot—isn't it?" *Stop it, Gina!*

He draped the requisite black smock over her, replying, "I rather think it's my gain. Perhaps, if you enjoy my treatment, you'll become a regular. Your slot would have a permanent place on my calendar." He grinned, running his confident hands through her hair from scalp out to the tips.

She tingled from his touch. *Oh, Gawd, help me!* This was not going to be as easy as she had expected. She wasn't counting on *him*, let alone his overt sexual persona. That only made it all the worse. Already she was feeling the same way that Frankie had made her feel on their first date at McDonalds when he fed her a french fry. This guy was a McDreamy.

"So what are we going to do to your beautiful tresses today?"

"I'd love to keep the length, but I'm looking for a new style. I trust you. You can do what you want to me."

"God I love when a client says that to me, especially the ones who look like models."

She couldn't help the unladylike chortle that exited her mouth. "A model? Gawd, that's so not true! Are you flirting with me?"

"I am." Rusty grinned mischievously, holding out his hand. "Come with me, and I'll wet you down," he said, making it sound as though a specialty treatment offered only by him.

Once settled with the back of her neck nestled against the porcelain wash sink, she looked up into his baby blues, and his hands began to work with the warm water spray. She wondered why one of the assistants wasn't doing the washing but as soon as he massaged the shampoo into her hair, she didn't care. Magic fingers stimulated her scalp, alternating between pressure and relaxation. Before her eyes rolled to the back of her head in supreme ecstasy, Gina noted that he had closed his eyes while working her. It was clear he was enjoying this as much as she was, and then it happened—sparks. Not the kind that happened when two hands meet for a shake, but the type of inner sizzle that occurred whenever she wanted to get it on with a guy. He rubbed her temples, the pads of his thumbs making slow circles and, by God, if she didn't think that his body was moving in erotic tandem with the rotation. It might have been her imagination but damn, if she didn't enjoy that image. She crossed her legs to keep the sparks at bay. She was near lifting off the chair, ready to pull him down upon her.

"How does that feel?" he asked.

"Like heaven."

"You have hair like an angel."

"I'm no angel."

She watched the slow smirk spread upon his lips, then his broad chest leaned over her, near enough to kiss as his massaging motions became more vigorous. His pelvis butted up against her hand as it rested upon the arm of the chair. He was no angel either. Rusty was quite the big red devil.

Her hand gripped the arm, immobilized as she tried to will herself not to give into the enticement. *One touch, just a little harmless brush. Perhaps my pinky could accidentally reach out and poke ...*

Then his talented fingers abruptly stopped and the sprayer of luke-warm water shocked her from her temptation.

Combined with the scalp tingling minty conditioner application, his hands presented a near orgasmic experience and suddenly Halo had a new appeal. Orgasm wasn't listed on the salon's menu because it was free of charge. No wonder the salon was packed; this Rusty's fingers weren't rusty at all. They worked fluidly, and she was a goner. Perhaps this was the customer service Yelpers had spoken of. In fact, she didn't remember seeing a single male in the establishment this afternoon.

PalHairMo could never compete with this. Wiping the tiny water droplets from her forehead, she considered, *Maybe we could. We do have Nicki.*

He wrapped her head with a beige towel and dried her neck before saying, "Let's head back to my place."

Yes, please, she thought to her mortification.

"Can I get you a coffee or spring water?"

"What I'd love is a glass of wine," *and a cigarette, even if I don't smoke.* "Do you have any?"

Rusty looked at her oddly. "Wine? No, but maybe you'd like to go for a drink with me sometime. There's a great wine bar over in Eastchester."

"Do you try picking up all your clients, Mr. Channing? Is that part of Halo's customer service?"

"No. In fact, this is a rarity. I just feel comfortable in your presence."

She didn't answer, chastising herself to stay focused on why she was here—to get information— not to get off, even if she needed that just as much.

They walked side-by-side through the salon to his cubicle and when she sat, he quietly asked. "Do you live around here?"

"Nah, I live in Belmont."

"What a coincidence. The new owners of that Tudor building across the street also live around that section of the Bronx." He uncovered her head then began combing out her long, wet locks as he continued, "You might know them. Their last name is Clemente."

"Nope." She blushed and fanned herself with her hand. Yeah, confession was going to be a bitch on Saturday. Now she had a lie to add to the growing list.

"Three sisters: Gina, Lizzy, and Nicki. I haven't met them yet, but I'm a little hesitant. We're a close-knit community here and well …"

"Yes?"

"They'll be my competition in a few weeks. They're opening a salon."

Gina gasped. "Oh dear! What will you do?"

Rusty removed his scissors from the pouch lying on his counter and leaned against the edge, facing her. She unexpectedly felt bad for him, not to mention guilty. His blue eyes suddenly looked cloudy.

"What can I do? I'll just continue to please our clients and hope that their salon services are different from ours here at Halo. I worked hard to build up my place and reputation, and I just can't roll over without a fight. That's for sure," he professed.

"A fight? You make it sound like a Mafia turf war?"

He smiled. "I will have to step up my game, but I don't think I'll be whacking anyone."

"Gosh, I hope not."

He walked behind her; his shears engaging with masterful snips. He was like Edward Scissorhands the way his fingers flew over her head as little slivers of blonde fell to the floor.

"How did you know it would be a salon?" she asked.

"Like I said, Etonville is like a family. My best friend's grandmother is a realtor and she's also on the village Board of Trustees. She keeps us merchants informed of any new shops and their owners."

"What's her name? My sister may be in need of a realtor soon. I'm trying to convince her to move back to New York from California."

"Stella De Luca."

And there it was, hanging in the air—that Russo De Luca woman. The devil's whore.

~**~

Unlike Capelli Belli, where even the blow-dry process couldn't drown out conversation and gossip, Rusty continued to work and Gina remained silent. She watched his backside in the mirror as he styled the front of her hair. The way he moved, how each turn and long pull of the round brush flexed the muscles in his back undid her. He had a great ass and his torso was equally impressive as he leaned in, mere inches from her face with each stroke of his tool. The man was gorgeous and she was feeling very ugly about her ruse, but not enough to tell him the truth of who she was and why she was there.

He suddenly looked away from his task and she could hear the jubilant tone in his voice.

"Hey, buddy! Great to see you."

Within the mirror's reflection, a dark-haired hottie stood opposite Rusty as he continued to work on her head between them. They talked, oblivious to the noise of the blow-dryer or the unspoken rule of the salon.

"What brings you into town on a weekday?" Rusty asked.

When this "buddy" turned his head and looked into the mirror at her, she could see clearly enough through the long strands of hair concealing her eyes. *Oh. My. Gawd! It's Lizzy's altar boy!*

For sure, she was determined to eavesdrop on their conversation even if the blow-dryer and club music conspired against her.

He smiled and Gina immediately understood her sister's instant reaction to him. Up close and personal, he was tall, fit, and stylish, wearing a designer suit and tie with ease. His appearance conveyed class and yet ... that smile showed him to be one highly passionate, maybe even a naughty, man. She admired his chiseled features and that deep tone of his voice was almost dreamy, penetrating the roaring air.

"I had a clear afternoon of patients and thought we'd go to dinner after your last client. I um, have something important to discuss with you," he stated.

"Oh, that doesn't sound good. Last time you wanted to talk to me over dinner was when my sister wanted to have her toes shortened to fit her thousand dollar shoes. Is this about her?"

"You know me well after all these years."

"Well, for you to break HIPPA patient confidentiality it must be pretty bad."

He's a doctor! Feet? Is he a podiatrist, too? Instantly excited, Gina nearly squealed.

"No, nothing like that, but it does have to do with Blair's visit to my apartment building yesterday. Between her and my grandmother, I'm having a few bad months and hope you can help me out of at least one sticky situation."

"Sure. I'll be finishing up with my new client Ms. Carpo in about twenty minutes and could use a drink after the day I've had. I asked her to come with me, but I don't think she's interested." He winked at her.

Again, Rusty's friend smiled at her, and she almost laughed feeling like Cousin It from the Addams Family. She waved, unable to make eye contact with him.

"You're in good hands with Rusty," he said politely. "He's too humble to tell his clients but he was voted #1 stylist in Westchester County three years in a row. He's also a great guy."

"I read that on Yelp," she spoke through the hair.

She liked this guy: courteous, handsome, a physician, faithful Catholic, complimentary of his friend, and friendly to a stranger. What more could a single woman want in a guy? Prozia obviously wouldn't consider him the wrong type of man.

Gina couldn't help blurting. "Do you know what strufoli is?"

The hottie quirked his head, bestowing her with an endearing smile, his intense eyes seemingly filled by a sudden recollection. "Sure, it's my favorite: Italian honey balls with sprinkles. My mother used to make them every Christmas." He kissed his pinched fingertips. "*Delizioso.*"

He's Italian-American! A no-no in Lizzy's book but a definite winner in Prozia's! I'll have to think on that.

"Well perhaps your wife could make it for you this year?"

His chuckle was the cutest thing, especially when he responded, "I have to find her first and if she can make strufoli, then she's a keeper."

Oh yeah, he's perfect.

Turning away from her with a grin, he looked at his watch and then craned his neck to glance out the plate glass window beside them. "I see the sign went up," he noted to Rusty.

"Yeah, about an hour ago. What a name: Pal•Hair•Mo."

"Clever. You think they're Sicilian?"

"That'll just piss off Stella even more. She asked me to sabotage their grand opening next month," Rusty remarked with a grimace.

Best friend? Best friend's Grandmother? Stella? As in De Luca? Good Lawd.

"Please, she's killing me with this Villa Fortuna war of hers. Even Ann was wearing a T-shirt that read 'Boycott Villa Fortuna.' I feel like I'm living in *The Godfather* now that Joey is investigating that Clemente family as a new hobby. Don't get involved, Rusty. Your reputation could be tarnished, and I'm furious at how she's handling herself. These poor women inherited an eighty-year-old vendetta along with that building. I only want to buy the place not dump them in the East River."

"I won't mind if it's the latter. I'm ready to go to the mattresses, ready for war. I hired a few new stylists and we've introduced fruit acid facials and ultrasonic cavitation to the menu, but I know what you mean. I near expected your grandmother to say 'Leave the gun. Take the cannoli.'"

"You have a great place here. Just don't get involved in her schemes and you'll do fine, my friend." He glanced at his watch again. "I have some errands to run, and then a stop in to see my hitman grandmother, the don. So, I'll meet you at Finnegans at 5:00, okay?"

"Yeah, sure. I'll see you then."

"Have a happy Thanksgiving, Ms. Carpo. You're hair looks lovely," the guy said with a genuine smile as he made a quick departure.

Holy Mother of Gawd. Lizzy's altar boy is the grandson of the devil's whore! He wants to buy Villa Fortuna, and she wants to destroy us!

There in the chair, practically in the window of Halo Salon and to Rusty's utter astonishment, Gina blessed herself.

~**~

Strufoli Neopolitan Style

2 ½ cups pastry flour
4 eggs
1 egg yolk
¼ cup leaf lard
½ tbsp. sugar
Dash salt
½ tsp. grated lemon peel
2 cups vegetable lard
1 ½ cups honey
1 tsp. grated orange peel

Place pastry flour on board. Make a well in center and place in well the eggs, egg yolk, leaf lard, sugar, salt and lemon peel. Mix well, working dough with hands, as in the making of noodles. Shape into very small balls the size of marbles and fry in hot lard, a few at a time, until golden brown.

Melt honey in saucepan and add grated orange peel. As soon as the little balls are fried, drop them into the honey mixture, take them up with a strainer and place on serving dish, piling them into conical mounds. Cool. Serves about 6

~Taken from: Page 242, *The Talisman, Italian Cook Book*, by Ada Boni (1929/ translated 1950)

~Eight~
Ritorno a Casa
(Homecoming)

At 4:30 in the afternoon, the yellow taxicab pulled to the curb and deposited Elizabeth in front of the Messina Pastry Shop in Belmont. Decorated for Christmas, old-fashioned colorful lights framed the interior of the plate glass window where a 1970s smiling plastic Santa stood bearing a tray of Italian cookies. The illuminated bulbs were as colorful as the rainbow sprinkles atop the sweets and the chocolate-covered Venetian tri-colored cookies. Behind the display of *dolcini*, she could see that the little shop was filled with customers awaiting service from the solitary, hair-netted old woman attending the patrons.

When the shop door jingled open beside her, Elizabeth breathed deeply, recalling the familiar scent with which she had grown up. The apartment and building might be all sorts of wrong, but in this instance, Gina had chosen wisely.

In spite of the winter chill, Elizabeth stood still for a time with an over-stuffed suitcase resting beside her ankle boots. At that dusk hour, the avenue had already come to festive life. She glanced up at the tacky red and green tinseled garland swagged from one side of the busy thoroughfare to the other. A lit star suspended from its center above the traffic reminded her of long ago Christmas Eves spent shopping with their father for their mother's gift. Music from the Dean Martin Christmas Album (coming from who knows where) floated on the brisk air reinforcing her conviction that in many ways, Belmont was a town that time forgot. She rolled her eyes as Dino's voice molested her ears with "A Marshmallow World,"—the quintessential soundtrack for a Hallmark Christmas movie.

She gazed around at the storefronts lining the avenue, most still open for business, and all busy with holiday shoppers. Many of them were holdovers from her childhood while others had been replaced with mom and pop boutiques or continental cuisine restaurants attempting to appeal to yuppie urbanites. The Salvation Army bell ringer tucked his chin down into his blue overcoat as he flicked his wrist with robotic inertia, obviously unenthusiastic. Narrowing her eyes, she noted that it was Vinnie the Turtle, her first childhood boyfriend. He had no neck to begin with—hence: "The Turtle."

The bell above the bakery door jingled again; a man balancing a red cellophane covered pastry tray exited followed by three children, each enjoying a piece of candied "coal." She smiled at the good-humored message to misbehaving children visiting the dessert shop two days before St. Nicholas Day. Elizabeth remembered how every December 6th, Nicki's stocking was filled with the "*carbone*" coal from the good St. Nicholas, patron and protector of children. According to Prozia, Nicki still deserved the *carbone*.

Seeing the children with their coal, called to mind how, as a senior in high school, she and Gina attended that "special" Mass for unmarried women on St. Nicholas Day and she hoped to God that Gina wouldn't make her attend this year. Lord knows, she wasn't a virgin nor in need or want of a husband. She was a career woman, a focused medical professional who would be in search of a new job when she got back to LA. The occasional uncomplicated hook-up was about the most she could handle. Not that she was superstitious about the special Mass and its bizarre ritual. Heck, she barely even believed in the *malocchio*, but one could never be too sure what might happen as a result of saintly meddling intercession.

She grabbed the handle of her suitcase and made for the apartment building's entrance, hoping that Gina or Nicki remembered that she didn't have a key. After ringing the intercom button labeled 4C, she waited in the cold, shoving her hands into the pockets of her wool coat. No answer came, and she pressed the button again.

"Dammit," she huffed, already annoyed at being back in the Bronx and bombarded with unwelcome memories. "Breathe, Elizabeth. Just breathe. It won't be bad. Remember why you are here. It's for Gina and Nicki. It's what you wanted. You'll attend the surgical conference, you'll network, and maybe you'll even find a great new position treating patients who really need you. There's a reason for everything."

She could see into the vestibule through the door window that an elderly woman was descending the stairs. Dressed in black from top to bottom, she wore a 1960s Jackie O. style mink hat and a boucle woolen coat with matching mink collar. Her low-heeled shoes were too tight for her pudgy feet, the tops spilling over like rising bread. Elizabeth furrowed her brow, concerned that the woman suffered from peripheral vascular disease or edema. She made a mental note to discuss this with Gina who might be able to encourage the woman to try wider shoes or see a vascular doctor for compression socks. After all, as her sister had vehemently declared three months earlier, they were "family."

The woman waved and yelled something that sounded like "wait" in Italian. Elizabeth quickly pondered which neighbor she was: the widow with cataracts and lasagna, the cat lady with the name of one of the Marx Brothers, or the famous boozing cross-dressing Toni with an *i*?

A curled arthritic hand pushed open the door and the woman's thick Italian accent immediately ruled out the cross-dresser. White and orange cat hairs clinging to her coat provided the proof that she must be Mrs. Zeppo from the third floor.

"*Ciao bella regazza.* You must be Elisabetta. *Benvenuta, bella.*" She pinched Elizabeth's frozen cheek.

Ah, yes, the Italian pinch, one that even the men knew well—only on another cheek. That, too, ruled out the cross-dresser.

"You must be Mrs. Zeppo on the third floor. It's lovely to meet you."

"*Si.* Call me Josie. Regina told me that you are arriving today."

"Are my sisters not at home?"

"No, they are at PalHairMo."

"Palermo, as in Sicily?"

"No, not-a Italy. It's their new beauty parlor ... for the hair, you know."

"They named the salon ... Pal*hair*mo?" *Holy Mother of God, what were you thinking, Gina!*

"*Si.* I have-a da key under my doormat."

"But if you were going out then how would I know where to look?"

"We all have-a da key."

"Everyone in the building has a key to my sisters' apartment?"

Josie looked at Elizabeth as though she had two heads, her expression a cross between confusion and possible insult when she replied. "*Si, certamente.*"

A woman's head peered down over the banister from three flights up as she called out with the typical Bronxite accent. "Is that you Toni?"

"It's Elisabetta!" Josie responded. "She wants da key."

Elizabeth assumed that the blonde woman above was Mrs. Genovese, the other third floor neighbor who made the door wreath. She started down the stairs, red-stained wooden spoon in hand, waving her arms in the air as she reached the vestibule. "There's no time. Primo needs help!"

The two older women broke into what Elizabeth referred to as a typical Italian argument: raising voices and moving hands. They obviously thought that she couldn't translate words, gestures, or facial expressions during their passionate exchange. In a language all its own, hands communicated even more than the discourse. Apparently, Toni had gone missing, probably drunk down at Saluté Bar and Grill, and Primo had telephoned for reinforcements. Elizabeth learned that Josie was on her way to church for choir practice, and the other woman had a pot of gravy and macaroni on the stove. Suddenly the two women looked her up and down each wearing the exact same expression that her mother used to give Nicki. Mrs. Genovese pointed to her knock-off Donna Karen slacks then pointed to her own head declaring, "*Sei pazzo!*" Apparently, she thought Josie crazy because it was followed by animated debate, at increasing volume, how black attire was unsuitable for the bakery and how the slacks she wore would be covered with flour in minutes. Josie won the argument by reminding her friend that the apron should cover everything—even her large bosom. Oh, and that, apparently, they both thought Elizabeth could use a big bowl of spaghetti to fatten her up.

She knew that the result of this exchange had disaster written all over it. "Excuse me, but it's been a long day with a flight delay. Is there any way I can get the key to my sisters' apartment? I'm exhausted." She faked a yawn as her nose began to tingle, eliciting that telltale finger scratch everyone in her family joked about, long ago recognized as "Lizzy's Lie Alarm." It always gave away her fibs, just like Pinocchio's nose.

Josie steepled her gloved hands in prayer, and Mrs. Genovese put her finger to her ear, pretending she couldn't hear a word Elizabeth spoke. She wagged the wooden spoon before her face. "No. You come with us."

"No really. I'd like to go upstairs."

A two-fingered pinch, which smelled like garlic when thumb met cheek coincided with the requisite onslaught of guilt when Mrs. Genovese said, "You're a good girl, skinny but good, and Primo needs help. He's an old man and …" She lowered her voice. "… got hit by the air. Come, before it turns to pneumonia."

Elizabeth sighed, recalling her mother's similar shame-inducing arguments. Why would Mr. Primo catch pneumonia in a bakery? In all her medical books, she'd never been taught anything called "hit by the air." *Whatever.* She knew it was a losing battle when she realized that Josie had already grasped the handle of the suitcase, and Mrs. Genovese had commandeered her arm. Both women tugged her out the door to the street, then into the crowded shop.

She resolved that she'd be helping someone who obviously had been left out to dry—not to mention, "hit by the air."

Every one of her senses became engaged the moment she crossed the threshold of the bakery. A lively Louis Prima Christmas swing song played overhead, which seemed to cause the baker's assistant to move in swift rhythm as she filled orders, boxing cookies and *dolcini*. Familiar faces, neighbors, and old friends, chatted patiently while waiting for their number to be called.

Against the wall, to Elizabeth's right, towered a four-shelf metal display lined with panettone and boxed Perugina chocolate. A table of cellophane wrapped gift sets and cookie trays looked as though it was about to topple over onto the crush of patrons. The aroma within the bakery was intoxicating—sweet icing and fresh bread. Her father once referred to this delicious scent as the perfection of the holy trinity – flour, butter, and sugar. He'd always had such a sweet tooth for Italian cheesecake, and this Little Italy was known to have the best.

Behind the counter, above the shelves of cakes and pies, one particular item caught her eye: the image of St. Elizabeth of Hungary, the patron saint of bakers, holding a basket of bread, offering a smiling welcome to pastry heaven. Beside the saintly image hung a 1962 ceramic plate depicting Pope John XXIII and President Kennedy, side by side blessing the elderly patrons with a *Pace Nel Mondo*. Elizabeth grinned remembering how her grandfather Vincenzo Clemente revered President Kennedy. Italians probably loved him more than the Irish. Hell, they probably loved him more than the Pope.

It seemed as though all heads had turned upon her entrance. She heard hushed whispers and a few gasps. The door's jingle bell followed by a momentary hush caused the diminutive Mr. Primo to exit the back room, coming around the display cases. His white baker's apron was layered with flour and streaked with red jam, most likely from the inside of the cookies and crostata pie. He wore a white hairnet, a beaming smile and, strangely, a colorful woolen scarf wrapped about his neck. She determined that his being "hit by the air" caused some sort of neck ailment or paranoia. He didn't look anywhere near as frazzled as Gina's neighbors conveyed, and she wondered if the whole thing had been a set up from that very first pinch. She considered her sister's new Machiavellian streak and thought … *hmm* with a twist to her lips.

As Primo approached, Josie grabbed her shoulders turning her to face Mrs. Genovese, who unbuttoned her coat, then slid it from her shoulders. Josie placed it over the luggage and quickly rolled it to a corner summarily shutting out any expected argument.

"*Bene.* Welcome, Lizzy, welcome!" he greeted, hugging her tightly followed by a kiss to both of her cheeks. "You're going to work with Rosa behind the counter."

"Hi Mr. Primo. I'm happy to help but I'm afraid I don't know anything about a bakery. Well, apart from satisfying my terrible sweet tooth."

She snorted a laugh, and he replied without batting an eye. "Then you know cannoli, cookies, pignoli, cream puffs, cheese-a-cake, and pizzelle. You put 'em in a box and take the money. Badda bing, badda boom!" He dropped the apron strings over her neck and Josie tied the back one around her waist. His happy smile warmed Elizabeth's cool, apprehensive demeanor and she thought for a second that this might not be so bad after all. She did want to help; already he felt like family.

Both ladies turned with a wave and a dismissive *Ciao bella* before departing. Elizabeth thought she heard one of them say something about a wolf's mouth in Italian and the other laughed raucously at the wish for luck. Yeah, she'd been played and instinctively knew who had orchestrated the game.

She rested her hand on the baker's surprisingly firm bicep. "Mr. Primo, are you feeling well? Do you have a fever or feel weak? Does your back hurt?"

"Such an angel to be worried." He pinched her cheek. "I'm fine, just baking in the kitchen, and my son did not show up for work. Besides, Gina tells me that you would like to move back to the neighborhood. This is your homecoming!" He deviously winked at her and took her hand, leading her behind the counter where an introduction to the standoffish Rosa took place. The ancient woman continued to work, halting in her path for a split second to push a white hairnet down upon her apprentice's chestnut locks.

Elizabeth felt all eyes upon her as Primo walked her through the process of filling orders. She tried not to focus on the fact that she remembered many of the spectators awaiting service. Feeling nervous, she pulled the cord to the ticket dispenser and announced, "Thirty-six. Who is next? Thirty-six?"

A smiling woman stepped through the crowd, rattling off her order as Elizabeth assembled two white pastry boxes then began to fill one with assorted cookies.

"You're Lizzy Clemente, aren't you?" the woman asked.

"I am. How did you know?"

"I'd recognize that beauty mark of yours anywhere. *Bellisima*! My son, Vinnie is single and lives at home. You must come for manicotti. A pretty girl like you should be married already."

Elizabeth walked to the scale and pressed a couple of buttons, thinking, *Dinner with Turtle? No friggin' way.*

"Lizzy!" Another woman near shouted. "*Mamma mia* you grew up! I remember you playing dolls on the stoop with my Connie! What good girls you were."

Elizabeth smiled in recognition at the mother of a childhood best friend. "Hi Mrs. Grappa. How is Connie?" She asked as she tied the twisted red and white bakery cord twice around the box, secretly grinning with satisfaction at the pretty bow she made on top.

"My Connie! She's very happy! She lives in New Jersey, now. Her husband works for the sanitation department, and I have six beautiful grandbabies—all boys!"

As expected. "How wonderful. Please give her my regards."

"Lizzy Clemente, is that you? Where did you go? Are you married? Did you move to Florida with your mother? Will you be moving back to Belmont?" Another customer asked without pause, though Elizabeth, smile affixed, continued filling the second box with crème puffs. She wiped her brow, feeling woozy from the heat of stares upon her and the heady smell of butter, not to mention her newfound superstardom.

After weighing the remaining box, she stood at the cash register, vowing to kill Gina the moment she came home, her ruse now obvious. Reading from the cheat sheet beside the old metal machine, Elizabeth depressed the large numbers, feeling as though she was re-living her Christmas past and, no doubt, that was exactly what her scheming sister wanted her to feel.

"You must come and see my Vinnie," Turtle's mother said, handing her over the money. "He's never forgotten how beautiful you were in your Holy Communion dress. Do you remember that afternoon at Our Lady of Mount Carmel (OLMC)? Such little angels practicing for your wedding day. You shouldn't have let him get away, but it's not too late."

"Thank you, Mrs. Balducci. Merry Christmas to you and your family," Elizabeth said, before turning to the ticket counter. "Number 38. Who's next?"

"I'm 38, Lizzy."

A handsome guy raised his hand. She groaned inside. It was him; for the love of God, it was him: Danny Tucci, the former love of her life and the very first cheating asshole who broke her heart the night of their senior prom. He had the sole distinction of being the one who taught her a thing or two about Italian men and their overactive libidos.

"Hi, Lizzy," he said handing her his paper number over the rainbow cookie display case.

"Oh, hi." Ugh, she hated that he was still good looking. Why couldn't he have lost his hair or something? Fat would have been even better. Yeah, fat and bald, maybe even missing a tooth in that perfect smile of his.

The patrons who knew Lizzy, comprising of ninety percent, watched the interaction.

"Are you back in town permanently?" Danny asked, his grin reminding her of all the hurts and all the joys at the same time.

Her lips drew to a thin line before speaking. "What'll you have, Danny?"

"A dinner date with you."

"And who else?"

"Still angry after all these years?"

As though watching a bocce ball match, the customers quieted and stood still, riveted by the exchange of these former high school sweethearts who everyone expected to marry right after graduation.

Some unknown man at the back of the shop complained. "Yo, could ya get a move on? I got someplace to be."

In complete accord, five women simultaneously turned to him, scolding in unison, "Shush!"

"No, I'm not angry. How is your wife? You know, the one you screwed in the back seat of the car on our prom night?"

"She's fine, I guess. We divorced last year. I'm temporarily living with my parents until I can find my own place. It's a good set up. Mom feeds me and takes care of my laundry."

She falsely smiled with mock intonation. "Divorce? Gee, there's a surprise. Did you cheat on her, too?"

Danny cleared his throat and uncomfortably toyed with the inch long gold horn charm hanging around his neck. "Yeah. How'd you know?"

"Once a cheater, always a repeater. Look, we have a lot of customers here, and you're wasting my time. What do you want from the bakery?"

"A pound of almond biscotti—your favorite." He reached into his pocket, withdrew a business card then rested it upon the glass counter. "I heard you were back in the Bronx for the month and I thought that, maybe, we could rekindle what we had all those years ago. I know how much you love Christmas, and well, the church is having a nativity parade. Here's my card. Why don't you call me?"

She chanced a glance at him, bowled over by his overinflated ego and ballsy confidence. He grinned. *Asshole.* What did he think she'd just fall back into his wandering arms after thirteen years? As curious as she was to examine the business card, she wouldn't give him the satisfaction. He was probably a dirty politician or worse yet, an ambulance-chasing lawyer. *Jerk.*

Elizabeth quickly turned her head, and snapped open a paper bag. She furiously stuffed the biscotti into it, eyes remaining focused on the biscuits lest she fell under that flirtatious spell of his. At all cost, she needed to resist his easy charm, unless she end up like Gina or his wife, what's her name.

"Who told you I would be back in Belmont?" she asked, covertly shoving a piece of candy coal in the bag.

"I read it in the church bulletin and there is also an announcement hanging up in the narthex as well as one at the Italian-American club. Someone even posted it along with your yearbook photograph on the Arthur Avenue Facebook page. Everyone in the neighborhood knows that you're back."

Gina! You should be nicknamed "The Mouth."

She stood before the cash register, pressing the numbers again, only this time with a little more force. Her dark eyes flashed. "I live in LA, and I'm not moving back to Belmont. No amount of biscotti or Tucci "The Stallion" seduction could induce *me* to change my mind. So, you better move onto another naïve victim with that business card of yours. I don't date Italian men. *Finito!*"

Vinnie's mother gasped and turned to stare Elizabeth down before crossing herself and heading out the door.

"That'll be $4.85," Elizabeth declared.

At that precise moment, Gina stopped dead in her tracks right outside the pastry shop's colorful window. She, too, gasped and grabbed Nicki's arm. "Holy moly! Look, Nicki."

The two sisters peered through the glass, staring in wonderment at the image of Elizabeth behind the counter: White flour anointing her brow and chin, hair falling from the nonna-like netting, and that telltale tightened line of disapproval that overrode lips when she was angry. Below the long apron, her black slacks were now dingy gray from bakery dust.

"Oh, no. She's talking to Danny," Gina said.

"Yo. Look how that dickwad is suckin' up to her. He's got nerve turning on that stallion bullshit of his. I hear his ex-wife caught him with Tina."

"Frankie's Tina? My ex-manicurist?"

"Yeah. She's like the village bicycle: everyone gets a ride." Nicki put her gloved hands on the glass to wipe away the fogging moisture and took in the whole scene in the shop. She snorted. "Lizzy is gonna kick your ass when she figures out what you did. All of Arthur Avenue is in there."

Gina deviously giggled. "Me? I didn't do a blessed thing?" She grabbed Nicki's bicep. "Nicki, do not—I repeat— do not, tell her about her altar boy being the grandson of that Stella De Luca woman."

"Why?"

"I don't know. I just have a feeling, that's all. I think he's the one."

"He ain't the one. He's Italian; she hates Italian men."

"Yeah, but maybe he's like fourth generation American or something. Besides, Lizzy doesn't know what's best for her anymore and it's up to us to set her straight. I think this guy—if she meets him again—might help her come back to her faith, her roots. Everything. He's not like the other guys she's met."

"But the dude wants to buy Villa Fortuna! That shit ain't gonna be happenin', Gina."

Gina clicked her tongue. "Details, details. Let's be patient."

Nicki glanced back into the shop, observing how Lizzy genuinely smiled as she shook the winemaker Mr. Graciosa's hand over the glass counter. "Like I said, she's gonna kick your ass."

*~**~*

Almond Biscotti

½ cup whole almonds, toasted
1/3 cup butter
¾ cup sugar
2 eggs
1 tsps. anise seed
¾ tsp. almond extract
½ tsp. orange peel, grated
2 ¼ cups flour
1 ½ tsps. baking powder
¼ tsp. salt

Chop toasted almonds into ¼-inch pieces. Meanwhile, cream butter and sugar until fluffy; beat in eggs. Stir in anise seed, almond extract, and orange peel. Mix together remaining ingredients, except almonds, in a separate bowl; stir into butter mixture. Stir in almonds. On a lightly floured board, roll dough into two ropes the length of a baking sheet. Place on an ungreased baking sheet; bake at 325 degrees, approximately 25 minutes until light golden brown. Removed from baking sheet and let cool 5 minutes. Slice diagonally into ½-inch slices. Lay slices flat on baking sheet and return to oven for 10 minutes to dry out, turning slices over halfway through baking. Cool. Store in a tightly covered container.

~Gardiner family recipe

~Nine~
Polpette
(Meatballs)

Rao's restaurant in East Harlem was one of those exclusive, authentic Italian eateries that didn't let just anyone in, and, if they did, it took an average of two years to get a reservation. Famed for its red sauce and meatballs, it was most notable for its famous (and sometimes infamous) clientele. Rao's was unfortunately also known for a mobster hit on "Louie Lump Lump" that occurred some thirteen years ago. That incident was an interesting factoid, to be sure. But if Mike had to drag Louie Lump Lump into the conversation with his dinner partner, the date was certainly dying a slow death.

He loved this homey place in spite of its mob connections; on any given night you were going to be rubbing elbows with a made man or, worse yet, a politician. Eating here was the closest he ever came to mixing with—or admitting—his great-grandfather's connected past. He was conflicted though—because of those connections he was assured of his standing reservation every other Wednesday night. Mike only dined here with a date, and tonight was one of those nights.

Surveying the diners seated beneath the many autographed photos lining wood paneled walls, he recognized some of the restaurant's regular customers at their usual tables. Because of the crowds, he couldn't quite make out the fireplace adorned for Christmas, but still he felt the undeniable holiday spirit. He loved Christmas and the feeling of joy that came with it.

His table was a cozy, dimly lit, narrow booth in the corner of the restaurant where he sat with his back against the wall so that he could control his environment. Above his head, a photograph of Gina

Lollobrigida stared back at his date. That, too, was deliberate. He didn't need any competition from an image of a young Chazz Palminteri or Robert DiNiro diverting her attention. The dating world was dog-eat-dog enough; the last thing he needed was to compete with a slick 8x10 glossy.

Although midweek, the bar crowd was two deep. The din of conversation combined with clanking dishware traveling in and out of the kitchen was jarring. On this crisp December night, holiday partiers waited for one of the frequent Broadway star patrons or the owner himself to break out into impromptu song while the jukebox played "The Mob Hits Christmas" album. At the moment, Connie Francis was singing "The First Noel," which somewhat calmed the nerves that always accompanied him on a first date. Forget that he'd gone on hundreds of dates in search of Mrs. Right; he never knew just how to act. It was always awkward. Should he behave as though on a job interview? A consult with a new patient? Chatting with someone in the produce aisle?

However, tonight's date felt relaxed. Maybe the holiday spirit took the edge off. But more than likely it was because he wasn't interested in Rebecca for anything further than this one dinner.

She was a full-figured, blonde-haired, blue-eyed, middle-aged woman he had met on eDating. Her first "wink" to him six nights earlier had been followed by a little chatting online. He learned that she was from Westchester County and, for some reason she felt it important to divulge that she was a natural DD. Not that it mattered and not that, here in the flesh, he was looking at her bosom.

All right, he was.

But how could he not? Her cleavage was staring him in the face, resembling a butt crack. He resisted shuddering. Her cup size was the only accurate description she had disclosed.

The photograph on her profile was most likely twenty years younger and airbrushed. She was his "type" on the computer screen but not in person. There was no way Rebecca was thirty-two. Fifty-two was more like it, but he couldn't slight her for bending the truth. Yes, the dating scene was tough, and like most men trying to impress, a woman has to do what she can to get noticed, too. That is, admittedly, at the heart of his medical practice and what kept his hefty paychecks rolling in. He couldn't deny that she was pleasant company, but they had nothing in common. *And* she was too flashy, similar to his step-monster. Definitely not his type, but a nice dinner date and, so far tonight, a woman who didn't flirt unabashedly, as if every word was an attempt to separate him from his pants.

During Rebecca's recitation about her cat Lola's eating habits, his mind wandered, as it did often these last three months, to his "type." He had seen her just that once at St. John's Church, and although he had gone back every Saturday evening since in the hope of running into her again, she was never there. The beauty had disappeared as if a puff of smoke. Perhaps the brunette had been a mirage, a wishful image following his confession that day.

"How on earth did you wrangle a table at Rao's? I'm so impressed!" Rebecca said, pulling him from his daydream.

"It's a long story, but essentially, I just got lucky in the end. I'm glad you like it. They're famous for their celebrity clientele and their cannolis."

She leaned forward, her breasts a fraction of an inch from the Marsala sauce on her plate. The image of the butt crack and brown sauce below it nearly gagged him as her fleshy mounds overflowed from the top of her dress. "I think that's Joe Pesci," she whispered.

"It is. He's a regular here. How's your veal?"

She leaned back, and then took a mouthful, her lips moving seductively as she chewed. "Delicious, so tender, like butter."

Loading her fork with more meat, she held it out to him. "Here try it."

Oh Damn! He hated when women did this. Why did they do this? He'd rather have his balls dragged through broken glass before he ate from a stranger's bacteria-laden fork. Her profile said she was disease free, but how could she be sure? How could he? He involuntarily shook his head as the threatening fork drew ominously closer, the meat growing larger and larger in its approach before it stopped at his tightly pursed lips.

"Oh c'mon. Open up. It's incredible. You have to try it."

"No, thank you. I'm really not a veal person."

He breathed a sigh of relief when she retracted the offending utensil with a shrug. "Okay, your loss," she said before her red lips surrounded the meat.

They continued to converse about her funeral home business in

Eastchester and some of her clients' odd last wishes for the disposal of their remains. Morbid conversation, but fascinating nonetheless.

And then it happened. Really the end game for any woman, no matter "type" or not, first date or fiftieth. Rebecca reached over to his plate, her fork tines poised for invasion. To his horror, she sliced one of the uneaten meatballs in half with the edge of her unhygienic utensil. She stabbed the saucy chopped meat and popped it into her mouth, followed by an enthusiastic, "Mmm, that's delicious."

Damn, he wanted to eat those meatballs! Now what? The entire remainder of his entree was now tainted by the act. He slid his plate closer to her. "Please, feel free to enjoy it all," he said with a mournful smile. "I'm quite through."

"Me, too, but that was incredible."

Mike signaled the waiter for two more glasses of vino. Pietro the bartender's homemade super-Tuscan red was guaranteed to loosen up most patrons, and particularly in this case, after an overly flashy, cleavage-spilling woman ate off your plate, defiling your food with her oral streptococci.

"I have a confession to make," she stated, smiling naughtily.

"That doesn't sound good."

"It's nothing terrible." She smoothed her hand down her side. "I actually looked you up before coming tonight. I … um … friended you on Facebook, *Michaelangelo*."

He wanted to groan but kept that false "date" smile upon his face. He should have realized that there was reason for her disclosure of bra size. *Breathe, Mike.*

"Who knew I'd be going to dinner with such a famous person. Your hands have changed many women's lives. Perhaps I'll have the opportunity to have them on me? I've already enjoyed your meatballs." She made a big cat growl, her fingers scratching mid-air like a fat paw.

So much for not separating me from my pants. He held back his shudder. "No way in hell" was the first thing on the tip of his tongue but he bit it back. It would be rude.

"Well, thank you for your interest in my practice. Should you ever find the need, call the office anytime, and my assistant will get you onto the schedule."

"I wasn't thinking surgery, silly. I'm very happy with my girls." She thrust out her boobs.

Mike downed the glass of wine that the waiter had just placed upon the table.

Thankfully, Mike's attention diverted to the restaurant's door. He watched as the crowd separated for someone smaller to walk through. Overriding Bobby Vinton's rendition of "Do You Hear What I Hear," he recognized the current bane of his existence command, "Step aside." He braced himself, involuntarily gripping the edge of the table for the red haired hellion. Holding his breath, he felt trapped by the one woman who had the uncanny knack of arriving on the scene when he was at his worst.

Rebecca turned her head to see what had stolen his absolute attention from her girls: an elderly woman encased in Blackglama mink came straight toward them, halting at their table's edge.

"She's arrived!" Stella declared with one hand installed upon her hip.

Mike sighed. "Stella. What are you doing here?"

"Your answering service told me where to find you. The last sister has arrived, Michael."

"Remind me to find a new service in the morning. Forgive me. Rebecca Montgomery this is my overbearing grandmother, Stella De Luca, and Antoinette, but you can call her Ann."

Rebecca's hand retracted when she observed how Stella gave her the once over with a raised eyebrow, her glower settling on the butt crack.

"Charmed, I'm sure," Stella said turning back to her grandson.

Ann, as usual, remained silent during Stella's tirade, her eyes fixed upon the remaining meatballs as though she hadn't had dinner yet.

Pondering the delicate, high fashioned blonde before her, Rebecca dissected Ann with a discerning eye; from the diamond jewelry to her perfect french manicure, Ann was quite a beauty. Her short golden locks were silky and shiny. On the lapel of her Louis Vuitton fur-lined winter coat was a bright red button that read, "Pal•Hair•NO!!"

"Grandmother, you can see that I'm having dinner. Why have you tracked me down? You could have called me on my cell, even texted me—not come all the way down to East Harlem."

Stella's gloved hand worked ferociously, raising in the air and gesturing as she spoke. "This is too important to telephone or even Skype you about. That salon's grand opening is in three days, and I need reinforcements. I want your commitment that you will be up in Etonville to hand out flyers. I've commissioned a special sign for you to carry. We will shut down those thieves before they even open!"

Thankfully, Rebecca remained oblivious to the conversation as she watched Ann's brown eyes hungrily examine the meatballs. "Would you like the rest? They're very good." She said, pushing the plate to the end of the table.

Stella turned to look at the coveting expression on her companion's face. "No, Antoinette! You know that red sauce doesn't agree with your digestion. You'll be up all night with the runs."

Ann's disappointed whine was barely audible as she abashedly diverted her eyes to the booth beside them, her focus now locking on the beef braccioli swimming in marinara on the table.

"As I was saying, Michael. I need your and Amelia's assistance."

"It's not going to happen. First of all, I'm in surgery the entire day, and second of all, I'm not participating in your campaign to bring down PalHairMo."

"That's the new salon opening in Etonville, isn't it?" Rebecca said. "What a cute name! I've already read fabulous things about it. There was an article in the *Daily Voice* about the owner's vision for a unique Italian family-styled salon in Snobsville."

Stella gasped. "We do not ever refer to our quaint village as Snobsville, and they are Sicilian *not* Italian! Family to them represents a lying bunch of thieving—"

"Shush, Grandmother!" Mike cringed. That last insult was bound to cross the threshold between rude and racist. "Don't insult Sicilians, particularly in here. You'll get us killed—and it's Christmas no less."

"Nonsense. Rao's was founded on Neapolitan roots! No one will be harming me in this establishment."

He lowered his voice to barely a whisper. "Oh yeah? Well this place is loaded with Cosa Nostra wiseguys, and even that didn't spare Louie Lump Lump's victim. He was one of Lucchese's men. Lest you want the same fate, I'd keep your racist, stereotyping remarks to yourself, or I'll be forced to publicly call you senile."

She perched her hand on her hip again, ignoring his threatening reprimand. "Joey tells me that you will be down at the Palace Hotel day after tomorrow." She looked to Rebecca, and spoke through tight lips. "I hope ... alone."

"If I tell you, will you promise not to track me down there and embarrass me like you're doing now?"

"Hmm."

"I'm going to a medical conference on reconstructive limb salvage."

~**~

Elizabeth forgot how physically uncomfortable it was to sleep beside someone on a full-sized bed. She lay awake listening to Gina, a foot away, snoring in unison with the car alarm outside the window. Unable to sleep, she yanked at the very blanket they had shared as children and turned to face her sister. Nothing in Belmont had changed, not even Gina's sleeping habits. The devious mischief-maker lay flat on her back, mouth wide open, snores rolling like thunder halting and restarting every couple of minutes. In the rare moments Elizabeth was graced with *near* silence, she cursed that car alarm, and the refrigerator's constant hum, not to mention Nicki's TV in the next room. It wasn't really any of those things keeping her awake.

With a sigh, she admitted it was the events of the last three weeks occupying her thoughts: quitting her job without another to fall back on, paying her school loan, fulfilling Prozia's behest, and now coming home to a slum over a bakery. She hated restless nights like this when the weight of the world kept Mr. Sandman at bay. In truth, she couldn't remember the last time she had a good night's sleep.

Tonight's stint in the bakery stirred something in her she couldn't deny. Forgetting Danny for a moment, she'd had a good time. Even Rosa came around, and it wasn't because Louis Prima or Jerry Vale had calmed the crotchety old woman. By the end of the evening, over closing and cleaning, along with Mr. Primo, the three laughed at how the "homecoming" and the matchmaking mammas were just what the pastry shop needed to kick off the Christmas season. It made her happy to see Mr. Primo overjoyed at the cash receipts and the empty pastry trays left on the shelves.

The number of people who recognized her, greeting her with such warmth and familiarity, was surprising. It touched her to know they had remembered her as a "good girl," "smartest in school," and "prettiest girl to crown Mary on May Day." Even a favorite teacher from high school had come into the shop to impart how proud she was of her and how, like her parents, she had been missed in Little Italy. One woman even mentioned that she desperately needed a good foot doctor because her calluses were killing her.

In total, seven mothers had attempted to play matchmaker for their prodigy—men she once would have jumped at the chance to date way back in the day, but now deemed totally unacceptable. Four of these prizes, at the age of thirty, she considered the kiss of death: triple *M*'s— "Mammisimo Mozzarella Men"— still living at home, soft, weak, and dependent on their mothers. Nevertheless, she couldn't deny being flattered that each of these eager mammas thought her good enough for their sons, and from an Italian mother's perspective, that was the highest compliment paid to any woman. LA definitely did *not* work this way. Further, that opinion wasn't drawn because she was Dr. Elizabeth Fairchild from Los Angeles. It was offered because they considered her *one of them, famiglia*, which, in a sense was true since she grew up calling several of them "aunt" even though they were no blood relation.

Elizabeth wiped at the uncharacteristic tear rolling down her cheek. The unexpected events of the evening pulled at her conscience. Had she truly become just what Gina joked: a snobby Doc Hollywood? Her admission to Father Mintern in LA haunted her, *"I want to be happy, and I'm not."* All her hard work at making something of herself had only left her unemployed, lonely, and without a family to pick her up off the floor when things turned to shit, as they always seemed to do. Her best friends had become her cell phone and medical journals; her holidays reduced to take out turkey from Boston Market. And when she found a moment to think about it, reconnecting with Connie's mother reminded her of all the good times they had shared in high school and how she was the one to introduce Connie to her now husband. Her friends were there that earth-shattering night when Danny screwed she-who-shall-not-be-named. That visual was burned forever on her brain: tangled legs, steamy windows, grunting, and that birthmark of his every time his ass made contact with the glass.

She shuddered. Seeing Danny had unnerved her. Today was her first sighting of him since the summer before she left for college, and damn if he didn't still look hot. He had stated he was determined to win her back. Over her dead body!

Gina produced another deep snore, and Elizabeth nudged her again with her foot, deliberately firmer than the last twelve times.

"Wha? What …? Is that you, Frankie? *Cazzo!*"

"No it's me. I can't sleep."

"Well, I can. Try to think happy thoughts or make some warm milk." She pulled her share of the blanket up and rolled to her side, giving Elizabeth her back.

"Stay awake and talk to me. I have a lot on my mind."

"Count your nights by stars, not by shadows. Count your life with smiles not tears."

She would have rolled her eyes at Gina's deflection using her father's proverb from the Old Country, but she felt too much like crap to react flippantly. "That's just it. I can't find my smile. I feel like someone put the *malocchio* on me."

Gina huffed, rolling back over to face her sister. The light of the full winter moon diffused through the window shears. "You found it tonight in the bakery didn't you?"

"Until Danny came in."

"Forget about that meatball. It did you good to be in the shop and see all those people who loved you."

"It did feel good. It reminded me of Christmas in mamma's kitchen and how she'd let us ball the macaroon cookies as we listened to Andre Boccelli. God she was obsessed with him."

"So you're not mad at me and Nicki for not being home when you arrived and having you end up in the bakery?"

"At first I was. I was near spitting nails, but how can I stay mad at you? Gina, you're such a good person. I know you wanted me to feel welcome even if you weren't here yourself … and I did."

"I could kiss your boss for giving you the time off."

Elizabeth didn't reply because if she did, she would have blurted out something unkind about that man. Something a lot more forceful than *Testa di cazzo!* There was no way in hell she was going to tell the girls about having to quit her job because he wouldn't let her come east. The guilt imparted would leave Gina crossing herself every five minutes. No, she'd keep her employment status a secret, never truly lying but just not saying. After this month, she'd return to LA and telephone some of her colleagues. She had a lot to offer and, surely, anyone would hire her.

"Rosa's a character, huh?" Gina yawned and stretched.

"If I heard once, I heard fifteen times that the three of us don't eat enough and that we should be married."

"Yeah. She's old school. She's been trying to fix me up with Toni, but how can I tell her that he'd rather get into my panties in a very literal sense?"

"I felt bad for Mr. Primo with Toni's disappearing act and all. That was so uncool."

"Oh, Toni didn't disappear. Mr. Primo knew where he was."

"So you and your friends totally played me?"

Gina grinned. "Of course. Toni was with Nicki and me at Villa Fortuna. He's going to be working with us at the salon four days a week. He's our receptionist."

"Will he be a male or female?"

"Who knows? I'm hoping he'll get a new lease on life and dump the sauce."

"You're so good, Gina. Are you nervous about the salon?"

"I am, especially since that De Luca woman is planning to sabotage the grand opening. I have it on good authority that she's going to picket outside, but Carpo promises he's handling that directly, something about him having a few of his friends show up."

"To do what?"

"I'm not sure. I guess to protect us in case the crazy woman gets violent. Apparently, Villa Fortuna has been the reason for a vendetta against the Clemente family."

"Then we should have the police on hand."

"No, I don't want to make a scene. I think Carpo has experience with this sort of thing."

The sisters laid there face-to-face and Gina took a deep breath. "I have a favor to ask, Lizzy."

"Anything, you know that."

"The salon needs a pedicurist. Will you do it until I find someone suitable before you leave? It's just that with the holidays, I know we're going to be busy with mani-pedis. I want a professional, someone who's not afraid of toenail fungus."

Elizabeth smiled in the moonlight. Gina always had a way of bringing her out of the doldrums and refocusing her worrisome thoughts. God how she missed this sharing with her big sister. They had slept together in the same bed for sixteen years until she ran from the Bronx.

"Sure. I'll do it."

"Are you sure it's okay? I know you've stated that you never wanted to be a podiatrist who only cut nails all day for a living, and that's why you studied so hard to become a surgeon to the stars."

"Don't worry about me. I'm happy to do whatever I can to make your salon a success," Elizabeth reassured enjoying the glow of happiness that suddenly lit Gina's face.

"Gina, did you name the salon PalHairMo?"

"Well, I had thought of naming it after Aunt Maria's ancestral home in Sicily, but I figured that 'Corleone' would make everyone think that we're the mob."

"Good idea. We don't want prospective clients to think we'll whack their hair. Speaking of hair, I love your new style."

Gina touched the messy tendrils and beamed. "Thanks. I met a guy with magic fingers."

"Uh oh."

"He's nothing like the men I've met before. This guy is from Etonville."

"Thank God! Will you be going out with him?"

"Oh, I plan on it!"

_**_

~Ten~
Caffè
(Coffee)

Before the business day began, Rusty stood on the ladder outside Halo—hanging twinkling garland over the windows and freezing his butt off. Etonville was quiet at this early hour when the morning held a bone-reaching chill as the sun had yet to rise above the village buildings. His unusual foul mood felt at odds with decking the halls.

Focused on the task at hand, he resisted the urge to glimpse over his shoulder at PalHairMo or toward his sister posing just inside of his salon window as she spoke to the evil receptionist. He wanted to fire that girl, but facing Blair's expected vitriol was the last thing he needed with the opening of the salon in Villa Fortuna scheduled for the next day—December 7th. Everything at Halo needed to be perfect and he rationalized that Emma's presence was better than no receptionist at all. Next week he would be better prepared to replace her.

As usual, Blair looked stunning, but that only pissed him off more. Mike's disclosure a couple of weeks ago over dinner had left him unsettled. He hadn't realized the growing level of his sister's obsession with his best friend. Her showing up at Sutton Towers, snapping photographs of his backside, and uploading them to Facebook had crossed the line. Tagging them with the words, "my hot god and his hot bod," was beyond the pale. Sure Mike was good looking and in great shape, but damn, the guy's mere existence seemed to drive women insane. That whole MAA Facebook fan page thing was the testament. Further, Mike's absolute humility prevented him from encouraging that behavior! His friend was clueless when it came to wooing or even flirting with a woman, but stalking was not going to get Blair anywhere.

After securing the center of the swag and affixing a red bow, he gave into the temptation to look over his shoulder. In the center of PalHairMo's decorative window hung a poster featuring an elaborate holiday updo headshot. *No one wants updos any longer,* he thought smugly. Inside, on the window glass, framing either side of the poster, Christmas trees were hand-painted in green, white, and red. Multi-colored lights finished the holiday display. He had to admit that it looked festive, even inviting, if a little tacky for Etonville. He'd only seen a couple of the salon's employees whenever he chanced a curious glance. He wondered if the owner was the blue-haired woman he'd seen inside.

Focus, man! Ignore them. You've replaced the Keurig, and now the salon serves iced tea as well. Halo is offering a heavenly Christmas sweepstakes, not to mention the frequent flyer punch card. Emma is even sending out holiday cards! Your salon is the go-to place for seasonal beauty, style, and class—not some ethnic excuse for a trip back to the 1980s.

Damn, he didn't like what this competition was transforming him into. He'd never acted this mean spirited, this Blair-esque before, not even when Redken opened their salon eight miles away and stole his best stylist. The characteristically affable and kind man he always considered himself resurfaced with the acknowledgement that living with Blair was turning him into an asshole.

With resolve, he descended the ladder then brushed his hands over his leather jacket. He took a deep breath, rearranged his scarf, and determined, "It's now or never—not tomorrow when you'll look like you're snooping. You better go introduce yourself."

Rusty stood, hands in his pockets, at the curb waiting for the traffic to clear. He could see, even at this early hour there were people in PalHairMo.

As he neared, he heard music playing inside and noted two women dancing. *It's eight o'clock in the morning for Christ sake! Stop it, man! You sound like Mike's grandmother.* That woman was going to be the death of him, too, and no, he would not be picketing tomorrow!

Chilled hands surrounded his face as he peered into the window. Just beyond the swirls of the painted Christmas tree … yup, they were dancing and singing along with a pop song. The shorter one with huge breasts was clutching a hairbrush as though it were a microphone and the taller blonde brandished a broom handle back and forth before her.

Both women were bumping, grinding and slapping their backsides to the beat and gesticulating lyrics describing something about their junk being in the right place. His eyes bulged slightly when the raven-haired one shimmied her chest, nearly giving herself two black eyes.

Rusty straightened and, thrusting back his shoulders, proceeded to the door. The sign mounted there read:

Grand Opening December 7
Eat, drink and be Italian Merry with a new hair style!
20% to benefit the Locks of Love charity.

Below the words, an image of Medusa laughed at him. Taking in a deep breath, he knocked on the glass. The music from within ceased instantly.

The shorter girl, poured into a tight black T-shirt, opened the door with a raised eyebrow. "Yeah? Whatta you want?"

"Um, hi. I'm your neighbor from across the street. Halo, the other salon."

"I know who you are Rusty Channing. Are you here to check out the competition?"

He couldn't help chuckling at the ballsy attitude emphasized by her heavy Bronx accent. Only an abrupt rotation of her surprisingly delicate hand as she spoke diverted his attention from her chest.

"As a matter of fact I am and, of course, to say hello, wish you luck, then tell you that I don't roll over and play dead without a fight."

"Well, that's a refreshing attitude in this town of Stepford Wives." She thrust her hand forward. "I'm Nicki, one of the owners. Come on in; we won't bite … hard."

It smelled like an Italian bakery and his stomach growled. On the long counter to his right sat one of those super-size imported cappuccino machines, all copper and shiny brass, ready to whip up drinks that he knew he couldn't possibly concoct or compete with. Deflated, he nearly groaned; his new Keurig appeared a cheap piece of shit in comparison.

The interior of the salon looked as though Mount Etna had erupted around the four stylist stations, and what the hell were those paintings on the wall supposed to be? Naked women with flowing red hair? The yellow painted walls were beyond cheery, screaming "yello!" and his eyes were captured by the tacky 1950s-styled Christmas tree lit up next to the receptionist desk. He noticed how festive accents touched almost every surface of the salon, even the shelving unit housing hair care products. Smugly, he thought how his product was top shelf, not this inexpensive supermarket crap. His eyes grew wide when he noted the six bottles of Giovanni shampoo and six bottles of Pantene. *Good God, is that Head and Shoulders! What's next, Prell?*

The taller woman came forward and shook his hand with a bone-crushing grip. "I'm Toni, PalHairMo's receptionist extraordinaire," she greeted him with a deep voice that more or less told Rusty, "I'm Anthony." The unibrow and five o'clock shadow ruled him out as an owner.

"Nice to meet you both. Are your other sisters here? I'd like to introduce myself before your grand opening, before the mudslinging begins and the knock down drag out fight ensues for ownership of Westchester County's hair."

Nicki smiled deviously. "One of my posse is in the back. The other ain't around today. Yo, Gina! Get your ass out here, someone wants to meet ya." She laughed, then walked to the coffee machine, and with a charming hostess voice offered, "Can I make you an espresso or cappuccino? It's on the house."

"Um, sure! That'll be great." He hated to admit that he was impressed and wondered if this Gina girl was as spirited as Tits and Vinegar now playing barista.

"Did you call me, Nicki?" Gina asked, exiting the office.

Rusty stood slack mouthed, folding his arms across his chest. It was her: the pink bunny whose slot he wanted to fill, the client who had hopped into his life as quickly as she hopped out. "You?" he finally managed, unfolding his arms then wagging a finger.

"*Ciao,* Rusty, nice of you to stop by." She coolly acknowledged him with a smile and humor sparkling in her eyes. She walked to the counter and held out a plate of disk-shaped cookies. "Can I offer you a pizzelle cookie?"

Her blonde locks were pulled into a ponytail and she wore a dated, baby pink velour Juicy Couture tracksuit. Though lacking confirmation as she strode toward him, he momentarily pictured the inevitable printed "Juicy" plastered across her butt cheeks. "No. No cookie! You were spying on me, Regina? You're one of the Clemente sisters? One of the owners of PalHairMo?"

She giggled, her fingers touching her lips as she shrugged both shoulders. "Yeah," she cooed, batting her lashes demurely.

"Guess she played you, pal," Toni said, walking to the laptop on the reception desk and clicking the music back on. The next song "Dear Future Husband" started the doo-wop gyration all over again as Toni picked up the broom using it as a standing microphone. Nicki held out the filled demitasse cup, her feet dancing toward Rusty. Her grin actually made him want to join the dance and it took all his composure to remain angry at his playboy bunny.

"Drink up, Red, and close your mouth. That hole of yours is catchin' flies."

"I'm sorry, Rusty. Lawd, I had no choice but to go undercover," Gina said, walking to him with a sweet smile as she twirled her ponytail hair in her finger. "It's just, we've heard a lot of rumors about Mrs. De Luca and this being my dream and all, I needed to find out what our chances are for success. Halo is so, like, the go to place, and I honestly didn't know if what we had to offer was a good plan, and then I visited and boy was I glad I did."

Afraid that his angry white-knuckled grip would snap the petite handle of the cup, he placed it down beside the tray of disk-like cookies and some weird looking, but heavenly smelling almond white nougat. He turned away from the desserts annoyed at her flippancy. "And what did your little deception reveal, Regina?"

"Oh you can call me Gina. 'Cause, you know, you've already run your fingers through my hair."

"Fine, Geeena." He clenched his jaw, the veins in his neck bulging. "What intel did you gain from my salon?"

"Well, I found out that Halo has nothin' over what PalHairMo will offer." She grinned, Italian proud.

"Oh, really?" Angry, he turned from her, storming to the door. "This means war!"

"Oh, don't be that way, Rusty. Here take some Christmas candy back to the salon with you. Torrone is far tastier than those boring peppermints you have."

Rusty looked up at the sign above the door that read *"Arrivederci."* His fury flared again and he spun around. "I liked you, Gina! You have great hair and the thought of you in those bunny earmuffs was ... well

… never mind. I retract my offer for drinks and dinner."

She looked at him and pouted, her hand still offering the torrone, and by God if his heart didn't melt. Purposeful steps brought him back to her, his face set in stone as he removed a piece of nougat from the red and green plate. He watched as the adorable pout turned into a genuine smile and he bit the candy.

"This is good."

"Of course it is, silly. My sister Lizzy made it last night. She's a baker at heart. Does this mean you're not mad at me?"

"No, it just means that I'm hungry and that image of you in those earmuffs is burned onto my brain." He chewed, forcing himself not to smile back. "This still means war, Gina."

"I know. May the best salon win."

~**~

Clutching a traditional New York City blue and white coffee cup in her gloved hand, Elizabeth stood between two identically decorated Christmas trees and three red-carpeted staircases in the lobby of the upscale New York Palace. She'd never before been in this hotel. In fact, she'd never been to most of Manhattan's exclusive accommodations. Sure she had walked passed them on her way to the subway as a young woman, but had never actually stepped within. This particular edifice on 51st and Madison Avenue always looked so formidable; its wrought iron gates seemingly discouraged people of her lowly station to enter into their famed forecourt. Always impressive, now it was decked out in holiday splendor with trees and garland adorned in tiny white lights that twinkled in the early morning. The huge white and red poinsettias greeted her and she found herself feeling welcome and optimistic for the day—St. Nicholas Day, as Gina reminded her before she left the apartment. She was thankful there would be no opportunity today for that special Mass her sister wanted to drag her to. Nope, just discussions of external fixations, limb ischemia, and soft-tissue coverage at the symposium.

Warming from the outdoor December chill, Elizabeth paused. Behind her, the central revolving door continued to woosh round, allowing the quick effusion of winter air to penetrate the lobby as visitors came and went. Gaining her bearings before seeking out the conference ballroom, her gaze was drawn to the unusual chandelier towering overhead. She briefly imagined herself transported to another time, a princess catching her breath before descending the grand staircase, about to make her entrance into a ball. Lost in her wonderment, she took in every detail of the stunning rotunda, from its ornate columns to its brass banisters and impressive golden statuary.

Today she felt every bit the professional Dr. Elizabeth Fairchild, and she buried the image of PalHairMo's shocking yellow walls and glossy white framed red and green contemporary artwork into the back of her mind. The uncomfortable thought that, just the day before, Lizzy Clemente had felt a teensy tiny bit at home in a hair salon determined to stereotype her, was disarming. She inwardly chortled at the irony that she now stood in a rotunda modeled after the Italian Renaissance.

Pleasant music discreetly infused the polished marble foyer, and the seasonal Christmas scents of cinnamon and pine added to the festive air. She was engrossed in her regard for the magnificence of The Palace where she stood.

As she sipped her black coffee, she continued to examine the glass chandelier that resembled floating golden champagne bubbles of varied sizes. But she was jolted from her admiration when someone slammed into her from behind, pushing her forward and spilling her coffee down the front of her camel wool coat.

"What the hell!" she exclaimed, holding out her arms in frustrated response, moving the dripping cup far from her person.

"I'm so sorry. Oh, Lord, I'm so sorry," the careless jerk said. "It was an accident."

"Sorry?" New York attitude ready, she turned, but her terse retort died as quickly as it came.

It was none other than her Etonville altar boy.

Her jaw went slack, not able to emit the words she was going to say. The sexy man she had often thought of for over three months, stood before her flustered as he fumbled to retrieve a handkerchief from his coat pocket, readying to dry her. Who gave a crap about the coat? It was a knock off anyway. But to have his hands on her attempting to swipe and blot—this coat was suddenly a prized possession.

"Did the coffee burn you? Are you okay?" he asked, still looking down at the violation to her chest.

"No. I'm fine. Really."

He finally looked up and their eyes locked with recognition. What dreamy, azure pools he had. She was immediately lost in them.

.   He smiled and so did she, enjoying the woodsy trace of his cologne.

"August 30th," he said, his astonished voice washing over her.

"St. John's Church," she replied with a nod and a grin that she just could not suppress.

"You didn't stay for Mass. You, um, never came back."

"No, I didn't." *He looked for me! Oh, my God!*

His hand hesitated between their bodies, unsure whether to depress the linen hanky. She, too, felt awkward, finally taking it from him, her gloved fingers brushing his. "Thank you."

"I'm so sorry. I didn't see you standing there. I just … I haven't been here since the renovation of the lobby and that chandelier just caught my attention as soon as I came through the door. It looks like champagne bubbles."

Elizabeth gazed up at the fixture and giggled at his similar description. "Yes, it does. It's spectacular. I have to confess that the champagne bubbles grabbed my attention, too. I was in another world and foolishly stopped when I entered." She continued to blot the coffee, alternating her attention between the stain and the gorgeous man looking so contrite and endearing, standing before her.

Handing him back the soiled linen, she thanked him followed by the removal of her gloves. There was no way in hell she was going to offer to shake his hand with any kind of barrier between their flesh.

At the same time, with outstretched hands, they said, "I'm …"

He smiled, chuckling modestly, taking her tingling hand in his. "Please, ladies first."

"I'm Elizabeth Fairchild."

"It's a pleasure to meet you Elizabeth. I'm Mike Garin, daydreamer, certifiable spaz, and destroyer of women's clothing. Wait, that didn't come out right. I mean … um."

She laughed, enjoying the feel of her hand cradled in his. Everything about him felt grounding and comfortable, even their shared nervousness. "I know what you meant. The pleasure is all mine, Mike, and don't worry about the coat, really."

He continued to hold her hand, seemingly unwilling to release it and that was just fine with her. It gave her time to note the missing wedding ring.

"I'll give you my card and, if the coffee doesn't come out, you can send me the bill for dry cleaning. If need be, I'll buy you a new one," he offered.

"I'm sure it'll come out. It was an accident."

Awkwardly, they released hands and then he looked at his watch.

"Looking to get away already? This meeting is too serendipitous to just run away from, don't you think?" she asked playfully, unable to resist the need to flirt, even unsure if she was doing it correctly. Lord knows it had been a long time since someone had caught her attention enough to put herself out there.

"Oh no! I'm not running away! I'm here for a conference and don't want to miss registration."

"The Limb Salvage and Plastic Reconstruction Symposium?"

Mike quirked his head as a sweet smile spread upon his very kissable lips. "Are you attending as well?"

"I am. I'm a foot and ankle surgeon."

"Beautiful, forgiving, *and* intelligent," he said.

She blushed. "I might say the same of you: handsome, penitent, and a podiatrist to boot!"

"I'm actually a plastic surgeon, but I'm in good company. I like feet. Do you practice podiatry near Etonville?"

"No. I live in LA. That's why you didn't see me again at St. John's. I was ... um ... just visiting family in the area for the weekend and ... So, do you live in Etonville?" she quickly changed the subject away from why she was in the village. Unwilling to lie outright lest the nose itching began, it was better just not to expound on the question.

"Like you, my sister and I were visiting family—"

"Your sister, the blonde girl in church?" she cut off, nearly audibly breathing a sigh of relief.

"Yes, my baby sister. Can I walk you to the conference, Elizabeth?"

"I'd like that. I always hate coming to these things alone, but I need my CME and hope to network a bit. It's nice to make a friend."

She watched that dreamy smile emerge again as they both stood thunderstruck by the other in the rotunda. Gentle Christmas music and twinkling lights under floating yellow, glittering bubbles provided the perfect beginning when he spoke with a nod, "Yes, it's *very* nice to meet you, finally."

"Finally?"

"Uh huh. I regretted not introducing myself in August and then you were gone."

"Really? I wasn't sure if you had even noticed me in the back of the church."

"Trust me, I noticed."

~**~

The guest speaker's lecture was fascinating, and if not for the stunning distraction beside him, Mike may have actually committed some of it to memory. Elizabeth's trace of perfume was currently doing a number on him and that stylish red suit she wore, set against her chestnut waves was affecting him in all sorts of ways. Damn if that occasional bump of her black pump against his calf every time she crossed or uncrossed her leg didn't act like a defibrillator to his heart. Yeah, he loved feet—after a thorough washing, of course.

What an incredible coincidence, her being here; he reflected that perhaps it was more like fate. He'd actually prayed to see her again, and had attended confession for *seeing* her in a compromising position (well, more than one position actually) in his imagination.

He closed his eyes and reveled in the sublime energy her body (only inches from his left side!) was generating. He resisted the urge to place the palm of his hand upon her stocking-clad knee by redirecting his focus to the image upon the presentation slide: a necrotic diabetic ulcer, which resulted in amputation.

It was for naught as Elizabeth leaned over and whispered to him, that puff of air against his ear, a sultry murmur, "Most likely peripheral arterial occlusive disease. I don't get to see this much in my practice," which reached his muddled psyche more like, "Let's go get a room. I'm wearing red garters. You can play Santa and give me my Christmas gift." That's how much she unhinged him, that's how useless he anticipated this symposium's lectures to be for the remainder of the day. With her beside him, learning about skin flaps and debridement was the last thing on his mind.

119

He felt a flutter of anticipation within his stomach when he whispered back trying not to show how affected he was by her nearness, "The vast majority of these wounds are due to venous insufficiency. I rarely get these cases in my practice, but I can see how an interdisciplinary approach can save limbs through extensive wound care and vascular intervention."

"I agree. My practice mostly focuses on vanity reconstruction."

Good Lord, they had so much in common. They seemed to click immediately; he had even foregone his obsession to use antibacterial lotion following their handshake. From the start, she seemed to like him for him, not for the same purpose that most women sought him out. Elizabeth didn't know anything about him or that insulting Facebook persona. She wasn't flirting unabashedly and even if she was undressing him with her eyes, it was no more than he was doing to her, and neither of them were obvious about it – unlike the last one hundred or so dates he had gone on. However, unlike those other women, he welcomed any overt attention that Elizabeth wanted to bestow upon him.

Unsure of how to proceed, he felt a tinge of perspiration under his arm. *Dammit!* He leaned toward her, his lips an inch from the curve of her ear waiting to be kissed. "Will you have dinner with me tonight?"

Her face glowed with excitement; the smile she gave him stopped his heart. God, if he could only bring that smile to her face time and again.

"I'd love to join you."

"Do you like Italian?"

"I love Italian."

Yes!

Just like that, they went back to taking notes, attempting to listen attentively to the speaker encourage the importance of integrating modalities: podiatry, vascular, and plastic surgeons in order to prevent amputation. Yes, a merger between podiatry and plastic was quite an appealing prospect, he thought.

From the corner of his eye, he admired the bone structure of her left hand as she took notes in the workbook provided to attendees. Her delicate fingers bent, executing loopy, slanted cursive, and that, too, fascinated him.

Fate. No doubt, it was fate. But Los Angeles—3,000 miles away from New York …

He surreptitiously observed her right hand accidently wrap around his coffee cup, thinking it was her own beside it; her attention remained on the projector screen like a laser.

His innate compulsion to cringe when her mouth touched the rim wasn't there. What normally would have been considered a disturbing desecration, felt strangely intimate when her luscious, red lips kissed his cup, drinking its contents. He watched that subtle movement in her neck as she quenched her desire for satiation. It was extremely suggestive and highly titillating. Germs or not, suddenly he, too, wanted to drink from the same cup, desiring to place his lips where hers had just vacated.

He had absolutely no misgiving when he did so after she rested the cup back down and he lifted it to his eager mouth. In that one action, he proved to himself that he wasn't a germaphobe. Ha!

"Oh my God. I'm so sorry!" she whispered, then raised her index finger to his lips, wiping away the transferred smudge of her red lipstick.

Was that a flirt? He nearly groaned at the *ahem* growing need that her simple touch to his mouth elicited. He smiled, powerless in his own flirtatious response. "No worries. It seems we are meant to have coffee shared between us." What followed from his lips took him by surprise. "Perhaps next time, it won't be the cup leaving the lipstick." *Did I just say that aloud?*

Elizabeth said nothing; her gaze locked with his in what he hoped was unspoken anticipation, and her pearly white grin lead him to believe that she—and he—welcomed this playful banter and the possibilities. Elated by the implication of her smile, he took unexpected pleasure at the fact that his brazen, uncharacteristic flirting hadn't offended—and that he had actually executed it seamlessly. For the first time in a long time, a romantic beginning felt natural. She didn't appear afraid to give into the exploration of their quiet attraction in a simple and pure beginning—over coffee, career, and then dinner—and maybe, if he was lucky, a kiss in the moonlight.

She shifted her bottom, re-crossing her legs, doing it again—that brush of her foot against his calf. Unable to resist the smirk that formed upon his lips, he glanced over at her and noticed she was saucily twisting her lips, too. Damn, if her footsie below the table hadn't been deliberate all this time! Confirmation: she had been flirting with him since nine o'clock this morning.

*~**~*

Torrone (Italian Christmas Nougat)

1 cup honey
2 egg whites
1 cup sugar
2 tablespoons water
1 lb. almonds, shelled and blanched
½ lb. hazel nuts, shelled and slightly toasted
1 tsp. candied orange peel, cut into small pieces
½ tsp. grated lemon rind

Place honey in top of double boiler over boiling water and stir with wooden spoon 1 hour or until honey is caramelized. Beat egg whites until stiff and add to honey slowly, mixing well. The mixture will be fluffy and white.

Combine sugar with 2 tablespoons water in small saucepan and let boil without stirring until caramelized. Add caramelized sugar to honey mixture a little at a time, mixing well. Cook mixture a little longer and when a little dropped into cold water hardens, add nuts, candied fruit and grated rind. Mix well and quickly before mixture has time to harden.

Line 2 or 3 6x8-inch loaf pans with wafer paper (ostia) and pour in mixture to a depth of about 2 inches. Let cool and cut into 2 long rectangular pieces. Wrap in waxed paper to keep. Makes 4 to 6 pieces.

~Taken from: Page 245, *The Talisman, Italian Cook Book,* by Ada Boni (1929/ translated 1950)

~Eleven~
Cibo dell'amore
(Food of Love)

Darkness had fallen on the Big Apple by the time the conference concluded, and Elizabeth found herself awash with nerves as their taxi slowly maneuvered through the southbound traffic down Madison Avenue.

Today is St. Nicholas Day.

The same feast day that, all those years ago, she had attended Mass and prayed to meet the man who would become her husband. Following that Mass, she had circled the church's seven marble pillars seven times.

Was my prayer heard? Had circling the pillars worked? Nah. That was a bizarre ritual that Father Rocco most likely thought up.

Admiring the holiday lights beyond the cab's window, she shook her head to clear it of such thoughts. St. Nicholas had nothing to do with meeting her altar boy—nor that they had clicked immediately … and were now headed to dinner together. Saintly intercession had nothing to do with any of this.

Reconnecting at a medical conference was purely coincidental. Yes, purely coincidental.

She blinked her eyes to snap her out of such silly musing, preferring to think on what an awesome day she had with Mike. Over lunch, they had discussed medicine, hopes for their personal career transformations, and the future of health care, which led to a conversation about politics. Usually a verboten topic (especially in LA if your opinions weren't with the consensus) they'd surprisingly seen eye-to-eye in their beliefs. Elizabeth's attention moved to Mike's hand resting upon his knee. He had beautiful fingers, long and strong. His nails were neat, possibly manicured. She had noticed earlier, but now, with the left side of her body leaning flush against his, she imagined them doing other things, instead of being uselessly adhered to his own thigh.

She glanced over her shoulder, admiring the contours of his face, the captivating blue of his eyes, and the charming quirk to his lips. Wanting to pinch herself, she couldn't believe she was sitting beside him on a date, an actual date.

"So where is this Angelo's restaurant?" she asked.

"Have you ever eaten down in Little Italy on any of your visits from the West Coast?"

"Um, no, but I'm open to anything." She scratched her nose.

Oh Lord, she wasn't off to an exemplary beginning with these kinds of fibs. Instinctively, she knew this could come to no good, almost hearing her sage father and pious Prozia instructing, *"Buon sangue non mente."* Good blood doesn't lie. She felt the same way, but she rationalized, *It's just a dinner date. Can't I just be Dr. Elizabeth Fairchild from LA who's visiting New York? He's a wealthy plastic surgeon of Anglo-American ancestry. His hyphen comes without stereotyping. His family lives in Etonville, the white bread village, and I'll likely not see him after December. Where's the harm?*

Promptly redirecting, she shifted in her seat, to look at him straight on. "Earlier you mentioned a sister; tell me about her."

The warmth of his smile reached his eyes, and she knew the siblings were close.

"Her name is Mia. We live together over on Sutton Place. She's a great roommate and probably my best friend, but even at twenty-four, she's painfully shy in public. It's ironic really, because she has a marketing degree from Columbia, but has a difficult time engaging with strangers."

"So she's not working then?"

"No. I keep reminding her that she needs to get out there, look for a satisfying job, and find a sense of purpose, but right now, her insecurities hold her immobilized. I fear I'm not helping the situation, but I just want her to reach her full potential and be happy. I don't think isolation and an unhealthy addiction to the internet is the path to a fulfilling future."

Yeah, she understood what it meant to love your family so much that you only desired their happiness, and would do anything for them to attain it. "I have sisters, too, and I know what you mean. They're the reason I came to the conference in New York, rather than the one in Arizona. I can understand you wanting to help Mia find her way. Has she discussed overcoming her shyness with a professional?"

"For years, but she stopped after college."

"It sounds like she's lonely, needs girlfriends, a support system, definitely an outlet to get her away from the internet. I know firsthand how hard it is to make friends, to put yourself out there."

"Oh I agree, and that's part of the problem. Up until recently, she's been hesitant to move from our current place, which I think would be the best idea—a fresh start, in a way. Maybe settling into an area of the city that is more trendy and upbeat."

His loving concern for his sister touched her heart, making her like him even more. "If you don't mind me asking, does Mia talk with your parents about her loneliness? Is your mom at least her best friend?"

"Long story there." His expression sobered slightly, eyes locking on hers. "I'll save that for our second date because I come with some baggage, and I don't want to scare you away yet."

"You're so sure you'll want a second date, huh? What if I do something uncouth like burp after my meal or eat from your dinner plate? Will you still want a second date?"

"I don't see why not. I survived you drinking from my coffee cup, so I might let you eat from my plate."

Elizabeth chuckled. "You are brave! I think that's my biggest pet peeve. I love food and unabashedly have a healthy appetite, and it's really the kiss of death when men assume you aren't going to finish your meal. I'm appalled when they stretch across the table and stab at my food. It feels like such a violation. Where I come from, food is sacred, even symbolic. Please tell me you don't eat from your date's dish and you may even get a third date before I leave."

His deep chortle tickled her ear. "I can assure you that I have *never* in my life eaten from anyone's plate—even my sister's. I totally get what you're saying."

"Whew. Sounds like you're a keeper and that my penne is safe from an overzealous intrusion tonight."

Mike raised an eyebrow with a naughty smirk, and his strong hand reached to take her gloved one in his grasp. Her heart hammered when he gently squeezed her fingers as he spoke in that deep seductive baritone voice of his. "Your penne, Elizabeth?" he ventured suggestively, feeling every bit like his Don Juan cousin, but that wouldn't stop him from flirting in the most salacious manner smoothly employing sexual metaphors for Italian food.

"My linguini and clam sauce."

"Your figs?"

"Oh behave, Dr. Garin."

"You make it very hard, Dr. Fairchild."

"Hard to behave?"

"I'm not going to answer that. It would go against my Catholic school upbringing." He chortled, looked down and then away from her heated gaze.

At any other time and with any other man, Elizabeth would have shouted, "Stop the cab! I'm getting out, you presumptuous ginzaloon. I see through your veiled seductive talk of penis (penne) and vagina (figs!) Do you think me so naïve not to know that Italian food is, in and of itself, one big metaphor for sex? Well, I'm not having it—any of it—with you. You're all alike! *Pezzo di Merda!*"

However, that wasn't her thought process or her physical reaction tonight. With a last name of Garin, Mike wasn't Italian—nope, not an end vowel in sight. And yes, she did want to have sex with him, repeatedly. Meatballs, penne, clams, figs, and melons. All of it. It was, after all, a feast day.

~**~

If a restaurant could be both romantic and fun, then Angelo's of Mulberry Street was the perfect eatery for a first date. Mike loved this place but very rarely came here, instead taking dates to Rao's as his safe haven, but tonight was different, very different. With little time left before Elizabeth would be back in Southern California, he hoped she would leave with the best impression of a memorable night: enjoyable company, excellent Neapolitan food, and the occasional waiter breaking out in song. Manhattan's downtown Little Italy at Christmastime was special to him and since LA didn't really have a community like this, he wanted the magic to touch her soul. With a last name like Fairchild, she most likely hadn't experienced the warmth of *famiglia* that Mulberry and Mott Streets embodied. In spite of his not-so-stellar relations that first settled here at the turn of the previous century, he couldn't deny the pull this small section of downtown Manhattan had on him. In some ways, he wished he was a member of one of those big Italian families that had 42 first cousins and everyone else was considered an aunt or uncle, not to mention having a nonna— a real nonna, not a diva whose tongue was razor sharp as a sword poised for castration with every spoken word. Sure, for many, turning 80 was license to remove all filters, but Stella had always been that way for as long as he could remember.

Elizabeth sat across from him in a cozy room with only four tables where terracotta toned walls cast an Old World feel in the dim ambient light. Behind the bar, swags of garland hung across the top of the mirror, and a small Christmas tree stood at the far end of the liquor bottles. Their little section of the restaurant was semi-private and their table small enough for his hand to hold hers before dessert would arrive. That is, if he got up the nerve. He'd been wanting to do it all night, but suddenly, he was internally panicking at having left his anti-bacterial bottle in his overcoat. Why now? Why was he feeling the need to protect himself? He'd already shook her hand and drank from the same mug as she had. He'd even allowed his fingers to brush hers when he reached to carry her briefcase at the close of the conference. If he was this freaked out about holding her hand, how the hell was he going to kiss her goodnight? It's been months since he last kissed a woman on the lips, but tonight he was drawn to the prospect like a pubescent teenager.

There were several key, pleasant aspects he noted during their meal, like the way she gave him all her attention. She hadn't placed a mobile phone upon the tabletop so there was no disconcerting checking of social media, nor, most important, had she spoiled his euphoria by eating from his entrée. Their conversation over the main course was everything he hoped it would be—both playful and serious, a real meeting of hearts and minds. Her concern over Mia and her commitment to making something meaningful of her career revealed her warm, giving heart. Sure, there was a physical attraction, but he found himself captivated by her intelligence and wit, her compassion and determination. Elizabeth was knock-out gorgeous and made him laugh. She was a bel-esprit, thus far satisfying all his dreams for Mrs. Right.

Elizabeth watched the waiter on the other side of the restaurant as he sang in Italian. Unconsciously she quietly joined in the few verses she knew and felt the grin she had lost weeks, months, years ago, stealthily return to her heart. When she noticed her date watching her, she immediately stopped singing.

"You know Italian?" he asked.

"No, not really. Just a few things I picked up over the years. My mother was an Andre Bocelli superfan." Well, that wasn't a total lie. Gina was the real *fluent*.

Again, she awkwardly diverted the conversation. "This place really is incredible, Mike. The company's not too shabby either."

A full-blown grin spread upon his lips as he blushed. "I'm glad that you're enjoying yourself as much as I am. I don't come down here very often but, during the holidays, it's pretty special." He paused, gathering his nerve. "Maybe, for our second date, we can come back when the tree lighting ceremony takes place in a few days. Sometimes it brings big names to Little Italy, and the church gets involved, too."

"I think I'd like that."

"Great!" He refilled her glass and then his own with more Chianti as he asked the dreaded question. "Do you attend church regularly?"

She couldn't help fidgeting in her seat, but was thankful he hadn't asked of her family roots.

"No. My being in St. John's that Saturday was, actually, unprecedented. I don't think I can even call myself a cafeteria Catholic any longer. Not quite an agnostic, but definitely not practicing."

Clearly disappointed he asked, "And why is that? Have you become disillusioned?"

She sipped her wine, mulling over just how much she wanted to divulge to him, resolved that she wouldn't be seeing him beyond the end of the month. But the issue of faith seemed to be an important one to him. She swallowed hard, readying to confess to more than she had in Father Mintern's office when she'd gone in adherence to Prozia's behest.

"Part of me believes that the choices I've made in my life have served to ostracize me from the Church."

"Sometimes the choices we make are very difficult, but they have to be made. No two circumstances are the same."

She took a deep breath.

"Well, I married in my second year of medical school because I got pregnant." *There* that's *out on the table*.

"He wasn't a Catholic. In fact, he hated that I was, and had I not put my foot down about going my pregnancy alone, he never would have proposed. Both he and his parents teased me mercilessly, even joked about most of our traditions. In the end, I suppose it was just easier to conform and walk away from the Catholic faith than to continue to defend myself to narrow-minded deaf ears. Shortly after I miscarried, we divorced."

Speaking about this part of her past was painful. She had deeply buried the initial joy of pregnancy and the simultaneous difficulties of it being unexpected in the midst of pursuing her medical education. The sorrow of miscarriage collided with her release from an intolerable marriage. The ramifications of those events determined her path. Lizzy Clemente had become Elizabeth Fairchild.

Mike felt ashamed by his insensitive question and embarrassed for her likely discomfort discussing her past. "I'm sorry, truly sorry that you had to go through that. I didn't mean to pry. One's faith walk is very private."

"It is, but … you asked a direct question about something that's important to you."

"I know it's none of my business, but I've always believed you can come home at any time. The door is always open."

Wow, Father Mintern in LA said the same thing.

She wistfully smiled and nodded, recalling her visit with the young priest. "Someone else recently told me just that. It means a lot, something I'll consider. Thank you." For a moment she thought of the peace she felt when she first walked into St. John in Etonville and then the subsequent visits to St. Clement in LA. Unable to maintain her gaze, she glanced to the archway and the few tables on the other side of the opening.

This time, Mike acted on his impulse, seizing the moment to reach across the table, taking her soft fingers in his grasp, his thumb brushing her skin in gentle strokes. The warmth of her flesh traveled the length of his arm. It was a sublime moment of honesty and tenderness, and he immediately felt something stir within him. "Elizabeth, I—"

Suddenly, her body went rigid, a wild flash appearing in her eyes as she retracted her hand, commanding, "Hold that thought!" In that instant she bent down to dig into her purse resting on the floor, her dark waves cascading, concealing her face.

"What is it? I'm sorry. I guess, I shouldn't have held …" he apologetically

129

stammered, feeling like a total jackass.

Panicked, her voice sounded stricken as she responded to him with her bent over body contorted and head remaining faced down. "No really, Mike, I'm glad you held my hand. It was romantic. I just... um... need my ... um sunglasses. Yeah, I need my sunglasses."

Elizabeth had just noticed a familiar man in the adjoining dining room: Frankie Puppino, Gina's slick ex-husband, the sausage wielding cheater. She was trapped with nowhere to go.

Of all friggin people! She sat in direct view of someone who knew Lizzy Clemente from Belmont very well, someone who could "out" her ethnic upbringing on the wrong side of the tracks. No doubt, that loser would have no qualms about cutting her down in a public place, as coarsely and loudly as possible. After all, she had encouraged her beloved sister to leave his cheating ass and had even paid to end that sham of a marriage. As if the adultery wasn't bad enough, he'd had the audacity to hit on her at the divorce proceedings.

Mike furrowed his brow in confusion when she slid the oversized glasses onto her face then gazed up at him with a smile.

"There, that's better," she said.

"I'd ask you if it's too bright in here, but being that we're sitting in candlelight, I know that can't be it. Are you okay?"

She scratched her nose before the lie even poured forth, "It's nothing, just a little ... Retinitis Pigmentosa."

"That's serious, Elizabeth. Have you had that since childhood?" He cocked an eyebrow and she wondered if he saw right through her lie.

"No. I'm fine really; no need to worry."

As the waiter placed their dessert and coffee on the table, she chanced a quick glance around his rotund form to observe her ex-brother-in-law chatting up the overly endowed Christmas bauble sitting opposite him. When she thought Frankie glanced in her direction, her head snapped sideways and she quickly grabbed the liqueur menu tented at the edge of the table, hiding behind it, pretending to read.

"Would you like to order something?" Mike asked with a tinge of humor to his voice, as he reached out turning the menu right side up.

She placed the menu back on the table then abruptly stood, moving her chair cattycorner to him, making sure her back was facing her sister's ex-husband. Dammit! She was having such a good time and didn't want this date to end, but Frankie would most likely blurt out something to the effect of "Well if it ain't Lizzy Clemente. What a surprise to see you in *this* Little Italy. What's the matta? You tired of LA and Arthur Avenue? How's my wife—the one you convinced was too good for her Italian roots!"

"Are you sure you're all right? You seem nervous," Mike asked.

"What could possibly be wrong? Let's eat! This tiramisu looks to die for. I love tiramisu!"

Mike couldn't help laughing, knowing full well that she didn't have the rare degenerative eye disease, which having usually begun in childhood would most likely have rendered her seriously impaired by now. He loaded his fork with a piece of cheesecake and, unthinking, held it up to her lips. "*Mangia, bella.* It'll take the edge off."

"I'm not edgy, just excited about dessert! I love sweets," she happily declared with a smile before surrounding his utensil with her lips, completely oblivious to *his* usage of the Italian language as well as the nervous anxiety coursing through his body when her moist lips slid along the tines.

"Are you going to tell me what's going on? While your eyeglasses are very stylish, they are, in fact, hindering my admiration of your lovely face."

"What's going on? This is great cheesecake, so creamy." She said with her mouth full as she sliced at the tiramisu before her then held a chunk of it up to his lips.

He deliberated. *Yeah, I can do this.* A delectable mouthful from her utensil followed.

Good Lord that was a liberating victory—french kissing should be a relatively painless endeavor now. He licked his lips at the thought followed by a wipe to his mouth with the linen napkin, noticing how she subtly glanced over her shoulder than snapped her eyes back to him.

"Do you know that guy?" he asked, finally putting two and two together.

"Which guy?"

"The one you're hiding from. The one who is making you go all incognito and shovel that tiramisu down your throat so you can make a quick getaway."

"Guy?"

Mike stilled her hand hovering over her plate. "Yes, Elizabeth, the guy with the blonde woman on the other side of the archway. The one whose stare is currently boring into your back with definite familiarity. In fact, he's getting up and coming toward us."

She dropped her fork then held her napkin aloft, covering her face. "Oh no! Shoot!"

He removed the linen and laughed. "I'm just joking. Still going to deny that you know him?"

Elizabeth relaxed her shoulders and lowered her chin to her chest. She laughed; the gig was up. "Unfortunately, I *do* know him. He's my sister Regina's loser ex-husband, and I paid for their divorce. On top of that, she's just filed for an annulment. So, let's just say there's no love lost between us. He's not the most eloquent or well mannered man of my acquaintance and, honestly, this could get ugly."

Mike effortlessly fed her another piece of his cheesecake. "You could have said. What do you say about me settling the check and we'll take this dessert to go?"

"Are you sure? We're having such a good time, and I don't want to ruin it."

Mike smoothed his thumb over the corner of her mouth, wiping away a smidgen of cream. "You're not ruining it at all. Selfishly, I don't want to share your attention with another man, especially one who is making you uncomfortable, someone you obviously dislike." He leaned closer to her. His sweet tiramisu breath was only inches from her cheek. "I want you all to myself and, like I said, I want to gaze into those alluring chestnut eyes of yours."

Elizabeth smiled. "You are quite a charmer, Dr. Garin."

"Not really. I just try to speak the truth. You captivate me, Elizabeth." Now she blushed.

Eight minutes later, sans their desserts and sunglasses, they stood at the curb in front of Angelo's, bundled up, trying to hail a cab. All around them, just like in Belmont, Christmas music floated in the air from some unknown location. The Santa-clad Salvation Army volunteer rang his bell in tune as pairs of lovers walked arm-in-arm along the sidewalks of Mulberry Street where red and green garland spanned the distance just like the decorations on Arthur Avenue.

Mike noticed a shiver of Elizabeth's shoulders and how she burrowed her chin into her Burberry scarf. Instinct removed all thought of propriety when he placed his arm around her shoulders and pulled her closer to him to keep her warm against his chest.

She didn't seem to mind and neither did he as the steam from their breath blended in the chilled air.

"It feels like snow," he said, his hand rubbing her back.

He could hear the nervousness in her voice when she replied. "It does. I miss the fall and winter. I miss getting snowed in."

"Yeah, I love that, too. Would you care to go for a nightcap?"

"Is that code for let's go back to my place?"

Everyone did it … one-night stands, jumping into bed on the first date. Why not him? He grinned, wishing he could be less honorable than he was, because the woman in his arms was tempting—very tempting.

"No. That's code for I want to spend more time with you before you head back to your hotel."

"Oh."

"Where are you staying?"

"I'm not staying at a hotel. I'm actually visiting uptown at my sisters' place." That, for sure, was not a lie.

"Well, what do you say about heading over to the Rose Bar at the Gramercy for an aperitif?"

"You mean I didn't scare you away with my forward assumption?"

Mike tightened his grip around her, enjoying how perfect she fit against him. "You didn't scare me. I'm just a man who likes to do things the traditional way; maybe that makes me old fashioned."

Elizabeth grinned. "I'm not used to tradition, but it's refreshing. You *are* a gentleman, and I meet so few of them."

"You may not think I'm such a gentleman if you knew my thoughts." Pursing his lips, he blew out a deep breath. "Elizabeth, I hope this doesn't scare *you*, but today, together … I haven't had such a great time in … I don't know how long."

"Me either. Thank you for asking me to dinner."

He admired the rosy chill on her cheeks, the sparkle in her eyes enhanced by her inner spirit not just a reflection of the holiday lights above. He almost stammered when he said, "I would really like to kiss you right now."

"So what's stopping you? Gentlemen still kiss."

His soft lips met hers in a tentative caress, and she couldn't help deepening their kiss as her hand clutched at his coat lapel, pulling him closer. Her mouth responded to his tenderness with an eagerness that her whole body demanded. Mike held onto her tightly, his mouth surrounding hers in matched perfection, his tongue breaching her softness with delicious probes.

Good God, this was a kiss. This was *the* kiss that every woman dreamt about.

Their mouths parted, catching breaths almost in unison. Dizzy from the encounter, Elizabeth barely managed to whisper, "Wow," overwhelmed by the delectable taste of him lingering upon her lips.

"Can I have another?"

"You don't need to ask, Mike."

A passerby whistled but it didn't deter eager lips or hammering hearts as he, most willingly, kissed her again.

~**~

~Twelve~
Inaugurazione
(Grand Opening)

Saturday, December 7th—a date that would live in infamy—in Etonville. This day would be remembered, in perpetuity, as *the* demographic
game changer of the staid Country Club village. The grand opening of
Pal•Hair•Mo would forever be considered the catalyst for the ~~corruption~~
revitalization of a community steeped in colonial history.

Bright sunlight reflected off the salon's display window, illuminating
the swirly painted Christmas trees and the updo poster. Spanning from
one end to the other of Villa Fortuna's storefront, a banner read: Grand
Opening Today. The old display window literally trembled from the
festivities and the sheer volume of the conversation within. As though
an Italian festival was taking place inside, the distinctly familiar song
"Funiculì, Funiculà," escaped through the door every time a patron came
or went.

On the front sidewalk, in groupings that flanked a gleaming red Vespa
scooter, three separate camps worked hard to hit pay dirt: The Salvation Army bell ringer for obvious financial gain, Stella De Luca and her
sidekick Ann for the ruination of the salon, and Salvatore Carpo along
with eight very sexy members of his hot-blooded Roman soccer team.
The latter, of course, was creating the greatest impact in the interest of
the hair salon's success.

Not a woman passed by them without becoming entangled in their
charming Romano net, getting chatted up with compliments and the
offered enticement of an espresso, glass of wine, or a free pedicure—possibly even a date, afterward.

The team's red and yellow athletic uniforms hugged those hard bodies just perfectly, which, of course, didn't hurt in rousing the response they sought. In fact, most of the women out shopping along Main Street deliberately crossed the thoroughfare to get a better look at the eye candy and be pleasantly assaulted with accented pick-up lines like: "Is your father a thief? He stole the stars from the sky to put them in your eyes."

The soccer team's Attacking Playmaker, Mr. Carpo, was greeting each female client at the door, suggesting his desire to place kisses on her palm, then depositing a bag of silver and blue foiled Perugina Baci chocolates. With gloved hands, the Goaltender held out a tray of dipped red, white, and green chocolate strawberries that looked like delectable Italian flags. He sauntered toward the corner in hope of breaching Stella De Luca's impenetrable front with a charming, *"Dolci per il dolci."* It had no affect on her whatsoever.

The woman was formidable, brandishing a picket sign that read: "Just Say NO to Pal•Hair•Mo!" Her mink-draped diminutive form paced back and forth at the far corner curb, while Ann silently trailed behind. Ann, however, remained unfazed by the competition and the fanfare. Vain creature that she was, she cared only for the attention and compliments her hooded glam coat and matching boots received from every coveting woman who passed by.

As soon as the door opened into PalHairMo, there was only one thing every patron smelled: Italian kitchen. Even the music, classic upbeat holiday and ethnic favorites mixed with well-known pop songs made the new clientele feel they were being welcomed home as *famiglia.*

The cappuccino machine worked overtime hissing out cup after cup of the good stuff. None of that "franchise piss," as Nicki had crudely called it. The Clemente sisters' salon used only imported coffee beans, and Josie Zeppo made sure that everyone had a taste. At the far end of the espresso counter sat two large, glass jugs, each now half-filled with Mr. Graciosa's homemade wine—from Gina's bathtub. Although only noontime, the wine supply had depleted faster than Gina could say *saluté,* and the proud winemaker himself stood at the ready to drive back down to the Bronx for replenishment.

Even Mr. Primo attended today's grand opening, having left Rosa in charge of the bakery so he could come to the sisters' aid, bringing with him his specialty cannolis, cream puffs, and mini éclairs, not to mention cookies of every variety.

Chatty and laughing clients filled every hairdresser's station. Gossip was flourishing all around and Gina couldn't have been happier because everyone knew that gossip united people in a beauty salon. A salon without gossip was doomed to fail because most women wanted to either be in the know or be known for being in the know! After parting the woman's hair in front of her, she surveyed the busy space through the reflection in the mirror above the vanity. Her heart swelled with pride, and she bit back the urge to cry with joy.

She observed Nicki escort another male patron to the reception desk for checkout. That dreamy look on his face said everything, and she chuckled at how quickly word must have spread about the sheer shirt and leopard leggings her sister wore. *Thank Gawd she ignored Prozia's will! Take* that *Mr. Rusty Magic Fingers and Stella "She-Devil" DeLuca!*

Even Toni had stepped up his game, dressed as a man and quite debonair, at that. As tempting as it was, he'd made it a point to steer clear from the vino.

Yeah, PalHairMo was going to be a success. Gina could feel the magic, the luck of Villa Fortuna, and the love of her family around her. She'd known at the time that Father O'Malley's blessing of both the salon and her sisters, two days before the opening, would bear fruit. Chancing a quick glance above the front display window, she smiled at the picture of the Blessed Virgin looking down at the goings on below.

Standing beside Gina, Dharma worked diligently blow-drying a client's long locks and, across the aisle, Mrs. Drago, the owner of Capelli Belli, effortlessly created one of those unique updos she was known for on Arthur Avenue. On this day, the motherly woman had closed her own establishment to answer the call to help her girls.

"I read about the salon in the paper. Are you excited about your grand opening?" the client in Gina's chair asked, snapping Gina from musing.

"Oh I am! My sisters and I are so happy. I feel like Cinderella! It's a dream come true!"

"Do they work here as well?"

"Yes, my sister Lizzy is in the back room giving pedicures and the youngest, Nicki, is the wash girl providing free scalp massages."

She snorted at the thought of how successful that particular service had turned out. Not a single male client had left the salon without first booking their next appointment. "She's very popular with the guys."

Both women observed the man remove a twenty from his wallet and hand it to Nicki, his eyeballs fixed downward upon the sheer mesh netting at her cleavage.

Gina's client chuckled before taking another sip of wine. "I'll say. He looks like he's gonna eat her alive."

"That's Nicki for ya'. She's always been the most wild of the three of us. Off the top of my head she's already raked in $385 for the charity."

Above the din of the salon, a lone voice cried out from the hair-dryer chair, waving a tabloid photo magazine in the air. "Hugh Jackman! This man is a god!"

Across the room, another client spoke above the noise of the blow-dryer, "And he can sing, but it's Pierce Brosnan who does it for me. A little bit more mileage equates to experience and know how ... if you get my drift. Oh what I wouldn't do for him to go all 007 on me just so I can go all Bond chick on him."

Even Mrs. Drago joined in the conversation with a hearty laugh. "You youngsters don't know a good looking man—Cary Grant was handsome. Marcello Mastroianni was a god!"

The blonde in Gina's chair fanned herself with her hand. "No, no. You're all wrong. You ladies haven't seen anything until you've seen the man I dined with the other night. Now, Michelangelo is a god!"

"Do tell!" The first woman demanded as the music pounded to Adele's "Right as Rain."

"His plump lips were as delicious as the meatballs on his plate. His eyes are as blue as the exotic Mediterranean! You want to talk backside, let me tell you ... that man's cheeks were so tight you could crack walnuts between them. He's a breast man and, well, he couldn't keep his eyes off my chest."

"Where did you find him?" Gina asked, measuring two pieces of hair for length.

"On eDating. His profile came highly recommended by an acquaintance of mine. She loved the attention he paid to her nipples. Every time she goes to see him, he tweaks them for her. I just knew I had to meet him. My girls are highly sensitive."

"He sounds like a Romeo, Rebecca. In fact, I know a few guys like him down in Little Italy. I was married to one."

"Oh no, he was quite a gentleman allowing me to savor *those* meatballs of his. I'm working on getting a second date, and I hope to have a recap for you—if you know what I mean. Maybe his sausage will be just as spicy as his balls."

Gina tried not to think of her ex. Spicy sausages always came with trouble.

~**~

Joey Falco spotted his grandmother from across the street and he honestly tried to look away from her narrowing eyes as he crossed with the light, but he could feel the malevolent heat of her disapproving stare. Avoidance was always best when it came to her, but he couldn't evade walking past her, once again, stunned by the ballsy audacity she exhibited for such a tiny woman. He'd always considered her the female version of Al Capone; the only things missing were the baseball bat, cigar, and fedora. Instead, her weapons of choice today were a picket sign and a bullhorn, which for the moment, thankfully, sat unemployed on a folding chair.

The tough detective in him would never admit to a soul, especially his cousin Mike, that their grandmother scared the shit out of him. Him! One of New York's Finest who went head-to-head with some of the most notorious criminals in the city. Without fail, she reduced him to a pansy-assed pussy every time he visited with her. But, by God, not today. Today he stayed focused on getting a scalp massage thanks to Rusty's intriguing phone call.

"Gran … Ann," he tersely greeted with a head nod, attempting to bypass her without a tussle.

"I might have expected you to visit the Sicilian trash. You and your cousin have an overactive fascination with breast size."

"Well, Mike *is* a plastic surgeon. Boobs are his business. As for me, I just like the look and feel of a nice rack."

"Crude, Joseph. Do you talk to my daughter, your dear mother like that?"

"I'm kidding you, Stella. Just trying to get that eyebrow of yours to move."

"Still, I should wash your mouth out with soap."

He laughed. "I think Mike might applaud you for that, but I'd like to see you try."

139

"Hmmph. Where's that trailer trash you're shacked up with? What's her name, Max, Al?"

"It was Sam, and she finally moved out."

"So you're here to find a replacement?" The brow remained fixed in place.

"No. I'm actually in Etonville because Mike asked me to keep an eye on you in his absence. He warned me what you have planned."

"He didn't! I'm doing this for him and he sends you like his lap dog."

"I'm no one's lap dog."

"Well, you know what I mean. Look, if you really want to be useful, you'll pick up that sign and march beside me. As a Russo descendant you have a vested interest in Villa Fortuna's return."

"No I don't. This is Mike's gig, not mine." He glanced over his shoulder at the soccer team working the sidewalk two buildings down. "I am impressed though that you've kept a respectful distance from the salon."

"Nonsense. I can reach more pedestrians at the crosswalk, not to mention the traffic light serves to give drivers a greater opportunity to read my signs. As I've stated time and again in my business, it's all about location, location, location."

"Well, PalHairMo seems to have the best location and has pulled out all the stops to get attention. Besides the obvious ploy, what is the soccer team giving away?"

"Sex."

"Well, that'll do it."

Joey pointed to the picket sign resting against the building. It read: Save Our Village from Dirty Sicilian Invasion. "You can't be serious. You do know that's considered a prejudicial hate crime, and I could haul you down to the station."

Stella strutted past him in a huff, her Poison perfume tailing behind her, leaving a plume as potent as any chemical warfare. "I'd like to see *you* try. If anyone is going to be arrested it's those women. I've already called the New York State Liquor Authority. They are illegally serving wine in there!"

"Can't you just let them be? You're never going to get the building, Gran. They own it. Get over it. This isn't the Christmas spirit."

"Yes it is. Just as St. Joseph returned to his ancestral home Bethlehem, so shall a Russo!"

He leaned closer to her despite the overpowering fragrance. "Well, you ain't no Virgin Mary, and if you don't pack up this sideshow of yours, I'll tell the town council exactly who Vito 'Scarface' Russo was. You'll be shunned from Etonville long before the Clemente sisters."

"You wouldn't!" she gasped, her index finger flying to the side of her mouth. That was Italian for "Keep-a your mouth shut … or else!"

He laughed, as he made his escape and left her standing on the corner. He heard her demand "Come here, Ann. You must walk beside me. Make sure they see the writing on your hood."

Poor Ann. If anyone was a lap dog, it was she who blindly acquiesced to his grandmother's commands without protest.

After snagging a chocolate-covered strawberry from the sidewalk server, Joey entered the salon, licking juice from his fingers. Once he crossed the threshold, the lingering scent of Stella's Poison dissipated and was replaced by the aroma of fresh baked Italian goods. The place was a hive of activity with blow-dryers and chatter across the aisle. A cute blonde wearing a red, white, and green apron, worked at the first station. He assumed that was Rusty's Playboy bunny. She was just his type, all sugar sweetness and wholesome ditzy when she cheerfully greeted him with a quick wave and a sparkling smile.

"*Ciao!* Welcome to PalHairMo! Have a zeppole!"

A raven-haired beauty sauntered down the aisle, the naughty grin on her face serving as the perfect accessory to the risqué outfit she wore. No doubt this was the wild woman who had caused him to drive thirty miles for a shampoo. Rusty was correct: she was one hot biscuit. It seemed as though the effervescent Doo Wop sound of Dion and the Belmonts filling the salon permeated her being.

Immobilized, he stood at the reception desk, his vision fixed on the smiling leopard-clad, mascara-laden Sicilian tigress bouncing toward him.

When she spoke, her broad New York accent matched his own. "Hi. I'm Nicki. Let me guess, you're here for a titillatin' hand job."

Hot damn! Already he had fallen for those plump *ahem* lips of hers.

"Something like that. Congratulations on your grand opening. I'm Joey Falco."

"Thanks. Nice to meet ya, Joey. Follow me, and I'll take good care of you." She laughed almost deviously, turning on her stilettos to lead the way toward the washbasin at the back of the salon.

"Is that an offer?" he asked, removing his coat then mindlessly handing it to the well-dressed guy manning the reception desk.

Flippantly, she glanced over her shoulder, her expressive gaze locking with his. "Duh, that's a bona-fide guarantee."

Bang zoom! Badda boom!

In the sink room, Elizabeth sat on a low stool at the foot of the deluxe pedicure chair, professionally removing a callus from her client's heel as though she were back in her medical clinic. These new clients weren't only receiving a pedicure with podiatry formulated anti-fungal nail polish, they were also receiving a full-fledged foot examination in the process. Although focused on the procedure, she couldn't stop her mind from wandering to Mike's incredible kisses the night before and the promise of more to come in four days. Her tummy fluttered in anticipation of their second date: a visit to his practice on Park Avenue followed by lunch. This cloud nine was a new plane of existence for her. She smiled, thinking of how his gentlemanly manner contrasted with those succulent lips of his, but she was pulled from her appetizing thoughts when she heard Nicki on the opposite side of the room.

"Are you comfortable?" Nicki asked her client, the water spray drenching his brown hair.

"I'm very happy," he replied.

Once the water spray ceased, her fingers rotated vigorously on his wet scalp, her breasts spilling over his face.

"How about now?" she asked.

"Even better."

Elizabeth chuckled. *Of course he's happy.* Her sister was adamant about wearing that low-class ensemble, but she'd learned long ago that when it came to fighting Nicki's petulance, it was always best to pick her battles with care. This one was a losing endeavor from the start. Apparently, Nicki and Gina had formulated a plan and, having observed the very first leering male client, she'd understood the method to their madness. It was no different from the soccer players parading outside the salon. Sex sells and everyone loves sex. Before leaving the apartment this morning, Nicki had stated it plainly – in her asset-less lifestyle, men only wanted *those* particular assets of hers, and well, if she could use that to the salon's advantage, so be it. Of course, with female clients she was considerate enough to put on an apron, but not with the guys. She wasn't so stupid not to know how things worked in the world and her personality was best suited to exploiting it—and herself —to get ahead. Elizabeth got that—didn't necessarily approve of it—but understood it. To each his own, but she couldn't help to admit that it was most likely her own assets that had landed her the job at WHPC. Her boss had implied as much on the day she had quit.

Nicki leaned further over the eager client, whose nose was just about touching the mesh of her shirt, her fingers delivering manipulating pressure.

"Do you work here every day?" he asked with a trace of hopefulness in his voice.

"Yeah. I'm one of those hands on owners. Lizzy there is the foot owner but not on Thursdays."

"Why not on Thursdays?"

"Cause it's bad luck to cut toenails on a Thursday."

"Are there any superstitions about hair that I need to be wary of?"

"Yeah, don't get a perm during your period."

"Well, I guess I'm safe on that one."

She slowly moved the pads of her fingers upward along his forehead. "How am I doin' so far—with your scalp massage?"

"I have no complaints. You're right; it's titillating."

"Good, 'cause I'm workin' for tips here. So get your fill 'cause all proceeds go to the charity, Locks of Love, for bald kids. Did ya' eat a zeppole when you came in?"

"Why? Is there a superstition about that, too?"

Nicki snorted. "Nothing official on the books, but … I'm told that if you eat an Italian zeppole ball, you'll get laid."

"Sounds like my kind of dessert. I have a thing for *everything* Italian."

"Yeah? Well, that's a good thing to hear around here. Those picket signs out front are givin' us a crappy image. So, whataya do for a living, Joey?"

"I'm a cop."

"Cool. I might have guessed that was a pistol in your pocket."

"That ain't no pistol, Nicki."

Elizabeth shook her head. She thought she witnessed the man lick his lips, which were only about an inch from Nicki's bouncing bosom as she scrubbed.

She had to admit, Gina was right. PalHairMo, with all its "culture," was on the road to success, and not just because Nicki had "a way" about her, but also because it was as though Little Italy had exploded on Main Street USA and the residents had responded with a resounding "yes!" What's not to love: Funds were being raised and locks of hair were being collected for a worthy charity that made wigs for children who suffer from hair loss; hot soccer players offering kisses; delicious, homemade pastries were everywhere; and Gina-trendy hairstyles were walking out the door on happy new customers. Only three hours into the grand opening and already it was clear they had become the go-to salon. Apart from Nicki's titilating-massage job, their father would be so proud! Moreover, she was proud because her sisters, with the help of Mr. Carpo and the tenants in their apartment building, did it all on their own.

~**~

One woman watched the grand opening from her perch within the empty Halo Salon: Blair Channing. With a pair of binoculars held to her eyes, she sat in a black director's chair facing the window. "I don't like this one bit, Rusty," she huffed. "Etonville is no place for an establishment like theirs."

"Blair, put down the binoculars. It's opening day for them; let them have their fifteen minutes of fame. The proof will be in the pudding. No amount of baked goods or espresso will make up for a bad haircut or an outdated updo."

"Yes, you're right. Big hair went out with the eighties, and clients will most likely end up here for you to fix the botched job. But they have soccer players! Hot ones and we can't compete with that." She placed the binoculars back up to her eyes. "Look at those backsides. I know of only one ass that could compete with those."

Rusty sighed. "Remember what I said to you about your behavior toward Mike?"

"Oh poo. Don't be such a spoilsport. His ass alone could bring women into Halo in droves." Her hand squeezed the air as though his tush was on the receiving end of her fingers.

"I'd like to think my hairdressers can do that."

Blair glanced over her shoulder and raised an eyebrow. "Obviously not this morning. Tonight is the first Saturday for holiday parties and you've had six cancellations and only three clients so far."

Rusty stopped his pacing and turned to gaze out the window. "You're making me feel worse, Blair. Stop it. I'll think of something."

"I'm telling you, your answer lies with Mike and getting him to do a few after-hour Botox parties with a little wine and cheese. They'll be coming out of the woodwork when word gets out that Michelangelo is visiting Halo."

"No. I refuse. I'll turn this around on my own." He paced. "I will not be ruined by a frickin' tray of cannolis or a bunch of ginzaloon soccer players."

**

~Thirteen~
Sorelle
(Sisters)

"I met a woman." Mike said into his phone, attempting to hold back his grin.

"And?" Mia asked.

"And, what? I met someone that's all, and you know what that means: time to put the condo on the market."

"No, that was so not what we agreed. The deal was for the spring, and you hooking up with someone isn't the same as finding Mrs. Right."

"I didn't hook up with her. She's someone I met at the symposium. We had dinner and I'm taking her to lunch on Wednesday."

"You went to that conference on Friday. You mean to tell me that you've let a whole five days pass before taking her out again?"

"She had important commitments. Wednesday was the soonest I could get."

He walked to the bar area of his office to wipe down the sink with an anti-bacterial wipe. Not that it was dirty, but facing his sister's resistance and his own anxiety over inviting Elizabeth to tour his practice followed by lunch brought out the compulsion.

"Wow, a second date with someone you actually like. I think I may need to post that on my Facebook timeline. This is totally unprecedented."

"You're tellin' me. She's the first woman I actually *want* to pinch my ass."

"Really? Oh, this is good gossip, definitely Facebook worthy. You do know that the number of my friends increased exponentially when one of your patients found out that I'm your sister and I've got to say, I am enjoying my sudden popularity."

Concerned, he groaned. "Many of them are not your friends, Mia. They're my stalkers, a few of whom need more professional help than I can give them, as evident by that MAA page."

"Whatever. Everyone likes what I have to say."

"I'm sure they do. You're brilliant, sensitive, and have a sharp wit. I just want you to be careful. I know you have a few good friends online, but it's just that there are a lot of mercenary woman out there who would use you to get to me. Posting anything about me on your Facebook is inviting trouble."

"I'm not fourteen, Mike. I know that. It's just ... I don't know. They don't know me. I'm protected behind the screen."

"You're not really protected, but I'll trust your judgment," he sighed.

"Did you go on a date with a blonde several nights ago?" she asked, the tone in her voice unnerving him.

"Whyyy?"

"She commented on the MAA timeline about your meatballs. The thread is up to 327 comments. Did you really get a blow job on a first date?"

"What? God, No! The woman ate from my entrée and I nearly hyper-ventilated." *But when Elizabeth ate from my fork ... well, that* aroused *me.*

"Whew. I never figured you'd be some woman's boy toy, but you have been a little desperate these days. It's hard to tell what's true or not on FB, especially since some of the things they say about you are so convincing. One woman posted 'Forget a nip and tuck, I only want to fu—.'"

"Mia! About the condo ..."

She laughed at how he cut her off. "My answer is no, not until you have something concrete to show me. Something along the lines of a five-carat Tiffany solitaire."

"I think you're putting the cart before the horse. You said for me to *meet* a woman, not marry one."

"That's semantics now. What's her name?"

Mike moved to his desk and then one-by-one removed the items from its surface, readying to wipe down the sleek top. "Elizabeth Fairchild. She's a foot and ankle surgeon from LA."

"LA? Bro, I'm definitely not giving up my Sutton Place address for a woman who lives 3,000 miles away. How long is she in the city for?"

"She's visiting her sisters for the Christmas holiday."

"Sisters…that's good. How old are they? Where do they live?"

"Stop with the inquisition! We didn't talk much about our families. So chill out."

"So then there is no chance for a quickie visit to the Justice of the Peace before she goes back to California?" she teased, deliberately provoking him.

"Mia. Stop this. I'm not marrying anyone. I want to get to know her first. We have chemistry, and she's intelligent, but for God's sake I only had one date." *One incredible date, which nearly ended up in a luxury hotel suite where, if I hadn't been such a gentleman, my tongue would have licked the sweet perspiration from her body. Germaphobe, my ass!*

Mia grinned, so sure of the tone in her brother's voice. This woman caught his attention, and that was monumental. "Don't screw this up," she said.

"Then don't push me."

"Fine, but if you do screw up, remember there are always those Clemente sisters up in the Bronx. Three to pick from!"

Mike shuddered when the image of chin hair flashed before his mind's eye. It must have been the connection to Mrs. Dixon that made him correlate the two. "Did you go to the grand opening?"

"No. There was a FB Bookalicious party I wanted to attend, but I have a haircut scheduled for today."

"At PalHairMo?"

"Yeah, sure. Why not? I'm long overdue for a cut, and I thought I'd check out the goods for you. See if you're making a mistake by not dating one of them. I read online that Sicilians are passionate people. I'm sure one, if not all three, would love to ride a Manhattan Mercedes and you might get a house in the process. Hint, hint: I'm with Stella on this one. It's an awesome idea."

Mike bent to inspect the desk. The agita in his gut was increasing with each turn of this conversation. Was it his imagination or was Mia becoming as goading as their grandmother? He paused, not quite sure if it was such a bad thing—her getting out of the house and all—and engaging with other women at a hair salon. Elizabeth had said that could be important for her. His reserved sister had always only felt comfortable at Rusty's place, so for her to venture to unfamiliar ground was unprecedented. No, he wouldn't dissuade this even if her intentions bordered Stella-esque.

"Have a good time at the salon," he managed, hoping the experience would prove liberating for her.

"It's just a trim."

"Yeah. I know. Maybe you should leave your iPad at home."

He couldn't see her roll her eyes, but was sure that she did.

"I think you should know something," she said, scrolling down her Twitter feed. "Blair tweeted that she's determined to break up you and Ann."

Snickering, Mike plopped into the club chair. His humor turned into a howl of full-blown belly laughter. "You're … kidding … right?"

"I'm not kidding."

"She seriously believes that Ann and I are an item?"

"Apparently so."

"Has she taken a good look at Ann?"

"Apparently not."

"You would think she's familiar with Stella's companion by now. Hell, she goes everywhere with Grandmother."

"One would think, but it's my understanding that Blair doesn't attend the town council meetings. She obviously hasn't had the *pleasure* of Grandmother's company since Ann came to live with her."

"What would lead her to believe that I would—um—even spend time with Ann?"

"I don't know. I once heard Rusty tell Blair how Ann adores you, and how she's constantly hot on your heels. I suppose the woman got jealous."

"Good Lord. See, this is what I'm talking about. Crazies. I'm gonna make another deal with you, Mia. Either you find a different outlet for your social life—get off the internet—or I'm moving out and leaving you there alone … with only the silicone-addicted cyber stalkers to talk to."

"You wouldn't dare!"

"I would." He stood then continued to wash the surface of the desk; he was sure he'd missed a spot—or two.

⁀**⁀

Gina leaned against the hair color counter observing Elizabeth's excessive compulsion to scrub every bacterial molecule from the pedicure whirlpool basin. During long minutes of silent scrutiny with a cappuccino cup clutched in her hand, she held back the smirk at the obvious change in her sister. It was more than happy Christmas spirit generated from yesterday's grand opening of PalHairMo. Something else had happened, and based on that twinkle in Elizabeth's eyes, it most likely involved a man.

"You've had that dreamy look on your face for a few days, Lizzy. What gives?" she finally said, watching her sister meticulously rinse the jets.

"Hmm. What do you mean?"

"You met a guy didn't you?"

Gina witnessed an easy smile then a subtle twist to Elizabeth's lips. She could see the emotion play upon her expression. "Yeah. You got laid. I don't know when or where, but you did it. Who was it? Vinnie the Turtle?" She gasped. "Or Toni? I knew it! You have that mystique, sis. You can make a gay man straight."

"Toni's not gay, Gina. He just likes to dress as a woman."

"Not gay? I was sure ... So, you did screw Toni? Wow!"

"No!" Elizabeth laughed. "I think he has a crush on Dharma."

"It was Mr. Carpo then!"

Elizabeth rose and stretched her back. She looked down at the sanitized chair and smiled, confident that no one would be getting toenail fungus at their salon.

"God knows Carpo tried. The womanizing man is as persistent as a wolf in heat. If he wasn't so protective and kind to us, I'd have to dislike him, too." Lizzy said turning to face her sister.

She removed the cup from Gina's hands and took a long draught.

"You. Screwed. Danny! I knew it! You fell for that stallion charm again." Gina cradled her forehead in her hand, shaking her head. "Oh, Lizzy, why did you do it with Danny? He screwed Frankie's Tina!"

"Would you stop being so melodramatic. You sound like Mamma. I didn't sleep with Danny. Do you think me that much of a pushover when it comes to him? Just because he sent flowers to the apartment and the salon doesn't mean I'll change my mind about him and every other ginzaloon who comes along."

"Thank Gawd it's not Danny. But, you know, Toni is Italian and you don't condemn him. He's not a ginzaloon or a Romeo."

"That's because he's only suave with Dharma, and she obviously likes it, dress and all. Besides, he's family." Elizabeth grinned. "Do you remember Altar Boy?"

Gina's mouth fell slack before she slapped her sister's shoulder, "No way!"

"Yes way! He's a physician, and we met at the conference the other day. We had dinner followed by a *chaste* nightcap, and I'm going to see him again on Wednesday for lunch."

"So you're taking off from the salon?"

"I checked the schedule. I don't have any clients."

Well paint me happy! The grandson of the devil's whore found Elizabeth! Yes! "Did he remember you?"

"He did! He said he looked for me these past three months. Gina, imagine that, he's the total package and he looked for *me!*"

"Of course he did. Did you kiss him?"

"Yes. Oh God, yes. Best. Kiss. Ever. It was just as Nonna used to say: 'The kiss is to love as lightning is to thunder.'"

"Lizzy, you met him on St. Nicholas Day!"

"Yeah, so?"

"The Mass! The circling the pillars at church!"

"That's preposterous and superstitious. One date doesn't mean that he's the one, just a great kisser and fabulous company."

"Did you tell him who you are?"

"Of course I did."

"I mean did you tell him that you're Lizzy Clemente from Little Italy, co-owner of an Italian hair salon?"

It didn't surprise Gina when her sister handed back the cup then turned away from her inquisitive stare. After opening a cabinet, she neatly arranged the cleaning supplies within, avoiding the question.

"Lizzy?"

Elizabeth suddenly turned with hands insolently fixed to her hips. "That girl from the neighborhood is not who I am. That's who you and Nicki are. I explained this to you more than once. For a decade, I've been Elizabeth Fairchild. I'm a physician and I live on Melrose Avenue, not Arthur Avenue. My life is orderly, not chaotic. I eat sushi and listen to jazz music. Guacamole is my condiment, not marinara and parmesan. You can't expect, in just six short days, for me to slip back into being the very person—the very stereotype—I ran away from. I am not that girl any longer."

She sucked in her lips, but Gina ignored the pissed off expression. "You're such a liar. Why are you fighting this, Lizzy?"

"I'm not fighting anything."

"He won't care if that's what you're so concerned about. Growing up in Belmont has made you who you are—your heart, your dreams, everything! You might be surprised—he may love that you were born Italian." The tip of her index finger pressed against her temple, twisting like a screwdriver. "You're out of your head! You're losing your compass!"

"I don't think I need to advertise I'm an Italian-American."

"Boy, that loaf of white bread you married really did a number on you."

"Yes he did. Do you know what it's like to be thought a trashy Italian whore just because you got pregnant, just because your father was a labor union rep for the Teamsters, just because you didn't grow up with a silver spoon in your mouth, but instead had a rosary hanging on your bedpost?" Elizabeth sighed.

"Gina, what's the point? I'm leaving on the 28th—back to my life in LA." *And an urgent job search.* She turned, opening a cabinet then dug into her handbag until she removed her wallet. "What does this say?" she asked, pulling out and holding up her driver's license.

"Elizabeth Fairchild."

"I rest my case. The State of California recognizes my name and that's what I go by. Would you like me to start calling you Gina Puppino again?"

Silence.

"Yeah, I didn't think so. That's not who you are any longer," Elizabeth retorted.

Nicki, oblivious, strolled directly into the smack down, wearing little more than a red Santa mini-dress. "I greeted your two o'clock and sat her in your chair, Gina. Girl's got a haystack of blonde hair that needs some serious shit done to it. Do we keep a lawnmower out back?"

"I'll be right out!" Gina uncharacteristically barked without even so much as a glance in Nicki's direction.

"Gina, calm down," Elizabeth said.

"Calm? I'm Italian—I can't keep calm!" Just as their mother had done for years, she jutted out her index finger at Elizabeth and shook it in her face. Her eyes bore into her sister authoritatively. "Mark my words, we're going to continue this later, *Dr. Elizabeth Fairchild*. If I've learned one thing from Frankie it's that, in the end, the truth always comes out, no matter if it's stuffing your sausage where it doesn't belong or pretending to belong where you really don't."

Now her hands were flying in this Italian argument. "Your home is where your heart is, and we are your heart—marinara, cannolis, church, and family—the whole shebang! Didn't yesterday's grand opening and the night at the bakery teach you anything? If you ask me, you're the one who's prejudiced!"

Gina placed her hand on her chest and took a deep breath, calming herself. She transformed her frown into that beaming innocent smile of hers; Elizabeth ran four fingers under her chin in a fast swipe, to which Gina responded by almost slamming the empty coffee cup down on the counter then storming from the back room.

She blessed herself and looked to heaven, mouthing *Aiutami, per favore* before her frustration dissipated at the familiar intro of Louis Armstrong's "Cool Yule" as she entered the festive stylist room. Dharma was busy with double-booked patrons, Nicki was sweeping, awaiting her next job as wash girl, and Toni was bringing coffee to two other clients, who sat conversing in the small reception area. Neither seemed perturbed or annoyed at the wait for service, and Gina's composure and happiness was restored when she noted how one of the women tapped her foot to the lively Christmas music. A young woman sat surfing her mobile phone as she awaited her consultation. Nicki was right: she had a ton of hair that sorely needed treatment.

"Hi. I'm Gina. Welcome to PalHairMo." She warmly held out her hand for a shake.

The client hesitantly took the offered hand and though her eyes didn't quite meet Gina's, a timid smile did emerge.

"Nice to meet you. I'm Amelia."

"Well, Amelia, what can I do for you today?"

"Um, I guess I'm overdue for a haircut."

Sensing the young woman's shyness instinctively, Gina attempted to put her at ease with the standard compliments that they taught her in beauty school. "You have such beautiful hair. I'm so jealous. What I wouldn't do for thick locks like yours."

"Thank you." The young woman glanced over her shoulder, taking in the shocking view of Nicki and the holiday inspired get up she had poured herself into for the day. "Is that … is that your sister?"

"Yeah, that's Nicki, the youngest. Lizzy, my middle sister is back in the spa room, preparing for her next mani-pedi client. Hey, would you like a glass of red wine?"

"But, but it's only two in the afternoon."

"It's always happy hour around here. I'll even join you." *'Cause I damn sure, can use one!*

"Really?"

"Sure. When in Rome! I've never read any cosmetology licensing regulation that said I couldn't share a glass of vino with my client." Gina left her sitting in the chair to fill two juice glasses.

"Well … um, okay, I guess." *Wine? In the middle of the afternoon? This was a first. Halo didn't serve wine. Rusty didn't even offer soda.*

Utilizing the minutes, amidst the blow-dryer being deftly wielded by the blue-haired stylist and a cool Doo-Wop song overhead, Mia surveyed PalHairMo, from its garish artwork to its checkered floor tiling. This place was fun—happy—and it made her smile. She loved all the kitschy details, the holiday accents, and especially the vintage glass ornaments on the Christmas tree. Even that freaky old woman doll holding a broomstick on the corner of the receptionist desk made her feel cheerful.

The music reminded her of good times spent at Grandmother's house before Stella got all crazed, obsessing like some mob henchman about offing Mrs. Dixon. It was all because of that Famizi weirdo who showed up with his dying father years ago. The old man claimed that his own father was once a bartender on Mulberry Street and had told a whole long story about Villa Fortuna being stolen from the Russo family. Mike was right: gossip stirs up a mess of trouble.

"Hey Amelia, do you want a cannoli to wash down the wine?" Gina called out.

"Sure." *Cannoli?*

So far, she loved this place—and this woman was so nice. Pretty, slender, and missing a wedding ring. She texted Mike: Marry the blonde Clemente sister. No chin hair.

Gina returned, balancing the good stuff, handing over the pastry first.

"Um, can I ask you something?" Mia asked shyly.

"Sure. What's up?"

"What's with the doll? She's kinda scary looking."

A giggle bubbled from Gina as she glanced over her shoulder at the desk. "Oh that's the good witch Befana. She stays out until the epiphany in January. It's an Italian Christmas tradition that my sisters and I grew up with. The legend says she was sweeping when the three kings showed up on her doorstep on the way to Bethlehem. Now she brings gifts to children. We used to joke that our mother was the Befana, but I don't think we meant it in a good way. She's in Florida now, and we thought it was funny to place Mamma Befana at the desk. Thank Gawd, unlike our mamma, she's silent!"

"I'm Italian and I never heard that legend."

"Not many people have, but we're proud Sicilians. So, Amelia, what are we going to do to your hair today?"

"I was thinking of just a trim, a few layers maybe."

"How about we go short? In case you missed the sign on the door, we are in the process of raising money and collecting hair for Locks of Love. They make wigs for kids with medical conditions that cause them to lose their hair. Are you up for it?"

"Gee, I don't know." Mia's fingers toyed with the end of a long tendril, as she stared at herself in the mirror, deliberating. It certainly would be an image changer, something new to kick start the year, and begin that fresh chapter Mike talked about. She resisted the reflex to post the question on Facebook and ask her friends what they thought.

"Yo! You gotta do it, sista!" Santa's helper shouted from across the room. "You'd totally rock the shit with short spiky hair."

"You think?" She gulped more wine uneasily.

"Let's ask Lizzy. She'll tell you like it is," Gina said.

Nicki disappeared into the back room, quickly re-emerging with the last sister on her heels. "She wants to know if ya' think she should donate her hair to those bald kids. I think she'd look better than Pink or Miley with some hip short look."

This Lizzy was the prettiest of all three. Dressed entirely different from the other two, she seemed classier right down to her french manicure. She walked toward the chair then sat in the empty one beside her, crossing her legs when she turned sideways. Her dark eyes and pleasant smile instantly soothed the anxiety that always came upon Mia being in the spotlight.

"So, you're thinking of going short? Or is it the wine talking?" the woman warmly asked without a trace of New York accent like the other two.

"I, um, I'm not sure." Mia could feel the heat of an embarrassed blush rising from the potent wine.

"You're a pretty girl, and you have such beautiful hair, but it's a shame you hide behind it. I think my sister Gina could give you a really stylish cut that'll give you a bit more confidence, but don't let them persuade you. What do *you* want?"

"I think I want a change."

"Change is always good. Trust me, I understand. Also consider that, if left untreated, trichoptilosis can destroy your entire hair shaft. Proper nutrition, leafy green vegetables, and frequent trims will help prevent them, so today's cut could start you on a pathway to healthier hair."

Gina chortled. Leave it to *Dr. Fairchild* to go all medical on the girl, "Tricho ... whatever. What Lizzy's trying to say is you've got ..." she whispered the diagnosis, "... split ends. I recommend mixing a cup of yogurt and a teaspoon of olive oil, applying it weekly as a conditioner. What you don't use on your head you can put on your face or eat."

"*Eat?* You mean ... no expensive product?" Mia asked.

"Nah, but you can buy the extra virgin oil here. We're organically Italian. We imported the best liquid gold from Sicily."

The receptionist came to stand behind the gathering and met Mia's gaze in the mirror. A red wrap-around dress hung ill fittingly but those chandelier clip-on earrings were the bomb, swinging back and forth as glam-length press on nails ran through her long hair. A deep voice took her by surprise but she tried not to laugh, when what was now obvious, *he* spoke.

"Do it, babe. Let the guys see that feisty side of you. With captivating eyes like yours, they'll be beatin' down the door. I'll be the first to take you out to paint the town red." He winked. "That's most girls' favorite color."

"But you're ..." *Oh this is so FB worthy! This place cannot—I repeat— cannot ever close!* "Okay, I'll do it." Bouncing with enthusiasm in her chair, she looked to Gina and declared, "I'm ready! Take it off. Take it all off!"

"Yeah, girl! Now you're talkin' my language, but I was born ready. Cue the strip music!" Nicki said picking up her discarded broom, readying to dance. Toni changed the song, increased the volume, and then joined her in their dance routine, his A-cup attempting, but failing, to jiggle like hers. The client in Dharma's chair rose to join them in the aisle, her black cape swinging to the music as she, too, gyrated.

Lizzy reached out and touched Mia's arm. "Don't worry, Amelia. You're in good hands with my sister. Not only is she a talented artist when it comes to hair but she would never lie to a soul. You're beautiful and you'll *feel* beautiful when she's through."

A perfect grin lit the woman's face, and Mia felt even more at ease. It took all her willpower not to pick up her mobile and text Mike: Brunette Clemente sister Lizzy is the one. She talks medical, too.

There was something special about PalHairMo, and Mia wondered if it was the free-flowing wine or the best cannoli she had ever eaten. She didn't think that was it. This salon was different from any other she had ever heard of. There wasn't even the obligatory expensive hair product sales pitch by the wash girl when she had your scull held captive in her hands. No, Villa Fortuna had some sort of magic, enhanced by sisterly love—and a cross-dressing receptionist.

After the dance performance and the massaging wash, Gina went to work on creating the new image. As she brushed, she carefully pulled Mia's hair into a smooth ponytail followed by a precision snip for donation. Strangely, she didn't feel uncomfortable about her security blanket disappearing, and she experienced even less anxiety about someone other than Rusty in his quiet salon attending to her style needs.

Over more wine, a few cookies, and several Christmas songs, they chatted like old friends about education and dating, which flowed into the lack of available men. Inevitably, the conversation turned to the whispered subject of Toni— *i* vs. *y*—and his penchant for polyester over silk, but not men over women. It was obvious that Gina had recently acquired that piece of gossip and was dying to share with someone. Even the one they referred to as Picasso stopped by the station to suggest adding baby highlights on her next visit.

The bell above the door jingled, and Gina turned to greet the patron, "*Ciao!* Nice to see you again so soon!"

Mia watched in the mirror how Nicki's expression transformed into a playful smirk as her fisted hand propped against a jutting hip. "Well,

well, well, if it ain't the eight-inch barrel pistol man. Are you here to handcuff me, officer?"

"Yeah, and then I'll pistol whip you. Where are the zeppoles so we can get this party started?"

Now *that* got Mia's attention, particularly the familiarity of the voice. She glanced over her shoulder to confirm who had prompted such suggestive repartee. Yes, it was none other than her playboy cousin, Joey.

A snort escaped her lips, and she shook her head. "Figures."

"Do you know him?" Gina asked.

"Yeah. He's my cousin."

Joey did a double take at the short-haired client seated in front of the owner as he walked down the aisle toward Nicki's come-hither look. He chuckled at seeing Mia in the salon, and was shocked by her sudden bravery to alter her appearance so drastically.

"Stella's going to kill you," he teased as he passed, without stopping to converse.

"I'd like to see her try. I'm donating to a charity and having a ton of fun in the process. She'll kill you first. You're older and supposed to be wiser than to cross her twice."

He glanced back over his shoulder. "Your hair is gonna look great."

"Thanks. I think everyone is going to be shocked."

Gina stopped cutting, looked to Joey then back down at Mia. "Did he just say Stella, as in De Luca, the she-devi—I mean the realtor?"

"Yeah. She's our grandmother. You won't hold that against us, will you?"

"Gawd no!" Gina's heart thundered, her mind working a mile a minute. *Oh, this is rich. This is too good a coincidence not to pursue.* She walked around to sit in the chair beside her client and leaned toward her, bridging the space between them. A whisper escaped her lips. "Tell me, are you related to a gorgeous, dark haired doctor?"

"That must be my brother Mike you're talking about. Do you know him?"

Gina's devious streak surged, the wheels of machination turning. "Kinda. What do you think of my sister Lizzy?"

A little more than tipsy and sensing where the conversation was leading, Mia snorted. "Is she a germaphobe?"

"Yeah. She's obsessed with diseases and germs."

"Then she's perfect. Perfect for him."

After a conspiratorial glance around them, Gina leaned closer. "Can you keep a secret?"

"Of course! I love secrets."

"Well, I have some juicy gossip for you then."

Mia leaned in. "Do tell, sista."

"Apparently, your brother and my sister have already hooked up without either of them knowing their *other* connection. He is the guy who wants to buy our building, and she is one of the Clemente owners ..."

~**~

~Fourteen~
Anima e Corpo
(Heart & Soul)

Even in the affluent section of Lenox Hill on Park Avenue, homeless people camped atop sidewalk subway grates and within any available vestibule or nook between buildings to protect themselves from the frigid temperatures. This always pained Elizabeth's heart and mind to witness. She wondered what impetus led to these unfortunate circumstances. Where were their families? Why do so many indigent take their chances on the street rather than in the city shelters during a freezing crisis labeled "Code Blue?"

The wind was strong today, whipping like a vortex up the avenue, and her own camel hair coat and worthless pantyhose did nothing to prevent the chill from attacking her exposed legs below. Without street vendors on Park Avenue, not even a warming cup of joe could be purchased for the young man bundled in threadbare layers, huddled in a doorway. His hair was matted and his eyeglasses patched with a Band Aid. She knew it was only a matter of time before someone escorted him from the entrance of the multi-million dollar apartment building. The entire scene seemed so incongruous to the efforts of the charity bell ringer on the corner of 58th Street.

Stopping before the man, she reached into her purse and withdrew ten of her twelve dollars, regretting that it couldn't be more. As she slipped the ten-dollar bill into the tin cup labeled "God Bless" in barely legible handwriting, she noticed the eyeballing disdain from the doorman within the glass and concrete sanctuary. She vowed that on her way back to the subway after her date with Mike, she'd bring lunch to this unfortunate soul.

This poor man on the cold concrete made her feel ashamed. For all her attempts at conveying worldliness and self-importance, his simple "thank you" and "merry Christmas," shot straight to her heart and filled her with deep humility. Blessed beyond measure to be home with her sisters, she wondered where this man would spend his holiday and what the New Year would hold for him. Did he have family out there somewhere? What did God's mercy and grace have in store for him? She prayed—yes, actually lifted up a prayer—that the mental health system or the city would come to his rescue—not only just for the night, but for whatever else his soul needed to re-write the course of his bleak future.

In a New York minute, the encounter had re-set the tone for her afternoon.

Two blocks north, Mike's building was a twelve-story structure that faced one of the many unique sculpture exhibits on the avenue's wide dividing malls. Elizabeth suddenly felt nervous for their second date, acknowledging that even her grey and pink winter suit ensemble wasn't enough of a confidence builder. She was about to rub elbows with patients and a physician exalted by wealth and society far beyond her B-listers at West Hollywood. This Lennox Hill neighborhood was filled with the crème de la crème of the society pages: world-famous movers, shakers, and corporate moguls from every upper strata realm.

Placing her gloved hand on her chest, she breathed deeply and entered the building through gold-toned doors. Quiet sophistication permeated the beaux-arts lobby where a lone uniformed guard sat behind a desk, watching security monitors. He glanced up with a smile.

"Hi! I'm here to visit Manhattan Aesthetic Associates."

Wordlessly, he handed her a visitor sticker, then pointed to the gilt framed elevator bank to the right. "Tenth floor," was all he finally conveyed.

Elizabeth entered the elevator, and when the burnished reflective doors silently shut, she immediately dug into her purse for lipstick followed by a hairbrush. She had just enough time to refresh, remove her scarf, and unbutton her coat before the bell alerted her arrival. One last primp and a quick smooth to her wool skirt were her last ditch attempts to relax.

In contrast to West Hollywood Podiatry Center, the elegant, warm décor in Mike's practice felt comforting. High ceilings and classic molding accented the rich brown upholstered seating area that flanked a welcoming fireplace. Obviously transformed from one of the building's original residential co-ops, it felt more like someone's living room than a medical office. Black and white photographs of New York City hung along one wall and, in separate alcove, a flat screen TV created an information viewing area with two comfortable chairs.

Her focus locked on Mike's onscreen image discussing non-surgical treatment for facial enhancement. God, he was gorgeous in that navy suit and pink tie. Professional, articulate, and according to *New York* magazine, one of 2015's best doctors with a bevy of impressive, credentialing acronyms following his name. Yes, she had Googled him, also discovering that he annually donated his reconstructive skills to an organization entitled Face to Face to help women marred by domestic violence. *Sigh* *Mike is a keeper...and I leave in a couple of weeks.* *Sigh.*

Elizabeth could feel the young receptionist's eyes assess her as she waited for the initial once over to pass.

"May I help you?"

Shirking her coat, she greeted, "Yes. Hi. I'm Dr. Elizabeth Fairchild here to see Dr. Garin. We have an appointment."

"Good morning, Dr. Fairchild. He's with a patient right now, but he's expecting you." The woman rose and walked around the desk, holding out her hand. "May I take your coat?"

Well this was already different from WHPC. Perhaps it was just because she was a colleague. She handed over the coat.

"That's a beautiful suit. Did you get that at Barneys?"

An uncomfortable smile formed and Elizabeth resisted the urge to scratch her nose. "Thank you! I purchased it in a little boutique in LA." *A discount sample store. I've never been to Barneys.*

"Follow me. I'll bring you back to Dr. Garin's office."

"Without him? I can wait here in reception."

"Those were his instructions. It's no problem at all. He must like you a lot to let you into his private sanctuary."

Elizabeth couldn't help fidgeting when a waiting patient turned her overly coiffed head at that last statement. Cold eyes scrutinized her, just as a jealous spouse might evaluate her husband's much younger mistress. Two other women of the same ilk glanced up from their magazines, ready to claw at her with their manicured fingers. Ignoring the women, she paused and pointed to a framed trade periodical cover hanging upon the wall. PSP, *Plastic Surgery Practice,* depicted a debonair man standing beside Mike's dreamy image. The article headline read, "Cutting Edge Family."

"Is this Dr. Garin's father?"

"Yes. Vincent Garin. He founded Manhattan Aesthetics in the seventies. Apart from Mike, I mean, Dr. Garin, he's a god around here as an innovative leader in facial and body reconstruction. He retired a few years ago."

They walked through the clinic down a wide, well-lit hallway lined with evocative black and white photographs. These were a series of tasteful abstract nudes delineating the contours of the body, nothing overt or salacious, but accentuated by discreet shadows. A subtle essence of orange citrus lingered in the hallway, infusing a refreshing uplift as she passed through.

The receptionist opened the door to a corner office with a view to Park Avenue. Bright and orderly, it was decorated in euro-styled furnishings of predominant steel grey tones. On the far wall, a floor-to-ceiling library case displayed books and journals, visibly arranged in size order. She assumed categorized, too. After having spent only one day in each other's company, she could tell Mike was fastidious; his office space confirmed it.

"Please make yourself comfortable." The receptionist swept her hand toward the leather club chair and the tray upon the coffee table. "There's sparkling water, some mini-pastries, and coffee for you."

"For me?"

The young woman smiled. "Of course, Dr. Garin was very specific. Oh! I almost forgot." She disappeared into a closet near the private bar. "He also had this made for you."

Again, disbelief came from her lips, "For me?"

"It's just a lab coat."

Elizabeth fingered the stiff white cotton then ran her finger over the blue stitching above the pocket. "Dr. Elizabeth Fairchild, Podiatric Medicine." This was more than an obligatory courtesy. In her opinion, this was bona-fide confirmation that Mike was a considerate man, who liked her not just as a woman, but respected her as a physician. There had not been any negative, glazed-over response when she told him she was a podiatrist. In fact, when discussing medicine at the conference, it was clear that he valued her knowledge and perspective. For over ten years of education and professional achievement, she had waited for that type of recognition from a colleague.

A small, humble "Thank you," left her lips and the receptionist smiled.

"It won't be long. Make yourself comfortable. My name is Gwen if you need anything." She took a few steps toward the door then turned back. "You know, forgive me for saying but, you're a lucky woman, Dr. Fairchild. Dr. Garin is one of New York City's most eligible and sought-after bachelors."

"He's … um … just a friend."

The woman chuckled as she departed the office. "If you say so. Well, whatever you are, he's certainly interested in you."

Embarrassed, Elizabeth grew antsy once the door closed. Riddled with nerves, the thought of sitting and eating the tempting pastry was out of the question. Investigation was paramount in calming these second-date jitters. The first item for inspection was the photograph above a medical journal clipping hanging upon the wall. The young Vincent Garin was handsome, and she could see where Mike got his good looks. Her curiosity was piqued to learn his story and accomplishments in medicine. She moved to a bronze statue of two hands nearing an embrace; her own hands trailed down the smooth digits in a reflective study of the anticipatory clasping curves. She recollected Mike's impromptu taking her hand in his upon entrance into the Rose Bar. Even with gloves, it felt so natural, so intimate—just like this statue.

Moving to the bookcase, her fingers brushed along the smooth steel shelf, her head tilting to read some of the titles. His taste was eclectic and each volume was alphabetized by title, everything from Classics to spy novels to surgical technique manuals and textbooks.

Startling her, the office door burst open and Mike stood at the threshold wearing a lab coat, checkered necktie, and navy trousers. The best thing he wore, however, was the smile that reached his azure pools. Her heart nearly seized. There was no doubt in her mind that he was overjoyed to see her.

"You're here!" he declared.

"Of course. Why wouldn't I be?"

He crossed the room, then bent, kissing her cheek. "I'm so happy you came."

"Me, too." Her stomach flipped.

"Your clinic is beautiful, Mike."

"Thank you. After my father retired, I did some remodeling so that the waiting and exam rooms would convey my philosophy about medicine. As I mentioned the other day, and I'm sure you see this in your practice as well, newcomers to reconstructive surgery are sometimes making life-altering decisions. I hope to make them at least feel comfortable, somewhat at home, as they venture into the unknown."

"That's exactly how I felt upon entering into the reception area."

"You were nervous?"

Already she could feel the blush rise as she moved to the club chair. "Yes. I was nervous," she said, sitting then crossing her legs. She could feel the burn of his gaze travel the length of her body from her grey pumps upward, and she smiled to herself.

"You look lovely, Elizabeth."

"Well, Park Avenue is a pretty ritzy address. Only my best for a visit with Dr. Michael Garin."

"I might say the same. You're a high class Hollywood physician slumming on 60th Street."

She snorted. "Hardly, but thank you for the compliment."

She could tell he was nervous, too, when he unbuttoned his lab coat, coming to sit opposite her. Almost immediately, he took a napkin in hand and wiped the edge of the coffee table. "I um... would like to think of this as something more than *just* a visit, maybe as our second date. I promise not to talk bunionplasty and fat pad augmentation all day."

"That, Mike, is actually one of the ways to my heart. It sounds as though you have a perfect afternoon scheduled."

"And what are the other ways to, you know, woo you?"

It was then that her heart slammed so loud that she was sure he heard it. "You've already guessed one of them. Pastry does it to me every time and the lab coat sealed the deal. Both were very thoughtful."

"It was nothing, really." He stood, taking the coat into his grasp and holding it open to her. "Shall we round?"

Again, she could feel the burn of his stare as he tried so hard to divert his attention from her chest when she stood, removing her suit jacket. Mike was failing miserably in his endeavor, and for some reason, she wasn't offended. Perhaps it was a plastic surgeon's natural reflex to examine every woman's bustline. She wasn't sure, but she did know that his attention to her pink, jewel-necked sweater was not unwelcome.

Sliding one arm and then the next into the coat sleeves, her back was only inches from his broad chest. Discomfited, her head turned slightly, gazing at him as his eyes locked with hers. She breathed in, inhaling the subtle trace of cologne. Time seemed to stand still when she straightened and felt his breath close to her ear, the heat expending from his hard body, her own fire igniting from his proximity. Her breath grew shallow when she imagined the sensation of his lips caressing the curve of her ear. She closed her eyes, thinking she felt a kiss. Maybe it was her desire sparking her imagination, maybe not. She was lost in anticipation.

Mike fixed her collar from behind, his fingers brushing below her hair against her warming flesh. "I'm so flattered that you came today."

She turned in his almost embrace, her body so close to his. A teasing smile played across her lips when she stood on her tiptoes before depositing a chaste, yet completely provocative, kiss.

Their lips separated and he whispered. "It's not too late to cancel my appointments and remain in my office eating pastry and playing doctor."

"Naughty boy."

"You're right." He kissed her with a tender peck. "We'll resume this on our third date."

"I'll hold you to it."

"Dr. Garin, Mrs. Hunter is in exam room number four." Gwen's clear voice came through the intercom.

He stepped away from Elizabeth to depress the speaker button on the immaculate desktop. "I'm coming now. Thank you, Gwen."

"Well, are you ready to meet the wolves?" he asked, turning to face Elizabeth.

"Oh they can't all be that bad. Even in Hollywood, there are a few who aren't obsessed with vanity."

He raised an eyebrow.

"Okay, maybe one in every hundred," she admitted.

"C'mon Dr. Fairchild. Let's introduce you to the House Wives of Lennox Hill and over lunch we'll compare their plastic addictions to the House Wives of Orange County."

~**~

Sitting in Amali restaurant, having consumed an incredible lunch, Elizabeth leaned back into the booth, her hand patting her stomach, experiencing the result of total gluttony. "God that was good," she declared.

"Yeah, it was. I love this place. With it so close, I dine here whenever I can break away. Lately, Gwen has been arranging for lunchtime delivery for the staff and me. It's justified since business has increased to insane proportions over the last year."

"Well that's great news. Anything you can attribute to the increased patient load? New procedures, advancements in surgery?"

"A few, but not the reason, I'm sure." *It's that damn MAA Facebook page!* "I think word of mouth. As much as I dislike surgery for the sake of feeding an addiction in going under the knife, I'm a bit of a cowboy and take on surgeries that others may steer clear from."

"Such as in a patient like Mrs. Hunter? I could feel your hesitance after viewing the outcome of her last surgery by her former physician."

Mike placed his drink back down on the table and leaned across to take her hand in his. "I abhor taking on botched reconstruction jobs, but for the sake of the patient and restoring confidence and giving her or him the ideal that they had hoped for, I do them. Many of my clients are old Blue Bloods listed in the Social Register whose photographs are regularly splashed all over the Society pages, women admired not just for their money and status, but also for their youthful appearance. A terrible facelift could send them into a reclusive life, making them a target for gossip mongers destroying their image and self-worth—as pretentious as that is."

"That's kind of you. I can see that, above all things, you value *total patient* restoration, not just of the physical type. It was evident by everyone you examined today. I was so impressed, so honored and flattered to be present, beside you."

"Same here listening to you allay Mrs. Abernathy's concerns about her possible diabetic ulcer scarring. You know a lot about diabetes," he said.

"Ah, well, type 2 diabetes runs in my family, and I've seen firsthand what can happen with chronic wounds such as hers: skin grafts, months of debridement, and hyperbaric treatment. Unfortunately, I don't have the opportunity to administer much of that kind of care at West Hollywood. I had hoped that my attending the conference might open that door."

He squeezed her hand. "It gave me great pleasure today to introduce you to my patients. Your employer is very lucky to have you."

Elizabeth tried not to fidget, just offered a wistful smile, unable to be honest enough with Mike about having quit her job three weeks ago. How would this heralded physician view her then? Would he admire her dedication to her sisters or see her as someone who couldn't play by the rules, a petulant junior associate who didn't get her own way so she quit? Maybe he would assume that her medical commitment to LA's equivalent of the Social Registry was mediocre at best. No, she would keep her job status in the vault. It was bad enough that her own self-confidence as to why Greenwald hired her in the first place was shaky.

She signaled the waitress who promptly came over.

"I'd like to make a to-go order of roast chicken and a side of kale caesar salad, new potatoes, and broccoli, and a pint of chicken soup. Oh, and coffee, too, please, all on a separate bill and boxed carefully."

"That's quite a doggy bag. I thought you were full," Mike asked, humored by the beefy order.

"It's not for me."

"Someone I need to be jealous over?"

"Nope." She grinned mischievously. "Would you like to find out?"

"Well, now you have my curiosity piqued. I have a couple of hours before my next patient, so I'm game."

"Good. *Your* contribution is at Pottery Barn on 59th and then we'll walk down to 58th Street."

"Home décor?"

"You'll see."

"You know, you are ... amazing. I don't know what to expect next from you: brilliant, sophisticated, professional, compassionate, and quite the mystery. Versed in Italian song, ex-brother-in-laws on Mulberry Street, sisters whom you avoid speaking of, a keen pastry addiction, and to go food that would feed an army."

"Mystery? No. There's not much to Elizabeth Fairchild. I'm just a girl from LA."

Twenty minutes later with one arm tucked into the crook of Mike's, they walked down Park Avenue bracing themselves against the wind hitting their faces. She tucked her chin into her knock-off Burberry scarf and snuggled closer to his heat, her free hand soaking up the warmth emanating from the bagged to-go boxes carefully clutched in her arm. Her legs were frozen, but all she could think of was the man in the doorway and the man on her arm.

"Are you going to tell me where we are headed with this down blanket? I hope your meal isn't cold by now," he said.

"No, it's still warm. I can feel the heat. We're almost there."

She breathed a sigh of relief at seeing that Mike's and her endeavor would find their intended recipient. The man she'd seen earlier was still there huddled in front of the luxury condominium building.

"Thank you, God," she said as they approached. "We're here."

Mike looked up at the building. "Here?"

"Not up there." She bent down toward the man. "Hello?" she softly inquired, attempting to gain his attention. She could sense rather than see behind her, Mike assumed a protective posture, readying if required, to shield her from harm.

"I'm not sure if you've eaten yet, but we brought you dinner. It's still hot. There's soup, even coffee."

He sat up. His eyes looked vacant, lips taut from the cold.

"You should get to a shelter, friend," Mike said.

"No. It's cool. Those places are dangerous."

Mike tentatively placed the Pottery Barn shopping bag beside him. "I hope this helps tonight, but if you can get to a shelter, it would be better." He took the food bag from Elizabeth's grasp and, careful not to spill its contents, placed it beside the shopping bag.

She could see a hint of something behind the stranger's muddied brown eyes and felt herself choke up as Mike reached into his wallet, pulling out a twenty, which he held out. "Merry Christmas." The expression on his face and the tone in his voice conveyed such compassion. Clearly, he was affected by the young man as well.

"Merry Christmas and blessed New Year," Elizabeth repeated.

A small smile crossed the young man's lips. "Thanks for coming back."

Elizabeth's heart soared. He remembered her from earlier, and she was so happy that she did what *she* felt best, ignoring all the admonishments against assisting someone commonly referred to as a vagrant. That wasn't what her father had taught.

She waved as Mike took her free hand in his, both hearing the rustle of the paper bag opening behind them when they turned toward the street corner.

169

"Let me hail you a cab from here," Mike offered.

"But I left my lab coat at your office."

"Good. I hope it entices you back to my practice." He wrapped both arms around her waist and held her close to him, the steam from their breath comingling in the air.

"As lovely as the coat is, it's *you* who is the enticement."

He bent his head, placing a warming kiss to her chilled, waiting lips.

"You are an incredible woman. What you did back there made me feel simultaneously on top of the world and humbled at the same time, just as we should feel at Christmas. Your gift was unconditional and I have no doubt that you restored some hope in him."

"You do that every day in your practice and with your pro-bono work."

"But this … this was different. You know how many times I walk by the homeless. It's become ingrained to just keep walking," he said.

"My father always taught me to give, even if the receiver spends it on booze or something other than it's intended. It's been a long time since I had the opportunity. I'm thankful that we did it together. Anyway … thank you for today. Every bit of it was perfect."

"Can I take you out again?"

She grinned. "Absolutely."

"When do you go back to LA?"

"The 28th."

"Well, I just might have to call West Hollywood Podiatry and tell your boss that someone wants you here." He raised his arm, hailing a taxicab and she scratched her nose.

"Unfortunately, that would be fruitless. He goes to the Caribbean for three weeks every December."

He wanted her to stay! Damn, meeting him was unexpected. She wasn't prepared for this, but in the silence of her heart she felt the rightness and allowed herself the thought. Enjoy it, while you have it. It's Christmas, after all.

~**~

~Fifteen~
Romantico
(Romantic)

The forecast threatened snow on the night of his next date with Elizabeth, but that wasn't the reason for Mike's worry. She had decided to take a taxicab up to the Bronx by herself stating it wasn't any trouble but it didn't sit right with him. She had vehemently protested against his offer to pick her up in his Lexus, even refusing his offer to send a towncar or an Uber driver. Now that she was late, he worried. Did she stand him up, or had something happened to her?

He stood outside the Enid A. Haupt Conservatory of The New York Botanical Garden; the blue glow of the domed crystal conservatory rendered the black winter sky a magical sight. The garden grounds twinkled with festive lights, and within towering dormant trees, white crystalline snowflakes swayed in the slight breeze. The piney scent of winter, along with the fresh scent of snow in the air, always thrilled him.

No doubt, Elizabeth's heart-stopping smile would be as resplendent tonight. He hoped to bring that out in her. That beatific expression, her laughter, and her sincerity in all things had bowled him over, and he was awash with anticipation for the night ahead. Over the phone he had heard in her voice that she, too, was excited for their date, but hoped she hadn't had second thoughts. Maybe inviting her to visit his office was a wrong move; maybe it intimidated her.

Another glance at his watch showed 7:45. She was fifteen minutes late, but he resisted calling or texting her. This dating thing was such a dance—getting it right, not pushing too hard. How should one appear interested without appearing too eager? Although he dealt with women all day long in his clinic, when it came to romance, they remained an absolute mystery to him. Would Elizabeth think him officious or endearing for checking in on her? She didn't seem to mind his presumption of having the lab coat specially made. That was a good sign, but maybe he had read her wrong.

He gazed out at the sea of adult visitors to the Bar Car Night event that the botanical gardens held every December; its primary attraction drawing thousands to see the Holiday Train Show. A vibrant red hat drew his attention as its wearer ascended the steps, and he sighed with relief at Elizabeth's safe arrival. She looked adorable with dark locks flowing from the bottom of the knitted hat, a matching scarf knotted at her neck.

She grinned and waved excitedly when she met his gaze. Nearly bouncing up and down, she pointed to the left, calling his attention to the ice-carving demonstration taking place in the garden. Illuminated in the moonlight, a nutcracker stood six-feet-tall as the sculptor chipped away to Ella Fitzgerald's "Let it Snow."

Mike chortled, also excited by that electric energy that came during the holidays, eager to experience it with a vivacious woman who had her own magnetism.

Elizabeth's gleeful laugh tickled his ears. He was sure that he looked like a love-struck fool. "You had me scared that you wouldn't show," he said.

"I'm so sorry I kept you waiting in the cold." She kissed his chilled cheek.

"It's okay. I was just a little worried about you, kicking myself for not being more insistent on picking you up and then I thought only for a second—well, maybe more like a minute—that you might have stood me up."

Furrowing her brow, she was taken aback by his honesty and concern, immediately regretting her decision to not let him see where her sisters lived. What was the big deal? Many people had an apartment in Little Italy. "You're so sweet; thank you. I wouldn't have missed tonight for anything, Mike. You *and* the gardens are a perfect combination."

"I feel the same way about you. The conservatory is magical at this time of the year. I hope you like it."

"You know, I grew up not ten minutes ... I mean, I've never been to the Botanical Gardens. I love that you chose this place for our date!" she said.

"Wait. You're from the Bronx?"

"I was born in the Bronx but left a long time ago."

Mike tilted his head, and she felt his eyes searching her face, looking for answers. She resisted the momentary panic. In her excitement, with a careless slip of the tongue, her thoughts had exited her mouth unchecked. Was it her subconscious? Apparently, Gina's guilt trip the day before had affected her more than she realized.

"Would you like to eat first or walk the grounds? There's so much to see and do," Mike asked.

"I think I need something to warm me up first. It's cold tonight."

He wrapped his arm around her, drawing her into his heated embrace. She looked up into his bright eyes, happiness evident there, though the quirk to his lips seemed naughtier than she had expected so soon from him. Apparently, he had thought of her over the last few days. Had his thoughts been as salacious as hers? Was there reason for him to make a trip back to the confessional? She suddenly felt nervous and her heart thundered with anticipation.

"Will this do in warming you up?" A gentle brush of his mouth against hers deposited a light, tender kiss. Even his constrained peck was raw heat. He pulled away too soon, leaving an electric tingle and a brief pang of disappointment in its place.

"Now I need ice water to cool me down," she said.

"Me, too. C'mon, let's get inside and get a couple of drinks."

His gloved hand slid into hers and she grinned, feeling butterflies—and not just in her tummy. Flustered by his kiss, she regrouped. "You've never been to this exhibition before?"

"Never. I always wanted to but my father was otherwise occupied and then my education became the focus. Too much schooling; too many expectations to meet. Every year I would promise to take Mia up here, but it never worked out. As I mentioned on Wednesday, my practice has become ... overwhelming."

"Sometimes I feel that way, as well. I'm trying so hard to succeed, yet I feel as though I'm on a hamster wheel, getting nowhere fast and missing everything else in the process. I'm weighed down by my own commitment to make my mark. Though, my family never had any great professional expectations of me."

"Be careful there, you'll end up pushing those you love further away.

I've recently come to realize that the sum of our lives is not measured by one's career. You know what they say: all work and no play…"

"Right. So even though it's a weeknight, let's play, Dr. Garin. I promise that I won't push *you* away."

He beamed. "That's my hope."

Hand in hand, they walked into the conservatory lobby then checked their outerwear and, after waiting on a long line, Mike presented their coveted tickets. He leaned down to Elizabeth's ear, whispering, "Thank you for coming here with me tonight so we can have some fun and get to know each other better."

This gorgeous, exciting, sensitive guy was thanking her—*her*! *She* was the lucky one, but a moment's shadow crept over her bright spirit when she remembered that she'd be leaving in two weeks.

"Thank you for bringing me." Their eyes remained locked for long seconds as they both recognized the fleeting time they might have with each other.

Within the magnificent glass house, hundreds of tiny blue lights soared high above four famous NYC bridge reproductions, spanning from one side of a pathway to the other. Standing below the Brooklyn Bridge, they looked up in amazement as a train zipped by on the trestles. All around them, handcrafted replicas of skyscrapers and mansions were placed amidst lush greenery. Each architectural model was constructed solely with gifts of nature: seeds, acorns, leaves, twigs, and the like. Plastic and metal trains of all types traveled over 1,200 feet of curved track. Elizabeth felt as though they were part of the scenic story of a snow globe, seemingly held captive by magic within a fantasy date. All around them, the sounds of the season transported them: train whistles, laughter, and music.

She studied Mike to gauge his response. Dressed meticulously, his slim-fit trousers and light blue sweater accentuated the dark waves that framed his forehead. His professional image and expensive apparel concealed the winsome man she believed was in his soul. He bent to admire the details of a miniature St. Patrick's Cathedral, and the changing expressions from wonderment to downright exuberance illuminated his pure nature. She couldn't help but to giggle that his elation was contagious; his happiness palpable—his backside looked oh, so perfect.

"I'm blown away," he said. "Look at the stained glass. It's amazing how they used berries in the spires! I'm in awe of the imagination."

Standing beside him, they examined the Channel Gardens of Rockefeller Center, astonished at the precise detail. "It says here that the angels' wings are made with okra pod leaves. Amazing, I'll never eat okra again without thinking of you and our date."

He pointed to a small train car zipping along a nearby track and laughed. "I love it! It looks like a bumblebee. It's the B line train!"

Together, in fascinated wonder, they moved amongst the whimsical displays and shared stories about visits to several of the landmarks, laughing about the memories.

Elizabeth removed the cell phone from her handbag and said, "I think we need to capture this moment with a selfie."

"Absolutely." Mike tucked his arm around her shoulders as they stood before a replica of the old Pennsylvania Station, its landmark inspiration, long demolished, forgotten by most New Yorkers.

He took the phone from her hands, their fingers brushing for only a milli-second but it was enough to set them aflame before he captured their smiling image.

After he handed the camera back to her, she gazed at the photograph. There was something unusual about it, sort of ethereal, as if a white halo surrounded them. With their heads leaning upon each other, their mirth jumped from the phone, their smiles lit with something she had never seen before—could it be … could it be the early stirrings of the *L* word?

"Can I see?" he asked.

Tentatively, she handed him the phone and it was clear from his expression that he, too, saw what she did. She was surprised when he tapped the screen and emailed it to himself. "This one's a keeper."

Mike meant what he said, in more than one way. Elizabeth is a keeper. No other woman had this affect on him before, and no other woman made him feel this way either. Kissing her wasn't some arduous experience that made him shudder with thoughts of the 80 million microbes of bacteria transferred when tongues played. Laughing with her wasn't in the hopes that she got his humor or fear that his jokes fell flat. No, they played off each other perfectly. Christmas spirit dwelled in her essence, twinkle lights played in her eyes. A fleeting thought crossed his mind: this was what love at first sight felt like.

She hooked her arm in his and his heart sang at the thought that maybe she felt the same way.

"How about that drink?" she suggested, sighting the bar as they walked the dimly lit pathway.

"Sure. So do you still have family in the Bronx?"

"Well, like most retirees, my mother lives in Florida but, um, my sisters live in the Bronx. They love it there and have no desire to move to LA to be closer to me."

"Hmm, and what of your father? Are your parents divorced?"

"No, my dad's deceased."

"Oh, I'm so sorry. He must have been pretty young. Was he ill?"

Elizabeth stopped walking and, not able to meet his gaze, bent to examine one of the miniature buildings. "Actually, his death was sudden, a shock to us all. Dad was run over on the street in front of my childhood home. Mamma, I mean … my mother was barely able to hold it together, and after a year of wearing black and mourning, she finally consented to move in with her sister who has a condo on the beach. They're very close. I think she's happy."

She continued to examine the details of the structure below her, but Mike saw through it. Speaking almost robotically, it conveyed her separation from the pain. He touched her back with a gentle caress and she rose. He took her hand in his. "I'm sorry for your loss, and I'm truly sorry to have reminded you of your pain, especially tonight. I also lost a parent. So I can relate. My mother was way too young, too."

Elizabeth tightened her fingers within their entwined embrace. "I'm so sorry, Mike. I usually never discuss my dad's death but coming back to New York has reminded me of some wonderful times with him, especially at this time of the year. I'm sure you cherish the same type of memories of your mom."

"I do." He cleared his throat. "She had leukemia. My sister was the miracle child the doctors swore she'd never have because of her illness, but she chose to stop treatment, and go through with the pregnancy. She died shortly after Mia was born. He smiled. "I miss her, but she left me with Mia and a true legacy of love."

"And that's why you're so close with her."

"Yeah. She's great. When my father re-married and eventually moved abroad, I became her parent, brother, and best friend all in one." Mike squeezed her hand. "Enough of this morose conversation. We're supposed to have fun. Some third date, huh?" They resumed their walk toward the bartender at the end of the pathway.

"Well, I'm having an incredible time witnessing that hidden little boy emerge from inside you."

She beamed, stopping him in his tracks, causing their hands to tug between them.

"What's the matter?" she asked, furrowing her brow, their hands remaining clasped across the gap between their bodies.

Thunderstruck, he said nothing. He took this moment to drink in that glorious expression he had hoped to bring about in her. With a gentle pull, he brought their clasped hands to his chest, over his heart, bringing her body against his. "This is the matter."

He let go of her grasp, tenderly moving his eager hands upward to cradle her cheeks, their lips only inches apart.

Without hesitation, his mouth descended upon hers, releasing the smoldering heat that needed expression. Oblivious to onlookers and phobias, he deepened their kiss, his tongue caressing hers. Elizabeth's mouth was made for his kisses. The way her soft lips responded set his heart and body aflame. Perfection. She was perfection.

Good God! He nearly moaned aloud. This intoxicating woman was bringing out his base instinct, but at the first sign of arousal, he gently ended their passion. Their dilated eyes remained fixed on each other as they panted. He could feel her heartbeat against him and reveled in the pressure of the rise and fall of her bosom against his chest as she caught her breath.

"I think I'm falling for you, Elizabeth."

"That's good because I think I'm falling for you, too. Is that too soon?"

He brushed a stray tendril from her temple. "I don't think so."

Her smile would have sparked another kiss, but he remained mesmerized.

"Lizzy is that you?" she heard from the other side of the George Washington Bridge suspended above them, breaking her from the spell of Mike's declaration.

No, no, no! Elizabeth tried not to flinch or react to the voice she knew well, attempting to remain encased in Mike's embrace, gazing intently at his endearing expression.

The voice drew closer. "Lizzy?"

Panicked, wanting to bolt, she reacted quickly. Threading her fingers through the back of Mike's hair, she brought his mouth to hers for another mind-blowing kiss.

A tap on her shoulder broke them apart as quickly as it began.

"It *is* you!" her ex-boyfriend said from only inches away, having already invaded their personal space.

Mike frowned at the stranger's intrusion, feeling Elizabeth's body go rigid in his arms, seeing her face struggle to maintain equanimity.

"As usual, your arrogance is astounding, Danny," she said in a tone that surprised Mike.

This Danny guy gave them both the once over, a crooked smile forming upon his lips when he held out his hand for a shake.

"I'm Dan Tucci, Lizzy's old flame."

Mike raised an eyebrow. *Lizzy?* "Michael Garin, Elizabeth's *new* flame." He tried hard not to let his annoyance show, but he immediately disliked the interloper. All slick and suave in his knock off Versace sweater and that obnoxious over-sized Italian horn. Jerks like him gave their ethnicity a bad rap.

Danny spoke as he toyed with the necklace, seeing where Mike's eyes had settled. "You're moving up in the world, Lizzy. Going all Park Avenue since you became an LA physician? Is that it? I should have known you thought you were too good for the likes of—"

"C'mon, Mike, let's go get that drink you promised. It's suddenly stuffy and getting very crowded in here. Excuse us, Danny."

"Yes. Let's get that drink. Nice to meet you, Dan. Have fun at the exhibition."

"Mike," Danny replied tonelessly clearly hating that he was dismissed when they pivoted in unison. "Did you get my flowers, Lizzy?"

Turning back, Elizabeth's voice softened but was adamant. It was clear to Mike that she didn't want to provoke this guy nor be misunderstood.

"I did. That was thoughtful of you. Thank you but, I'm sorry, my answer is still no."

"I won't give up. I'll wear you down until you go to dinner with me. We have a lot of catching up to do."

Now aware that this man saw himself as a rival for Elizabeth's affections, and she apparently was unwelcoming of that attention, Mike stood to his full height, puffing his chest.

He took a step closer to Danny, his blue eyes boring into the challenging browns of his opponent. He hated competition but in this case, it was "game on." "Elizabeth is taken, Dan. I'm sorry, pal."

"Don't be so sure about that. I was once her stallion." The interloper competitively scanned Mike up and down.

Stallion? More like jackass.

Elizabeth came to stand beside Mike, taking his hand into hers. "I only look to the future, Danny. I never, ever revisit the past." She gazed up at the man who had claimed her heart minutes earlier, and he leaned down unable to resist the urge to kiss her.

"Sure you do, or else you wouldn't have come home. I'll see you around the pastry shop or at family night at Our Lady of Mt. Carmel (OLMC)—just like old times." With an overconfident chuckle, he walked away from the kissing lovers.

The kiss ended and Mike continued to hold her. He frowned. "Are you okay?"

"Sure. He's just a ghost from the past, nothing to worry about."

"That guy couldn't be your ex-husband, right?"

"No. Just someone I used to date. I ran into him the other day, and he's been a bit persistent."

She glanced down the pathway, staring at Danny's retreating back. Her voice was low and thoughtful. "I wonder how he knew that I was here."

~**~

~Sixteen~
Catturate
(Captured)

After their long days at the salon, the sisters routinely made a quick stop at the Arthur Avenue Retail Market to purchase fresh meat or fish, which usually ended with Gina in front of the stove. But like most other independently owned salons on the planet, PalHairMo was closed on Sundays and Mondays, giving the sisters a much-needed opportunity to breathe—without the others. Sisterly love was great, but it had limits. To Elizabeth, at times it felt suffocating, though at other times there was an incredible warmth of security that she appreciated, the polar opposite of her independent LA existence. This was a fact she would never admit to anyone.

On this particular Monday evening, Carpo had called a last minute dinner meeting at an inconvenient hour to discuss the salon's business model and marketing plan for the coming year. This meant that her very first visit to Barneys (suggested by Mike's receptionist) was cut short. She was sure that her sisters were just lounging around today, and would have no problem coming into Manhattan for the dinner. Perhaps they could visit Rockefeller Center and see the famous Christmas tree after dinner and head back to the Bronx together.

Unlike the last time she visited a luxury hotel, she was not dressed as appropriately as she would have liked for The Bull & Bear Prime Steakhouse, which was located at the Waldorf Astoria Towers. Of course, then she had worn her power suit, and when Mike spilled coffee down the front of her coat, it had called forth her New York bravado. However, today she was at the iconic Waldorf—the Park Avenue palace of dreams where Marilyn Monroe once lived, a salad was named, and kings and queens stayed on state visits. Yet, here she was, casually dressed in trendy blue jeans and a ribbed, red turtleneck sweater about to dine at a power restaurant in Manhattan: a place known to see and be seen. It was just the type of eatery she always aspired to visit and, of all people it was Carpo about to treat them! She hoped her sisters had the foresight to dress up.

Elizabeth wished tonight's dinner could be with Mike, but was resolved to make the most of this meeting because, frankly, she couldn't lie to herself any longer. She knew that LA and all its allure could be replaced in a New York minute following Mike's admission in the conservatory. *"I think I'm falling for you,"* he had said, and that admission was tempting, very tempting. She, too, had admitted the same to him. But she wanted a professional reason to stay in New York.

Passing through the center of the lobby, she admired the understated holiday decorations displayed against gleaming black marble. A live pianist on the lobby floor added to the ambiance entertaining tourists, Wall Street moguls, and chic urbanites drinking at the bar. Her vision took in the elegant splendor, the famous antique clock as its focal point.

Following signs through the block-long hotel, fine boutique spaces dotted the wide hallway that crossed inside from Park Avenue to Lexington. Hollywood instinct prompted the impulse to peruse the boutique display windows showcasing exclusive, expensive arrays of perfect Christmas gifts. Elizabeth gazed at the jewelry in the Cellini window, however the diamonds within failed to captivate. Her attention grew distracted by the niggling sensation of eyes boring into her back. Any reflection in the pane of glass was lost by the bright light and platinum bling within. She touched her temple and covertly glanced around her fingers peripherally, but that revealed nothing, except for the visitors and business professionals searching out banquets and conferences. Now that she thought about it, she had a troubling sense that someone was following her at Barneys on Madison and 60th—nothing concrete, just the same discomfort she typically felt whenever she was in a spotlight. Jumping into the first cab that pulled up at the clothing store, the feeling had disappeared until now.

Maybe it was Danny. He'd been a total pain in the butt since "accidentally" running into her and Mike at the botanical gardens. Gina's unguarded disclosure of her whereabouts had sparked more flowers, tweets, and FB tags on photographs of them together at the prom. That idiotic maneuver was beyond the pale, a total insult, given that the only memory she had from the prom was his bare ass kissing the backseat glass as he screwed "she-who-shall-not-*ever*-be-named!"

Elizabeth snapped her head around, hoping to catch whoever was staring in the act, but to no avail. The scent of cheap cologne reached her. *Ugh—is that Brut?* That odor always brought to mind one of her father's labor union friends.

A crowd brushed by her; she tagged alongside the group and made her way to the restaurant.

Salvatore Carpo waited at the entrance of the steakhouse and, upon seeing her, grinned like the Cheshire cat. She'd seen that type of grin from him before: *I am a Romano man, ergo, I want to make love to you.* She couldn't deny that he was one incredible looking and sounding man, delicious in fact. His designer suit conveyed class. Without a tie, his open collared shirt revealed a smattering of dark chest hair.

"*Ciao, Bella.* You are right on time." He kissed both her cheeks. "Thank you for meeting me on short notice."

"Sure. We haven't seen you since the grand opening. Is everything okay?"

"*Sì.* It is nothing, just a quick trip to Rome. It is romantic this time of the year."

She surmised what that trip was about, having spoken to his receptionist three days ago. Her disclosure that Ms. Donato accompanied him on the trip left little doubt that the beautiful woman was more than his legal assistant.

"Come. I have a table awaiting us."

She removed her coat, draping it over her arm and noticed a slight twitch to Carpo's lips.

"Have my sisters arrived yet?"

"No … no. Not yet," he stammered. "*Andiamo, bella.* They will meet us."

The restaurant was packed, although the overall din was subdued and offered an intimacy for the diners despite the crowd mingling at the bar. As in the lobby, Elizabeth took in all the details from the leather tufted, half-round booths to the magnificent chandelier and floral arrangement at the center of the historic restaurant. Masculine décor rich in mahogany set the mood for power brokers and mergers, but simultaneously conveyed warmth and romance in the dim lighting.

Escorted to their table, she noted Carpo's guiding hand lightly touching upon the small of her back. It seemed an insignificant thing that men often did as a courtesy, allowing the woman to lead the way. Stopping at a window table overlooking Lexington Avenue, she asked, "Will the girls know where our table is?"

"*Si*. Of course," he said, settling himself across from her once the maître d' had pulled out her chair. "You look like a movie star tonight, Elisabetta."

"Thank you, but I feel a little uncomfortable. I'm definitely underdressed for the venue. I hope the girls think to dress up. You know Nicki."

"She loves sensation."

Elizabeth snorted. "Yes, she does. She always has, ever since we were children."

"You are all so different, but so very much alike, too. Your prozia would be so proud."

He signaled the sommelier over. "We'll have a bottle of the 500."

It became apparent that Carpo knew the wine list by heart when the expert concurred, "Ah yes, your usual Mr. Carpo, an exceptional choice. I think the lady will enjoy the Barbaresco." His eyes raked over her when he said, "Cherries, licorice, and gorgeous fleshiness."

"Of course," Carpo said in a voice implying he knew how to pair wines with women well and dismissed the man with a wave of his hand.

She folded the menu and placed it beside her bread dish. Something was fishy here and it wasn't coming from the kitchen. "They're not coming are they?"

Carpo smirked, his lips drawing into an adorable smile.

"You stinker," she said.

"You cannot expect me not to try, Elisabetta. You are a beautiful woman with the body of Botticelli's Venus and the soul of an angel, but you are in need of a passionate man to set you free. I am that man. The fullness of your lips intoxicate me. Like in the book *Thirty Shades of Red*, I feel like Icarus flying too close to the moon."

"You mean the sun ..."

"*Si*, yes, that is what I meant, the sun."

His cheesy pick up lines would have made her giggle, but her lips remained fixed when he reached across the table and took her hand in his.

"So you have read the *Thirty Shades of Red*?" he asked then raised an eyebrow, smiling with obvious delight.

How could she not laugh aloud at this attempted seduction? Like both Vinnie and Danny, he was trying too hard—doing so was his nature. Had she not believed that all along? Italian men were born to love and seduce women, married or not, and Carpo was 100% full blooded, straight from Italy's capital. She easily recollected, upon their initial meeting in August, being rather inclined, on a carnal level, to worship at the altar of this modern Roman god.

"I think every single woman has read that book," she said. "It's not my cup of tea, though."

"And why not? I enjoy the feel of silk ties."

"Salvatore … if you read it, which I don't think you really did … the woman-lover in you would have been offended by the abusive tone the male character took when addressing his lover. It wasn't romantic at all, and no one should ever disrespect someone like that, especially a *paramour*."

"I believe in romance. It is in my blood."

"I know."

She was relieved when the waiter came with bottle in hand, promptly pouring two glasses. A slight nod of Carpo's head signaled removal of the other two plates, his hand still holding Elizabeth's at the center of the table.

Trapped (but amused), she knew she would be putting her foot down in a few minutes. The fact remained that she liked Carpo and appreciated everything he had done for her and her sisters. He'd been with them through thick and thin these three months, going far beyond normal attorney-client parameters. Reproaching him would be offensive. She'd tactfully have to let him down. It wouldn't be the first time, but this little seduction of his had crossed the line.

He let go of her hand then raised his glass. "To PalHairMo and your beauty. *Buon Natale*."

"*Cent' anni*," she finished as they clinked.

As she drank, a chill ran up her spine again, just as it had at Barneys and then again on her way to the restaurant. She thought she saw a flash go off near the glass, but figured it was someone taking souvenir photos of the famed hotel. Her eyes scanned the passersby outside, her vision locking on a nearby outdoor vendor filling a paper bag with chestnuts.

"Salvatore. You're sweet to lure me to dinner, but ... but apart from the very real fact that you are married with four children, I'm in a relationship with someone special. I'm flattered, but I'm sorry I must disappoint you. I hope I didn't lead you on or anything."

Stunned, he sat back in his chair, bringing the drink to his lips. Finally, she could see humor play in his eyes, followed by a hearty laugh. "I tried." He shrugged. "Who is my competition?"

"An incredible gentleman; he's a Park Avenue surgeon from Sutton Place. I noticed him when we visited St. John's in August and then I ran into him at that medical conference I went to the day before the grand opening."

"*Destino.*"

"Maybe, but it's new and of course, short-term since I leave soon. However, it just wouldn't be right being with another man, allowing intimacies I have yet to share with him."

"Lawyers make better lovers than doctors."

She chuckled. "Perhaps, but a surgeon's hands are very skillful."

"An Italian man will worship at your feet and make love to you wherever and whenever you desire, many times a day."

"But *any* man in love would do the same. Italian men don't own exclusivity on passion and romance. In fact, he's not Italian." *Even though he kisses like one.* "Aaand, he's not married. So the wherever and whenever isn't restricted to luxury hotel rooms, after hours," she countered with a smile.

"You have me there."

"Yes, I do. I'm starving; let's order."

"So, you are not mad with me for trying?"

"No. I'm not. I'm flattered, but please don't do it again."

"What's-a this man's name?" he asked before taking a drink.

"Dr. Michael Garin." Elizabeth grinned, feeling on top of the world.

Carpo's wine suddenly sprayed from his mouth.

"What name?" he choked out.

"Garin, Michael Garin."

He coughed, wiping his mouth with a napkin.

"Are you okay, Salvatore? Do you suffer from dysphagia or esophageal spasms?"

"No, no. It is nothing. Just hit by the air."

"That's what you get for not wearing a scarf."

She removed her phone from her purse and scanned through the photo gallery then proudly held out the image taken of them at the Botanical Gardens. She beamed. "This is Mike."

Carpo sighed. Confirmation: The grandson of De Luca, the guy who has been trying to purchase Villa Fortuna for the last year. *O mio Dio!*

~**~

The best day of Ralph Famizi's life was when he received a phone call from a *compare* on Arthur Avenue informing him that the third Clemente sister had returned to the Bronx. Before even contacting his employer, he drove north, balls to the wall, from Mulberry Street straight to Messina Bakery. He'd heard a lot about Little Italy's legendary beauty, Lizzy and had to see for himself. *Mamma mia!* Like the goddess Sophia Loren, she was va-va-voom!

That night of her arrival, he stood at the back of the crowded shop, listening to Louis Prima and all about her life as told by old acquaintances. The guise of waiting customer was the perfect ruse for his surveillance. Only he hadn't expected to be spellbound by her. Even the flour on her cheek inflamed him. She was *dolcini,* and the thought of her naked and rolled in confectionary sugar became a hot, sweet topic of his imagination these last two weeks.

This De Luca gig was just like watching soft porn from his 78' El Dorado. Every guy wanted a piece of those tits and ass of hers, including him. It was lonely watching her with other guys from his ride or in an empty alley on snowy, dark nights. Stella's grandson, at least, was getting some liberties the others were all failing at.

Just the night before at the Botanical Gardens, Garin's secluded make out session, under those twinkle twinkle tree lights on the garden path, gave him a flaming hard on. He just wanted to shout out "Take it off, baby!" but that would have blown his cover. It was bad enough that he was hiding beside a damn holly bush that scratched his face whenever he craned his neck for a better view. He almost hated asking for payment for this job, but Stella had promised him thirty grand if they got Villa

Fortuna and that kind of dough was nothing to sneeze at.

The other two sisters were also interesting subjects for surveillance. The eldest was just his mother's type and, had he any sense at all, he'd make a play for her since she was obviously single. Living with his mamma's daily nagging to find a good wife had become a real ball breaker. Gina was pretty and angelic, but what hot-blooded man in his right mind wanted an angel? Now the youngest … holy Toledo! He was sure she knocked boots with Garin's cousin in the back seat of his Jeep Cherokee under the Whitestone Bridge two nights ago. Judging by the way the Jeep was rocking, he was sure she screwed like a rabbit and if it wasn't for the steam on the windows he would have taken pictures, even if Falco was a cop.

Now, squatting beside the cart roasting chestnuts outside the Waldorf, Famizi snickered. His compares with the Family would love to get their hands on photographs of Joey Falco, detective with the Intelligence Division, getting it on with Tommy "The Mouth" Clemente's great-granddaughter. But again, thirty thousand smackas was enough to keep him silent on that account. Stella was paying for his loyalty to her. Real mobsters adhered to the omerta, the code of honor and silence, and so would he.

He snapped a few more photographs when Carpo took hold of Lizzy's hand across the table, then the clink of wine glasses, and her laughter when he made a joke. His boss was gonna' love these shots. They were just what she was lookin' for.

~**~

Ann had been homeless before she came to live with Stella and, in her opinion, living with the old woman was a double-edged sword. Those days of sleeping in the cold, curled up behind dumpsters or huddled into corners had been replaced by a warm, soft bed and companionship. In the homeless world, making friends had been difficult, territory firmly marked and only the most sought after and most attractive were allowed to snuggle up with the studs who ruled the street life. Hers was a lonely existence until Stella found her shaking outside Finnegans restaurant, taking her in, providing a safe home and eventually, spoiling her beyond all reason.

That was where the other side of the sword came into play. Ann adored the attention but to put it frankly, Stella's strict diets had no appeal to her. Those dumpsters behind Etonville's fine restaurants had kept her belly full with incredible food, but since moving in with the old woman, hunger and pangs of gas plagued her from the healthy organic shit served daily. She didn't care about fine china, no matter how much Stella did. She needed real food, actual cooked meat, ribs, burgers, and french fries—none of that frou-frou French crap. Not to mention, she missed the freedom that came with living on the streets, adhering to no one's rules. Sometimes life with Stella wasn't worth the warm bed and expensive accessories.

Gah! In the name of pleasant breath and white teeth, trips to the dentist were her bane of existence! At times, she rued the day that she came to live at Hillside Manor, wanting rather to reside with Michael. She'd follow him anywhere, employing any trick she knew to woo him. She'd do anything for him. Not to mention that his cooking was to die for. He was kind and warm with a smile that came from his heart, but she knew he would never dress her as lavishly as Stella. To be honest, she loved the clothes. What girl wouldn't?

It must have been midnight when Ann awoke, padding quietly into Stella's suite, walking toward the side of the bed. Good, she had her eye mask firmly in place, the snores and wheezing reverberating in the room. It would be hours before the old bag awoke to use the bathroom.

Promptly turning, Ann walked back out then bolted down the staircase. She turned a corner followed by a silent slip through the basement door left ajar after Angelo hung his driving coat on the inside hook. She barreled down that staircase, too, running straight to the unlocked dormer window above the old wooden storage shelves. The means of her escape fortuitously was not wired for alarm.

Within minutes she was free again, free to roam the streets as she once had and, come first light, she'd return to her warm bed and organic breakfast. Having snuck out undetected for months now, Stella would be none the wiser.

~**~

~Seventeen~
Visitatori
(Visitors)

For two weeks, every appointment slot on the schedule for both Gina and Dharma was filled. In fact, the salon was so busy that they had to institute a wait list. And, just yesterday, Toni had booked a bridal party before the wedding set to take place at St. John's R.C. Church on New Year's Eve. On opening day, one of Mrs. Drago's clients had been the bride giving PalHairMo an incognito test run. The girl had come away that day proclaiming that no other salon in the area could proficiently execute updos, while providing such a damn good time in the process.

Gina stood looking out the shop door window before the ten o'clock opening. As usual, music played overhead and she could hear Elizabeth loudly singing "A Marshmallow World" from the washroom. Arthur Avenue had been piping out that song for the last two weeks, but the singing was an unusual occurrence and definitely a good sign. She wondered about that old wives' tale: one sings from the heart when one is full of love. Could Elizabeth be in love already? As far as she knew, her sister hadn't sung a note since leaving the church choir when she began dating Danny in the ninth grade. That should have been a prophetic tip off.

Danny … now that was turning out to be a total mess. How was she to know that he'd follow Elizabeth to the conservatory when it came up in conversation? Big sister fight. Huge. However, Doc Hollywood got over it by the time she was through baking Christmas fig biscuits to serve in the salon.

Unfortunately, Danny had become relentless in his pursuit.

With a double espresso clutched in her hand, Gina observed her sexy, red-haired competitor inside Halo's display window as he decorated a

Christmas tree. His salon had been practically dead for the better part of a week; she felt bad about that. She didn't expect that she would, but feeling that little inner triumph of PalHairMo's success played on her Catholic guilt. Rusty was a good guy and here she was inadvertently putting him out of business. She'd have to talk to Father O'Malley about those feelings. On the bright side, Halo was becoming a little more festive each day. Obviously, she had pressed his competitive button, and he realized the need to make some changes. Rumor had it that he got rid of that ugly bowl of worthless mints and replaced them with cupcakes! But ugh!—Cupcakes were old news. How did Elizabeth put it? Passé. Cannolis and strufoli had become the hot new thing in Etonville.

Well, at least Rusty was upping his game, if for no other reason than to provide better customer service to his Yelpers. She liked Rusty, and wanted to get to know him, maybe go for another magic finger massage and do the unthinkable: ask him out for a date. Prozia would frown on that, but Prozia, although dead, was on her shit list right now. Dealing with the De Luca woman was giving her agita. Gina blessed herself, feeling guilty for thinking of her great-aunt in that manner. After all, she did give them Villa Fortuna, the luckiest building on the planet!

Rusty exited Halo to admire his handiwork, and his hands rubbed his opposite biceps in the chilled weather. "It looks festive, Rusty. You did good even if you're a little late. Christmas is in four days!" She gulped her coffee then giggled. "I think I'll pay him a visit today, bring him some Christmas cheer."

"Yo, Gina. There ain't no toilet paper in the john," Nicki called out from the bathroom.

Turning, Gina sighed, but not three steps from the door she stopped, hearing a rapid knock on the glass. With an anticipatory smile, she glanced over a shoulder, expecting it to be her big red devil from across the street coming to call again.

For the love of Gawd! It was the other red devil, Stella De Luca and her sidekick, both wrapped in fur and standing with their respective noses high in the air.

"Nicki, use paper towels. You and Lizzy need to get your butts up here immediately. We have a visitor and she looks pissed awf. Of all days for Dharma and Toni to be late. He's our Wonder Woman!"

False smile in place, she unlocked the door then opened it wide.

"*Buongiorno!* Mrs. De Luca, Merry Christmas."

The woman's sickening sweet perfume preceded her into the salon, causing Gina's hand to fly to her nose, attempting to cover her nostrils.

"Good morning, Miss Clemente," she replied filling the doorframe with her big attitude and small stature. Ann brushed by, immediately settling on one of the yellow leather reception chairs. She looked tired, but nervous; she attacked her manicure, furiously biting her nails. Gina could relate; the woman was almost driving her to do the same.

Elizabeth stood straight, putting her business face in place as she exited the sink room, and Nicki emerged from the bathroom wielding her cordless Black and Decker electric drill, poised and at the ready for destruction. She pulled the trigger releasing a threatening sound as the bit spun in place. Elizabeth shot her a deadly look, chastising her younger sister in a tone that brooked no opposition. "Stop it, Nicki! This is serious."

"That's why I've got the big gun here. No one's gonna ef with us or I'll put a hole in their chest."

"You must be the other two Clemente sisters," Stella decreed, giving them the once over from top to bottom. The oldest and middle were not as she had expected, and it surprised her that Famizi's information was so incorrect. However, the youngest, the one holding the power tool looked like stereotypical trash standing there with her curled lip and spilling bosom. *She must be the puttana Joseph is lusting over.*

The blonde introduced them all, and for a moment, she felt more akin with her fastidious grandson, wishing for an antibacterial wipe or anything to sanitize herself with. Who knew where those hands had been.

"Can I offer you an espresso, Mrs. De Luca?" the prettiest offered.

"No, thank you. My visit this morning is strictly business, not a social call." She walked around the reception area, eyes settling upon the old woman doll upon the desk. At first glance, she imagined it to be an effigy of that Dixon witch, but then remembered a similar doll she had as a child. It had been years since she'd seen a Christmas Befana, recalling with fondness the one her mother purchased for her on Mulberry Street before they moved from Little Italy. A colorful ceramic platter of *s*-shaped cookies beside the doll distracted her. "Are these buccellati?"

"Yeah, Lizzy made them," Nicki replied, churning the drill bit, followed by Elizabeth yanking the tool away from her.

Stella licked her bottom lip, resisting the temptation. The traditional cookies smelled heavenly, and the music and festive decorations, including that Christmas tree were all conspiring to undermine her personal pride, as well as her formidable resolve.

"Take one, please. We have more in the back. They're an old family recipe and out of this world," Elizabeth stated.

"No thank you. In spite of my better judgment, given how your family acquired Villa Fortuna, I'm here to make you a generous offer."

"We refuse," Gina said. "But thanks anyway."

"Don't you want to hear what it is?"

"No."

She strode past Gina in a huff, circling the holiday-decorated table stacked with bottled extra-virgin olive oil. "Are you running a beauty parlor or a restaurant here? Because I can assure you that this building is not zoned for a restaurant—it's retail and residential only. If you persist in serving food and beverage, the village requires health department inspections on a monthly basis and, of course, rezoning after you pay a hefty fine."

Gina walked to the desk then reached under the counter. "Then you'll be pleased to know that we have all the necessary paperwork, and have applied for our liquor license, too. Would you like to try our homemade vino? It's the best in the city." She gave Stella an innocent grin.

This blonde was good, very good. In the real estate business, she'd make a killing: sweet as sugar and diabolically manipulative at the same time. In fact, she hated to admit it but the Trinacria seemed well suited for the three of them. All visually different and most likely embodying divergent skills, but connected by that big Medusa head, hell bent on their destructive mission.

"I have a silent investor," Stella said. "And he is prepared to offer you an overly generous $2 million for Villa Fortuna. He is determined to acquire it before the New Year and since you are more than likely barely scraping by in your first two weeks, now would be the time to cut your losses and sell."

Elizabeth cleared her throat, walking toward their diminutive nemesis. "I'm sorry, Stella, but my sisters and I are here for the duration. We are not 'barely scraping by,' as you say. Regina, how much did we bring in our first fourteen days before the donation to Locks of Love?"

"Oh! Off the top of my head we grossed $39,462.85."

Stella's chin nearly went slack, and Elizabeth continued, as would any professional who had experienced dealing with a *testa di merda* such as her former boss.

"So you can see that Etonville has responded in a positive way to our opening on Main Street. I think it just may be you and your investor who want us gone and if that is the case, I wonder at you being on the village Board of Trustees. Certainly, your loyalty should be questioned. Tell us, what would your buyer like to do with Villa Fortuna should we agree to sell to him?"

Stella's arm swept out theatrically, "This building would return to its original splendor, just as my father envisioned before your great-grandfather stole it from the Russo family. Etonville needs luxury condominiums right here on Main Street. An aesthetically appealing lobby with a 24-hour doorman will be in this *space*."

Her gaze lit upon Ann slowly settling into a relaxed recline. "Antoinette! Sit up straight, legs together! We do not expose ourselves in such fashion!

"As I was saying, my investor already has consulted one of the top architects in Manhattan. That is how confident he is that you will accept his offer. He's prepared to do whatever it takes to acquire Villa Fortuna."

"No dice, Red. We ain't sellin' to some money bags who wants to shit on our parade. We got plans, too, and they don't involve some architect."

Aghast, Stella's hand flew to her chest. "That's Mrs. De Luca."

"Whateva, lady."

"*Stella*, what my sister Nichole is attempting to say is that, although we appreciate your investor's offer for purchase, Regina's dreams are not for sale. She has a God-given gift and, therefore, PalHairMo will be a success. As sisters, we have confidence in her and are committed to helping her make her mark." Elizabeth smiled at a teary-eyed Gina. "That's what family does, and we'll use every tool in our combined arsenal to entice people into her world until she builds a solid following in Etonville. Whether it's buccellati, wine, or soccer players—we'll use the whole shebang. Once clients arrive, Regina's talent will do the talking and *our* 'aesthetically appealing' *space* will make them feel right at home—Sicilian style—just as our great-aunt intended."

"Bah! Your great-aunt knew the history of Villa Fortuna. Yet when I presented her with notarized testimony, she laughed in my face, denying that her crooked, chiseling father 'Tommy the Mouth' was connected to the Black Hand, the Sicilian Mafia!"

She pinched her fingers, rocking them before her face. "For eighty years your family has enjoyed the house of good fortune, which was meant to be a part of my Neapolitan heritage."

"Then why sell it to an outside investor?" Elizabeth asked.

Gina approached the furious woman, causing Ann to stand up moving to defend her mentor. Placing her hand on Stella's mink-clad arm, Gina calmly steered the question away from who the investor was. Now was not the time to divulge the identity of her sister's new love interest. She needed more time for that revelation.

"Mrs. De Luca, we've never heard about this Mafia history or anyone named Tommy the Mouth, but I'd like to talk to my sisters about this undeniably awesome opportunity you've presented today."

Elizabeth gasped. "We're not allowed to sell it, Gina!"

"Say it ain't so, sista!"

"Go on. I'm listening, Miss Clemente."

"It's just that Christmas is such a special holiday for the three of us, and we'd like to have more time to talk about our options. For girls like us, from the neighborhood you know, $2 million is a ton of money. We could finally take that trip to Cancún we've been dreaming about, but maybe we can compromise by giving you our answer in the New Year?" She smiled those pearly whites of hers, holding out the plate of buccellati.

And there it was, that Machiavellian inflection in her voice that tipped off Elizabeth to Gina's bull. She had heard that tone used with Father O'Malley in the church, and the result on him had been magic. When he came to sprinkle the building with holy water, the man was all that was gracious and accommodating. Any disappointment he may have felt about not inheriting Villa Fortuna for the church's youth center had vanished. The Irish shortbread cookies and free haircuts for a year sent him off a happy priest. What was Gina planning now? Why the ruse and the stalling? Obviously, she had a scheme because there was no way in hell that the three of them would even think about selling Villa Fortuna.

Diverting the tension, the bell over the entrance door jingled and in sauntered Toni, dressed in an all-white ensemble: a 1960s mod swing coat and plastic go-go boots. His blond wig was teased at the crown behind a red headband and, like Stella, his scent preceded him. The blended stench of sex and Mr. Graciosa's Chianti was unsuccessfully masked by a liberal application of Uomo cologne.

"Hey, dolls," he said in that deep Bronxite voice of his as he batted super-long false eyelashes.

Gina observed Stella look him up and down when Nicki said, "Rad outfit, Tone. Is today Doo-Wop day?"

"It's sixties mod beat day," he replied giving Stella a reciprocal once over. "For our older clients who might need a reminder of when life was groovy before they went all uptight, country club suburban." He hiccupped and made his way to the reception desk where he removed his coat, revealing a white and red striped mini dress.

He was in rare form today and Elizabeth audibly sighed, "*mamma mia,*" which escaped her lips at the same time as Nicki said, "Cool! I'm all over that." Her sister rotated her skintight jean-clad hips, doing some sort of freaky dance when Toni clicked on his new playlist.

Stella adjusted her collar uncomfortably. "What kind of establishment are you runn—?"

Her question died on her lips when the bell jingled again and Dharma strolled in wearing a shit-eating grin and a blue-haired Twiggy geometric bob cut. Modeling her own 60s mod ensemble and newly acquired "eau du Toni," she looked clear-eyed, ready to conquer the fully scheduled day.

Gina giggled. *Yeah, Lizzy was right; Picasso is knocking go-go boots with Toni!*

"Hi kids!" Dharma said with a little lisp, dancing to the beat toward her stylist station. "Are we ready to rock out today?"

Stella did a double take when the trashy sister and the blue-haired pixie with a nose ring began to dance around the olive oil table as though performing some primitive fertility dance. "Ann! We're leaving!" Both bee-lined for the door.

"Nice to see you again, Mrs. De Luca," Gina called out, holding back her laughter. "Have a Merry Christmas! See you in the New Year!"

"Bah!"

"Hum bug," Elizabeth finished under her breath as they stormed out onto the street. Snow had just begun, and so had this crazy Saturday.

_**_

During the week, if possible, Toni tried to keep the lunch hour free. Whenever this scheme was successful, the team at PalHairMo locked the door and ate together in the reception area, laughing and gossiping. On more than one occasion, Elizabeth had laid out a fantastic antipasto spread of all the sisters' favorites: anchovies, deli meats, roasted peppers, and cheeses, without a dollop of guacamole in sight. Apparently she, too, enjoyed visiting the Arthur Avenue Retail Market (which was unfortunately located next door to the Puppino sausage shop). Gina was convinced that with Elizabeth's condiment choices in transition, it was only a matter of time before each and every marvelous thing about Belmont would re-engage her sister's heart as well as her digestive tract. She wasn't sure if the driving force was the unavoidable immersion of all things Italian or, perhaps, this Mike guy and all his perfection. At any rate, she'd never seen Lizzy so happy since she was accepted to medical school in Connecticut.

After today's disturbing early-morning visit, Gina decided to spend her lunch hour spreading Christmas cheer instead of gossiping and speculating about the devil's whore. Crossing Main Street, snowflakes began falling as she balanced a cellophane-wrapped tray of sprinkled cookies. She had made sure to include the intricate tri-color ones that the three sisters made the night before with Josie.

Approaching Halo, she could see through the decorated display window that the salon was a hive of activity. Little people ran amuck, and she wondered what on earth was going on in the normally, sedate establishment. She peered through the glass and giggled. "Good Lawd!" It looked as though the country club version of Chuck E. Cheese's had exploded in the middle of Rusty's salon. Misbehaving kindergartners ran wild from station to station, as others spun in the unmanned stylist chairs. She could hear the howling laughter like a heathen cacophony coming from within.

Gina took a deep breath and entered the mayhem, stopping on the threshold in shock as the evil receptionist, Emma, sat there surfing the internet, completely unfazed by the chaos around her. Rusty's newly erected Christmas tree was tilted over to one side, shattered bulbs surrounding it, and poor Santa had been turned on his head and stuffed into a wastebasket. Even the Hanukah Menorah on the magazine-laden reception table hadn't escaped violation. A child sat banging the candles as drumsticks on a cupcake, smashing it to smithereens causing cake to careen into the air.

At the washbasins on the far wall, three five-year-olds were having a water fight with spray hoses, the minimalist paintings hanging behind the sinks getting drenched in the process. Three other hellions sat cross-legged on the floor, stacking expensive product into pyramids. Several shampoo and conditioner bottles had come open in the endeavor. Forty-dollar-a-bottle thick, blue liquid oozed menacingly across the tile flooring, inching toward the blow-dryer chairs. A fourth child made handprints upon the floor using the azure liquid, and Gina could see that they led a path to the stockroom. She shuddered at the thought of what was going on back there.

Competing with the blaring club music overhead, she addressed the receptionist. "Good Lawd, what on earth is happening in your salon?"

"Sign in on the iPad please," was the toneless reply, her eyes remaining fixed on the computer screen.

"You need to get off the internet and take some action here. Where's Rusty?"

Emma robotically lifted her arm, pointing along the front aisle.

Gina placed the tray of cookies down beside the lone half-eaten cupcake remaining on a fancy dish. She commanded, "Guard these with your life," before striding to the group of children building an Egyptian empire on the floor. Taking hold of the "architect's" flailing arm, she spoke in the most stern, adult voice she could muster. "Up. These are not toys. You're making a mess."

"This is my birthday party and I can do what I want! Get off me!" the spoiled birthday girl said, tugging her chubby limb from the gripping hand.

Gina frantically looked around the salon for any adult supervision attached to the children, but sadly, the only adults present were employees attempting to keep the holy terrors still as they cut hair. Scissors flew with lightning speed over small heads, their little bodies propped on old phone books stacked on the hairdresser chairs. No Sicilian proverb could fully describe this level of hell Halo had descended into.

Scanning down the front aisle, she saw Rusty standing at his station:

inert, hair coming free from his ponytail, face frozen in shock as carnage ensued within his salon. Poor guy looked like a deer caught in headlights. Pink icing and blue shampoo stained the front of his formerly immaculate white shirt.

She ran to him, narrowly avoiding a collision with a little girl whizzing down the aisle on the pedicurist's rolling stool. The wild thing jeered, "Get outta my way, lady!" with such fury that Gina near expected her head to spin around.

"Rusty, what the heck is happening?"

In slow motion, his head turned to look at her, his mouth gaping open. She noted a split second of relief pass in his eyes until he finally spoke through clenched teeth, his face matching the shade of his hair. "I knew I should have fired that receptionist. I know we needed the business, but c'mon … she booked a birthday hair party and never told me that it was for 20 *five-year olds*. Not 25-year-olds! We don't do children at Halo! We are not kid friendly—only animal friendly."

"Obviously, but today they are one in the same."

The preschooler in the chair beside them stood on the expensive leather. Chocolate icing covered his mouth. In his small hand, he clutched the crumbling remnant of a cupcake. His other hand was smearing globs of chocolate all over the back of the chair, right before reaching out for her pink faux fur coat, little fingers opening and closing as he whined, "Bunny! Gimme!"

"Holy Mother of Gawd!" She blessed herself, stepping back from the boy as though he was Rosemary's Baby and his fingers were the moving prongs of Satan's pitchfork. "Are these kids sugared up?"

"I guess. They cleaned out our gourmet cupcakes and all the specialty chocolate in about five minutes and found my stash of mints in the bottom drawer of the reception desk. All hell broke loose about ten minutes after that."

"Boy, they must be desperate if they turned to your mints."

"Ha. Ha."

Suddenly finding humor in it all, she snorted, pointing to the brown stains on his shirt. "You know, there's an old Italian saying, 'Who takes care of children will get dirty with shit.'"

He didn't laugh, just narrowed his eyes menacingly at her flippant observation.

"What can I do to help, Rusty?" she asked with sincere sympathy in her question.

"Gina, I have no frickin' idea. They won't listen to me or anyone on my team. Blair came over from her shop to help, but I think they tied her up in the massage room and might be playing with the hot wax. One of the assistants went back to check on her but she, too, never came back!"

"Calm down, Rusty. It'll be all right, trust me."

"Calm down? I'm scared shitless!"

She walked to the window and gazed across the street at PalHairMo, intentionally quiet at lunch hour, blissfully playing Dean Martin to the passersby on the street. Making a snap decision, she reached into her back pocket and removed her phone. "Toni, I need you and the girls to come over to Halo. Rusty needs our help. Tell Nicki to bring her power drill and that duct tape she loves so much. You better bring over a jug of wine, too 'cause these people need it. *Pronto!*" Clicking off the phone, she turned and ran to the reception desk, calling back to Rusty, "Don't worry, handsome. PalHairMo is coming to the rescue!"

Gina's commands, reminiscent of their mother, were forceful when Italian phrases mixed with English poured from her lips as her hands flew around her with violent expressions all their own. The receptionist leaned back in fear, then vacated her seat, experiencing for the first time what true New York-Sicilian pissed off looked like.

Gina was a remarkable sight when she commanded, "Be of some use and go check on your boss's sister in the spa room, you lazy good for nuthin'!"

Minutes later, Halo's front door swung open, and in its frame stood Elizabeth with hands on her hips, flanked by the mod squad. Nicki pulled the trigger of the power tool, the sound of which harnessed a modicum of attention from the cross-legged pyramid builders. "Yo! Step back from that shampoo, or I'll drill you all a third eye! Get up, now! *Capisce!*" She drilled again, snapping four miscreants to standing attention as only a proficient military drill sergeant could command.

Elizabeth took in the scene before her and immediately moved to the computer, accessing YouTube. As if by magic, the soundtrack from the movie *Frozen* replaced the pulsating overhead club music, and within the first few notes of a song, several hellions stopped dead in their tracks, the wild flashes in their eyes instantly calming. Looking to the ceiling they screamed, "Frozen! Yay!" and began bouncing and dancing in place, singing along to the lyrics. Within seconds, the inert computer screens at every stylist station came to life, broadcasting Sponge Bob, literally rendering each fidgeting child immobile, transfixed as though group brainwashing had ensued.

Toni and Dharma separated, one to the left, the other to the right. As only a schooled prodigy of an immigrant Sicilian baker and Albanian mamma would do, Toni simultaneously pinched the ears of two wild boys, dragging them to the reception waiting room. He duct taped them together, back to back, cursing them out in Italian with a booming voice that none of the women had heard from him before. Children cowered and silenced; Elizabeth cringed more than once when she heard the verboten *cornuto* escaped unguarded. She surmised that Toni's drunken high this morning was now giving him a rocking headache, which these misbehaving culprits served to aggravate.

With the music and Sponge Bob acting as a high-tech super nanny, peace gradually descended upon Halo, the adults gaining ground over the wild mob. Elizabeth came to stand beside Rusty as he poured wine into a Dixie cup, his hand shaking in the process.

"I'm so sorry this happened to you. I think you should fire your receptionist."

His eyes bore into Emma on the other side of the salon. "You're right, and I will. What a mess."

She glanced over at the blue shampoo now being mopped up by a couple of his employees.

"What a terrible first impression I must have made on you," he said.

"Not at all. I think most people would have been overcome by this swarm. Sugar combined with the lack of parental supervision is a recipe for disaster. By the way, I'm Elizabeth—Gina and Nicki's sister."

They shook hands. "Great to finally meet you. Thank you for saving my salon and keeping me from having a nervous breakdown. How did you know what to do to tame unruly children?"

"Ah, well, in my 'other life', back in LA, I'm a physician, and my path crosses with children on occasion. During residency, I did an externship in pediatric orthopedics. They're quite obsessive when it comes to Disney and Pixar movies."

"So you're an orthopod?"

"Actually, I'm a podiatrist."

Yes, even Rusty gave that glazed-over expression. "Oh. Right. Cool."

She glanced at her watch and grinned. "Well, lunch hour is over, and we have to open back up. I have pedicures to give! Are you good here? Got everything under control?"

"I think we'll be able to handle it now."

"Rusty! Look what those little monsters did to me!" Blair yelled as she exited the spa treatment room."

"Oh dear," Elizabeth murmured.

Toni laughed, Nicki snorted, and Gina covered her mouth to hide her giggles.

Blair was missing an eyebrow.

Elizabeth touched his arm. "I hope her brow area was at least sanitized first. Double dipping that wax stick could have transferred infectious organisms. Maybe I should take a look at that burn to her forehead."

"Thanks, but I think she'll be all right. You've all been kind enough to come to our aid."

"It looks minor but make sure she sees a physician, *pronto*."

"I have no doubt that she'll visit her plastic surgeon as soon as these kids leave."

"Well, since it's Saturday, if she can't get an appointment, just let me know. I have a friend who might be able to see her quickly in an emergency, especially since the snow is starting to accumulate."

"I appreciate that but, no doubt, my sister will make it a point to see him as quickly as possible." He moved closer to her, lowering his voice. "Blair looks for any excuse to see her physician. She's probably secretly reveling in her misfortunate ... er ... um ... deformity." He shook her hand then waved to the PalHairMo team, his eyes locked with Gina's. An easy smile lifted the corner of his lips, and he winked. "Thanks everyone! I owe you, big time."

~**~

Buccellati

Biscuits filled with figs, nuts, chocolate, orange, and lemon peel
4 cups flour
¼ cup lard
1 egg
½ cup sugar
Grated lemon and orange peel
½ cup milk
1 packet yeast (powder)

For the filling:
1 ¼ cup dried figs
½ cup chopped almonds and nuts
½ cup honey

Preheat oven 400° Mix altogether the flour with the lard, the egg, sugar, the grated peel, milk and yeast and kneed thoroughly. Let it rest covered with a tea towel. In the meantime, chop finely the figs and add the chopped almonds, nuts, and honey. Mix well (you need a little elbow here.)

Thinly roll out the dough and cut out rectangular forms on which you place the filling in the center and carefully fold the pastry over the filling and making sure that it is sealed good and also the ends should be sealed. You can make different forms: a round or 's' form or as you wish. Place them on a baking tray lined with parchment paper and bake in a warm oven for about 30 to 40 minutes or until they are gold brown. You can if you like cover them with icing prepared with egg white, icing sugar and lemon juice whisked together until stiff.

They should be covered when they are still warm and sprinkle some colored sugar pearls and then let them cool. Serve when cold. Buon appetito

~Rizzo-Paganno Sicilian Family Recipe

-Eighteen-
Paraggi
(Neighborhood)

In Elizabeth's limited dating experience, even when physical attraction existed between two people of like minds and character, there was always an intense nervousness preceding the much-anticipated fourth date. The first date represented a test run—that awkward, putting-your-best-foot-forward, laughing-at-his-jokes-even-if-they-stink kind of date. Accepting a second date usually was confirmation a man had made a good impression and just might receive a good-night kiss, provided he had nice breath. Date number three was the "Okay, you don't kiss like a reptile or a cannibal, so let's see if the first two dates were just pretense." Then there was date number four. Back in LA, the granting of a fourth date would speak volumes—had she ever gotten that far. In her mind, date four meant "Hey, you passed the respect and personality tests, and I like you enough to proceed to dates five and six." No one had reached that mark since ... well, since ... her residency two years ago.

Mike had surprised her. From the get-go, the sensations of comfort and compatibility had led to passionate kisses (in public displays of affection, no less!) and her unprecedented desire to sleep with him. Heck, they had eaten from each other's forks on the first date! Their second date represented mutual professional respect, and an undeniable electric current that ran between them throughout the entire day. Date number three took them both by surprise with not only PDAs but also unexpected declarations and a nice bit of territorial posturing on Mike's part. God that felt good. A man, and not just any man, publicly staked his claim upon her affections to a challenger. Confronting Danny with steely, yet gentlemanly behavior behind a dazzling smile showed Mike to be protective and kind.

Mother Nature almost caused the cancellation of tonight's date due to the forecast for a snowstorm. Already the accumulation meant dangerous driving conditions, but Mike had texted that he'd pick her up, come hell or high water, at her sisters' apartment, which only added to the anxiety she felt already. Date three had ended with him dropping her off at Dharma's place near Fordham University—a much safer address for concealment of all things Lizzy Clemente. But tonight, he was coming to Belmont.

Staring out from Nicki's bedroom window, her eyes surveyed Arthur Avenue and she couldn't help the roiling in her tummy. She was nervous reflecting on Gina's assured declaration: where they lived wouldn't matter to him.

She could hear her sisters chattering to Mrs. Genovese in the hallway. Much like the delicious aromas from the woman's kitchen and the bakery below, garbled voices penetrated the plaster walls, destroying any expectations of privacy. The girls were going to help decorate their neighbor's Christmas tree tonight and, strangely, Elizabeth felt a twinge of disappointment that she'd miss the opportunity to assist, saddened that the sweet woman's own children and grandchildren lived so far away. The holidays must be very lonely for her, and her neighbors had become, just as Gina explained, a replacement family.

Apart from the muffled conversation and the hissing of the radiator as the heat came on, the apartment was quiet. Tapping her fingers against the windowsill, she contemplated the festive beauty of Little Italy beyond the sheltering glass. How had she not truly noticed the Avenue before? How could she possibly have considered the cascading garland tacky? Twinkling red, green, and white lights magically enhanced the now falling crystal snowflakes. The illuminated dangling star reminded her of long ago Christmas Eves when she and her sisters gazed out the window in hopeful anticipation of Santa's arrival. Nicki never believed, but Gina had, even after mamma let it slip that St. Nicholas, a real saint, existed centuries ago, but Babbo Natale, otherwise known as Santa Claus was just a fat old man in an ugly red suit.

The apartment door slammed and someone turned on one of those radio stations playing Christmas music on continuous loop for the last three weeks, but Elizabeth's vision remained locked upon the street, watching cars inch down the avenue through the accumulating snow.

Principessa Boutique's neon sign flickered on cue when a city bus stopped and several passengers slowly disembarked. She took a deep breath attempting to calm her nerves, praying silently that Nicki would be on her best behavior and be wearing something appropriate, also hoping that Gina would control her Gawds and Lawds. Tonight was huge— *huge*. Mike was coming *here*. Maybe she could meet him downstairs at the door to the building.

The bus pulled away just as his sleek, silver-gray Lexus parked in front of Messina bakery. She watched from above as he got out of the car looking all sexy even with snow falling down upon him. Her heartbeat stuttered in unison with the erratic hiss of the radiator. Quickly, she grabbed her coat and purse and ran through the apartment toward the door.

"Love you both, don't wait up!" she said hurriedly, passing Nicki eating ziti with her fingers, lowering a three-day old macaroni tube into her mouth.

"Is he here?" she asked. "Cause you know, I've been dyin' to drool over that tight ass of his again."

"Not tonight. Gotta go."

The buzzer sounded and the three sisters simultaneously bolted to the speaker box on the wall. Amidst giggles and "get outta my way," fingers fought with slaps for dominance on who would get to depress the "talk" button and speak first. Elizabeth butt checked Gina, which left Nicki's sauce-tinged fingers closest to seize victory when her sister hit the wall.

Assuming a mock Asian accent Nicki greeted Mike through the speaker. "Fong's Chinese Kitchen. What you order?"

"Um … Hi. I'm Mike. I'm here for Elizabeth."

"Do you want lucky fortune cookie or just get lucky? Chinese proverb say: she one hot cookie and you get lucky."

He laughed when Nicki added, "Five minute!"

Elizabeth pushed her aside, depressing the button. "I'll be right down and meet you in the hallway, Mike." She buzzed him in.

"Lizzy, aren't you going to invite him up?" Gina asked.

"What, and expose him to Nicki's belly ring and Prozia's plastic covered chair in the corner? Not on your life."

"You're embarrassed by us. Aren't you?"

"No, Gina. I'm not. It's just … look, he's waiting. We'll discuss this tomorrow. Okay?"

"Sure, but remember what I said. No matter how fast you run from yourself, you can't outrun being Italian. It's like mamma's wooden spoon. It's gonna reach out and smack you in the ass eventually."

"What? What kind of metaphor is that?"

"You know what I mean. One day soon, he's going to be in Etonville and overhear someone refer to you as Lizzy Clemente, physician to the stars *and* co-owner of PalHairMo, born and raised in Little Italy with a cannoli in her mouth and a hot Sicilian temper. Then I'd like to see how you're going to backpeddle. If you like Mike as much as I think you do then you should tell him."

"I don't see what the big deal is, Lizzy," Nicki said, "I'm from the neighborhood, and I'm a damn fine catch for any dude, Italian or not."

Elizabeth ignored them both and opened the apartment door. She looked out into the hallway where Mr. Graciosa stood wearing a white sleeveless undershirt, menacingly holding a baseball bat. The rundown corridor felt about a hundred degrees. "Hi, Mr. G. Is everything okay? You don't look so well. Have you been hit by the air?" she asked in Italian, unaware that her voice reverberated down the three flights of stairs.

After the buzzer released the lock, Mike turned the doorknob to enter the building, and immediately wiped the perceived bacteria from his fingers with his handkerchief. Elizabeth's singsong voice traveled down the stairwell straight to his heart and, when she addressed someone in Italian, it sounded to him like an aria. Using the square of white linen, he grasped the unstable looking banister and craned his neck, catching a visual flash of the tan coat he had accidentally stained with coffee the week prior. He could hear a note of concern in her voice speaking to a neighbor, an older man he believed, something about a turtle and an offer to help him into his apartment so he could lie down.

Glancing around, he noted the state of disrepair of the tenement hallway. Given the growing real estate values in Belmont, he thought it was a shame the owner hadn't invested a little money in the building. In spite of his grandmother's opinion of *this* Little Italy, its demographics were changing fast, and he had lately considered it a suitable location for a potential investment. Like Mulberry Street, Arthur Avenue revered its immigrant history, and an endearing vintage past of Doo Wop musical fame that collided daily with urban modernism. This locale still embraced its Catholic roots and many considered it the true Little Italy, but he was sure gentrification was in its near future, just like its downtown counterpart community.

As he waited in the sweltering heat of the hallway, he heard the opening and closing of apartment doors above, and distractedly read names on the metal mailboxes, also ancient and in serious need of refurbishment. A mix of Albanian and Italian names most likely read like every other listing of occupants in this section of the Bronx: Graciosa, Zeppo, Primo, Mangiacapre, Tolaj, Genovese, and Clemente.

He scratched his head, thinking it a small world, but Clemente was one of those common names, like Davis or Smith. However, the Clemente sisters were from this neighborhood.

Outside, in the gathering snow, an old woman dressed in all black was attempting to enter the building, pulling a wire-framed handcart. She struggled with the heavy door, and Mike rushed to assist her. "Please, allow me," he said, opening it wide. Immediately taking the metal handle of the cart into his grasp, the grocery-laden aluminum frame clanked and banged up the two steps into the vestibule.

"Oh *Madonna mia*. It is snowing so much," she spoke with a thick accent. "*Grazie, grazie.*" A black gloved hand touched his cheek. "Such an *angelo*."

Now this woman embodied a nonna. She looked and sounded like the real deal, right down to her chin hair and the remnant cat fur embedded into her worn, woolen coat.

"Can I help you to your apartment?"

She searched his face before speaking again. "You are here for Elisabetta?"

"Yes. How did you know?"

"Your eyes. They give-a you away. She's a good girl, skinny, but sweet like *dolcini*. She is most happy in Messina and Palhairmo."

He leaned toward her and whispered. "I'd like to one day take her to those places. I hear Sicily is very romantic."

The old woman chuckled and shook her head, proceeding up the steps as she held onto the rickety railing. "*Andiamo.*"

Three flights up a door shut then stairs creaked just as Mike lifted the paper bag-filled cart and began to follow the old woman upward.

"Mike, I'm here!" Elizabeth shouted down. "I'm sorry. This is the second time I've kept you waiting. It's just that—" She met them on the second floor landing, and he thought he saw embarrassment in her eyes.

"Oh! Hi, Josie. I see you met my date. Mike Garin, this is Josie Zeppo."

"Zeppo, like the youngest of the Marx Brothers," he smiled.

Josie shrugged her shoulders. "Elisabetta, your *innamorato* is helping me to my apartment." She tugged on his coat. "Don't let this one get away. *Molto bello!*"

Elizabeth blushed, her face glowing as their eyes locked, and he couldn't help grinning like a sap, loving that this stranger just referred to him as Elizabeth's sweetheart. "I'm afraid I'm the one who is going to have to keep her from getting away. She's leaving in a couple of weeks to go back home to California."

"Ah!" Josie said something in Italian, waving her hand beside her head.

In her head, Elizabeth recognized the Italian proverb: Love with someone who lives far away is like putting water in a basket.

Mike furrowed his brow, not understanding the translation but it was clear to him that Elizabeth did. He noticed her smile momentarily diminish as though she'd heard something sad.

When they reached Josie's apartment, he admired the pink wreath hanging upon her door. Tucked within its foliage were Italian and American flags beside a tiny plastic Babbo Natale. "What a pretty wreath," he commented.

Elizabeth's head snapped up and she looked at him with a surprised expression, maybe humored or pleased. He genuinely meant that compliment, not because of the artificial carnations or the arrangement but because the wreath expressed home and welcome. The old woman rewarded him with a proud smile and a pinch to his cheek. His heart leaped for making her so happy by his simple compliment. *If only Stella was this type of nonna for Mia and me.*

"You two go now on your date. Be careful and, Michelangelo, make-a sure she eats something. It is good for love and passion."

He would have cringed at her usage of that abhorrent nickname but understood it was meant as a term of endearment. She had just called him an angel, but the last thing he needed was for Elizabeth ever to see that embarrassing MAA Facebook page and make a connection. It surprised everyone, even himself when he leaned down—without a single fear of germ transference—and kissed Josie's cheek. "Merry Christmas, Mrs. Zeppo. It was wonderful to meet you." He whispered in her ear,

"And yes, I will make sure she eats."

She winked at him then unlocked the door with Elizabeth helping her drag the cart inside. After exchanging a quick hug and wishing Josie a sweet *buona sera*, she exited the apartment.

As soon as the black door closed behind her, Mike swept her into his arms, feeling—he couldn't be sure—familial, filled with emotion. They kissed hello in a deeply evocative lip lock.

"Hello to you, too," she breathed forgetting all about the embarrassment associated with being in this building.

He breathed deeply, gazing intently into her eyes, inhaling her intoxicating scent. His heart hammered. "It's very sexy when you speak Italian."

"I'm not any good at it. I fake it well."

"It sounded pretty authentic to me—and *you* can't fake sexy."

"Charmer." She rewarded him with a peck to his lips.

"Was everything all right earlier? Is one of your sisters' neighbors having trouble?"

"Everything is fine. Mr. Graciosa, their next-door neighbor was a bit confused. He's a winemaker and, well, he probably imbibed a bit too much on his newest batch. Earlier this afternoon there was an unwelcome visitor and when he heard you arrive, he came to our protection."

"Unwelcome? Did you call the police?"

"Nothing like that." *Just Vinnie with flowers and his presumptuous lips and pickle breath!*

"Is he okay now?" He took her hand and they carefully descended the stairs side-by-side, eyes locked on one another.

"Yes. He'll sleep it off, and Regina will check in on him."

"I'd like to meet them."

"Who? My sisters?" She looked over her shoulder toward the top of the stairs. "Well … um … They're not there."

"But I just spoke to your funny sister over the intercom no less than ten minutes ago."

"I mean, they're here, but not in the apartment. They're visiting with another neighbor, decorating her Christmas tree."

"That's nice. I like this building, the tenants, and how you all seem to care about each other."

"You do? Really?"

"Sure. Why wouldn't I? I don't have anything like this sense of community on Sutton Place. Not to mention that the scent of baked goods all day is worth its weight in gold."

Elizabeth grinned, never expecting to hear that from a wealthy, sophisticated Manhattanite. For a second, she considered that maybe Mike wouldn't stereotype her ethnicity as her ex-husband had. Maybe he wouldn't be so prejudiced against all that came along with an Italian-American girl from the Bronx: the assumption that everyone was mob related, the talking with hands, the raised emotions, the obsessive eating and, lest she forget, the belief in silly superstitions. Even the saints they honored and some of their traditions were different from those in the "outside" Roman Catholic world, but this was Mike, a good man with a generous, caring heart.

As though her vision came into focus, she admitted, "I like this building, too. The people, colorful as they are, have become my sisters' family in my absence. I think they made a wise choice in moving here."

He held the door open, allowing her to exit onto the sidewalk first.

The snow had tapered to just gentle puffs of white floating in around them. She could hear the Salvation Army bell faintly ring in the distance, but resisted glancing over her shoulder to see if it was Vinnie the Turtle. Oh, that wouldn't be good. He's probably still smarting from that slap to his cheek when he tugged at her and tried to slip her his lizard tongue. Between him, Danny, and Carpo—all in hot, horny pursuit—she was totally convinced, now more than ever, that all Italian men thought about was sex.

"Where are we headed?" she asked.

"Someplace special nearby so that we don't have to navigate too far in this dangerous snow."

Oh shit! I hope I don't run into someone who knows me.

In another gentlemanly gesture, Mike opened the car door for her and she slid onto the soft leather. The aroma of new car and his distinct scent blended within pleasantly, and she breathed deeply thinking someone should bottle that combination.

After settling beside her, Mike slowly drove down the avenue, eventually crossing through the Botanical Gardens then down another main thoroughfare. Feeling nervous, she remained quiet, just watching him drive with such caution, his strong grip upon the steering wheel. He broke the awkward tension. "Are you familiar with the Christmas House?"

"I am. I hear that it's a fantastic display. The biggest in the city. Is that where we're headed?"

"I hope that's okay."

"Okay? That's great! It's a perfect night for it."

Another pause hung heavy in the car.

"Have you ever thought of moving to New York City, Elizabeth? Being closer to your sisters? I mean, LA must be lonely for you."

The Christmas lights on a passing house provided a deliberate distraction as she considered his question, acknowledging that her white lies and her avoidance of total disclosure were wrong. "I ..." she took a deep breath. "Very recently, I have thought about moving here. I quit my job so that I could come east to be with my sisters this holiday season. So, I really have nothing permanent to go back to—just a lifestyle that I've grown accustomed to."

"I'm surprised you didn't tell me when you came to my office. Why not?"

"My sisters don't even know. I guess, the truth is, I'm embarrassed."

"Embarrassed? Why?"

"I realized that the head partner didn't really care about my education or the skills I brought to the clinic, just what I wore. Honestly, I didn't expect sexual harassment in this day and age. I just assumed that I was on par with all the other physicians at the practice. That's a blow to the ego—a total kibosh to my dreams at West Hollywood Podiatry. I thought if I told you, I don't know, you may have thought less of me, a loser, even naïve."

He looked over at her, and she could see true empathy there. "You? A loser? No, Elizabeth. I'm so sorry. What a jackass your boss must be. He lost an ambitious, talented physician as part of his team, someone who *is* on par, even superior."

"Thank you. I guess it's better that I found out only sixteen months in, than later when I might miss the opportunity to take my surgical boards due to lack of cases. But I'd be lying if I didn't admit that something has changed while I've been away from LA."

"Changed, as in you maybe staying in New York?"

"Perhaps." She grinned. "You know, the other day I met a girl just a few years younger than I am who was so afraid of change, so shy, but she took a brave leap of faith and was so happy that she did. Just meeting and talking to her and seeing her transformation was inspiration. Change is good. My mother always said that when God closes a window, he opens a door."

"Would it sound selfish of me if I asked you to walk through the door?"

"Maybe a tiny bit, but I won't mind hearing it." She gave him a coy, sideways glance. "Will you be waiting on the other side of the threshold?"

The Lexus stopped at a red light and Mike reached over, taking her hand. His voice felt like warm caramel flowing over her. "Consider remaining in New York, and I promise I'll be here waiting."

"I'll consider it. You certainly are excellent incentive for changing the status quo, Mike." *Oh. My God!*

"And so are you. More than you know."

"Uh oh, that sounds like it comes with a story. You didn't forget to tell me about a wife or something salacious, did you?"

"No! Nothing like that. As of about a week ago, I'm off the market. I'm such an optimist that I closed my eDating account."

Taken aback, she furrowed her brow. "You're on an online dating service? I wouldn't think that ..."

He laughed before letting go of her hand when the light changed. "It's been a challenge to meet a woman that I could click with, but it turns out that I didn't need eDating after all, just a little CME."

Feeling the same way, she said, "Who knew medical education would come with such perks? Meeting someone in LA has been hard, too. A few of my colleagues have tried to fix me up, but I've been pretty focused on my career."

"I hear ya'. My grandmother has even attempted to play matchmaker. The stories I could tell you about her club and latest schemes, especially lately. She says that 'I look for hairs in an egg'."

Her eyes widened slightly. "Really? My great-aunt always said the same about me. In fact, she took me to task in her Last Will & Testament, on video no less, with that exact phrase."

"That's funny. Must be a generational thing."

Up ahead, the two-story Christmas House lit up the residential one-way street, as cars inched along with their occupants gaping in curious fascination at the unique decorations. Mike pulled into the first available parking spot at the curb then exited, walking around the car to help

Elizabeth out. The snow had temporarily ceased, but the sidewalk holiday revelers were few and the fresh drifts many. Brenda Lee's "Rockin' Around the Christmas Tree" grew louder as they approached. Holding gloved hands, he gripped her tightly making sure she didn't slip on the pavement.

Bathed in pink from thousands of tiny bulbs against the black night, the house was fantastical. On the top balcony, a giant crèche moved under direct spotlight, and celebrity statues dressed in eveningwear danced below in a simulated ballroom. Every square foot of the house and front lawn was filled with gaudy, twirling figures and lights.

Elizabeth's fingers grasped the chain link fence separating the holiday admirers from the displays. Though fascinated, she could feel herself going into sensory overload. She hadn't remembered the display being this colorful, this large before, but it was years ago when her parents took them to see it.

"It seems odd that a statue of St. Michael should be standing beside Liberace and his piano, doesn't it?" Mike asked with incredulous humor.

"It does. Is he your patron saint?"

"He is. My mom was exceptionally devout."

"That's nice to hear. My father was quietly pious, but my mom is a church lady. She wears her religion on her sleeve but not so much in her heart or actions." She snorted. "But who am I to judge?"

He smoothed the hair at her temple, smiling wistfully, and she earnestly wished she knew what he was thinking, but instead changed the subject.

"The nativity display is the largest I have ever seen, but even that has Mickey Mouse at the end. Thank goodness they didn't put him in the manger."

"I read that something special happened to the family on Christmas Eve in 1973 and that was when they decided to praise God every Christmas season with this display."

"With a mannequin of Superman holding Lois Lane? Well, it is fantastic—all of it—and makes me smile, just as Christmas should."

Pointing through the fence, Mike leaned down. "Even Michael Jackson is present for this celebration."

"Oh my God!" She beamed up at him, proudly declaring like a schoolgirl, "I can moonwalk, you know."

Fortuna

He raised an eyebrow then laughed. "Let me see."

"No way! Not here. Not now!"

"Do it. I dare you."

"Never dare a Cl—Fairchild."

Mike hummed "Billie Jean" egging her on with his hand tapping his thigh, his body moving with a little dancing rhythm. Yeah, she thought her heart would stop on that one.

Elizabeth bent her legs with jazz fingers spread at her side. Her pelvis thrust once, then again. One leg snapped out and three fingers tapped that knee. Moving her feet in place, she free-styled mini kick push glides then pointed at Mike, and smiled saucily before launching into full-fledged moving moonwalks, black boots suddenly sliding backward etching pathways in the snow. Her arm swept beside her with the momentum.

"Where did you learn to do that?"

"Aquinas High School. Sister Margarita's math class, uniform and all!" She laughed, feeling released, as Lizzy Clemente danced joyously back into the stoic, focused life Elizabeth Fairchild had ruled these many years.

Mike cheered her on as nearby Christmas House spectators turned smiling faces toward the fun of the dancing brunette in a red scarf. Upon execution of her last walking glides back toward him, she lost her footing. Her jazz hands frantically grabbed onto him, crashing them both down into a snowdrift. Her body lay upon his, faces so close, cradled in his embrace and they laughed raucously. She doubted that she was ever so happy.

They stopped laughing, their eyes locked, their breaths held. He kissed her.

~**~

~Nineteen~
Ardente
(Desire)

The Christmas House, moonwalking, laughing, and more laughing led to late-night dining at a Dominican restaurant not far from the holiday display, which led to wine and more wine. Mike should have known better, particularly since the off and on snow began again during dinner. Still, they didn't rush to end their date. Dessert followed and it hadn't surprised him to witness Elizabeth devour the flan, but it did surprise him when she finished hers and attacked his. Genuine laughter was his response, assuming her tipsiness was the culprit for the voracious sweet tooth, not to mention carrying out her very own date pet peeve. Although Rebecca had done the same at Rao's, he hardly felt Elizabeth's action a violation and continued to eat from his plate after she helped herself, particularly since she had moaned when doing so. The sound did something to him and he realized that he'd gladly share everything with her because there was no doubt in his mind—he had fallen hard.

Moments after they departed the restaurant, the lights dimmed and the staff began stacking the chairs. The late hour and heavily falling snow had cleared the roads of travelers; the silence upon the city was romantic. Again, he held the car door open for her, feeling regret that their night was coming to an end.

Once installed in the driver's seat, he placed his fingers on the key in the ignition, readying to turn, but paused glancing over at Elizabeth. He admired the alluring flush to her cheeks, maybe there from the excessive wine or the chill in the air, neither of which mattered. She was a vision and the look she gave him, he had yet to see. There was wanton desire in her chestnut eyes, dark and dilated. The seductive tone in her voice confirmed it.

"Mike, I had a wonderful time."

"I did, too."

She was full of surprises tonight, especially when she bridged the separation between them to kiss him. Her hand grabbed the lapel of his coat and pulled him close to her for a deep, passionate kiss. Unwilling to deny what he had been wanting to do all night, he responded in kind, giving into the influence of wine and love. Yes, he was sure he was in love with her on only their fourth date.

The sensation of her soft malleable lips against his flesh was rapture. Turning in his seat, he held her as close as the console between them allowed, loving her with his lips, smoothing a hand under her open coat to caress her shapely form. He had no restraint and ignored the internal voice in him that said *stop*. Desire and anticipation ruled over him.

Elizabeth unbuttoned his coat and continued to unhurriedly kiss him. She tasted like succulent summer grapes, and his body responded in pleasure. He shifted so that her hand could glide over his body, and a fervent moan escaped when her palm brushed over his nipple. He was sure she could feel his rapidly beating heart when her hand caressed over his chest.

Her mouth left his and she leaned back, gazing into his eyes. Seeing those parted luscious lips and the rosy flush to her cheeks, it was clear she felt what he did: intense need. A little quirk of a smile preceded her move closer to him. She leaned over the console, their lips meeting in consuming flame.

Passionate kisses exploded into deep exploration, her hand traveling upon his chest and abdomen in gentle glides. He did the same, eager to discover the heated flesh below his hand, from the curve of her waist up to those glorious breasts he had admired the first time he saw her. Feeling every bit the horny teenager, his hand cupped a mound, gently squeezing the soft, natural fullness, reveling in how it spilled from his grasp. The sensation of her pebbled nipple was his undoing when a single brush of his thumb against her taut peak caused her to arch her back, welcoming his touch. A breathy "yes" escaped her lips.

This impassioned woman in his arms had ignited an arousal the likes of which he hadn't had in a very long time. Damn it felt incredible, but when her eager hand brushed over his erection, he knew he had crossed the line. Slowly, he ended their kiss, although still enjoying the feel of her palm gliding upon his rigid shaft, secretly yearning for its release, its satiation.

He barely was able to catch his breath. "Elizabeth."

Her hand slid upward, away from the caress undoing him.

"Hmm," she moaned.

"I adore kissing you and feeling you in my arms, but we have to stop."

She kissed his chin then deposited a peck to his lips. "We can continue. It's okay. I want to."

"Believe me when I say I want to as well, but not tonight. We've both been drinking."

He noted the foggy windows and remembered where they were; she followed his gaze.

"You're right. We're necking in a car. I don't know what came over me."

"I do, because the same came over me." He kissed her tenderly. "We will resume this. I promise you."

Rising from his body, Elizabeth righted her sweater and coat, then did the same to him. Her tender regard and embarrassed expression made him want to pull her back down. Instead, he sat up and took her hand from fussing. "I love … that you kissed me like that, that you want me so badly. I want you just as much." The yearning in his heart and body was undeniably the strongest he had felt for someone. His fingers brushed her cheek then both hands cupped her face, before he deposited a gentle kiss.

"I should take you home now."

She nodded, the desire still prevalent in her eyes.

"Elizabeth. I … um … you should buckle up. The roads are unsafe tonight." He thought it best not to express what he really felt: that taking her home was not what he desired, but making love to her all night long was. Taking that kind of emotional step in a new relationship represented a commitment and until she decided what and where her future would unfold, his propriety, and yes, religiosity said, "wait." Of course, his libido said something entirely different.

~**~

Elizabeth couldn't believe the words, "You shouldn't drive home," exited her mouth, but they had. The roads were terrible and she could see the stress on Mike's face as he navigated the treacherous, unsalted streets: his jaw flexed and his hands white-knuckle gripped the steering wheel at two and ten. The snow was now coming down with ferocity as the Lexus pulled up in front of Messina Bakery, double-parking with its red hazard lights blinking.

"Are there any hotels around here?"

"No, silly. Come up. Stay over, and I promise not to take advantage of you."

"I don't know if I like that particular promise."

"Is that an invitation?"

"Perhaps it is, but I can't impose on your sisters."

"It's no trouble. The sofa is big and the place is warm."

What? Are you on drugs, Elizabeth! Is this your conscience or sexual desire talking? She smiled brightly and hoped he saw her sincerity. She *was* truly concerned for him and whatever apprehension—or fears—she felt about exposing him to her loud, ethnic upbringing seemed inconsequential when it came to his safety. Of course, the temptation of holding him in her arms and touching him again could not be denied. She certainly wouldn't lie on that account. Cutting short their make-out session left her feeling frustrated. It wasn't the wine—it was 100% Mike.

"Are you sure I won't be any trouble? I'll be out early in the morning. I don't snore."

"I want you to stay, and my sisters won't mind in the least bit." *Trust me, they won't.*

She looked at her watch: midnight. They'd both be asleep by now, or Nicki might be up watching television in bed. Gina would never hear them; her own snores were like white noise to any goings on.

"Well, so long as you're sure. While I find a parking spot, why don't you go up and let your sisters know that I'll be crashing overnight?"

He re-tied the scarf around her neck and brushed his index finger over her cheek. "I won't be long."

If one could describe the pounding in Elizabeth's chest at the thought of her two worlds colliding, they would have said sonic boom. She could hear it in her ears—feel it in her bones—as she made for the apartment building. She slid the key in, pushed open the old, heavy door, and bolted up the steps—some two at a time until she stood before the new plastic holly Christmas wreath on the door. Chuckling to herself, a sweet thought crossed her mind: Mike would probably like it.

Apart from brilliant snow accumulated on the two front windows and the multi-colored lights defining the perimeter of the fire escape, the apartment was dim, and not even the illumination from Nicki's TV escaped under her closed bedroom door. She must be dead to the world. Gina was, as evident by the freight train steamrolling in unison with the hissing of the radiator through the apartment.

Frantic to make the best impression possible, Elizabeth shrugged off her coat, pulled off her scarf, and then ran through the living room, hiding whatever screamed tacky, Italian-proud, or Clemente-addressed. She tossed a crocheted lap blanket over the plastic-covered chair and headed to the kitchen. The round fluorescent bulb flickered with a buzz when she switched the light on and she gazed up at the stained ceiling tiles, then looked down at the mismatched linoleum and sighed. There was nothing she could do about them, but she could do something about the stove and countertops, promptly wiping them down with a fresh dishcloth. Surely after Nicki's late-night cooking attempt—apparent by the stacked pots and dishes—there might be salmonella, or possibly even listeria present! There was no time to tackle the sink or dishware. She'd have to take her chances that he wouldn't think them low-class slobs. Slobs yes, but never low class. Her eyes spotted last week's article in Etonville's newspaper about PalHairMo's grand opening stuck to the refrigerator; she quickly banished it into a drawer along with the mock-up design of the Trinacria and six or so magnets.

Ready as she could possibly be for Mike's anticipated buzz to the speaker, she paused, backlit by the fluorescent lighting as she gazed at the crucifix above the sofa. The black and white family photographs beside it reminded her of good times and one in particular caught her eye: she and Nicki eating gelato at a street festival under the Little Italy welcome banner. Remembering that day with fondness, she smiled at how the three of them wore T-shirts that read "FBI – Full Blooded Italian." *Ho-ly crap!*

She climbed onto the sofa and removed the photograph, quickly shoving it under the plastic seat cushion of Aunt Maria's chair.

As her panic set in, the buzzer sounded. With a trembling hand, she buzzed Mike up and left the apartment to meet him in the hallway. Poor Mr. Graciosa may well be hung over, and she didn't want to startle him. Each creaking step that grew nearer made Elizabeth more panicked at Mike's arrival. She glanced down over the banister and grinned nervously.

"Hey beautiful," he whispered, reaching the top step. She put her finger to her lips then pointed to Mr. G's door before they slipped into the dimly lit apartment.

Mike entered, removing his coat, which she promptly took and hung in the closet with an immediate apology. "That's Regina's snoring. I'm sorry." She made a face, crinkling her nose. "The place is kinda messy, too. Nichole is a tornado."

She assumed that Mike's silence, as he scanned the apartment, was either condemnation or perhaps simply because he didn't want to wake her sisters. A slight smile touched his lips when his eyes drew to the crucifix on the wall and the image of St. Padre Pio above Prozia's chair.

"It feels homey," he whispered before kissing her sweetly and walking into the kitchen.

Once he stepped into the dingy room she really wanted to crawl into a hole and die. That bathtub still had grape juice rings around it. She watched as Mike looked at everything with a discerning eye, just as she had on her first visit back in August. Only she prayed that he was less a snob than she at the time. Yes, he would be kind she reminded herself—this was Mike Garin, not Richard Fairchild her ex-husband.

He pursed his lips and turned to her, whispering. "Do you have something to drink? All that wine has made me parched."

Relief emitted a delicate sigh. "Of course."

The refrigerator hummed when she opened the door to retrieve a coke.

"My fridge does that, too," he said pulling the soda can's tab with a pop, his eyes settling on the dish filled with rainbow cookies.

She took the plate in hand before he had the chance to look up at the ceiling tiles, then grasped his hand in her free one, leading him from the kitchen. She wasn't so blind not to have noticed his slight obsessiveness with germs and how he kept his hands in his pockets or held hers when in public. No doubt, he'd be thinking E. Coli or Stemphydium mold and would bolt at first sight of those stains above the stove. Lord knows, she thought that the first time she had come back to Belmont.

She flipped the kitchen light off and whispered, "I'll be right back. I need to get you some sheets and a blanket ... and something for you to sleep in."

"Just a blanket is fine, Elizabeth. Really, don't go to any trouble."

"It's no trouble. I'm happy you're here." She placed the cookies on the dilapidated coffee table.

"Are you? You seem, I don't know, anxious. Is it because you brought a guy into your sisters' apartment for the night?"

"No. That's not it. It's just that their place is different from mine, and I'm sure quite unlike yours on Sutton Place. Living in an old tenement like this just takes some adjusting, that's all."

He shrugged his shoulder and moved to sit on the sofa, taking her with him with a tug to her hand. "This apartment is great. Space is over-rated, and that claw-footed tub in the kitchen—is that where your neighbor makes his wine? Many of these older buildings still have them from when they were coldwater flats. They're highly sought after."

If a grin could light Times Square, hers could have lit the world. "Yes. Mr. G is here a lot. Regina invites him for dinner twice a week. When I first saw the tub, I assumed that it was for bathing, but she set me straight."

"This is the kind of building Mia and I need."

She followed his gaze, their eyes settling on the colorful lights upon the fire escape. "Well, based on what you told me over dinner about her finally getting out and making a few new friends, and how happy she seemed, this type of building—even in this neighborhood—*would* be good for her. Trust me, there's no chance of her invisibility on Arthur Avenue."

Mike placed the soda on the table beside them and turned, bringing her into his embrace. It felt so natural, and she couldn't believe that he displayed no disgust at the rental she had once considered a slum.

His voice was filled with heartfelt appreciation when he said, "My taking your sound advice to encourage her in making some female friends outside of her virtual world made all the difference. It's because of you that she took that first step. Next thing I knew she came home with a smile and a haircut, feeling on top of the world."

"I'm so happy to hear that. A place like this, with roommates, would be perfect for her. In fact, there are a couple of vacant apartments in the building."

She gave him a thoughtful smile. "My sisters are great neighbors."

Mike looked up at the wall above them, the obvious missing photograph perplexed him, and he wondered why exactly she seemed so embarrassed by the apartment—maybe even her family. If anyone should be embarrassed by family, it should be him. Stella was insane, obsessed with her new roommate Ann and the reclaiming of Villa Fortuna. Her old mob connections and incessant badgering about him finding a wife didn't help to make a case for normal. Hell, he was even reticent in discussing his father's lack of familial concern and the gold-digging step-monster.

His thumb smoothed over the pad of Elizabeth's hand. "I'm sorry I sidestepped the issue when you asked about my father over dinner. I guess I'm not too dissimilar from you when it comes to discussing my family dynamics. I say that because I get the feeling there are some issues about your family that you want to avoid, and I just want to say that whatever they are—whenever you're ready—I make a good sounding board. I have experience in dealing with embarrassment, both personally and professionally."

"Thank you. And I didn't mean to pry about your relationship with your dad. Really. As far as I go, it's just that my family, well … it's complicated. It's not really them; it's me. This is the longest I've been back to the city since my father died and before that—I don't know when—Spring Break or something … years."

"Is that why you had me drop you at a friend's apartment after the Conservatory?"

She nodded then reciprocally touched his face. "You know, I'm also a good listener. Do you want to discuss your dad? I'd be honored to be the shoulder you choose."

"I struggle a lot with guilt for not thinking of him more kindly, for not accepting some of the decisions he made following my mother's death. His demands and expectations of me I've learned to brush off these many years, but when it comes to his conduct where Mia is concerned, I harbor a lot of resentment toward him. I can't sit idly by allowing his disregard of her and the guilt I feel over my anger with him stabs at my heart."

"And that's one of the reasons you are so close to her?"

"Yes. He remarried someone who was more after his assets than to be a part of his family. Mia, only three then, ostensibly became baggage to the lifestyle he found himself enjoying with a much younger—healthier—woman than my mother. Dad has a penchant for younger women. My mother was fifteen years his junior."

"Is it that you view his new wife as replacement of your mother?"

"In part, but not all. Mostly, it's that I cannot accept his abandonment as Mia's father because this woman has no desire to *be* a mother, or even a friend to her. He has forgotten my mother and the promises he made on her deathbed. Candy, the woman he married, is primarily responsible for Mia being such an introvert."

"I'm so sorry. Mia is blessed to have you for a brother. It seems to me that she has the best of everything in one man—one good, compassionate, loving man. I'll pray that your father has a change of heart and that good women will come into Mia's life to reverse the affects of a bad step-mother."

He softly kissed her then said, "Thank you."

Although it felt liberating to share that bit of himself and the guilt he felt burdened by, he, too, looked for a change of topic but hoped that his example would give Elizabeth confidence whenever she became ready to talk about her family.

"You know, Italian rainbow cookies are one of my favorite," he said, eyeing the plate of colorful cookies.

"Really?" She reached over to the plate and selected a perfect cookie for him. She held the delicious combination of chocolate-covered red, green, and white cake to his smiling lips and fed him. Heaven. Just like her kisses and company.

"What do you think?" she asked, grinning at his obvious satisfaction. He would have moaned if they weren't attempting to be quiet.

"The best I've ever had. I'll have to stop into Messina's before I leave in the morning. Mia would love these."

"They're not from downstairs, although theirs are to die for. These, I made. I love to bake."

"Another impressive quality." He took one more from the dish and fed her in return, his finger remaining embraced by her lips until she sucked the chocolate and jelly from it. The seductive expression on her face broke his resolve to keep his hands, and emotions in check. Leaning toward her, he wove his fingers upward through her locks. His breath was shallow when his lips brushed against hers in a throaty whisper. "I love you, Elizabeth."

He kissed her full on, neither waiting for her reply nor her possible rejection. Her kiss back to him was enough confirmation that what was in her heart closely matched his.

"Lizzy ...?" Gina asked standing in the archway, flipping up the light switch. She rubbed her eyes. "What's going on?"

Elizabeth and the god whose lips she couldn't get enough of abruptly stood. As if they were teenagers caught necking by the resident adult, she stammered, "I'm so sorry we woke you, sis. This is my date—Mike Garin. He's going to crash here tonight due to the snowstorm. Mike, this is my older sister, Regina."

Well, well, well. Gina thought, damn glad she woke up when she did. "It's nice to finally meet you, Mike."

Flushed, Mike walked toward her holding out his hand. "And you. Elizabeth has spoken of you often."

She couldn't help but to snort. "Right. Sure she has."

He was looking at her strangely. Tilting his head to the left. He examined her face—or messy hair. Or perhaps it was the racooned mascara under her eyes. Suddenly her sleepy fog cleared, and she hoped he didn't remember the time they kind of met, but didn't officially meet: Halo Salon, before Thanksgiving.

"Have we met before, Regina?" he asked, furrowing his brow obviously trying to recall her face.

"Nope. Not unless you recognize me from St. John's Church back in August, but you were probably too focused on Liz ... Elizabeth to remember me."

"No, I don't think that's it. It was more recent."

Not only could she feel his examination, but also Elizabeth's eyes boring into her flesh, her lips forming that telltale thin line when she sucked them in.

"Well you can be damned sure, Mike, that had I seen you, I would have kept you for myself." She tried not to smile, tried not to give herself or Elizabeth away but damn if it wasn't tempting just to blow the lid on this foolish mask of her sister's. God how she wanted to turn around and blurt, "You know, her real name is Lizzy Clemente, and she thinks all Italian men are liars and cheaters. But you're Italian, aren't you? And you're not either of those things." She laughed aloud at that thought and brushed past them in her T-shirt and pink furry bunny slippers toward the kitchen.

Mike finally blurted, "Carpo!"

Gina and Elizabeth froze.

"You're Regina Carpo, Rusty's client at Halo Salon. We sort of met before Thanksgiving. He asked you for a date."

From the kitchen, she replied in as thick a Bronxite accent as she could muster. "Yeah. Rusty Magic Fingers. I wanted to see how the other half lived so I took a trip up to Etonville. I remember you now." Even separated by the wall of the kitchen and the running tap water, she could feel Elizabeth's rolling anger for never divulging that little bit of information. *Good. She did this to herself.*

"So Carpo is your maiden name?" Mike asked Elizabeth. "Or is it Regina's married name?"

"Um—"

"Well you lovebirds, have fun. I'm going back to bed." Gina giggled, walking past them with a glass of water clutched in her hand. "Keep the moans to a minimum. I've got to go to Mass at the crack of dawn tomorrow." She flipped the light switch again and was gone with another giggle, leaving them in the dark. "Have fun!" she declared as she walked down the hallway.

"Small world," he said.

"Hmm. Very small. Let me get you that blanket." *I'm gonna kill you, Gina! You met him! What else haven't you told me?*

_**_

Not every superstition in the Clemente family was born from old Sicilian wives tales. In fact, some of the more whacky ones originated from their mother's crazy side of the family—the one-quarter Maltese side—yet others were things she had just made up to keep her three daughters in check and in fear.

Nicki had always pushed the buttons and challenged the crazy superstitions, and from that developed her defiant, brash personality and unusual habits. Waking at three in the morning was one of those habits. Her internal clock was set on automatic pilot for the last fifteen years, always waking with the dead. Mamma had repeatedly claimed that the spirits came out to haunt naughty children and teenagers at that ungodly hour because the "plane of spiritual separation" was at its thinnest. It sounded like a bunch of bullshit in order to keep them from sneaking out. No friggin' such plane existed, but when she heard noises coming from the living room at 2:45, curiosity got the best of her. It was either their dead father, Vinnie the Turtle stalker, or a robber coming to steal the flat screen TV they just purchased. Two of the three might well require a phone call to her personal law enforcement officer.

With baseball bat in one hand and her mobile phone in the other, she padded out into the dim living room, wearing a tank top and underwear.

She stopped dead in her tracks, her jaw dropping. *Holy. Shit!*

Rubbing her eyes, she wondered if she was sleepwalking or perhaps that superstition was true and the dead had delivered her Christmas gift early. One supremely fine, half-naked god slept on the sofa with a blanket pushed dangerously low to his waist, exposing a beautiful bare chest with hard nipples. She licked her lips. His muscular arm lay bent above his head, provocatively displaying wispy armpit hair. Her vision traveled downward to the treasure trail of hair leading the way to probably something extraordinary. Closer inspection was required. Absolutely.

Abandoning the bat against the wall, she tiptoed toward his sleeping form, standing only two feet from him. He stirred slightly, shifting in the moonlight, the Christmas lights playing upon his smooth chest. She licked her lips again, moving her tongue back and forth, up and down, as though licking remnant chocolate from them.

Good Lawd! He was Elizabeth's altar boy, but with a body like that, he ain't no saint. His body was made for sin and sin alone. *Yeah, baby!*

Nicki snapped a few photographs and he stirred again, readjusting, the blanket pushing lower. Curiosity was killing her. She had to know— boxers or briefs—and what was in them.

With poised fingers, she bent, delicately lifting the linen to peer under.

Light blue boxer briefs. The waistband couldn't even contain the soft tip of a raging hard-on the size of sopressata salami.

As though scalding hot, she dropped the blanket, her hand flying to her mouth to keep from either touching it or saying "come to mamma, big daddy" before suppressing the temptation of climbing on for the ride of her life. She kissed her pinched fingertips as if to say "*magnifico,*" then looked at Mike's impressive appendage again—just to be sure that her eyes had not played a trick on her. She needed confirmation. Yeah, that's it, confirmation. Another lift to the blanket: *Mamma mia!*

She resisted the urge to photograph it. There was no need; the image was forever burned on her brain. Besides, she's not *that* tacky.

On her way back to bed, feeling *ahem* inspired, she wondered if anyone would hear that new toy of hers, then shook her head thinking, *Lizzy, you are one lucky girl, so long as you don't ef this up.*

~**~

A chill came over Lizzy as she stirred awake at four in the morning beside Gina. She turned her head to glance at the window and noted the accumulated snow upon the window sash. Pulling the blanket up to her chin, she burrowed down thinking how the clanking steam radiator was failing miserably. Warm arms (Mike's arms, to be precise) were less than twenty feet away, separated from her by only the closed bedroom door. Aroused by the recollection of his scorching lips whenever they touched her flesh, she shifted uncomfortably. *Good Lord.* She writhed slightly, replaying in her mind the delicious kisses on the sofa and then his quiet declaration of love. That alone was cause for excitement. She hadn't expected it, and when he said it, she felt almost giddy—followed by that hot kiss of succulent moisture! A tingle sparked fiery heat that quickly spread to her apex, her legs suddenly feeling restless, and her body needy.

Wanting him so badly, yet having him on the other side of the door was sheer torture. She abruptly pulled back her side of the blanket then grabbed the crocheted throw at the foot of the bed. He was most likely chilled out there. Yes, she was sure he needed another blanket.

Quiet tiptoes brought her to the darkened living room; she simultaneously held her breath and the implement to her ruse in folded arms across her chest.

She stopped beside Mike's sleeping form, afraid to breathe lest she wake him. Her hungry eyes drank in his bare chest, causing her to run her tongue over her upper lip involuntarily. His tilted head was surrounded by folded arms, broadening his chest, accentuating the muscles on both. Mike was stunning in the moonlight. The white snow framing the two large windows on both sides of him cast an ethereal glow across the smoothness of his skin.

The winter chill was doing a stimulating number on his taut nipples, but she carefully draped the blanket over him, torn between covering up his chiseled physique and leaving him exposed for her pleasure. Standing over him, gazing at his magnificence, she again pondered his earlier declaration. Yes, she had fallen in love with him, too. He was everything a man should be: He made her laugh and was intelligent, thoughtful, sexy, and great company. Unable to resist the need to touch him, she reached out and smoothed her hand over his cheek.

He moaned opening his eyes. "Babe? Are you okay?"

He'd never called her babe before and her heart slammed against her chest. No, she wasn't okay. She was revved up and ready to go.

"I'm sorry to wake you. I … um … just thought you might be cold."

Their eyes remained locked and he quirked his lips into a seductive smile. "I could use warming."

An inviting lift to the blankets and a shift of his body against the back of the sofa was all she needed to give into the provocative temptation of feeling him pressed against her. She wondered if he would give into his base desires, which was fine by her, or would he worry that her sisters were only feet away. Or … would his religiosity stand in his way? Nervously, she climbed onto the sofa, sliding alongside him, her cold, bare feet instinctively entwining with his; a little giggle escaped her lips when they did so. His chest was smooth and cool as she snuggled facing him, their mouths so close, open and waiting. She could feel her nipples brushing against her T-shirt and his pecs. His nearness caused a heightening of every sensation.

Elizabeth's trembling hand languidly smoothed upward to his shoulder, molding around it then gliding down to his bicep. She brushed the protruding vein. Mike's breath was warm against her cheek as he pulled her closer, his arms circling her waist.

"Are you comfortable?" he whispered.

"Yes, are you?"

"Very. I was dreaming of this, wanting you beside me all night."

"Me, too."

"We ended things in the car, sooner than both of us would have liked."

She reached up, touching the tendrils at his forehead. "Can we continue?"

Mike's kiss was full of all the heat and desire coursing through her veins. His strong hand slid to her panty-clad backside, and she was sure she would die in his arms particularly when he pulled her hips closer to him—and his arousal. *Holy God!*

She couldn't help moaning when he deepened the kiss with fervor, devouring her mouth with his, his tongue probing in passionate repartee with hers. Her hand slid down his perfect backside when he laid her upon her back, and just as he had done, she pulled his hips closer when she felt the hardness of his arousal between them.

His eager hands burned the flesh of her waist with their ascending caress as they slid up the sides of her T-shirt, raising it upward. Arching her back to release the fabric's confines, she wasn't self-conscious exposing her nakedness to his eyes. Finally the white cotton was discarded to the floor and her sensitive peaks relished in the feel of his bare flesh against hers.

Was this a dream? Because, *those* had become increasingly hot. She was floating, yet grounded in Mike's loving embrace. *Oh God!* She bit back at the first sensation of his lips surrounding an aroused nipple, suckling then alternating between nibbles and tongue flicks.

Mike moaned, grinding his erection against her and that was confirmation: this was no dream. Dreams weren't this good. His lips, combined with the gentle ministrations of his caressing hands upon her body and his impressive arousal, caused a tightening within her that she hadn't felt in a long, long time. She was ready to explode very soon. The man's mouth and fingers were skilled, bringing her to a higher ground than ever before. Her mind begging: *Remove my panties, now!*

"I want you so bad, Mike. Make love to me. I need you," she whispered in the moonlight.

Mike gazed up from his lovemaking with the sexiest smile she had ever seen. His hair was tousled, his cheeks flushed as he breathed heavily. "Are you sure?"

"Yes, Oh God, yes."

He kissed her nipple, licking it again and she arched meeting his mouth. She mewed. "Oh yes, I'm sure."

"Do you have protection?" he asked.

"No. Do you?"

Small kisses grazed her chest upward until he kissed her full on the lips, then suckled her bottom lip before sighing in disappointment. "I don't. I didn't think …"

"I know. I didn't either."

Mike shifted his body, lying beside her. His fingers walked down her tummy, each placement tickled her heated skin as he neared her apex. He kissed her ear before whispering, "Let me make love to you another way."

~**~

~Twenty~
Svelare
(Reveal)

Leaving Elizabeth's company in the morning felt tortuous and, to be honest, a little unnerving, but escaping the apartment as soon as he could was necessary. He should have stayed and inquired about his discovery when he removed his coat from the closet, but he needed to make an immediate getaway and thankfully the snow had stopped so he could do so.

This particular Sunday morning with Elizabeth's sisters was a little too chaotic for him on a day that he ritualistically spent in solitude with an espresso, the newspaper, and classical music. He liked to ease into his mornings—gently. Even Mia knew it was a good two hours before he became conversant, which was fine with her because she spent the morning catching up on overnight internet happenings.

Between the clanking radiator, Mr. Graciosa's Mario Lanza music seeping through the walls, the youngest sister's rap music colliding with some crazy Sci-Fi movie on TV, and Regina's loud departure for church at seven, he was nearing sensory breakdown. And it wasn't just the noise. Nichole's overt staring was more akin to ocular devouring; a thick tension emerged between Elizabeth and Regina; and the scent of fresh baked bread from the bakery below made him slightly nauseous. Finally, in the harsh light of morning, not even Elizabeth's delicious kisses could drive away the thought that the kitchen was covered in E. Coli. No. No, he could not eat that entire omelet.

Flight was paramount and he felt bad about it, but knew that she understood also feeling mortified by the situation, which made him feel even more terrible. All of it was overwhelming, and had he not been hung over *and* sexually frustrated, he might have tried to stay longer, pull Elizabeth aside for a quiet make-out session in the bathroom, maybe even make a few jokes about Nichole's sweatshirt that read: "Trust me they're real."

Waking with Elizabeth entangled with his body wearing nothing more than a T-shirt, panties, and a good morning smile nearly shattered any resolve he needed in order to not demonstrate how much he wanted her. Their almost-lovemaking and her position within his arms for the night caused him to awake with a raging erection, which, of course, meant that he needed to stay where he laid—covered—until he could break free to use the bathroom without detection. Talk about awkward.

After shoveling and salting the building's front steps, he whispered into Elizabeth's chilled ear how sorry he was for leaving so soon. He wanted to say the *L* word again to confirm that what they did last night had meaning to him, but the morning had stressed him out too much.

Now, sitting in the Lexus with tires crunching over the salted city streets, he reflected on the discovery in the closet. Elizabeth had other suitors, and not just the ex-boyfriend they had run into at the conservatory, but also someone named Vinnie. The bouquet of fresh flowers carefully concealed on the floor of the coat closet attested to it. The card confirmed it with the words "Lizzy, Remembering our first kiss. Come for lasagna. Love, Vinnie"

He resisted the urge to laugh at the total lack of charm conveyed on the inscription, thinking Elizabeth wouldn't date a guy who says "come for lasagna." *Come for dessert or come to discuss the advances of diabetic wound care, yes, but not lasagna. But maybe that's one of those food sex metaphors. Hadn't we joked about that in the taxicab on our first date?*

Clenching his jaw, he gripped the steering wheel; not because the roads were icy from the snow, but because there were two other guys trying to win her affection. Again, competition wasn't his bag; there was never any use for it in his opinion. However, now he didn't have a choice. Elizabeth was worth the fight.

"Come for lasagna! Gee, what a guy! Elizabeth is high class and deserves better than carnations. Jerk. I can do better than that. I'll send her exotic flowers."

Driving down Belmont Avenue, he passed a brick Catholic Church decorated with Christmas wreaths and pine swags. Our Lady of Mount

Carmel's center arched door remained open to the latecomers climbing the recently shoveled steps. He turned the wheel, quickly making a snap decision to attend Mass on this stressful, yet beautiful snow-kissed morning.

The name of the church he recalled from when he and Elizabeth met suitor number one and his offensive horn necklace at the conservatory. He was from this neighborhood but implied that "Lizzy" had lived here for a better part of her life. Even her comment about where she learned to moonwalk niggled at him. If memory served from his high school basketball games, Aquinas Catholic High School was in this section of the Bronx. Was she from this neighborhood? Did she grow up here before moving to California? Or perhaps he was just tired, hung over, and annoyed that there was another man on the scene that he didn't know about. He knew he was searching for things that weren't there. Surely, she would have mentioned it. His mind wandered to the mailboxes in her building. What did her sisters do for a living?

"Nah, stop it Mike. You're just tired and looking for hairs in an egg. These two other guys are nothing—they just have good taste. She's perfect for you and has already admitted that she's fallen for you. For God's sake you told her how you felt last night in more ways than one! Stop this."

As he parked the car, the mobile phone rang, and he depressed the speaker button. "Hey Rusty. What's up?"

His friend groaned. "Can you meet me for dinner tonight? I'm having a bit of trouble with this PalHairMo competition."

"Have the sisters gotten under your skin, too?"

"Personally they're great, but … that's the problem. They're kicking my ass with cannolis and gossip, and I need your help."

"You're barking up the wrong tree. I don't style hair, just perform hairline scalp reductions, and I definitely don't bake or gossip."

"But you do Botox. I hate to ask but I'm hoping to convince you over a bottle of wine to come for an injection party."

Mike chortled. "That's not normally something I do. Are things really that bad at the salon?"

"Bad isn't the word. My business is tanking and at this time of the year, I can't afford to lose clients. I even saw your sister and cousin go into PalHairMo. Talk about a blow to the ego."

"I'm sorry. Both were actually doing a little damage control. When were you hoping to do this Botox party?"

"The day after Christmas. I promise to make the night lucrative for you. We can discuss the details over dinner at Finnegans, if that's okay."

"Don't worry about me. I'll do it if you really—truly—need it."

"I do. You could be my ace in the hole for New Year's preparation."

As much as Mike disliked the idea of catering to his clients "off hours," he could hear the desperation in his friend's voice, and in friendship, he'd put aside his reservations. "Then you have my word. Just telephone my assistant at the office and give her the details so she can get in contact with some of my clients who might be interested in attending. I'm sure Gwen could get you at least twenty or so up in your neck of the woods."

"I owe you, Mike."

"You don't owe me anything, but I will be happy with a bottle of Bryant Bettina red. Just kidding. I'll see you tonight at seven."

"Great. Thanks a shit-load."

Mike hung up and an immediate incoming Skype transmission beeped. He glanced at the church steps, observing the last person enter and the door firmly close. If not for his thinking it Mia calling, he would have let it go, and immediately regretted hitting the accept button the second he did so. Stella's face (sans make-up and taped at her crows feet) appeared on the screen. He turned off the ignition and sat back, the anxiety growing behind his placid demeanor, as he wrung his fingers spreading anti-bacterial liquid.

"Good morning, Michael."

"Grandmother. Good morning."

"You look tired. Were you up all night?" Surprisingly her eyebrow cocked.

"It was a late night."

"Where are you?"

"About to enter church; you should be doing the same."

"Bah! I have other business to attend. Besides, O'Malley is on my shit list for not helping me bring down Villa Fortuna."

He looked at his watch. "Can you make this quick? I'm already late. Is everything all right?"

"How was your date last night?"

"What date?"

"The one in the Bronx."

The agita began, the knife turning. "And how would you know about my date?" *I'm going to kill you, Mia! It's most likely all over Facebook.*

"I have my sources. I need to see you over lunch today. There is much we need to discus. I'll be at Sutton Towers at one."

"I have to do my Christmas shopping, and I have plans uptown with Rusty for dinner. Is there any chance I can take a rain check?"

"No chance at all."

Mike could see Ann's delicate features behind his grandmother; the vibrant color of the scarf she wore shocked his eyes. Damn, this morning sucked and, unfortunately, he couldn't control the unusual vitriol as it spilled unchecked from his mouth. "Will you be coming for lunch alone or will I need to meet Ann's stringent dietary restrictions, too?"

"Sarcasm does not become you, Michael. You're growing more and more like your insolent cousin, and I would appreciate you keeping your voice down. Ann is not deaf, you know."

"I'm just saying. After the way you chastised her at Rao's over that meatball, and my splitting headache, I'm in no mood to start cooking French nouvelle cuisine to accommodate *anyone's* irritable bowel syndrome, not even yours."

"You're going to have to accept Antoinette as part of my life now, so stop acting childish."

"I apologize for offending you, Grandmother. I gotta go. I'm late for Mass."

"Yes. Well, your apology is accepted, and I will come alone if that is your wish. While you are attending Mass, you should thank God for your grandmother's formidable shrewdness because I have information that will *guarantee* you Villa Fortuna. I'll see you precisely at one."

She clicked off, and Mike sighed before exiting the car.

~**~

Apart from St. Patrick's Cathedral, Mike had never seen such a magnificent church as Our Lady of Mount Carmel. Its brick edifice hardly conveyed the classical beauty within. The scent of old wood and incense filled his lungs as soon as he entered, evoking a sense of calm. The restored religious frescos high above the traditional marble altar transported him far from the disharmony of the morning.

He blessed himself after dipping his fingers into holy water and promptly found a place in the back of the church beside the confessional. Immediately he felt comfortable in a community comprised of young and old, families and singles. Made up of every ethnicity, this church family embodied the heart of a city built by the hands of its immigrants. Dotted within each pew, several older women displayed traditional black or white lace head coverings. He couldn't help but wonder if the Clemente sisters were in attendance, even imagining Maria Dixon wearing a chapel veil attending Mass here before her death.

Morning sun streamed through the one-hundred-year old stained glass windows, shining down on the congregation as the lector read the first scripture. Keeping one ear trained on the Word and the other on his greeting to the Almighty, he silently recited his penitent prayers that would normally be on bended knee. Asking forgiveness for his shortness with his grandmother and his lack of patience in just about everything this morning was paramount before receiving Holy Communion.

He relaxed, hoping and imagining that one day Elizabeth might be sitting beside him—open to the liturgy and the children's choir angelically singing Christmas choral pieces. With only three days remaining until Christmas, the peace of the season filled his heart and upon Mass's conclusion an hour later, he felt a thousand times better in facing the afternoon ahead.

The congregants filed into the aisle, many smiling as the pipe organ's music filled the nave. Shuffling toward the back of the church where the priest stood shaking the faithful's hands at the door, Mike inched closer in the crowd of worshipers, not caring that his hand touched the edge of the wooden pews as he passed. He freely acknowledged that he never fretted about germ transference when it came to drinking from the Communion cup—or Elizabeth.

Finally, in the narthex, he took a weekly bulletin from a small table then glanced up to the wall beside the right entrance door. A white poster centered amidst other church flyers and announcements caught his attention and, well, his curiosity was piqued. Through the crowd, he made his way past the priest, proceeding to the section of wall labeled: Monthly OLMC Parish News.

He knew that beautiful face. Shocked, his mouth opened agape, eyes widening.

No way! Impossible!

In colorful red and green lettering, surrounding a graduation photograph of Elizabeth was the announcement:

OLMC and Aquinas High School's Class of 2003 Valedictorian Lizzy Clemente will be returning to Belmont on December 4th. Welcome her at Messina Bakery between 4:00 and 7:00 and tell her how much she has been missed in Little Italy. Once the little girl who crowned the Queen of Heaven on May Day, now a physician to the stars in Hollywood! We are so proud!

Anger, guilt, and anxiety washed over him. Mike shoved the now twisted bulletin into his coat pocket and removed a small bottle of anti-bacterial wash. His thoughts were a jumbled mess.

Dr. Elizabeth Fairchild is Lizzy Clemente, Italian-American, just like him. She is one of the owners of Villa Fortuna, a building he is trying to take over, one of the very women putting his best friend out of business. Someone his grandmother is attempting to ruin because they'd stolen the Russo family home. A woman whose own family is so connected to the mob that her father was whacked in broad daylight only three years ago. Elizabeth had stated that her father had been run over, just like Stella has stated. No wonder she was so secretive about her family

He sighed after his mind scrambled to put every connection together.

No, he was no longer looking for a hair in an egg. This was not just one hair in one egg. This was a full dozen of rotten, stinking eggs, and if she found out who he was—the man who wanted to turn Villa Fortuna into condos—the shit would surely hit the fan.

Yes, Tom Hanks and Rusty said it best, *The Godfather* is the sum of all wisdom: "Revenge is a dish best served cold" would become Elizabeth's motto.

Rusty. Oh No! He'd just committed to engaging in salon-warfare against the woman he no more than an hour ago vowed to fight for—an incredible woman he had verbally declared was perfect for him. The one he loved!

He'd have to think on that; her family was Cosa Nostra—an absolute game changer.

However, one thought stuck out among all the others: Elizabeth and

PalHairMo were the reason his sister returned home so happy from her freeing haircut, feeling confident and determined to overcome her shyness.

He needed space, Mozart, and an espresso and only had three hours to calm before Stella's invasion downtown.

~**~

"Did you notice that creepy dude sitting in the red Cadillac in front of Principessa?" Nicki asked gazing out the living room window.

"What guy?" Gina asked coming to stand beside her.

"He's been there for at least two hours, drinking coffee and eating. Doesn't he have to pee by now?"

"Maybe he's waiting for someone?"

"Yeah, maybe, but I don't like the look of him. He's got pervert written all ova his face. I watched as Lizzy went downstairs to help Toni in the bakery and he couldn't keep his eyes off her when she exited the building. He was there when you came back from church, too."

"I don't know. Just ignore him. Everyone looks at Lizzy." She walked from the window, preoccupied and still smarting from the lack of conversation between Elizabeth and her. Her sister's tight lips without the anticipated confrontation, was the worst possible outcome. She'd never seen her so angry and all because she hadn't mentioned that Mike was at Halo Salon when she had her haircut. Well then, she sure as hell wasn't going to tell her that Amelia was his sister or that he's trying to buy the salon.

"The guy looks familiar, like I've seen him recently."

"Guys like him all look the same, even Frankie."

Gina plopped down into Prozia's plastic-covered chair, hearing the snap and crunch of glass under her butt. "What the heck?"

She rose, lifting the seat cushion to reveal the missing photograph. "Look, Nicki. I found it."

"Damn, and I looked good in that picture. Now it's ruined."

"Everything is ruined. I don't know what to do. I've tried it all. I really, truly thought she would have come around by now, but I was mistaken. Lizzy is so pig headed!"

"I think it was a step in the right direction, you know, her allowing him into the apartment," Nicki said.

"Yeah, but when morning came, you can just tell how she regretted inviting him to crash on the sofa. Of course, your rap music and that sweatshirt didn't help the situation."

"Hey, I am who I am and I don't put on no airs. Don't be such a downer. It's gonna take a sopressata to move Lizzy back to Arthur Avenue, not no pastry, or even all the other things that make our world so awesome … not even *our* awesomeness."

"Sopressata is awesome."

Nicki laughed, nodding. "Yeah it is. It worked for Ronnie Greco."

"What are you talking about?"

"Mike and that sopressata of his. Lizzy just needs to get laid. Shit, she's half in love with him already; all he needs to do is slip her the salami and we're home free."

Gina cocked an eyebrow. "And how do you know he's got a sopressata?"

"Neva you mind."

"Is that why you were staring at him this morning? I swear, you made him so uncomfortable."

"I didn't make him uncomfortable. It was probably his massive hard-on getting in the way of his walking."

"Nicki!"

Continuing to look out at the street she replied, "Alls I'm sayin' is that with a body like his, he's gonna rock her world when they finally get it on, and Doc Hollywood'll finally realize that Italian men deliver the goods with passion. There ain't nothing wrong with them."

"I still want to know how you know about you know …"

"I looked when he was asleep last night. *Mamma mia!*"

"You didn't!" She looked to heaven and blessed herself.

Nicki clutched a hip and turned. "Were you under some notion that those three Masses where going to transform me into Miss Goody Two Shoes? 'Cause if you were, you got it all wrong. Of course I looked, and I'd have no prob looking again. That new toy of mine ran out of battery power last night and, just think, Lizzy could get that every day if she would just pull the pole outta her ass."

"I can't believe you looked! Did he see you? Did you touch … I mean …"

"No I didn't touch. Geez, I'm not that nasty, but I did go back and snap a few pictures to inspire me. Wanna see?"

"No!"

"Your loss. So what's on the agenda for today? Christmas tree decorating or are we going to get stuck helping in the bakery again?" Nicki asked, her eyes still riveted on the grease ball exiting the vintage Cadillac.

"Let's decorate the tree tonight. We better get downstairs to help until Mr. Primo gets back from church. I'm sure the line for bread is crazy long and I don't want to upset Lizzy any further." Gina sighed, her thoughts trailing off as she rose to stand beside Nicki. "She'll be going home soon."

"Yeah. We need to do something drastic. Maybe I'll email her these photos of the sopressata."

"Don't you dare!"

~**~

~Twenty-One~
Il Vero e il Falso
(Truth & Lies)

The Sunday before Christmas was traditionally Messina's busiest day and, as was the norm, Mr. Primo and Rosa faithfully attended church. In the past, Sundays always inconvenienced Toni. It wasn't that he disliked assisting his father, and it wasn't that he abhorred the people or pastry—no, on the contrary! The simple fact was that he was usually hung over. But something in the last two weeks had changed, and Mr. Graciosa's specialty grape juice failed to be the means of escape. Nothing in the recipe had been altered. That stuff was still as potent as ever, demonstrated by Mr. G's binge last night. No, something else was responsible for the alteration in his mornings. He felt more at peace than ever. His proclivities had always caused anxiety—some days deciding to dress by the widely accepted norms of society, and other mornings wearing whatever the hell he felt like. On those days he always made sure to protect his father's sensibilities, making sure the dear man never saw the dresses or handbags. Old school respect and familial love were the impetus behind his concealment, but he hoped that one day he would feel free to discuss his penchant with his papa.

Today's crowd in the bakery felt like a renewal of sorts. With clear eyes and an even clearer head, he interacted with every patron, laughing and singing as he boxed sweets and slid loaves of bread into paper sleeves. A decade of drunkenness had dulled the beauty of the neighborhood where he had grown up, but lately he felt more alive than ever—thanks to the job at PalHairMo.

Dressed as Tony with a *y* wearing his father's bakery apron and hat, he stood at the register, listening to Mrs. Dardani go on and on about her son's Las Vegas elopement, and he chanced a surreptitious glance at Elizabeth boxing cookies beside him. She, too, had changed in the last two weeks. On this morning, she was all smiles with flushed cheeks and eyes that sparkled like diamonds. Even her normally fashionable attire had been replaced with one of Gina's red velour sweatsuits, and her carefully styled hair was now tied in a casual ponytail; she looked youthful and at peace. Given her evident joy, she must have gotten over her anger at Gina for secret-keeping. Of course, that look upon Elizabeth's face wasn't wholly unfamiliar to him. It was love and, by God, he hoped that one day it would come back his way, maybe with Dharma.

"And I told him he could get divorced as quickly as he got married!" Mrs. Dardani exclaimed, slamming her palm against the counter for added emphasis.

"That's what my mamma once told me too," Toni said.

"See! She was right! Mammas usually are."

He looked to Elizabeth, again. "Sisters are usually right, too."

She glanced up at him then smiled, brushing her fingers under her chin.

"Those are fighting words, Lizzy!" someone called out from the crowd.

"You know, that's what I love about being Italian. I don't need to say a blessed word and can let my hands do all the talking," she replied, moving over to the scale.

"That's right!" another patron confirmed.

Toni raised an eyebrow. "Girl, did I just hear you say that you love being Italian?"

She swept a hand upward across her body, giving him a look that said, "I'm gonna smack you one."

Side-by-side they joked, filling orders and singing to Christmas pop songs, Toni's choice of music until his father arrived. The mood within the bakery was light and festive and neither thought anything about airing their laundry to the gossiping friends of Arthur Avenue waiting for service.

"You're in exceptional form this morning, Toni," Elizabeth said.

"It must be the holiday season."

"Or perhaps Picasso?"

"I could say the same of you and that guy you've been going out with. I don't think I was dreaming when I saw him leave this morning looking a little worse for the wear."

A blush spread up her cheeks.

Confirmation: Lizzy Clemente was in love.

"Are you going to tell him that you're not who you say you are?"

"Are you going to tell your father that you're not who you pretend to be?" she challenged.

"That's different—it's complicated. I'm dealing with Old World traditional values born out of generations of narrow-mindedness not to mention religious beliefs."

She turned her back on him to make a cappuccino for a patron but suddenly stopped then took a step toward him. Standing beside him, she leaned close to his ear, placing a comforting hand upon his forearm. The look upon her face conveyed compassion and he welcomed whatever she had to say.

Elizabeth spoke quietly, "Toni, I understand. It's exactly my reason for … um de-Italianizing myself. I can't deal with the stereotyping and bigotry. I shouldn't have to. I am not defined by my ancestors or the neighborhood I grew up in."

"I hear you; my character and worth shouldn't be devalued or limited because of what I wear, but I don't want to break the old man's heart. It's a stereotypical machismo thing, like wife beater T-shirts and mistresses."

"But, your father loves you, just like Dharma. He'd accept you and your miniskirts no matter what."

Toni closed the cash register drawer and bid his customer good-bye. "Number 31," he announced before replying. "And I bet this Mike feels the same way about you. It's no different at all."

"Ha! You're just using my argument to make your case as it applies to my love life."

"And you're using my argument to make your point. We're two of a kind, Lizzy. Dharma is the first person to accept and love my uniqueness. My ex-wife couldn't and she left me over a decade ago. You might be surprised by this guy. He hardly acted the macho type when I opened the apartment door wearing a Japanese kimono."

Elizabeth gasped as she placed a cannoli into a small white box. "Was your father home?"

"No he had left for church already."

"Well, Mike does love Italian pastry and … and … our building and the tenants. That's a good sign, and I'm sure he thought nothing about your robe."

"Exactly my point."

"Yes, exactly my point about your father. How about I consider being completely honest with Mike, if you give thought to being honest with your father."

"After Christmas," he vowed with a head nod.

The bell above the bakery door jingled, but instead of greeting the new customer, Elizabeth turned to Toni, and placed the box on the counter. She smiled. "Yeah, after Christmas. Do we have a deal?"

"Yeah, we have a deal."

The customer with slicked-backed, wind tunnel tested hair, pushed his way to the front of the crowd then depressed the number dispenser lever. He leaned against the glass cookie counter.

Elizabeth wiped a hand on the front of the apron she wore as she walked toward Toni. Right there to a unison "aww" from the onlookers, they hugged each other.

"Please keep your word, Lizzy. You'll be back in LA on the 28th. Tell him before it's too late. Give him the opportunity to prove you wrong before you leave with regret."

~**~

The den at the Garin family home was a comfortable space that Mike had redecorated specifically for his and Mia's taste upon the departure of Candy and his father. A leather, contemporary sectional faced the gas fireplace and flat screen TV at the center of two floor-to-ceiling, recessed bookcases filled with their favorites. He sat in the club chair, enjoying the soothing relief of an espresso as the fire held his sole focus with Mozart's "Sleigh Ride" playing around him. Although he appeared to watch the dance of flame in the grate, his thoughts obsessed on the situation now before him. Meeting Elizabeth had been an absolute serendipitous occasion; he was sure of it, but felt unsure if she would see it the same way. It seemed contrived and opportunistic on his part, wooing the woman to acquire a piece of property. Wasn't that what Stella had wanted all along? He wondered if Elizabeth already knew who he was. Maybe *she* was playing *him*.

"What do you think of this holly here?" Mia asked, snapping him from his intense stare.

He looked up, barely acknowledging her question about the swag she held against the mantle. "It's nice."

"Gee, that's helpful. This is so unlike you to not take part in holiday decorations." She placed the holly bough on the coffee table then sat on the sofa opposite him. "What's up with you? Is it about your big *sleepover* last night?"

"Sort of. Did you tell Stella about my date in the Bronx?"

"What are you kidding? I didn't even put it on Facebook. I swear! I'm trying to go cold turkey."

"That's good." He paused, swirling the coffee in the demitasse cup. "What ... did you think of PalHairMo?"

"Why? Are you having a sudden change of heart about buying it?"

"I'm just wondering. Rusty is having difficulties and I've offered to help him out with a Botox party at Halo on the 26th. The Clemente sisters did a nice job on your hair, and I'm looking for a little feedback about them."

She abruptly stood. "Don't do it. I love those girls. They're just what Etonville needs."

"How so?"

Her hands and arms began a diatribe with movements the likes of which he had never seen from his sister. "First off, look at this haircut. It's awesome, and my followers on Instagram agree! Secondly, I felt like I was one of their own—*mi famiglia*, ya know! We ate, drank, gossiped, and they played the coolest music. I danced!—hell, we all danced, even their cross-dressing receptionist, *and* I received a pedicure to die for. They've got one hell of a marketing strategy!"

She kissed her pinched fingertips with ethnic proficiency, and he couldn't help but to snigger.

"Lizzy is *magnifico*!" she exclaimed. "I'd love to have the Clementes as sisters—they're that cool! The oldest, Gina, well she's got the hots for Rusty—big time—She calls him her big red devil, and Nicki, the youngest ..." Mia sat down again and whispered loudly, "She's brash and fun and dating Joey of all people."

"What!?"

She laughed. "You heard me, and I heard *her* call him her pistol man when he came into PalHairMo the day I got my haircut."

Mike downed the espresso. "You've got to be kidding?"

"I'm not kidding. If you buy that building and close their salon, I'll be seriously mad at you. I'm totally girl crushing on all of them and hope they'll be a success. The gossip alone is friggin' worth the trip up to Westchester County. Who the heck needs Facebook when you have PalHairMo!"

He placed the red cup down with a clink upon the saucer. "You liked this *Lizzy* person?"

Mia raised an eyebrow. "Why?"

"Just wondering."

"You wonder a lot of things. Yes, I liked Lizzy. She's the salon's pedicurist …" She began to back out of the room with a sly grin. When she reached the threshold of the door leading into the foyer, she burst out laughing. "… and I think she'd make a great sister-in-law provided you can convince her not to move back to LA. *Then* you can sell the condo."

Shocked at her assertion, he shouted, "Mia! Get back here!"

"Sorry, Bro. I think Grandmother is here."

Astounded, Mike rose and walked to the fireplace. Placing one hand upon the mantle, he gazed down into the flames below. "She knew Elizabeth was a Clemente, but did Elizabeth know that Mia was my sister? She's acting as a pedicurist. Well I'll be damned."

Stella entered the study at the pronouncement of his last sentence.

"Why will you be damned?" she asked, actually conveying a modicum of concern in her voice.

"Hello, Grandmother," came from his lips with warmth and sincerity in spite of the events of the morning and Mia's disclosure. He kissed her cheek. "You look lovely today."

"Don't bullshit me. Why will you be damned, Michael?"

"No reason, just work issues, the holidays. You know, the usual stresses this time of year. Are you hungry? I made shrimp and mushroom risotto. I hope that's okay?"

"It sounds delightful."

So far, so good. She seemed in an amiable mood. He looked around her to see if Ann was in attendance.

"Antoinette is at home. It's just as well. Late last night she had decided on a snack from the pantry and is now suffering from severe flatulence. She's an obstinate, headstrong bitch."

"Whoa. Those are harsh words."

"Yes, they are. Tomorrow I will be spending a fortune, taking her to a holistic doctor to address her digestive issues. Who knew that when she came to reside with me that she'd bleed me dry!"

"Unfortunately, you took her in as a companion before getting to know her. At your age you should have thought that through."

"My age! Bah!"

Mike led the way from the den to the never-used formal dining room where three place settings were laid out. Ever attentive to their grand-mother's hoped-for nonna triggers, Mia made sure to use their mother's Waterford goblets and Tiffany Christmas china, a set Theresa received from Stella on her first wedding anniversary. Mia even managed to put together a last-minute centerpiece using candles, ribbon, and holly.

"The table looks lovely, Mia. You outdid yourself."

Mike smiled, secretly thanking his sister. In spite of her anger over Ann's gas, they were two-for-two in pleasing the red-haired hellion.

Lunch commenced with Mia serving. She was more than happy to be a third wheel in this conversation as it unfolded.

"I wanted to discuss this issue of Villa Fortuna with you personally, not over the phone. I apologize for upsetting your plans this afternoon, but there are things I need to *show* you," Stella said.

Mike shifted in his seat, resting his utensil down upon the side of his dish. "I've been doing some thinking about my investment as well and …"

"Let me finish. I know that I'm not one to give compliments freely, but in this case, I want you to know how proud I am of you." She placed a forkful of risotto into her mouth.

"Um. Thank you?" Yes, it was a question because he wasn't quite sure if he heard her correctly.

"This risotto is sublime. Authentic Tuscan. I'm impressed, Michael. Your culinary skills are superb."

Mia's eyes widened at the compliments flowing from Stella's mouth—even with food in it. She looked to Mike and their eyes locked. A slight smile formed upon his lips.

"Thank you, Grandmother."

They ate in companionable conversation with Stella even going so far as to flatter Mia's new hairstyle, adding that Rusty is the best in Eton-ville. It was wise not to contradict her; they had made such strides this afternoon.

"What is so important—apart from your generous compliments today?" Mike finally asked, his meal nearly complete, so sure that he would have lost his appetite earlier. Stella never came with good news, even if the compliments were diversionary.

She rose from her chair then walked to her briefcase from which she removed a large envelope. "As I said this morning, I am delighted that you took my advice by acquiescing to date one of the Clemente sisters. I have proof that the return of Villa Fortuna to a Russo heir will be easily attainable following your nuptials."

"Nuptials?"

"Yes, to the middle sister—Lizzy."

"If you don't mind me asking, just how did you find out that I took her to dinner last night?"

Stella's lack of expression said everything: I'm Stella De Luca. I know it all. "My source, a man of great skill and information has, at my instruction, proceeded with active surveillance."

"And who is 'this source'?"

"You know him. Gino Famizi's grandson is the private investigator who began it all."

She slid a thick stack of 8x10 glossy photographs from the envelope. "These were messengered to me first thing this morning. They attest to the fact that family is low class dirty Sicilians."

Mike shook his head then ran his fingers through his hair. "I have to object to these slurs, Grandmother. Elizabeth is not—"

"Your acting proficiency, as evident from these photographs, is convincing," she cut him off, holding out a few slick photos for his examination.

Taking them in hand, he was appalled to see his memories with Elizabeth on film: Elizabeth and him holding hands, embracing at the Botanical Gardens, and even kissing her in the snow in front of the Christmas House. Each one of their four dates was captured for posterity.

"Three days before Christmas and this is what you bring into my home?" A deep sigh left his lips before Mia tugged the photos from his tightening grasp.

"Smooth kiss, Mike. How'd you get her to lie down in the snow?"

He tugged the images from her fingers. "We slipped! All right? Stella, this is beyond the pale. You've had me followed and photographed like

I'm some criminal, or worse yet a celebrity stalked by the paparazzi!"

"It's not like you're not used to it. Even I read about your dating and carousing activities on the MAA Facebook page," she huffed in defense. "For God's sake, you're like a dog in heat! Thankfully you are putting that Italian passion of yours toward financial gain and revenge."

"I'm getting a headache. Let me see the rest of those."

She held them back from his reach. "The point I'm making, Michael, is that you have set up the perfect scenario. Marry this woman and you have all the evidence you need for a quickie divorce. She's a cheating *puttana*."

"And I suppose the so-called evidence is what you are holding—those photographs?"

"Of course, these are only the stills. I have the video surveillance on my iPad if you would like to see."

He snapped. "Just give me the remaining damn photographs!"

Stella laid out the images one by one. At least a dozen of them revealed Elizabeth in various incriminating positions with four different men. All twelve images looked damning to his eye. The first, whom he already knew about, was the idiot they met in the conservatory. The photo showed them standing in front of the apartment building, then another caught his kiss to her cheek as he held her hand. Apparently, her ex was making strides in re-gaining her affections. Several others captured another guy also holding flowers that looked like carnations and of course, a kiss. This must be that Vinnie the lasagna jerk. There was also a third guy behind Messina's bakery counter—more hugging and kissing. He recognized him from the apartment building this morning. The last photographs, the one that gutted him, was a suave looking business professional. In one image, he kissed Elizabeth's hand. In another, he was touching her hair. The look upon his face spoke seduction. Mike sorted through the five photographs of this guy, his face growing more flushed with each one. The last one nearly broke his heart. Wining and dining, the guy held her hand across a restaurant table during … a romantic setting at … at … The Bull and Bear Prime Steakhouse at the Waldorf! He'd know that chandelier and décor anywhere. Crestfallen he bowed his head. She went to a hotel with him.

"That last one is Salvatore Carpo."

"Carpo!"

"Yes, the lawyer. She's having an affair with Dixon's Romano lawyer." Stella raised an eyebrow.

Her iPhone buzzed within her purse and she turned her attention from the shocked looks upon her grandchildren's faces."

Mike looked to Mia.

"Mike, I'm so sorry. I didn't know. I swear."

He narrowed his eyes, hoping she understood his wish that she keep away from PalHairMo.

After retrieving the mobile, Stella smiled, her red lips twisting. "Apparently, she didn't waste any time after you left the Bronx. This was taken by Famizi at ten this morning."

She held the phone out to Mike and his heart sank deeper; Elizabeth hugging guy number three in Messina Bakery.

"Didn't I tell you, Michael? She's a cheater and a liar, and lucky for you she has a thing for Italian men. You being number five. You've been played my boy, and she played right into our hands!"

_**_

~Twenty-Two~
Rimorso
(Remorse)

Finnegans restaurant in Etonville was usually packed on Sunday nights, especially during football season. Dark paneling and wood benches created an authentic Irish pub environment, especially with its large Guinness sign stretching from one end of the bar to the other. Famous for its extensive selection of craft beers on tap, this was the joint where local husbands flocked to for escape with like-minded buddies who, come Sunday evenings, couldn't wait to break free from their society wives and spoiled children. Very rarely did Westchester County's women venture into Finnegans even though their prices and food quality kept with the exclusivity of the village. Or maybe the hot barmaids made them feel uncomfortable. Besides, women hated restaurants with televisions broadcasting sports—and this place had twelve of them—and the faint stench of beer.

As upscale and relatively clean as Finnegans prided itself, it still always skeeved out Mike whenever he ate here, most likely because it was a veritable man cave. Not every business professional in the suburbs was as fastidious as he. Rusty was a prime example. Their European backpack trip the summer between sophomore and junior years of University attested to that fact. By his standards, the man was still a total slob: two day old socks on the floor, week old take-out boxes on the counter, leaving the toilet seat up. It was no wonder he loved the homey bachelor feel of this place. He shrugged. Maybe he had changed when Blair moved in with him.

The din was loud and boisterous as men of all ages cheered on their teams and examined their betting stats displayed behind the bar for each game. As soon as Rusty departed for the restroom, Mike, once again, wiped down the table with a napkin, feeling out of sorts. The entire day had passed and he had yet to call Elizabeth, only returning one of her texts with a brief "merry Christmas." He scrubbed at an invisible spot with his napkin, convincing himself that he had expressed his appreciation for the hospitality after he salted the apartment building's steps.

She was a cheating woman from a mob family, yet he still was attracted to her. His heart hurt and he silently chastised himself for not focusing on the all the positive things that made him fall hard for her in the first place. Condemnation without hearing her side of the story was unlike him, but he felt betrayed by what was evident in those photographs and further betrayed by the abandonment of his natural proclivity to look for perfection. He had an excuse though: she spellbound him from that first time he saw her. Admittedly, it was love at first sight. Had he not felt something deep for her then he never would have let their intimacy progress the way that it had on the sofa. He groaned audibly. Good God, the memory of the softness of her skin made his hands tingle. He licked his lips recalling the feel of her taut nipple surrounded by his mouth. Her seductive words whispered in the darkness echoed back at him, *"I need you, Mike. I want you."*

Rusty stood over him with a twisting smirk to his lips. "What's up with you, man? You're fidgeting tonight." He slid opposite Mike into the booth. "Are you trying to get out of the Botox party already?"

"No not at all."

"Lady troubles?"

"One in particular."

"I hope not Blair. I tried to reason with her, but it didn't do any good. She commissioned a Warhol-style Diptych of you for her condo. It's hanging in her bedroom, and I don't want to know why it's at the foot of her bed."

"She needs help." Mike sipped his beer.

"Or something."

"Not from me. I'm thinking of releasing her from my practice, actually. It's too much for me to handle. She telephoned last night when I was on a date, leaving a message about her missing an eyebrow. It was a Saturday night for Christ sake, and there I was kissing a gorgeous woman when my phone vibrates in my front pocket. It was, um, uncomfortable to say the least."

Rusty chortled. "I knew she'd call you. There was an accident at the salon and well, she ended up getting an eyebrow completely waxed off. Nothing a little penciling can't correct while she hibernates until seeing you for a hair transplant. I don't expect her at the Botox party."

"That's the best news I've had all day."

"You don't want to do it, do you?"

If asked that question about the party eight hours earlier, Mike's answer would have been a decided "no," but the events of the day changed that. "I can't think of anything I'd rather do more than help you kick PalHairMo's backside across Etonville, down to Little Italy, and back over to Los Angeles."

"Really? Why the change of heart?"

"You need help at the salon," Mike lied.

"Yeah, right. I'm sorry to say that's not enough incentive to get you to malign or compete with anyone. You only play dirty pool when it comes to your father, your step-monster, and Kyle Petty when he stole Olivia Hasselbeck from you in the tenth grade."

Mike sighed. "Well add Elizabeth Fairchild to that list. I'm ready to roll up my sleeves and get ugly."

A furrow to Rusty's brow made Mike correct himself. "Lizzy Clemente."

"What about her?"

"*She's* the woman I was kissing." He cleared his throat. "Man, I thought she was *the one*."

"What do you mean *the one*? The one who's destroying Halo with those medical anti-fungal pedicures she's giving? The one whose baked goods are so incredible that they make my cupcakes taste like packaged processed shit? The one whose smile and beauty mark can disarm any man harboring ill will?"

"Yes, those things—except maybe the last one—but she's also the one I have fallen in love with over the last three weeks. The one I seriously thought was *the* one."

Stunned, Rusty set his drink down on the table and sat back. "Holy shit. You're in love with Lizzy the sexiest leg of the Trinacria? Did you know who she was when you started to date her?"

"No! I just thought she was a visiting physician from LA, having met her at a surgical conference. She goes by her married name and barely shared anything about her family. Only just yesterday I met her sisters at their apartment in Little Italy, and I can see why she kept them a secret."

"That sounds judgmental. It must be the beer talking."

"That's not what I mean. *She* was ashamed. She's different from Nicki and Gina, but it doesn't take away the fact that she lied about other things, a lot of things."

"You know, your grandmother is going to kill you for fraternizing with the enemy. Does she know?"

"Yes and she's pleased about it! She came for lunch this afternoon happily bearing her photographic arsenal of Elizabeth with all her other lovers. I saw the proof right there: she's been in town only three weeks and has a string of guys on the side while dating me. I'm number five."

He bowed his head again, his hand gripping the beer glass. "I should have known she was like all the others. Every time we went out, she was the aggressor wanting to jump in the sack on our first date. She's no different after all."

"Wow. She was so nice. They came to the aid of the salon yesterday when all hell broke loose. Wait … does she know that you're the one trying to buy Villa Fortuna? Shit! Do you think Gina told her? She was sneakily at the salon that day when the PalHairMo sign went up. There's no doubt that she overheard our conversation."

"I don't know, but I'm assuming she does. I feel so played. I thought she was different from all the other women I've dated. To make matters worse, Joey confirmed that the Clemente family is mob, which puts my cousin in a tenuous position since he's screwing the youngest sister. Both her grandfather and father were labor union executives with the Teamsters."

"As in Jimmy Hoffa Teamsters?"

"Yeah. My grandmother tells me that the Clemente sisters' father was whacked. Elizabeth confirmed it in a roundabout way. Poetic justice since Joey's investigation into the family revealed the strong possibility that their great-grandfather 'The Mouth' killed my great-grandfather 'Scarface' in '36."

"Mike, I gotta tell you, this is the best damn gossip I have ever heard. It's like *The Godfather Part Four*. To think, my little blonde Easter bunny comes from a rough crowd. All that sweet sugar and fluffy goodness, and she's connected to the Cosa Nosta and a hood nicknamed 'The Mouth'.

It does things to me. I wonder if she packs heat."

"You're happy about this?"

"Of course I'm not happy. I just don't give a shit and neither should you. Just because their father may have run with wise guys, doesn't mean the Clemente sisters do. Shit, your own grandmother has a history with them, so what should you care?"

"That's right ... you're Gina's big red devil. Rusty Magic fingers," Mike snarkily said.

"What?"

"Of course you're sympathetic. You're sleeping with the eldest sister."

"No!" Rusty looked away from Mike's heated gaze. "Well, not yet, but that's the plan. I'm going to invite her out for dinner and dancing on New Year's Eve."

"Do you hear yourself, Rusty? You want to kick her salon's ass yet you want to date her! Jeez, what's with these women? They've put a spell on the entire village, captivating every man and woman who comes in contact with them. Even my own sister is girl crushing, forbidding me from buying Villa Fortuna."

"Of course she's crushing. It's 'cause they have Sicilian blood in them. Sicilian women are incredible!"

"Since when have you developed this exalted opinion about Sicilian women?"

"I've always had it. I just never counted on them being such talented business women, too."

"Yeah, well, Elizabeth is all those things, but she's still a cheater and I don't date cheaters." Mike bowed his head, expelling a deep breath. "I really fell for her."

"I'm sorry, man."

"I'm ashamed to say that I'm so angry with her, that I want to put them out of business and am excited to throw my hat into the ring of salon warfare. The quicker she leaves town the happier I'll be." *Do I really mean that?*

Mike's phone beeped an incoming text from Elizabeth.

His face felt flush, either from the beer or the rising unprecedented anger as he read the text: *Call me. I'd like to invite you to something special.* He didn't reply. His heart was breaking. With a tap, he turned off the phone.

_~**~_

Mistakes in the beauty business are common occurrences, especially in Hollywood, but Alfred Greenwald was in the foot business, not facial reconstruction. Hidden within a shoe, screw-ups can't readily be seen, but everyone notices a gimp, and in this town that could destroy a career. But there are other screw-ups that aren't so obvious—those of poor decisions and regret.

His dimly lit home office felt like a comforting lair as he thumbed through the magazine in his hands. His wife called up the stairs stating something about meeting him in bed. She was going to read for a while. It was best that she didn't see the strain to his brow or the anxiety behind his eyes. How on earth had the practice gone to shit in just four weeks? He knew how: that Andrews woman, the one with the kid, who possibly has CP, made a stink, contacted the newspaper citing discrimination and demanding treatment by none other than Dr. Elizabeth Fairchild. Yes, it was Elizabeth's fault for promising the woman the world. He had all but fired her that day, but she had taken the bull by the horns herself, packed up her desk, and stormed out of WHPC in those knock-off Jimmy Choos of hers.

The other partners had been livid when she quit, no thanks to his mismanagement. One even felt confident that the junior associate would slap the practice and him with a sexual harassment lawsuit, given his history with other young, attractive interns and patients. What could he say? He loved women and had a thing for sexy feet. But he could acknowledge that he had hired Elizabeth for more legitimate reasons: her diagnostic skills and professionalism. Her curriculum vitae, among all the others submitted, had been the most impressive. Yet he failed to give her the opportunities to prove herself and excel at WHPC—all because he secretly wished she would attempt to get ahead by demonstrating *other* skills. That girl was all business though—all idealistic wanting to get the world walking—and she missed every one of his passes for lying down.

Greenwald ran a hand through his grey hair and sat back in his chair, once again, reading an article that *Panache* magazine sent to him via messenger on Friday afternoon. Advance print copies worked that way whenever publications mentioned West Hollywood Podiatry Center.

He didn't need to read it again, knowing it by heart now. Angered, his fingers twisted the magazine's edge. Of all the Cinderella bunionplastys performed by his practice's notable physicians, it would be Elizabeth's surgery on the B-lister back in August that would make it into one of the fashion world's most respected magazines. Scheduled to hit the stands in one week, he needed to hustle with some serious wooing. Greenwald had to get Elizabeth back. He'd do anything because once this article hit the stands, there were going to be a lot of disappointed, even angry film moguls, agents, and stars.

He turned the slick page of the fashion magazine, shaking his head as he looked at the image of those half-million dollar bridal stilettos made famous by Elizabeth's acumen at hiding scars. Who would have expected that Ms. Rhonda Mills, supporting actress of her first movie "Gwendolyn's Trashy Vampire," was marrying one of Bollywood's biggest A-lister stars in a multi-million dollar musical wedding broadcast on India's Zoom TV! It was the wedding of the year and every Hollywood and Bollywood celebrity had been invited. He read it again:

The bride credits her West Hollywood foot and ankle surgeon for making this day possible. After suffering for years with painful bunions, the ugly bump at the side of her foot, she finally decided to take the plunge into podiatric cosmetic surgery. "Everyone does it in Hollywood, face lifts, scalp reduction, lipo, but I resisted. I mean, it's not as if I can't stand on my own two feet when it comes to beauty or acting, but literally, I was having a difficult time getting into my 142-carat diamond sandals for the big day. Honestly, Dr. Elizabeth Fairchild saved my life, even postponing her travel plans to accommodate my tight schedule. Filming of "Trashy Vampire" was coming to a wrap, and I had barely enough time to breathe—or enough Vicodin for the pain to get through dance lessons for our Bollywood theme, but she was there at the ready. I had very little recovery swelling and my wedding day was pain free. Thanks to her, Deepak and I danced all night! I can't stress enough, if you want the best, you go to the best, and Dr. Fairchild is the best in the business. If only she did faces, I know quite a few women who are paying the price for a botched job.

Laying the magazine down, he sighed, ready to eat humble pie. He opened his laptop, focusing on this vital, career saving email, praying it wasn't too late.

~**~

~Twenty-Three~
Comunicazione
(Communication)

The cheery sounds of "Winter Wonderland" filled PalHairMo with Christmas spirit as blow-dryers worked their magic and Toni excelled as hostess with the mostest. They were so busy that Gina had to contact a few of her former classmates from Angelina's Beauty School to come to the rescue as temporary stylists and manicurists. Honestly, the sisters could not believe the sudden rush, the begging insistence for an appointment before Christmas, demanding trendy styles and highlights by the now famous Picasso.

Sitting in the office awaiting her next client, Elizabeth could hear the laughter at the front of the salon, three women cackling at a joke Nicki had made when guy number 14 entered the salon. That girl had made eight hundred dollars last week in tips, a lot more than she would have made working in Atlantic City—on her feet, that is.

She smiled thinking things were finally where they should be for her sisters. They had found their niche and the neighborhood embraced them and all this "culture" they brought with them. She knew first hand that one can never resist an authentic cannoli or a good time with girlfriends, finding both on her return home. Yes, home, and in spite of the second fight she had with Gina over all these secrets *both* of them were keeping, erecting the fresh Christmas tree and telephoning their mamma seemed to set everything right. She hadn't felt this happy in a long time when it came to accepting who she really was. Returning to the foundation of her life had changed her, and now, standing on the precipice of decisions, she considered telling her sisters that she was staying in New York permanently. She wanted what they had!

Lost in number crunching, Elizabeth tried not to think of Mike, feeling bereft that he hadn't called after leaving the apartment the morning before. Last night's two word text hardly was romantic, and she had hoped that he'd call her following her own text. As proud as she was of her sisters, she couldn't help the niggling suspicion that they—and the apartment—scared him away. Although, his usual polite self, she could see how at breakfast he picked up his fork using a napkin clenched between his fingers. Just as she had always believed, bacteria would be a Clemente's eventual downfall. She hoped she was jumping to the wrong conclusion now that she decided to tell him that she wasn't All-American Connecticut hoity-toity, and that the hyphen in her ethnicity usually came with uninformed, hurtful negativity. She sighed in realization that she, too, had enacted that same prejudgment during her absence. He'd be compassionate but she was sure that he couldn't relate.

Her phone beeped and she jumped, hoping, nay begging, that it was Mike on this beautiful Monday morning, two days before Christmas. Disappointed, she saw that it was an email from the *cazzo* Greenwald of all people. A tap to the phone brought it before her.

Dear Dr. Fairchild,

The partners and I would like to extend our sincere apology for my unprofessional conduct last month.

From the beginning of your employment at West Hollywood Podiatry, we have been impressed by your patient care, each leaving satisfied with the outcomes they had sought. Your compassion to every individual's fears and desires was tantamount to forming medical relationships that will extend into second and third generations of care.

I acknowledge that I was mistaken in referring patient Brandon Andrews away from your expertise and management. I was wrong to have rescinded your vacation, as promised by me three months prior.

In a nutshell, we would like for you to consider returning to employment at West Hollywood. The partners have agreed on a new well-deserved contract, elevating you to Senior Podiatric Associate with a compensation package of equal pay ($185,000) and full benefits to our other physicians (Profit sharing, 401k 100% match, school loan payment.) As a senior associate, you will have the option of full partner within three years, should you choose to pursue that opportunity. A new office is awaiting you, as well as a patient load that *reflects your vision of podiatric medicine and surgery.*

WHPC is committed to meeting the needs of all patients, not just those seeking cosmetic alteration. You will be the solo sub-specialist within our practice to handle ankle and foot reconstruction, wound care, and other lower extremity orthopedic surgeries deemed necessary by you.

I hope you will think about our offer, Dr. Fairchild. We regret the events of November and humbly ask for your thoughtful consideration to rejoin WHPC as a valued team member.

Sincerely,

Alfred Greenwald, DPM

Elizabeth's heart raced. *Holy shit.* She had worked hard for this compensation package. This was the career track she had always imagined. *Holy shit.* Acknowledgement, respect, success in Hollywood!

Mike was the only telephone call she wanted to make.

After pressing speed dial, she listened to the hopeful rings, praying it wouldn't go to voicemail, willing him to pick up. Bubbling over in excitement, she nearly bounced in her seat, her spirit flying in anticipation. She wanted to laugh and clap her hands with glee! *Pick up! Please pick up!*

"Hi Elizabeth," he answered. Blood rushed to her temples upon hearing his bland greeting.

"Hi Mike! I'm so glad I got you between patients. How are you?"

"Busy. I'm actually running into a consultation. What's up?"

"I um … did you get my text last night?"

"Oh did you text? I'm sorry, I was out with a friend, and I must have missed it."

Trying to stifle the crack to her voice, her heart seized. "I did. I wanted to invite you and your sister to Our Lady of Mount Carmel church for midnight Mass on Christmas Eve. It's a big thing in Belmont, and I was wondering if you'd like to go with me." *There I did it, taking the first step to complete honesty!*

"Our Lady of Mount Carmel, huh? I don't know. I'll have to see."

The chill in his voice paralyzed her, that cold brush-off that usually came when men moved on or were cheating, but she clung to the little hope in her heart, believing that Mike wasn't that kind of guy. "I know it's probably a little forward of me to ask you for a date, but I'd love to usher in Christmas with you. Maybe we could go to dinner beforehand. There's a fabulous Italian restaurant on Arthur Avenue."

"Like I said, I don't know. What time for dinner?"

She swallowed the lump in her throat. "Maybe nine, but you could come early to the apar—"

He cut her off, "I have to go. Thanks for calling and, I'll, um, try to work it into my schedule. If not, I hope you and your sisters have a merry Christmas."

Her heart sunk at his obvious kiss-off and a hand went to her forehead. Try as she might, the despair was evident when she spoke. "Right. Well, just call me if you'd like to go to dinner, okay. Maybe I'll see you at Mass. Anyway, um, thank you for a wonderful date Saturday night."

Biting her lip, she tried to keep it from quivering, the tears unexpectedly welling when he paused.

Silence ensued for long seconds as she waited, holding her breath and listening to the thundering in her chest. The pain strangled her and she wiped the tear from her cheek. *Say something. Say yes. Say you had a good time. Say you miss me. Say you love me. Say anything, but just don't say goodbye.*

Mike sighed and quietly said, "Goodbye, Elizabeth."

He clicked off before she could wish him a Merry Christmas. A second tear trickled down her cheek, the silent phone remaining pressed to her ear. He had rejected her. The burgeoning love she felt for him was left to burn, unrequited, in her heart.

Unwilling to relinquish the phone, it remained clutched in her hand when she cradled her forehead upon her arm resting on the desk. She wept.

There were no words to describe the feeling of being on top of the world one minute then devastated the next. What went wrong? What happened? She should have asked, confronted him, but it was apparent that he was in no mood to discuss anything and it would have been unprofessional to get into it on his way to a patient. So much for her considering going through that open door—he wouldn't be on the opposite side waiting as he promised. Clearly, Sutton Place never mixed with Belmont, even if it was her sisters' address. Being honest with him about her upbringing was moot now. Telling him about her job offer, pointless. He had acted just as she feared he would when even a modicum of Lizzy Clemente exposed herself.

~**~

Ten minutes later, Elizabeth dried her eyes then cleaned the lipstick smeared across her cheek, determined that no one would be the wiser when she emerged from the office. She hung onto her father's saying from the Old Country: Smile even if you are sad, because there is nothing sadder than someone who doesn't know how to smile. With her Hollywood Face in place, she walked into the styling room with a false million-watt smile on her face.

Toni walked past her in the aisle between stylist chairs as he balanced a tray with three glasses of wine and two plates loaded with cream puffs. He loved his job and it showed. Today's outfit was a funky 1970s bell-bottom pantsuit. He looked like he belonged on re-runs of Soul Train with that black afro wig and hoop earrings he wore. Today was Funk Groove day, and boy, was her heart in a funk.

"You okay, doll?" he asked.

"Sure, what could possibly be wrong? It's Christmas!"

"Yeah, well the only time I've seen bloodshot eyes like that was when hashish brownies kicked my ass, and I know you don't do drugs."

"I'm good. Don't worry about me, just a little Retinitis Pigmentosa." She grinned even brighter, refusing to succumb to the overwhelming heartache.

He handed her a glass of wine then offered one to two women chatting in neighboring stylist chairs. "Now go easy with this stuff," he advised to one of the clients. "It's caused me to lose my way too many nights."

"Oh darling, I can drink with the best of them. I play bunko, and that's not for lightweights," the first woman said.

"Don't say I didn't warn you. Have some cream puffs." Toni danced away to Earth, Wind and Fire's holiday rendition of "September," his hips moving to the funk.

Hiding behind the rim of the wine glass, Elizabeth tried not to meet Gina's traveling gaze as she passed her station, so sure that her sister would ask about the bloodshot eyes. The blonde in the chair was one of the salon's first clients, Rebecca, the funeral home director, and Elizabeth caught a snippet of conversation.

"Did you get your second date with that Romeo?" Gina asked.

"No, but I'll be seeing him the evening of the 26th at Halo. They're having a special event. I'm hoping to make an impression on him. That's why I just had to see you Gina. You're single, you understand what it's like out there. A woman has to do whatever it takes to capture the man she wants."

"Don't I know it, girlfriend."

Elizabeth smirked hearing that tone in Gina's voice. Who was she kidding, she didn't have to do anything to get Rusty's attention. After PalHairMo's first bridal updo party, he was taking her out on New Year's Eve and all she did to secure that date was to bat her eyes and bring him some rainbow cookies. Oh, and save his salon from child demolition. The guy was putty in her hands, and honestly, she was happy for her. Gina really liked Rusty.

"Why I'm not even opposed to standing naked on a street corner to get that man's attention!" Rebecca blurted as Gina continued to cut her hair.

One of the women, Sandy, whose head was covered with layered foil packs of hair, turned. "Oh my! Did you hear about Ann?"

Everyone stopped dead, giving her all their attention because the whole village knew Ann—because everyone knew Stella.

"Do tell, darling. I love good gossip about Stella De Luca. She's one of my least favorite people in this village," Ellen, another client said.

"Well ..."

The blow-dryers turned off and everyone leaned in. Nicki popped a cream puff in her mouth, grinning as she chewed.

"It turns out that Ann has been sneaking out of Hillside Manor every night. Personally, I haven't seen her, but my husband has on several occasions, usually late Sunday nights when he leaves Finnegans after the football game. She's been hanging around the pub, trying to cozy up to the men as they come out."

"What a hussy!" Toni laughed with Dharma adding, "I wonder if she got lucky!"

Gina snorted. "Oh Gawd, I bet the devil's whore would die if she knew that. I'm sure Finnegans isn't fine enough for her discerning palate."

"Devil's whore?" Rebecca asked.

"Yes, just something our great-aunt used to call Mrs. De Luca."

"I can relate. I met her at Rao's and she was evil personified."

"Wait, there's more." Sandy continued, "The other night, someone spotted Ann sleeping in the gutter by a street corner in Eastchester. Her coat was torn and her hair was matted and dirty. She smelled like a brewery and cheap cologne. The sheriff described her as being disoriented and confused without identification. Thank goodness one of the deputies recognized her and drove her back home to Stella's."

"I'm sure Stella will be ending that relationship very quickly," Elizabeth chimed in. "I met someone the other day, who mentioned that the woman spends thousands on Ann's holistic medical care."

"It's true," stated a client in the reception area, coming over to participate in the gossip about the woman who ruined her husband's home inspection business. "Ann farts everywhere."

Now that got Elizabeth laughing. God this was great stuff to temporarily distract her from Mike.

"Yup, that's right." Ellen agreed. "We could be sitting in the Town Council meeting, and she'll break wind right there. Sneaky toxic fumes that smell like baby poop. Once, we had to move to another conference room then she farted there, too. The president wanted to banish her from the room, but Stella wouldn't hear of it."

"I met Ann at a restaurant and the poor thing was obviously starving so I offered her the leftovers. Of course, meatballs from Rao's are nothing to sneeze at. I could see it in her eyes, she wanted those balls," Rebecca declared. "I wanted my date's balls, but she wanted a different kind of meat."

"It's a shame, really, because Ann isn't such a bitch; she's very sweet when you get to know her. I'd run away from Hillside Manor just to get some lovin', too," Ellen said.

"Yo, I actually dig the way she dresses. She's got awesome outfits and those pink sunglasses and matching hoodie are rad. It's her jewelry that sucks. That Pal•Hair•NO!! button totally pisses me awf," Nicki said.

"That's just what the devil's whore wants to do—piss us awf and make us leave," Gina said.

The front door jingled and a dark haired guy wearing a suit and overcoat walked in holding a briefcase. Everyone turned.

"*Ciao*! Welcome to PalHairMo," Gina greeted as Toni strolled over to the visitor.

"I'm looking for the Clemente sisters," the diminutive man said as he nervously toyed with his bowtie.

"I'm Elizabeth. How can I help you?"

"I'm John Zavanella, Inspector with the New York State Liquor Authority. We have received a complaint that your beauty parlor is serving alcohol. I've been sent to investigate." His left eye twitched.

Toni nodded to Nicki before stepping forward to play hostess. "Pal, can I take your coat?"

"There's no need. I can see the illegal wine on that counter there."

"But we've already filed the necessary paperwork through the proper channels," Toni said.

"Paperwork? Application? Nothing crossed my desk. My report will only take a few minutes." His eye twitched again.

Nicki walked through the crowd of gossiping women, mumbling under her breath, "We'll see about that." She pulled her sweater down a bit, thrusting her shoulders back with determination. Number 15 had just walked through the door and she had better make this a good one. "Step aside, sistas, and watch the masta work her stuff on how to win a guy over." Her thumb pointed to her chest. "If you can't dazzle 'em with brains, baffle 'em with boobage."

Blow-dryers came back to life and business as usual commenced with Elizabeth shaking her head. She was going to miss this if she went back to LA. As of twenty minutes ago with Mike's cool ambivalence and brush off, she was now undecided.

"Hi I'm Nicki, the youngest-with-the-mostest sister. Is this your first visit to PalHairMo?" she asked sauntering up to him as he removed his coat.

"It is, and not a moment too soon. You're serving alcoholic beverages without a proper permit. I could have you arrested, fined at the very least."

Nicki twirled the end of her dark hair in an index finger and put on a sweet baby voice. This act was a new one for Elizabeth, having not seen this level of naughty manipulation from her sister before.

"Yeah, well you can't slight us girls for spreadin' a little Christmas cheer. We aim to please in our salon." Her foot playfully twisted slightly as she jutted her hip invitingly. She bit her lip and batted her long lashes. "*I* aim to please."

No doubt, Prozia turned in her grave.

Gina blessed herself, the scissors almost poking an eye and nipple out.

Elizabeth thought she heard Toni say, "Work it. You go, girl," as if a prostitute in the movie *Pretty Woman*. She tried to ignore that implication, remaining focused on the twitching left eye of Mr. Zavanella trained on the boobage.

"Follow me, big guy, and I'll give ya some cheer in the back," Nicki said, taking the tip of his red bowtie between her fingers. "My specialty is a titillatin' wet scalp massage followed by one of Gina's blow jobs. Are you in?"

"In? Blow? Um … I have a report …"

"Don't you worry about nuthin'. That wine ain't goin' nowhere and neither is your report. You deserve to chill out for a bit. I'm sure your job is very demanding."

"It is. I should chill. Is the homemade wine good?"

"Yeah … real good."

Like a lost puppy dog, he followed Nicki down the aisle of the salon, his eye twitching, and his stare to the exaggerated sway of her backside, obvious.

She glanced over her shoulder. "So tell me, was it Mrs. De Luca who cawled you?"

"Um …"

Nicki stopped, turning to face him. Her painted fingernails skimmed through his short hair. "You can tell me. I won't bite … hard."

"Yes. Mrs. De Luca," he gave up the second she winked.

"See, was that so *hard*?" She turned on her stilettos. "Toni bring us some of that vino, *pronto*."

Thirty minutes after the boobage manipulation and a Gina blow out, the inspector stood below the *Arrivederci* sign above the front door. He hiccupped. "I like your hair salon, Nicki. It's very friendly and the wine is the best I've had in a long time."

"So you won't be givin' us no summons or whatever it is you give?"

"No. I'll send your license by FedEx as soon as I get back to my office on Mulberry Street."

"You have an awefice in downtown Little Italy?"

"I do. I'm connected to some powerful people who are connected to Mrs. De Luca, but you won me over. I'll put in a good word for you ladies."

"Yeah? I won you ova?"

"Sure, you're a brilliant businesswoman, and cute too. I enjoyed talking with you."

"You mean ... I dazzled you with brains?"

He handed Nicki his business card. "You did. I could use an undercover investigator like you, someone who thinks fast and uses everything at her disposal to uncover the truth. Too many establishments are serving alcohol without permits. If you're ever considering a career change, give me a call, or if you're interested, call me anyway and I'll take you out for dinner."

Nicki snorted. "It would only be dinner 'cause I don't give it up for just anyone." She leaned closer to him. "Don't tell my sistas, 'cause they think I'm easy, but ya know, I'm all talk and no action."

He smiled. "That's good to hear."

"Are you Italian?"

"With a name like Zavanella?"

"Well *that's* good to hear. Do you like zeppolis?"

He chortled and fidgeted with his bow tie. "Merry Christmas, Nicki. Call me, and we'll paint the town red, green, and white."

"Merry Christmas, Johnnycakes."

Folding her arms at her waist, she stood watching his retreating back through the door. He was the first guy to see through her bullshit as they talked over his scalp massage. Not even Joey her pistol man recognized that she had a brain above her boobs, but maybe that was her fault. Investigative work wasn't for her, even if she had the skills. She'd never leave PalHairMo; the Trinacria depended on three legs.

⁓**⁓

Italian Cream Puffs

½ cup shortening
¼ teaspoon salt
1 cup water
1 cup sifted all purpose flour
4 eggs, unbeaten

Place shortening, salt, and water in medium saucepan. Bring water to boil and stir until shortening is melted. Add flour. Beat in saucepan over heat with mixer at low until mixture forms smooth mass and comes away from sides of pan, about 30 seconds. Remove from heat. Add eggs one at a time. Beat mixture at medium for 30 seconds after addition of each egg, scraping sides and bottom of pan with rubber spatula occasionally during mixing.

Drop by spoonfuls 2 inches apart on greased baking sheets. Bake in oven 450°F for 10 minutes. Reduce heat to 400°F, bake for 25 minutes longer.

Makes 18 large puffs

Filling
¼ cup sugar
1 egg yolk
¼ cup flour
1 cup milk
1 tbsp rum
Lemon peel

In a medium pot add sugar and egg yolk, whisk together then add flour and a piece of lemon peel, approximately 1 inch, mix together. Heat milk in a small pot on medium heat. When it has almost started to boil, remove from heat and slowly add to the egg, flour mixture whisking until well blended. Heat mixture stirring continuously with the whisk until cream becomes thick. Remove from heat, add rum and continue to stir for a couple of minutes. Place in a bowl and cover with plastic wrap, making sure to touch plastic to cream so it doesn't form a coating on top. Bring to room temperature then fill pastry.

~Taken from Bressan family recipe

~Twenty-Four~
Vigilia di Natale
(Christmas Eve)

Christmas Eve should never feel lonely, particularly when one is surrounded by friends and family, but for Elizabeth, it felt gut wrenching and empty. Worse than how it felt for the last eight years eating leftovers alone in her rental. "The Messina Famiglia," as she referred to all their friends in the building, arrived dressed with bells on at Mrs. Zeppo's tiny apartment. With wine and gifts in hand, they beamed in the resplendent joy of the holiday. The gifts of love, life, and family burst from their hearts upon entering the festive apartment filled with Italian song. Even Dharma attended, arriving on Toni's arm, both dressed wearing floral print dresses and dazzling smiles.

That alone had been cause to celebrate. Toni had kept his word, discussing with his father and the priest at OLMC his proclivity for women's apparel. No one at the dinner table gave particular scrutiny to his outfit, although Mr. Graciosa did a double take, rubbed his aged eyes, focused, then downed a juice glass of wine. Apart from that, it seemed as though everyone had already known for years, including Mr. Primo, and they certainly hadn't condemned Toni for being in touch with his feminine side. They loved him, and as Elizabeth had conveyed to him two days prior, they didn't judge—unlike Mike. Toni had been sadly wrong on that account.

The traditional Italian Christmas Eve meal consisted of seven fishes, right down to the smelly bacala codfish Mrs. Zeppo had prepared with proficiency. Her guests didn't mind the three cats or being squished together at an antique table and two connected card tables. Instead, they laughed, ate, and enjoyed being together. Closing the holiday festivity with Mrs. Genovese's special dessert, one of Gina's favorites, frozen biscuit tortoni topped with a maraschino cherry had been a delicious highlight. There was no denying on Elizabeth's part that the night would have been perfect if not for her empty heart missing Mike.

Following dinner and after opening gifts, she and her sisters had traipsed in the cold and snow to Midnight Mass. Elizabeth remained hopeful, anticipating his arrival to services, diligently sitting at the back of the nave so as not to miss him when he came in, but it was for naught. Mike hadn't shown. With each passing tradition of the liturgy, her heart sank a little more. Twice she almost cried: first listening to the recitation of the Gospel and again when offering her pew neighbors the sign of peace by kisses and handshakes. When the angelic voices of the children's choir filled the traditional church, she was sure she would lose it, convinced that Mike would have loved this celebration of the Nativity. They had yet to attend services together and, truth be told, this was the first Christmas Mass she'd been to in over a decade, but the hope of his arrival propelled her to take the step. Attendance on his arm would have taken away all trepidation. Mike's previous words about coming home resonated in her heart opening it once again to visit the foundation of her youth … her faith. She wanted to attend Mass with him every Sunday.

That night of her true return to church coincided with the sorrow she felt at his brush-off seemed entirely appropriate. Receiving the Holy Eucharist felt like an all-encompassing embrace of forgiveness, love, and understanding, but it hadn't been enough to take away the emptiness of unrequited love.

Now, at almost three in the morning, she focused on how much she had to be thankful for this Christmas: first (and most importantly) her sisters and this time that they had had together; and second, the career she had dreamed of was waiting for her back in LA. She was also grateful for the time she had spent getting to know Mike and how he had made her trip home special, something that she was sure would be a fate worse than death. Up until this heartbreak, it had been the happiest she'd felt in a long time, considering she had feared returning home without her father awaiting her.

Since sleep was impossible and Gina's snores added to her distraction, she found herself in the kitchen doing what she did best: baking. Her eyes welled as she took her sorrow out on the batter-filled bowl before her, the beater doing a number in fast, furious rotations. With her back to the threshold, it was easy to block out the cheerful, colorful bulbs and the Christmas tree in the living room. Tonight there was no space in her heart or mind to focus on the holiness of the holiday. That feeling of childlike anticipation, which always came even as an adult, was nowhere to be found at this hour.

She marveled at her sidestepping ability not to let her sisters know about her heartache—but she had hid a lot of things, hadn't she? Then the tears flowed. Big, sobbing feeling sorry for herself tears at having let Mike get away fell into the cake batter. She hadn't counted on falling in love, but did. Oh God did she! Only he didn't want someone whose family wasn't as proper or wealthy as his. This was just as she had feared!

"What are you doing up, Lizzy?" Nicki inquired from behind, jolting Elizabeth.

"Oh! Nicki! You frightened me." She quickly dragged her free forearm over her face, wiping her tears.

"Sorry. Why are you baking?"

"I couldn't sleep. I'm just thinking about Daddy, life, my coming home, my leaving."

Nicki walked to the small countertop and dipped her finger into the batter, followed by a long suck to her index finger. "You're making panet-tone?"

Elizabeth glanced over her shoulder, meeting her sister's eyes. "Yeah. I realized we hadn't picked one up for breakfast and with Messina's closed for Christmas. ... it just wouldn't be a family holiday without it."

"You'll be at this all night. It takes foreva."

"I know," Elizabeth said stifling a sniffle as she changed the attachment at the end of the beater followed by the addition of flour to the mixture.

"I'm gonna miss you," Nicki blurted. "Don't go back to Tinseltown."

"I'll miss you, too, sweetie. I didn't think returning to the Bronx would be so fulfilling and I certainly didn't expect to like living with the two of you."

"It's 'cause Gina and I are awesome."

Elizabeth chuckled. "Yes, you are. I'm so proud of you both and so is Mamma. So, too, would Daddy and Aunt Maria be."

"I don't know about that. Prozia thought I was a *puttana*."

"Well you have to admit you do put out that vibe."

Nicki slid the vintage step stool chair beside Elizabeth. After taking a seat, she popped a few raisins into her mouth. "I know I'm a tease. I should work on that image. Johnnycakes wants to take me to dinner. I think he wants a good girl, and I don't want to ef this up."

"The liquor inspector guy?"

"Yeah. He's cute with that bow tie of his."

"Wow."

"I know, right. He said he likes my brains."

Elizabeth poured more flour into the bowl. "Deservedly so. You know, Nicki, you don't have to continue this pretense of yours. You may be ballsy with a mouth like an open sewer, and dress like a stripper, but apart from Ronnie Greco being your first lover, I don't think you're as slutty as you pretend to be."

"And what makes you so sure I don't have a string of dudes?"

Standing the hand mixer on its end, Elizabeth gazed up deciding to be frank. It was about time she did so. "Let's just say, it takes a fake to know a fake, and as much as it kills me to say it, Gina was right—loving who you *really* are and being yourself are the most important things to personal happiness. You don't give yourself enough credit, sis. You don't have enough confidence in your brains over your boobs, so you devalue yourself. I'm coming to realize myself that if people can't or won't accept you—the whole shebang—well then, you're better off without them." *Do you hear that Mike? I'm better off without you!*

"Hey, I accept who I am, but I have so much more fun watchin' people's eyes bug out. Like Toni, I dig the shock factor."

"I don't think that's what drives Toni. I think he feels happiest just being himself, and dresses make him happy."

"Yeah?" Nicki paused, scratching her head as she knit her brows until finally she said, "Maybe you're right. So, what else are you fakin' beyond your ethnicity?"

Here it goes. "Well, you know those shoes you borrowed tonight, and how you kept complaining that they were highway robbery because they hurt. Along with everything in my wardrobe, they're knock offs. I bought them from a street vendor for $6.95. They're plastic because I can't even afford grocery money half the time."

"No friggin way! You're shittin' me!"

"It's true. I've convinced you all that I'm some hotshot, wealthy doctor, when in fact up until yesterday, I was unemployed when I arrived back in Belmont. I'm a fraud."

"Holy guacamole! You sure fooled us. So does this mean you're not going back to California?"

"No. I'm going. The practice I worked for made me a huge offer to come back and, let's face it, you and Gina are settled now. PalHairMo is a great success and Gina has found another pedicurist to take my place. Everything worked out as I had hoped." *Except Mike.*

"Huge? What's huge?"

"One hundred and eighty-five thousand a year. Maybe now I can buy *real* leather shoes."

Nicki's jaw went slack before proclaiming, "You could buy friggin' Prada!"

She rose from her little perch, walked to the refrigerator, and then banged the side of the appliance to silence the humming. "Wow." Nicki took a deep breath. "As long as we're being honest … I only got it on with three guys in my life. I didn't even sleep with that Joey cop guy. He wanted to and was a damn good kisser, but there ain't no way I'm gonna have sex with anyone in a Jeep under any bridge. That's why I dumped him—a girl's got her principals."

Well, her sister had her on that one. She had nearly given it up on the front seat of Mike's Lexus and then again on the living room sofa the other night. Removing the bread dough from the bowl, she plopped it into the floured center of the formica kitchen table. After mixing in the raisins and other ingredients, her hands dug into the squishy goodness. Comfort and warmth washed over her. She loved the feeling that came over her when her fingers and palms kneaded something that would be yummy when it came out of the oven.

"You're a far more principled girl than I am, Nicki. Much to my shame, and I am sure Mike's repugnance, I attacked him in the front seat of his car after dinner the other night. You're more an angel than I am."

"I bet he loved it 'cause you know it runs in the blood, all that hot sausage Italian passion."

"I don't understand. Mike's last name is Garin. He's, I don't know, English or something, not Italian-American."

Nicki furrowed her brow. "Yeah he is. That Joey's a total horn dog, and I just found out that he's related to altar boy. I guess he's not such an altar boy after all if you attacked him."

Elizabeth gazed up, her expression frozen. She could feel the heat rise to her cheeks as her hands gripped the dough oozing up between her fingers. The words came slowly from her mouth. "He's … what?"

"Oh shit. Um … didn't you figure that out by now? Mike is Joey the cop's cousin; they're devil De Luca's grandsons and Mia, Gina's client, is Mike's sista. I wasn't supposed to tell you because Gina and Mr. Carpo—"

"Carpo? Carpo knew, too!?"

"Yeah, you showed him Mike's picture the night he tricked you into dinner. He and Gina were convinced that you were in love and that everything would be cool. You'd go back to church, stay in the Bronx, marry him, and then the devil would get awf our backs 'cause Mike's the one tryin' to buy Villa Fortuna."

"What!?"

Nicki backed away from the table the moment she saw her sister's lips draw into that thin pink line of pissed-off. The satanic flash in her eyes matched the bright red burn to her cheeks. The woman was gonna blow like Mount Vesuvius and she had no intention of being turned to ash.

"I'm sorry … I thought you knew, Lizzy. I thought that was why you were such a sorry sack of shit tonight. Confused about what to do."

Dough flew through the air fast and hard, missing Nicki's cheek then backside when she ran from the kitchen. Elizabeth screamed bloody murder. "You all knew and didn't think to tell me?"

More dough careened into the living room as Nicki yelled back. "He's in love with you! Mia said so!"

"No he's not! He dumped me! He's a conniving, lying piece of scum like the rest of them! He was sucking up to me for the building!" Elizabeth screamed.

"But he's got a soppressata!"

At this point, safety was paramount, and Gina's bedroom was the only room with a lock. The door slammed behind Nicki, separating her from the *pazzo* woman on the opposite side. She leaned against it, breathing hard, her hand resting upon her chest as Elizabeth continued her Christmas Eve tirade. Finally the harsh swear words came. When did her sister learn German?

"What's going on?" Gina asked rubbing her eyes.

"Oh Gawd, she blew."

"What did you do to Lizzy to make her so angry?"

The doorknob jiggled violently when Gina switched the lamp on.

"I know you're in there, Nicki! Open up. Now!"

"What happened?" Gina repeated.

Then the pounding fist against the old door began, propelling Nicki to leap onto the bed and duck under the covers. "Don't open the door. She knows. She knows it all and she knows you knew and kept it from her. Like I told you, she's gonna kill you *and* me!"

"She knows about what?"

"Mike being De Luca's grandson, him being the investor guy."

Gina looked to heaven then rose from the bed. "I better talk with her."

"Not if you value your life. She threw dough at me. It's everywhere. I haven't seen her this mad since Tucci the Stallion on prom night, and he ended up with a black eye."

"Calm down, sis," Gina admonished through the door, pressing her ear to the wood. "You're going to wake Mr. Graciosa."

Both fearful sisters looked at each other when they heard Elizabeth crying. "Lizzy ... talk to me."

"Not unless you open the door."

"I don't think it's safe for us to do that right now. You're giving into your animal instincts."

"I knew he was too perfect, and I knew *you* had a Machiavellian streak running through you."

"Look, I'm sorry we hid the truth from you, but it wasn't to be mean-spirited. I really felt that Mike was the one for you, and I needed time for you to see that. He's everything Prozia would want for you in a man. You met him on St. Nicholas feast day, and I've even been praying a novena."

"Saintly intercession is worse than the *malocchio*. The only thing circling those pillars accomplished was getting me dizzy."

"Now you know that's not true." Gina placed her hand on the door. "Do you love him?"

Silence.

"If you do, then it shouldn't matter if he's Italian-American. Heck, everyone has a little Italian in them, and he hasn't shown himself to be a player like Danny or Frankie. He might be as dreamy looking as Carpo, but he's a good man. He's in love with you and would never cheat. I'm sure of that. As for the building, well, I just thought that when you found out who he was, then it wouldn't really matter. You might even laugh about the coincidence. What did you call it? Serendipi-doo or something like that. True love is supposed to be like that, right?"

"Said the naïve woman whose ginzaloon ex-husband had been sleeping around since their wedding reception!"

"What?"

"Nothing. It's not important."

"No, Lizzy, what did you say?"

"I said that Frankie slept with one of your bridesmaids. I walked in on them in the bridal suite when you were taking photographs."

"She did not just say that!" Nicki yelled. "Low blow, sista! You were supposed to keep that in the vault til death!"

Gina released her breath, her own lips drawing into an uncharacteristic line, too. Unsure of who to be more mad at—Frankie for his lying and cheating, or Lizzy for having kept it a secret for so long.

"Did you know about Frankie, Nicki?"

"Yeah. He even screwed Cousin Maria when she visited from Malta. I also saw him makin' a play for the funeral director's assistant at Daddy's wake. You picked a winna, Gina. He couldn't keep his sausage in his pants if his life depended on it. I'm surprised it hasn't fallen awf by now."

"Did he make a move on you, too?"

"No but he made one to Lizzy at your divorce proceedings last year. She stepped on his foot with one of those knock-awf sandals she wears and told him to go ef himself."

Sitting on the edge of the bed, Gina cradled her head, breathing hard. She broke out into a sweat. This wasn't about Frankie, or the secrets her sisters kept from her. After all, she had kept secrets, too.

~**~

Biscuit Tortoni

3 egg whites
¾ cup sugar
1 ½ cup heavy cream
¾ tsp. vanilla
¼ cup blanched almonds
1 ¾ tsp. almond extract
6 maraschino cherries

Let egg whites stand at room temperature for one hour. Mix ¾ cups sugar with ¼ cup of water, bring to boil. Continue boiling to thick syrup consistency.

Beat egg whites at high speed until stiff peaks form. Pour hot syrup in thin stream into egg whites as you continue to beat until very stiff. Cover and refrigerate for half hour.

Toast blanched almonds then chop fine. Place in small bowl and add 1½ tsp. almond extract. Whip cream with vanilla and remaining ½ tsp. almond extract until stiff. Fold into egg white mixture. Spoon into aluminum foil cups, top with almonds and ½ cherry on top. Cover and freeze.

~Taken from Bressan family recipe

~Twenty-Five~
Esposto
(Exposed)

"Talk to me, Lizzy," Gina insisted.

"No."

"We can't keep this up. You're leaving in two days."

"And not a moment too soon," Elizabeth snapped, changing the music in the salon to a much needed, soulful Norah Jones playlist after a busy eight straight hours. Even the salon's 50s theme— Elvis Presley day—could not break the tension between the eldest Clemente sisters. Toni and Dharma, knowing what went down, walked on eggshells in matching saddle shoes.

Elizabeth audibly sighed and her sister obviously took that as a sign of acquiescence, pouring two glasses of wine, placing one in front of her.

"Let's have a drink."

"No thanks."

"But this is Mr. G's super Tuscan. He made it especially for the New Year." She grinned in that sugary sweet manner that everyone caved at, only Elizabeth knew better. If the woman blessed herself one more time, she was going to smack her one with the back of her hand because Gina was proving herself as adept at bullshit as Nicki. Her father's Old Country proverb "A drunk man's words are a sober man's thoughts" was the reason for the wine.

Downing the vino, Elizabeth hoped that the harping to make up would end and that she could keep her emotions and words in check when the homemade recipe kicked in. The salon closed in twenty minutes and the ride home in that small car of hers would feel like drunken torture. No doubt, she and Nicki would fight for the back seat.

Gina continued to grin and poured them both another glass.

"You have to drive home," Elizabeth chastised. "And given our genetics, you need to be mindful of hyperuricemia due to the elevation of serum uric acid levels. You've been drinking like a fish since we opened PalHairMo."

Obviously, Gina was feeling as petulant as Nicki and downed her glass of red, following up with a wide grin.

"Suit yourself. I'll be 3,000 miles away when you get gout or diabetes, but maybe *Dr. Garin'll* take care of you."

Dammit.

Her sister had her talking now, *and* mentioning Mike! It amazed her how Gina's anger, unlike Nicki and hers, could dissipate so quickly. She never held a grudge, even as a teenager.

"Fine, let's talk." She swallowed the knot in her throat. "I apologize for being so insensitive when I said what I did about Frankie the other night. Please know, I didn't really want to hurt you. It was wrong of me." Reaching across the counter, she took her sister's hand in hers.

"*And* I'm sorry that I went to the movies alone on Christmas day. Old habits die-hard, and that's what I've been doing on holidays for a few years. I shouldn't have let my anger get the better of me, but I just needed to have my own pity party." *There, I said it!*"

"*And* ... " Gina asked with a raised eyebrow.

"And I love you and know that what you did, you thought was for the best—even if you played right into Mike's deceiving hands."

"I don't think they were deceiving, Lizzy. I know for a fact that he didn't know who you were, and that he felt bad about all this. When I first met him at Halo, I overheard him speaking about how upset he was over his grandmother's underhanded tactics. He's a good man and genuinely interested in you, and you can't deny what you feel for him."

"Even if that were true about him not knowing that I'm one of the owners of Villa Fortuna, in the end, he broke it off with me for unknown reasons. I invited him to dinner and midnight Mass but he blew me off." Elizabeth shrugged. "So much for his gentlemanly piety."

Gina squeezed her hand. "I'm so sorry."

"Even before my invitation, I hadn't heard from him since Sunday night with his brief 'merry Christmas' text. It's been three days, without any word from him. He would text me like five or six times a day before that. He'd telephone me every morning and every night. Now nothing. If I didn't know any better, I would think he was cheating." *Or stuck up.*

Her eyes welled with tears. "I … my … foolish heart fell in love with him in this short time. He was the total package, everything I ever dreamed for in a man. Mike did and said all the right things and they appeared so genuine, right from the heart, just for me."

Nicki swept by with her broom, slowly rotating her shoulders to "Love Me."

"So cawl him, sista," she said.

"No. The ball was and is in his court."

The salon door flew open, the bell ringing violently over the song. Everyone stopped and gazed up at the wild-eyed woman with her manicured hand upon her fur jacket.

"*Ciao*, Rebecca!" Gina greeted.

"He's here! Michelangelo is at Halo. You wanted to see him, Gina, so hurry! Oh that backside of his!"

Rebecca waved them all to follow her as she teetered on the icy sidewalk in her trendy black boots. In single file, the team exited the salon into the cold, foregoing outerwear, and ran across Main Street toward the competition.

Gina rubbed her arms and stepped over the slush puddle at the curb. "Rusty already took down the Christmas decorations. Doesn't he know about the twelve days of Christmas? Beffana hasn't come yet!" She clicked her tongue.

"I think he's focused on New Year's now," Elizabeth replied, noting the candlelight glowing from the plate glass display window as they neared closer. "It does look magical and romantic inside. What does this Michelangelo do? Is he a massage therapist?"

"No. He's a body sculptor."

At first thought, Elizabeth assumed a personal trainer. "Gina has a four-floor walk up. We thankfully don't need one of those."

"No you don't. Honey, your girls are perfect. Now Toni might need a little help with that A-cup of his but Michelangelo doesn't swing that way. He's all testosterone."

"And what's wrong with my girls?" Toni asked, thrusting back his shoulders and smoothing his hands over his poodle skirt.

"They need a little hands-on love by the number one boob man in the tri-state area. He has a thing for nipple erection. In fact, I think his hands have been on more breasts than Hugh Heffner's."

"I told you, Rebecca, this guy sounds like a Romeo."

Nicki snorted. "He sounds like Joey the cop!"

Eight faces peered into Halo's front window, hands surrounded cold faces as breath steam fogged up the glass.

Within the salon, gorgeous women of all adult age were dressed to impress, just as Rebecca had expected. Westchester County's society babes held champagne and wine glasses while gossiping and enjoying the uncharacteristic and outdated sounds of Irish new age artist, Enya.

"Look, there's Blair! I wonder if she had her eyebrow fixed?" Gina noted.

The crowd of women standing beside Rusty's sister moved, and everyone outside the salon watched as Blair's hand slid down a man's toned back. Another woman, on the opposite side of him, touched his arm and laughed, throwing back her head at a joke he must have made. A third touched the tendrils at his forehead.

"Do you see him?—There in the red sweater!" Rebecca effused. "Michelangelo is a god and he's going home with me tonight!"

Elizabeth wiped her forearm over the steamed glass then gasped when her eyes locked upon a backside she knew very well. There were two men and at least three dozen women fawning all over Mike. He was eating the attention up.

"Lizzy …" Nicki said slowly.

"Yeah … I see him." *Oh God! The pain. Take it away. Michael isn't an angel at all!*

She swallowed hard then bit her lip to keep from yelling out as her face squished trying to stop the tears. *Was I truly nothing to him?*

"Good Gawd, guess he ain't no altar boy after all. You almost got some of that ass, but by the looks of things everyone else has already," Nicki declared with a curl to her lip.

On a dime, Elizabeth's pain turned to anger. Her heart pounded; her face burned bright. "Yeah … look at that *ass* hole."

"It looks like an orgy is about to start," said a new stylist.

Gina removed the shocked hand covering her mouth, barely managing, "C'mon gang. We need to close up PalHairMo and get home." She tucked her arm under Elizabeth's, nearly dragging her away from the hurtful almost prophetic vision of Mike as a cheating, womanizing *cazzo*. "There's nothing more to see here. Have fun tonight, Rebecca."

Elizabeth stopped dead in her tracks, and turned to their client. She stammered. "If, if you don't mind me asking, why exactly is *Michelangelo* at Halo?"

"Oh! It's a Botox party! He's good friends with the owner of the salon. I received a personal phone call from his assistant and then a few of the girls from the MAA Facebook page were talking about it in chat. I knew I had to come. His reputation for pleasing women is impressive. Like I said, he has a thing for breasts."

"Right. Breasts. What's MAA?" She sucked her lips in.

"We're a satisfied group of ladies who can't help sharing our stories about our visit to Manhattan Aesthetics Associates and Dr. Garin's hands-on, yummy treatment."

Toni took Elizabeth's other arm, supportively escorting her back to their happy little place in Etonville.

"Look at that sack of shit," Nicki proclaimed. "What a *testa di merda*! He's got huge …"

Pinched fingers zipped across Gina's lips, silencing any further discussion on the matter.

"He's nothing, Lizzy," Toni said. "A guy like that isn't worth your time. Be thankful you didn't sleep with him. Who knows what diseases he carries?"

"Get me to a computer and that Facebook page!" was all she could think to say, controlling the boiling rage.

⁓✳✳⁓

Mike leaned close to Blair's ear, making sure the other clients present didn't overhear him. "Please remove your hand from my backside."

"Oh Mike, you know how tempting it is."

He closed his eyes, in an attempt not to stare at her penciled eyebrow. "I won't ask you again, Blair."

"Fine, but I won't give up. I have known ever since I was a teenager that you and I should be together."

He sighed, feeling defeated. Tonight was a nightmare. Rusty had lied about Blair not attending this little soiree. Not only was Blair *not* to be here, but he had been promised that he would see these clients in an orderly manner. Instead, Blair and 30 other women were clamoring for a piece of him—and not … vials.

He recognized almost all of the party's attendees from eDating—as well as their winks and private messages. One of them, he was sure, was the creator of that infamous, denigrating Facebook page. Never in all his years had he felt more objectified than tonight, and he couldn't help his thoughts from traveling to Elizabeth (for the millionth time) on how she must have felt everyday at WHPC. Her boss was a jackass—an insult to the male gender, the medical profession and humanity for harassing her, making her feel that her only worth was a set of *ahem* fine eyes.

With each female touch to his body, his flesh crawled. He needed a shower.

He stepped away from Blair, giving her his back, and his eyes met those of a long-time patient's as she walked toward him. Angela's car accident reconstruction had been a success story, just the type of plastic surgery he hoped to focus on in his practice. Now with minimal scars remaining, she was a sixty-year old vision and a balm to his unhappy soul. An earnest smile spread upon his lips.

"It's great to see you, Angela. Merry Christmas," he said with a hug. That he could tolerate; she, no doubt, was disease free—and married. Hugging her wouldn't taint him in any way. Down to earth, she wasn't one of these society babes, nor was she born blueblood, only marrying into it. Of Venetian descent, she frequented his grandmother's club: the Metropolitan Italian-American Center.

"Mike, I'm shocked to see you here, but I'm delighted, nonetheless! When Gwen telephoned, I jumped at the chance to have a holiday drink with you. Patrick didn't even mind my spending the evening with one of New York's hottest bachelors."

"Hardly the hottest, but judging by tonight's show of single women, I'm assuming sought after. You're a sight for sore eyes and looking wonderful!"

"Thanks to you. You look well, a little tired and I'm sure stressed, but well. Are you burning both ends of the candle?"

"Trying not to."

She raised an eyebrow. "Have you found Ms. Right?"

He shifted his weight and toyed with the edge of his sweater sleeve. "I thought I did, but it didn't work out."

"Oh I'm sorry. Don't worry the right woman'll come along. So tell me, are you still doing charity work with Face to Face?"

"I am, and I'm also considering a change to my practice to reflect that direction," he replied thankful that she was sensitive enough to move on from the topic of the Elizabeth dating debacle.

She looked around the room, her gaze settling on an overdone social-ite sipping champagne. "Yet you're here giving Botox injections. This isn't your style, Mike."

"I know, I know, but Rusty is a friend and needed my help. Christmas spirit and all that."

"I imagine he's having a difficult season with the opening of Pal-HairMo. Such a quaint salon with a brilliant marketing scheme. It's good to see those young women from the old neighborhood get a leg up, but it's even better to see a little of the old neighborhood up here in Westchester County."

Mike tilted his head, furrowing his brow. "Old neighborhood?"

"Yes, I grew up on the opposite side of the Bronx Zoo in the Van Nest community. When my family lived there, it was all Italian, but like most areas of the city, its demographics have changed."

"I have a feeling that PalHairMo will be changing Etonville; it has already."

"I hope so. I knew the Clemente sisters when they were little girls and couldn't wish them more happiness. They're a breath of fresh air up here in Snobsville."

Shocked, he took a step back, running his hand through his hair. "You know them?"

"I do. My brother worked alongside their father in the Teamsters Union. Thomas Clemente's death was such a tragedy."

"Yeah, I heard he was whacked by the mob."

"Oh Mike! You have a vivid imagination. Why is it anytime men hear Italian and Teamsters they automatically think Mafioso? It's as though *The Godfather* has brainwashed them! Yes Dr. Garin, the poor man was hit by a bus. Almost blind from his diabetes and wearing those clunky diabetic shoes, he tripped off the curb into the street right into an oncoming city bus."

He took a step back from her, searching her face, his own blanching. "Is that true?"

"Why would I make something like that up? It made the newspapers. His wife passed out at the wake."

Shocked, his fist flew to his mouth, his skin immediately responding in a cold, clammy flush. *What did I do?*

"Mike, are you okay? You're as white as a ghost."

"You're *positive* that the family isn't Cosa Nostra?"

Angela put her hand on his bicep. "Yes, of course. Did you really think the Clemente sisters' father was Mafia?"

He could feel the perspiration immediately bead upon his brow and under his arms. *Good Lord!* He had done the unthinkable—he believed gossip and lies. Falsely prejudiced, he most likely broke Elizabeth's heart, even if she had broken his with her sleeping around …

Or had she? Perhaps, there was more to those photographs of his grandmother's than met the eye, too.

Oh my God. I must make this right!

"No, of course I didn't think that. I never listen to damaging gossip or rumors. They usually prove to be false."

In spite of his poor attempt at controlling his expression, he could tell that Angela saw right through him when she gave him a sideways glance with a narrowing of her eyes. It was one of those looks his mother used to give whenever she knew he was lying. How could she not see that he was lying? He was breaking out in a cold sweat.

Confession at the end of the week was going to be difficult. Apologizing to Elizabeth, a woman he declared to love yet callously blew off because of his assumptions was going to be worse. Ashamed and disappointed in himself, his gut pained him, the agita growing at how he hurt her by his prejudgment.

Glancing at his watch, he shook his head. PalHairMo had most likely closed. Dammit! He needed to clear the air between Elizabeth and him *now*—not in three hours—when the party was over. He anxiously glanced around the room, needing to get on with the injections if he intended on calling her at a reasonable hour. He hoped to God it wasn't too late to apologize; she was leaving New York in only two days.

~**~

Immediately upon entering PalHairMo, everyone ignored "Hound Dog" playing overhead. Dharma poured the wine and Toni stormed to the laptop. The electricity of the song and the anger running through the family's blood felt explosive to the new beauticians who didn't know Elizabeth and her history.

"Hurry, Tone!" Nicki demanded. "Before I run back there and put a hole in that good fa nuthin' and his tight ass with my Black and Decker. Nobody disses my sista!"

Elizabeth groaned and Gina clicked her tongue followed by, "I never thought that nice altar boy would play so dirty by conspiring with the enemy. Who woulda thunk it. I guess you really don't know people, huh? Rusty'll probably clear at least $5,700 with that little party of his, thanks to Mike."

"Gina!" Lizzy barked. "Did you not hear the woman? He's no altar boy. His hands have been on more breasts than Hugh Heffner! He pleases all his women with his talent at nipple erection. And don't I friggin' know it."

"I heard her, but I'm trying to distract you."

"How can you possibly distract me from her proclamation that she's going home with him tonight? Didn't you see Blair's hands all over Mike?"

"Yeah. Lizzy didn't even get to *eat* that soppressata, and now Rebecca and Blair are goin' afta his meatballs."

Elizabeth dropped into the chair at the counter then cradled her head in her hand, groaning. "Stop with the food analogies."

"Lizzy, Nicki doesn't have food allergies," Gina stated.

Elizabeth slugged back the wine. "Please, fill it up again, Picasso. I intend on getting extremely trashed tonight."

"Whoa," Toni said in shock, reading the MAA Facebook timeline. "This dude's a verifiable sleaze. He seduces his patients! I want his job for a day." Dharma slapped his arm as she stared at the screen from over his shoulder.

Nicki stood dumbfounded beside him. It was the very first time Elizabeth observed her sister speechless, her chin nearly dropping to her chest, her hand installed upon her hip.

"I don't think I should read this to you, Lizzy."

A wave of Elizabeth's hand said, "Sock it to me." She could feel the burn to her face and it wasn't the Tuscan red; it was most likely the effects of the *malocchio*!

"Look, Tone! Someone posted that Mike is dating a new girl. Says here that she read it on Mia's Facebook page! I guess the new girl is Lizzy, 'cause there's a comment from that Blair saying he's too good for 'her kind.'"

"Stop talking like I'm not here! Read it all!"

Toni bent over the laptop, scrolling down. "Don't say I didn't warn ya'. There are whole threads about how skillful his touch is. One doesn't want the nip and tuck but only wants to, you know, fill in the rest. There are at least a half a dozen photos of his ass, even an up close and personal one of his boys. Man, I'm jealous. Look at that bulge. I wonder if he uses a sock?"

"Yup. I told ya'. That ain't no sock. The guys packin' some serious meat." Nicki nodded.

"This patient said that she exploded right there on the table when he—in quotes—'examined' her va-jay-jay with those long, talented fingers of his."

Gina blessed herself, mumbling something in Italian as though Satan had entered the room and she was performing an exorcism.

Elizabeth abruptly stood, downed her second glass of wine and declared. "See! Italian pig! I have to get out of here."

"But … but … maybe it's not as it seems, Lizzy," Dharma said. "I don't know what the procedure is called but lots of society women are pursuing vaginal rejuvenation. Some women even bleach it and several actresses now have it steam cleaned."

On her way to the back room, Elizabeth stated emotionlessly, "It's called a labia minora reduction,"

"Yo! What are you sayin', Picasso?"

"Well, um, they do it to make their lady bits smaller."

"Are you shittin' me? Putting kitty unda the knife 'cause it's lips are too big? That is so wrong!"

"Dharma, baby, this dude is all hands on *and* getting it on, kitty surgery or not. Listen to this one from two months ago. 'I went on a date with Michelangelo after finding his profile on eDating and sending him a wink. I can confirm to my fellow MAA Dr. Garin fans that the man is *very* skillful. Italian dinner, vino, and a nightcap at the Rose bar followed by … well you get the picture.'" Everyone's head turned almost simultaneously to Elizabeth.

That's where he took me! Her heart stopped, and then she stormed straight to the office. Slamming the door, she released a scream that nearly shattered glass.

~**~

~Twenty-Six~
Corsa
(Running)

Not even watching the movie *Clueless* could make two Clemente sisters smile, both feeling terrible about the outcome of the day's drama. A plate loaded with cookies sat uneaten on the coffee table before Gina and Nicki. The Christmas tree lacked illumination. Their spirits as dim and low as the ambient lighting in the living room. Poor Lizzy. Eyes locked when they heard drawers opening and closing within Gina's bedroom. They knew what was coming next.

"She's gonna bolt," Nicki said.

"I know."

"Should I show her the pictures of Mike sleeping on the sofa?"

"Stop it. Now's not the time for your stupid jokes."

They both knew running was Elizabeth's way of keeping her heart safe, cutting it off from everything or everyone that engaged it on a personal level, especially following their father's death.

"Did you know she lost her job in LA?"

Gina's head snapped to take in Nicki's expression. "Is that true?"

"Yeah, but her boss offered her a shit load of money to come back. There's nothing for her to stay here for."

"There is. There's us and PalHairMo."

Dressed in the attire she had arrived in, Elizabeth stood with her suitcase at her feet under the hall archway. "Well, this is it, kiddos. I'm going home."

"But, Lizzy, you have one more day with us, and we planned something special in the salon. Dharma was going to put the highlights in your hair remember? Everyone from the building and even Mr. Carpo were going to come up to Etonville and we had a sort of festival planned!" Gina begged, rising to stand before her sister.

"No. I have to get back. One more day won't make a difference. Thank you for the thought though, but I have important things waiting for me. Give them all a kiss for me and thank them for everything. Make sure Mr. Graciosa wears a scarf so he doesn't get hit by the air and see that Mrs. Zeppo gets those compression stockings we talked about. Her pedal pulses are good, but the edema worries me."

"You betta stop running, sista. Just 'cause some guy did something shitty doesn't mean you need to leave the only place where you belong— your real home—your family. We love you. We want you to stay. What will we do without you? The Trinacria can't stand on only two feet!"

Nicki watched as a wistful smile quirked Elizabeth's lips. She was obviously struggling with the pain that Mike caused. "I know he hurt you, Lizzy, but won't you consider staying for us?" she asked, the tone in her voice near begging, her accent softening.

"I can't. It's done. It's over. I emailed my boss, accepting the offer and well … I promised to be there on the 29th. I don't want to miss this opportunity of a lifetime. They miss me and obviously see my worth now that I've been away."

"You didn't tell me that you lost your job," Gina stated, rising from the sofa.

Elizabeth shrugged a shoulder. "I didn't want to worry you, but I quit, and I'd do it again if anyone attempted to stand in your way of happiness. My boss rescinded my vacation the day before Thanksgiving, so I told him to go scratch in Macy's window."

"You did that for us, sis?"

"I did but don't go blessing yourself or feeling guilty about it. I was glad to come back to the Bronx." (Nose scratch) "Glad to help your dreams come true and happy to witness how Etonville embraced you— and our ethnicity. I had a great vacation."

"*Our* ethnicity?"

Elizabeth smoothed the hair from Nicki's face. "Yes, our ethnicity. Both of you and our little Messina family—not to mention going back to church—helped to change most of my opinions. Sadly, Mike confirmed others. I was just one of many. But I don't want to talk about him. I have a flight to catch back to a life I began a long time ago."

"You began this one first, Lizzy. You're a different girl now."

"Yes I am, but I still have a career to focus on, and a mountain of debt to tackle. Those school loans still have to be paid."

Nicki wrapped her arms around Elizabeth's waist and squeezed. "Be careful that you don't suffer from Takotsubo cardiomyopathy 'cause it'll kill ya'."

"Where'd you hear about Broken-Heart Syndrome? I'm shocked Nicki!"

"I looked it up, Doc Hollywood. It's about time I start using big words. I don't wanna ef this up with Johnnycakes."

"You won't mess anything up. Like I told you the other night, just be yourself, your beautiful self, and he won't be able to stop from falling for you. Trust me; masquerades are only good for Carnevale. I'm proud of you."

She glanced at her watch then sighed. "Well, my Uber car will be here in a minute, so I better wait downstairs."

Tears streamed down Gina's face and it nearly broke Elizabeth's reserve and resolve. This was harder than she thought. It gutted her to say good-bye. Three weeks ago, she couldn't wait to leave. Now she only wanted to stay. Once again, head and heart were battling like they did when her father died, just before she took the job at WHPC. No, her heart would be safe from ever experiencing Takotsubo cardiomyopathy again.

Reminiscent of the scene at the airport back in August, the sisters hugged and then Elizabeth allowed her own tears to fall before grasping the handle to her suitcase. She wheeled it out the door and didn't look back.

As she descended the steps, wiping her tears, she was startled to see Mrs. Zeppo standing on the landing holding a brown paper bag. The woman nodded her grey head. "Elisabetta, you are leaving us."

"*Si.*"

"I'm a gone-a miss you. You're like my daughter but she no come to see me." She pinched Elizabeth's cheek. "Take care, *bella*. I'll-a say a rosario for you. You know the rosario?"

"Yes, Josie. I have my great-aunt Maria's in my pocket for good luck."

"No such-a thing as luck, only blessings and destiny. Your Michelangelo is your destiny. Like I said: Far from one's eyes, far from one's heart. He is your *innamorato*."

She snorted then smiled wryly. "I'm hoping that Italian proverb is correct because he's not my sweetheart anymore. It seems as though Mike is *everyone's innamorato*."

The old woman patted her cheek, a tender smile attempted to console her. "Do not worry. No man can-a resist a Sicilian woman. He will come back to you and you alone. He's a good man."

Whatever. It would have been rude to roll her eyes, but this wasn't the 1940s. Mrs. Zeppo still lived in the world of her imagination and memory where men were gentleman in an era when they held open doors and respected a woman.

"This is for you, a meat-a-ball sandwich for the plane. You are too skinny."

Elizabeth's phone vibrated letting her know that the Uber was downstairs waiting. She bent and kissed Josie's cheek, bidding her good-bye feeling as though the woman had become her grandmother these three weeks. "*Grazie. Arrivederci, Nonnina.*"

~**~

Never before in his cautious life had Mike driven with balls out speed on the precarious Bronx River Parkway from Etonville to Belmont. Each of his illegal texts went unanswered by Elizabeth, and each phone call went straight to voicemail. The outgoing message astounded him; the caustic recording was in an accent that sounded similar to Nicki's: "If you have finally decided to cawl, Dr. Garin, this message is for you: Go screw yourself, you cheatin, manipulatin *cazzo*! Go scratch that perfect ass of yours in Macy's window! Or better yet have one of your *fans* do it!"

Yup, *The Godfather* was correct: "Sicilian women are more dangerous than a shotgun."

After the third message, the *agita* over what most likely brought about that recorded reply was gutting him. His hands gripped the steering wheel when he gassed the Lexus, moving to the left lane to pass a car going too slow. "Dammit!" he shouted, so sure that he had, as Mia previously expressed, "Screwed this up."

"Please, please be home," he begged in the empty car.

Ten miles felt as though one hundred. Twenty minutes as though hours. All of it placing Elizabeth too far from his embrace and contrition. He had acted abominably, allowing faithless cynicism to enter his heart, dumping an incredible woman based on false assumptions and misleading circumstantial photographs. On the issue of other men, well, why not—had he not dated many women at the same time, too? Elizabeth was knock-out gorgeous and intelligent. Of course men would pursue her.

Reaching up to the dashboard, he tapped the screen, placing a call. Joey's Rambo screensaver face appeared as it dialed.

"Finally, a worthy distraction from Santucci's midnight screwfest. What's up, Mike?"

"Did you perhaps leave out a few details about the Clemente family?"

"What kind of details?"

"The ones that exonerate Thomas Clemente as a wiseguy? The ones that tell how he was hit by an MTA bus three years ago?"

"I'm a cop, not a genealogist, and the details of *his* death weren't in the precinct archives. What did you think, I was so obsessed with these women, I'd run down to the city's municipal building and scour the death records for their *father*? My research was about their great-grandfather, which ultimately led to a shit load of information about our great-grandfather. Now you want to talk piece of shit mobster, Stella was near crapping in her Valentino suit when I dropped the name 'Scarface'."

"Are you alone?"

"Yeah. My partner went for a cup of joe."

"I guess I thought that you were investigating the entire Clemente family. I assumed you had the inside track on *all* of them."

Joey snorted. "Just one inside track and that went off the rails."

"What do you mean?"

"Nicki and her little c.t. ways turned out to be a bust—all talk and no action in the end."

Mike sighed. He was glad to hear that, and thought that maybe Elizabeth's dating persona, as portrayed by the photographs and Stella's "information," was false, too. "I'm glad she sent you packing then. Your womanizing is starting to emulate the subjects of your stakeouts."

"At least I'm upfront about it. It gets lonely in this van."

"Then sign up for eDating or get a Facebook page."

"Ha. Ha."

Mike pulled up to the curb across from Messina Bakery; it was now one in the morning, and the neighborhood was dead silent. With the exception of a lone display light in the bakery window and the colorful Christmas bulbs strung along the fire escapes, the building was dark, but that wasn't going to deter him.

"I have to go do some making up now. Thanks to you and Grand-mother, I was easily swayed into thinking the worst of Elizabeth."

"Hey, you assumed and you know what they say about assumptions."

"And you inferred. I'll call you tomorrow." He hung up and with one last pump of the antibacterial liquid, exited the car.

Nearly frantic to talk with Elizabeth, he ran across the street, readying himself for the argument he knew was sure to follow.

After buzzing for entry, he stood in the cold, waiting to hear the heated reply from the speaker box outside the door to the apartment building. Two anxious minutes passed before buzzing again. "It's Mike. Please open up. I need to speak to Elizabeth," he spoke into the silent box, anticipating the click and response buzz, which finally came only without greeting.

The stairwell light turned on as the vestibule's overhead round flores-cent flickered, working up to full illumination.

Beside him, the kimono guy he greeted the Sunday prior opened his apartment door. "She's gone, pal," he said raising three pinched fingertips and narrowing his eyes as if to say, "You jerk."

An old man grasping a cast iron frying pan exited from the neighbor-ing apartment.

Mike couldn't help glaring at the first guy smashing his fist into his palm. He also remembered him from the photographs taken at the bakery, the hugs and kisses to Elizabeth.

Josie peeked her head down the walk up. "She's on-a da plane," fol-lowed by a series of tongue clicks and a shake to her gray head. She said something in Italian that he was sure meant having pine cones instead of a brain. Yes, he could concur. He had acted stupidly.

Brandishing a wooden spoon above her hair rollers, another woman exited her apartment, coming to stand beside Josie. "Whats-a matta with you? You got your head on backwards? *A fanabala!*"

Nicki descended the steps, wearing nothing more than an oversized T-shirt, but she gripped a cordless drill and depressed the trigger. The sound of the rotating bit echoed off the dirty plaster walls. Her five-foot-three inch form blocked the stairs to keep him from ascending. "Yo. You ain't welcome here. *Michelangelo!*"

"It's not as it seems, everyone. Really." He fidgeted, shoving his hands into his pockets as he stood in the hallway. His face burned with embarrassment. He was about to be beat up by three senior citizens, a petite woman, and a cross-dresser with a unibrow. Nothing could be more degrading.

He gazed up the four flights and could make out another old timer leaning over the banister brandishing a baseball bat. Gina came to stand beside the man, calling out. "She left a few hours ago to take the red eye home, Mike."

"I screwed up, Gina."

"Yes you did, but so did she. Looks like our aunt Maria was wrong. I'm not the only *stupido* one around here. Nicki, let him up. I think we need to set him straight and get to the bottom of that Facebook page."

"Elizabeth saw that?"

"Yeah. She left for California 'cause of it and what we saw at Halo."

"Damn!"

"Guess you didn't go home with Rebecca afta all," Nicki added, spinning the drill again.

"Rebecca?"

"The one who ate your meaty balls."

"Nicki, stop it! Let him up!"

"You try anything on me and I'll drill a hole in your chest."

"Don't bother, one is there already. It caved in when I let your sister go."

Mike took a step up, holding onto the banister, feeling all eyes boring into him.

"Hey pal. If you mess with my girls, I'll mess with you. You better fix this or you'll be sleeping with the fishes."

"I hear ya'. I love Elizabeth. The last thing I wanted to do was hurt her. You have my word, I'll make this right."

Ascending the staircase, Mike gazed up, noting the way the winemaker tapped the end of the bat against his palm; the look in the old man's eyes scared the crap out of him. Yes, these people and this building would be great for Mia.

Nicki glanced over her shoulder. "Where's the vowel?"

"What vowel?"

"The one in your last name. You had huh fooled into thinkin' you were English or something."

He couldn't help but to chuckle. "It's of Austrian descent, before that part became northern Italy. Why? From what I've seen it doesn't seem that Elizabeth takes umbrage with Italian men."

"Are you kidding? She hates 'em. Swore off dating them years ago. So you can imagine what a shock to her ticker it was to find out that you were a friggin' ginzaloon *and* the grandson of that De Luca woman to boot."

Oh Lord ... I really did jump to conclusions from those damn Famizi photographs, her kisses, and her forwardness! That's right, now I never even stopped to remember—she was downright frigid to that jerk at the botanical gardens. No wonder why!

Gina stood at the top of the stairs with a hand clutching her hip. Her body language spoke pissed off but the expression on her face looked as amiable as ever. "It's okay, Mr. G. Mike is harmless. We'll take over from here," she said to the old man.

"Sorry to wake you, Mr. Graciosa," Mike apologized, but the wine-maker scowled back, narrowing his venomous eyes.

"You betta get in the apartment before they whack ya," Nicki said.

Like an Italian mamma, Gina pinched Mike's ear and pulled him into the apartment toward the kitchen. No one had ever done that before—not even the red-haired hellion. He felt five-years old when she demanded that he have a seat at the Formica table. Trying with all his might to ignore the water-stained ceiling and the press and peel tile that caught under the chair leg, he removed his coat then sat at her commanding pointed finger.

Entirely upset, he ran his hand through his hair. "When did she leave?"

"Not too long after that show you put on over at Halo. Traitor."

"I'm sorry, Gina. Rusty and I have been friends since grade school, and when he asked for help, I just couldn't deny him. Truly, at the time of his request when I committed to him, I didn't know that you girls were *the* Trinacria."

She smiled a devilish grin then held out a dish of pignoli nut almond paste cookies. "Cookie?"

"No thank you."

"Yo, dude, we saw those women feeling you up and read all about your manwhoring. What do you say to that?"

"I don't know what you saw, but it was most likely circumstantial evidence, attention certainly not welcomed. If you're gonna go there … well … what of Elizabeth's other men, anyway? I've seen proof of her dating no less than *five* guys in the short time she's been in New York."

Gina sat across from him, munching on a cookie. "Whatever you saw, that was circumstantial, too. Every guy wants her, they always do. That's Lizzy, but that doesn't mean she wants them. Mr. Carpo, The Turtle, and The Stallion have been working hard to woo her, but she's in love with you—even if you *are* Italian-American."

"What about the guy in the bakery? The guy in the first floor apartment."

Nicki laughed, "Toni? He's our best bud, the receptionist at PalHairMo, and Mr. Primo the baker's son, you idiot. They own the building!"

"Oh. And, and … what about her lying to me about being the co-owner of PalHairMo?"

"Gawd, you really are a dope. She didn't know who you were, just some hot-shot hottie surgeon from Sutton Place. Lizzy didn't lie, she just didn't say 'cause—as she repeatedly cautioned, and you have confirmed—*some* people tend to stereotype us as low class girls from the neighborhood then bolt when they assume Sicilian blood means Mafia and crazy mammas with chin hair who talk with their hands."

"Yeah, just like you obviously did! As an Italian-American you should be ashamed of yourself!" Nicki said, coming to stand behind Gina in unity. She jutted her chin in his direction, "Bet you don't see a single hair, do ya?"

"Um … no. I don't think that at all!"

"And what about you, *Michelangelo*? 'Cause you ain't no angel either."

Mike reached over and took a cookie in his hands, playing with it. "Did she make these?"

"Yeah. Don't try to blow off my question. We wanna know about that Facebook page of yours," Nicki challenged.

"The entire situation is mortifying. A patient started that Facebook page. It's all innuendo and falsehoods. I'm calling my lawyer in the morning."

"Well, thank Gawd for that! Here I thought I had misjudged your character. I tend to do that with men."

He bit into the cookie then smiled. "Does Elizabeth really love me?"

"She wouldn't have left if she didn't. That's Lizzy's way, running from the pain and focusing on matters not of the heart. It's what sent her out of state to college after Danny cheated on her. Then she went to medical school in Connecticut and licked her wounds, hiding after that *cazzo* ex-husband of hers did a psycho number on her. There was no way she was going to come home to her Italian-Catholic roots after Richard Fairchild made her feel like a loser. Then Daddy died, followed by Mamma moving for Florida. There wasn't any "home" to come to even if she wanted to, not that she wanted to. She took that job in California, running from the memories of being our father's favorite and all the good times she had in the Bronx."

She sighed. "Just when we thought she'd stay in Belmont, you go and pull this Michelangelo crap and now she's back in LA—all because of you."

"And what of her dislike of Italian men?"

"Gawd. Where do we start with that?" Gina ticked off on her fingers. "Danny, her first boyfriend screwed Anita, one of her best friends, whom he ended up cheating on after they got married. Then boyfriend number two, in her first year of college, cheated with her roommate. Then some cray-cray doctor she knew cheated on his wife. The last guy she dated a couple of years ago was married—and she didn't know it. My loser ex-husband cheated on me and then hit on Lizzy at the divorce proceedings. Both his brother and his father have mistresses. Turns out my ex slept with one of my bridesmaids at our reception and banged the funeral director's assistant at our father's wake. So that's seven off the top of my head. Oh! And don't forget Carpo and Vinnie. Newsflash: they are all Italian, just like you. So yeah, she's a little judgmental."

"Oh God." He cradled his head in the palm of his hand. "She never told me any of this. I mean she briefly told me of your father's accident, but never went into detail, never said anything about her dating history. I mean, we only touched on her ex-husband. In fact, she never discussed her childhood. I feel like a total shit."

"Oh, you *are* shit," Nicki agreed.

"But that job … the harassment … their disrespect to her."

"I don't know anything about that, but they made her a Senior Associate and are paying her more money than Gawd."

"Don't go all soft on him, Gina. He doesn't deserve to know any of Lizzy's business. She cawled him to share the good news, and invite him to midnight Mass, but he blew her off and ruined her Christmas! I wanna know what Mr. Congeniality here intends on doing about Villa Fortuna. We ain't given up our new digs. I'd rather be in Etonville than go on that trip to Cancún any day!"

Gina cocked an eyebrow, waiting for Mike's explanation.

"I don't want to buy your place any longer. I have never approved of my grandmother's antics and first thing tomorrow, I will be giving her a piece of my mind. If there is any future that I want to invest in it's one with *Elizabeth*, not Villa Fortuna."

"It was the marble pillars," Gina stated matter-of-factly, folding her arms across her chest.

Mike leaned back in the rickety metal kitchen chair. "What pillars?"

"The ones in Our Lady of Mount Carmel that we circled seven times every year on St. Nicholas Day following Mass. You first saw Lizzy at church, then met her on St. Nick's feast day when you went to that conference. I started saying a novena nine days earlier that she'd come home and back to the Church. That she'd find her sweetheart and let her heart rule ova her head for a change."

"You're right. Elizabeth is my destiny, heaven sent. I'm head over heels in love with her. So now what do I do?"

"Be patient. Be persistent, and pray that the good witch Beffana works some magic on her on the Epiphany. In the meantime, I'll start another novena that she keeps going to church and sees the light." Gina slid the plate closer to him. "*Mangia, Bello.* You look skinny. Are you hungry? Can I make you a bowl of spaghetti? I have some meatballs."

~**~

~Twenty-Seven~
Successo
(Success)

LA hadn't changed during Elizabeth's three-week visit back to the Bronx, but West Hollywood Podiatry had, and she finally felt vindicated. Greenwald was not kidding when he said that she'd have a full patient load waiting for her. New clients, and notable ones at that, were scheduling appointments every day. Her daily grind barely reflected cosmetic surgery, except for the A-listers and agents who insisted upon Dr. Fairchild as their physician. Right now, she was soaring high in her career. The unexpected article had seen to that.

When she walked into her new oversized office on December 29, the glossy issue of *Panache* was placed in the middle of her new desk. At the time, she didn't know which to be more excited about: the write up or having an office window. So happy to be moved out of that closet, she didn't mind the alley, dumpster-filled view. Her quilt art, which wasn't the *only* genuine thing she now owned, hung center stage on a long wall. This office, its furnishings, and her promotion superseded the view, but none of it really filled the Mike-shaped, aching hole in her heart. Missing *him* hadn't gotten better with time or distance; nothing could replace that.

The New Year at WHPC had begun on the right foot, and she remained focused on her overnight medical stardom. Her very first scheduled surgery was to Brandon Andrews. A complete success, he was recovering without complications. And although her new position as Senior Associate precluded her from taking hospital calls, she insisted upon it. She introduced herself to Cedars Sinai hospital's vascular doctors and established herself as the consulting physician on all presenting diabetic wounds. Not that she had received any calls, but at least she had put herself out there. Every day since her arrival back to LA, she attempted to convince herself that the symposium in New York had served a valuable, educational purpose. Thank God she hadn't let Mike's brief presence in her life cause her to lose her determination to make it big in LA.

Ah, who was she kidding? Privately, she wished for another outcome, but it hadn't happened. What was a girl to do but focus on career?

Her day at WHPC was just beginning as she awaited her first patient when the practice's manager popped her head into the office with a pleasant smile. "Dr. Fairchild, Dr. Greenwald asked for you to stop by exam room six in twenty minutes. He's consulting with that hot Australian actor from "Dawn of the Apocalypse."

"Did he say why he needs me? I have a new patient in thirty minutes."

"The actor asked for your second opinion."

Although feeling quite proud, she simultaneously could not help but to wonder if it killed Greenwald to consult her. Leopards of his ilk never changed their spots.

The woman departed, and Elizabeth sat back in her leather desk chair, deciding to kill the time by checking emails, her only link to the outside world. There was always something in her inbox from her sisters or Toni, but never Mike. Since her arrival home five weeks ago, she had blocked all communication from him, determined to get over her heartache by not looking back. Not that he'd try to contact her, but she had hoped that by blocking the cheater the day she left New York she would cut off that part of her heart. Still broken up over her discovery of "Michelangelo" and his typical Romeo manipulations, "Hell hath no fury like Elizabeth's scorn or grudge holding" had become her mantra. In vain she tried to shut out Prozia's deathbed words about her perfectionism and stubbornness. And as if Prozia's sentiment weren't bad enough, her own heart had turned traitor: "talk to him about it" urged her.

She opened an email from PalHairMo and smiled at the stilled image upon the attached video: Nicki wore a jeweled and feathered *Colombina* Venetian mask and a tight black and white costume. Toni appropriately wore a hand-painted *Gnaga* cat mask symbolic of a man who dressed as a woman.

After tapping play, a smile immediately spread to her lips.

Most likely on their lunch hour, the expanded salon team greeted her in unison with raised wine glasses. "Lizzy!"

Dressed for Italy's Carnevale "Fat Tuesday's Mardi Gras," which had come early this year in the first week of February, some smiles hid behind masks, but she could hear the jubilation in their voices. The costumes were as detailed as the masks, and made even more spectacular by the gold and black streamers and small mirrors dangling on red ribbons from the ceiling. The girls had laid out quite a spread with Italian dishes of all kinds tempting clients from the barista station.

Gina stepped from the crowd, wearing a feathered *Volto* mask, three-cornered hat, and matching black cloak. "We miss you, sis, and we are so proud of you and your promotion! Since you can't be here to celebrate with us in person, we're bringing the party to you. Oh don't worry; we're not getting into *too* much mischief, just having a blast."

"Yeah, don't you worry about us. We got news!" Nicki said.

"Ann is pregnant!" Dharma shouted.

"Guess she got lucky on one of those midnight strolls of hers," Toni added.

Gina continued, "So Stella has been very busy and keeping out of our hair. Of course, it helped that Mr. Carpo slapped her with a harassment suit and well, it turns out that Nicki's boyfriend the liquor inspector guy …"

"Johnnycakes!"

"John talked to his wiseguy friends and they told her to back off, too! Turns out that our great-grandfather was a mobster after all! Just like Stella said, but the name "Tommy the Mouth" is venerated like St. Anthony down in that *other* Little Italy. He made a respectable name for himself by moving up to Villa Fortuna. He was the only made man to get the blessing of the Black Hand to leave the Mafia. She won't be bothering us anymore!"

OMG! We were Mafia? OMG! We were *mobsters after all!* Elizabeth bounced in her seat, clapping her hands even if they couldn't see her hysterical laughter. This was an absolute hoot! Six months ago, she would have found this a blemish like no other on her past, but after all she had been through back in Belmont, the irony of it was too much to not find humor in.

The music in the salon was Dean Martin and her spirit soared at hearing the lyrics to "That's Amore." Everyone looked so happy and, to be honest, she felt left out, wishing she could be there. She could hear

Mike's caution on their third date in the back of her mind: *Be careful there, you'll end up pushing those you love further away. I've recently come to realize that the sum of our lives is not made up by career. You know what they say, all work and no play.*

Toni elbowed Nicki and she stepped forward, holding her juice glass up high. "We're gonna toast you, Doc Hollywood, because there's more, thanks to you. PalHairMo was voted Best Cultural Experience and Best Hair Salon in Westchester County! We kicked Halo's ass all ova town. Don't worry about Rusty—he was still voted number one stylist and his magic fingers are gonna do some re-vamping to make his salon a bone-fide day spa. He's gonna leave the hair and bake goods to us and lease a stylist station in PalHairMo once a week."

Now Elizabeth's tears came. A full-fledged blubber was about to begin but she quickly squashed it down. All her dreams for her sisters had come to fruition thanks to Prozia and Villa Fortuna. Even Mr. Carpo helped them to reach their full potential. She wanted to shout at the computer, "You did it! I'm so proud of you!" Her cheeks hurt from grinning so wide.

"Everyone in the building is asking for you," Gina said with a mischievous grin that tipped Elizabeth off to something being afoot, but she discounted it.

"My dad came into a windfall, and the bakery as well as the building is getting a facelift. Just like what you and the salon did for me and the girls, Lizzy," Toni added. "You gave us wings to fly!"

"Now don't let us fool you too much, 'cause it wouldn't be *Carnevale* without *some* mischief making, and you know just how good I am at that," Gina continued taking off her mask. "Remember: "A *Carnevale Ogni Scherzo Vale*"—anything goes at carnival! We are kicking awf Lent and it's a time of renewal. It's not about denying yourself pastry or wine."

Toni gasped.

"It's about tearin' down walls and opening your heart to everything from Gawd. Part of *our* continued reinvention is that we hired a marketing director to help PalHairMo get on social networking. She's someone who loves us and the salon, someone we consider part of *famiglia*, and she has a few words about Villa Fortuna's so-called investor. So listen to her and your big sister and embrace Lent tomorrow when you get your ashes." Gina wagged her finger. "Today is the last day of your masquerade.

We all love you and we want you to be as happy as you deserve, as happy as you helped us become. Stop hiding and take away the mask, sis, 'cause you know in your heart where you're happiest and who makes you happy. Don't forget Daddy's advice: 'A happy heart is better than a full purse.'"

A shorthaired blonde woman wearing a traditional full-faced *Arlecchino* (harlequin) mask stepped forward. She shifted slightly and clenched both hands before releasing the tension to remove her mask.

Elizabeth thought her heart would stop. Mia waved at the camera with her free hand. "Hi Lizzy. Do you remember me? I'm Mike's sister, Mia. I just wanted to tell you that he thinks about you a lot, like all the time. That article in *Panache* magazine is even on the refrigerator. Lizzy, he's not the man you might think he is. That MAA Facebook thing was very misleading, all of it lies, and he took legal action against the slander. Check for yourself; the page is gone. Mike's not a player—he is and always has been a one-woman man, you being the woman for him. He told me so!"

Elizabeth's tears fell as her heart clenched at that last proclamation. She paused the video, walked to her office door, and then closed it. *Could I really have been so very wrong about him?* That was a rhetorical question, of course. She knew: Danny Tucci started that bias, Richard Fairchild reinforced it, and Frankie Puppino and Salvatore Carpo and a myriad of others along the way perpetuated it, but *she* had succumbed to *her* stereotyping all on her own. The second she heard that Mike was of Italian descent she convicted him of philandering, never allowing the consideration that his being touted as a "breast man" was simply because he was a cosmetic surgeon. She never even considered this circumstantial evidence as entirely false. Mike had never behaved in such a way—had never disrespected her—but she refused to remember the good things, the true things about him.

Swiping at her cheeks with one hand, she settled back down at her desk, her heart thundering.

The tears renewed when Mia continued. "He misses you so much, and he's not interested in Villa Fortuna, only one of its owners. I know you're thinking that he sent me to do his dirty work in the hopes of making things right between the two of you, but he didn't. He's been emailing you every day since you left without a reply to his apology, and I was thinking that maybe they went into your junk mail. Gina said that you blocked his texts, so I'm assuming you did the same for his email. He's truly sorry for having dissed you the way he did. You see … my grandmother had these photographs taken of you and well, Mike thought that *you* were cheating on *him*! Isn't that cray-cray?"

"So what she's sayin', sista, is get off your sorry ass, remove the pole, and read those emails 'cause that man is in love and you need to come home 'cause you're in love, too."

"Yeah, what she said!" Mia shouted as she put her arm around Nicki and everyone moved together hugging one another.

"We love you, Lizzy! Come home to Belmont. Come home to Villa Fortuna and PalHairMo!" Toni cheered.

"Come home to Mike!" Mia said before the video went to black.

Elizabeth closed the email then shut her eyes, taking a renewing breath. Gina, in all her "stupid" wisdom was the smartest woman she knew.

Admittedly, she had almost everything, yet still had absolutely nothing. Those Italian proverbs were friggin' brilliant! It took only three weeks in Belmont to transform her life and wants, never before realizing just what she truly needed. Mike was the missing, long desired, final piece of her heart but family, friends, and caring for and celebrating with them was what made her soul sing. As Gina had once said, she had lost her compass. Homeless, she had wandered in the desert for far too long and as though rescued, she was now thinking straight. No wonder she felt so much for that homeless man back in New York; she could identify with the isolation, hers was self-imposed and a result of unwarranted embarrassment and broken heartedness.

Clicking the junk folder, there were at least sixty e-mails from Mike Garin amidst spam mail staring back at her.

Feeling the blood surge to her temples, she scrolled downward, and although she had to leave her office for Greenwald's consult, she could not help herself in opening the oldest first.

Dear Elizabeth,

I just left your sisters' apartment. In fact, I'm sitting in the car hen-pecking this message on my iPhone. My hand is shaking because I'm so upset by what has transpired between us. I tried to telephone you, but you're most likely still in-flight on your way back to LA. I need to talk with you. I need to apologize for my treatment of you, and explain why I acted in such a reprehensible, rude manner. I am such an ass! Everything—including what you think you saw and read about me—is entirely untrue. However, one thing is true. I meant it when I said it that night at the apartment. I'm in love with you, Lizzy Clemente, and I want you to stay in New York—with me, your Italian-American innamorato, your destiny. Please call me when you land in LA.

Yours, Mike

Frantically she opened the next message:

Dear Elizabeth,

I know you're mad. I know how it seems, but it's not what you think. As I told you the night we went to the Christmas House, I closed my account on eDating. I'm not interested in anyone but you. That humiliating Facebook page has been growing over this last year. Started by an obsessed patient, she and her friends have found great humor—and lust—at my expense. Everything is deliberate innuendo, all of it lies. I'm so sorry that it hurt you and sorry that you think I deceived you about Villa Fortuna. Truly, I did not know who you were other than the woman I fell in love with you the moment I saw you. What we did, the things we said, how we felt were real and from the heart—all of it. Please believe me, Elizabeth, that man you assume me to be is not who I am. Look into your heart, and it is there that you will find the truth. I'm crazy mad in love with you and I want to make you as happy as you deserve.

Please telephone me. We need to discuss the foolish assumptions that we both *made from damaging gossip and appearances. Please give me a chance to make this right. I won't give up on something that was so right from the start.*

Yours, Mike

Oh God! Her hands flew to her face and she wept, holding in the cries.

"Dr. Fairchild, Dr. Greenwald is ready for you now." The manager spoke over the desk telephone intercom.

Elizabeth looked to heaven and wiped her tears, biting her lip. Now hungry to devour each word of Mike's to forever banish away her pre-conceived notions and foolish discrimination, she needed hours to tear into every one of those emails.

"I'll be right there. Thank you, Mary."

Pushing away from her desk, she stood and decided to stop fighting her heart. Forty-two days was long enough. Opening the desk drawer, she removed her cell phone then scrolled through the photographs until finding the one her soul yearned to gaze at: that magical night she and Mike visited the Botanical Gardens. Yes, it had been the first stirrings of the *L* word. Once again, fighting the tears, she smiled wistfully at their image. *Help* me *to make this right, Lord. Show me the truth. Ready my heart for Lent. Help me make amends for being such a total jackass to this wonderful man.* Taking a deep breath, her finger trembled when it touched the screen smoothing down Mike's face. "I will make this right."

Four minutes later, with her heart still thundering, she walked down the hallway toward exam room number six, passing the pharmaceutical closet. Two senior associates within were having a hushed conversation, but one word caused her to stop and linger: Elizabeth.

"Of course they're asking for Elizabeth. That article has doubled our patient load. We're damn lucky she came back to WHPC, and thanks to her, I've been booking some prime surgeries."

"She's easy on the eyes, too. Hell, if I didn't think Melissa would find out, I'd have tapped that months ago."

Another cheating *cazzo*! She heard the other physician chuckle and her face burned with anger. Torn between curiosity and her knee-jerk reaction to storm in, she held back, needing to hear the whole story.

"Marriage hasn't stopped you before. Look, don't get yourself into the same position that Al found himself in. We're lucky "Tits" didn't slap us with a sexual harassment lawsuit. Thankfully, the partners appeased her with that shit office none of us wanted. Without her, there goes some of Hollywood's biggest talent with terrible feet, so keep your dick in check."

"Yeah, I know. I heard from Al's secretary that they pulled out all the stops to bring her back. The other partners said that if he didn't do some major sucking up, he was out. They weren't about to miss the opportunity the article presented."

"Yeah, but there's a physician on the East Coast who's been telephoning her, trying to woo her back to New York. Al gave reception strict instructions that Elizabeth isn't to receive any personal phone calls.

There's a list of questions callers must answer before connecting to her. We can't take the chance on her having second thoughts."

"I heard that, too. Apparently, he's a plastic surgeon sending her flowers—as though that would be enough to entice her away from West Hollywood. Although, if I recall, Al sent Melissa and me symphony tickets when he was wooing me. Women are suckers for music and flowers."

"That would be a sweet gig for her. How did they know he's in plastic?"

"Simple Google search. Manhattan something."

Elizabeth audibly gasped, promptly covering her mouth with one hand and balling the other into a fist at her side. Now Greenwald was messing with her love life! Well, not that she actually had one. Said love life with said plastic surgeon was currently in need of resuscitation. *Flowers! Are they the ones sitting on the reception desk four weeks in a row?*

Down the hall, Al stepped out of the exam room. "Dr. Fairchild, we're waiting on you," he said.

Taking a deep breath, she put her shoulders back. "Right. I'll be right there."

She opened the closet door, met by two surprised physicians she knew to be first class a-holes before this demonstration of male chauvinism. "For your information, *gentleman,* I wouldn't sleep with either of you if you were the last men on earth. But with that said, I thank you for the information you so unguardedly voiced. I can see I was misled into coming back to WHPC. Perhaps, my place *is* back in Manhattan." She took a step away, but doubled back with a smile. "Perhaps, I'll take that plastic surgeon up on his offer. A lab coat with my name on it is already waiting for me."

~**~

"You're sure about this, Mike?" Gwen asked. She and their nurse stood at the reception desk dumbfounded.

Mike rested his elbows on the counter and smiled proudly. "Yeah. I'm sure. I've thought hard about it over the summer and now's the time. We'll close the practice for the months of April and May, regroup and rebrand, and then re-open June 1st practicing very little body sculpting. Mia is going to work with me on *re*-social networking, website creation, and marketing, and I'll work on establishing my credentials outside of *cosmetic* surgery. My lawyer has already taken care of that Facebook issue, and I hope within the week to hire a firm to send out letters to our patients referring them to Dr. Anzalone. I count him as one of the best contour physicians in the city."

"And your pro-bono work?" Meghan asked.

"Nothing will change there—if anything there will be an increase. But overall things will change in regard to my private practice. Within a year, I hope to have built a clinic on solid, life-enhancing plastic and reconstructive surgery. In time, I'll bring in other adjunct physicians."

Gwen grimaced. "What about your dad?"

"It was a fight, but it's done. The MAA corporation has been dissolved. The practice is solely mine. I hope you are both still on board, still interested in hanging around with me … only this time building something truly meaningful." He looked at Gwen, giving her a hopeful expression of pleading.

"Of course I'll stay on board. You're the best boss in Manhattan, and to be honest, I'm sick of these society women. Can we institute a casual Friday?"

"You got it." He looked at his watch then smiled, feeling as though the weight of the world had been lifted this last month. "I gotta get out of here. The closing is in a couple of hours downtown."

"Oh that's right!" Meghan effused. "I bet you're so excited to be rid of the condo."

"I am, but mostly I'm excited for Mia. It's remarkable what a job and new home in a different section of the city has done for her self esteem. I'm so proud of her, and so thankful to the Clemente sisters for the marketing position they gave her at PalHairMo. Maybe I'll bring them a puppy next month. Their salon feels like home to so many of their clients and Mia that I bet *un cucciolo* would fit right in. Thankfully, they've moved on from my grandmother's antics."

"So you're speaking to Mrs. De Luca again?" Meghan inquired, having been present in the office when the shit hit the fan the day after Dr. Fairchild left for LA.

"How can I not forgive her? She's a master at Italian guilt. I believe she recognizes the damage her lies wrought, and I'm going to hope that she's sorry for them. Perhaps Ann's unfortunate circumstance is forcing Stella's nonna-esque manner."

"So you're happy, right?" Gwen asked.

"Don't I look happy?"

"On the outside, but I think you're still pining for that Dr. Fairchild."

He shrugged. "I might always. Misjudging and offending her will be the greatest error of character in my life. You know, when growing up, I was given good principles by my mother. So I honestly don't know why I chose to believe gossip and slander over the character of the woman I adore. If I can't right that wrong with her personally, then I'll make amends in other ways. Breaking her heart and letting her go was the biggest mistake."

"But if you *could* make amends, what would you do?"

"I tried everything, even telephoning her practice, sending her flowers, texting, emailing, calling her cell. There's never a reply. Her sister, Gina says that she just needs a little time. I'm afraid the ball is in her court."

Meghan reached out, careful not to touch his skin. She knew how obsessive he was about contact, even more so this last month. "Go after her, Mike."

"I've thought about that, but her career is taking off. All her dreams have come true. I don't know that she has room in her life for me, and I don't want to be a distraction. She's worked hard for the success she has now. My showing up would only complicate her life. Elizabeth is extremely focused in her career."

"I'm sure not *all* her dreams have come true. She's a woman. I don't care what you say; every woman hopes for their knight in shining armor—career or not."

Mike gazed at the framed professional photograph of the Botanical Gardens newly installed in the reception area. He smiled. "Maybe I will go after her. With the office temporarily closing and the two of you in charge of the details, it'll be the perfect time to visit the West Coast."

~**~

"Grrr! That man is infuriating!" Elizabeth complained behind the closed door of her private office. Al's "consult" was no consult at all, just one stuck-up A-lister who thinks himself God's gift to women. He had leered at her bosom, making one sexual innuendo after another as Al sat idly by with that smug look upon his face. Obviously, the jackass's nose was out of joint when the actor asked for her second opinion. Therefore, any actual medical advice to the man was shot down by the senior partner as soon as it exited her mouth.

"Nothing has changed! Nothing at all!"

This was the first opportunity she had to blow off the steam. Immediately after said consult, she was called into exam room number two where her new patient waited for her. Keeping her cool and replacing the telltale thin lips with a million-watt smile was difficult, but she managed to comfort the woman suffering with post-polio syndrome.

Now, standing at her desk, she placed her hand above her heart attempting to quell the furious beat, but it was for naught. Her head was reeling from that fortuitous eavesdropping. Had she not been called for the consult, she would have missed the information imparted, and still been delusional about her value in the practice, about her friggin' windowed office! Not only was she wooed back to WHPC under false pretenses, but Mike had also telephoned and sent flowers—repeatedly over these five weeks! That alone caused a burning anger to her cheeks. She breathed heavily, willing herself to cool off before making a rash decision. Her hands balled into tight fists at her side until she gripped the edge of her desk to keep from storming into Al's office. No, she needed to be calm and cool when she quit this shit practice for the second time. "Focus, Lizzy. Calm your temper."

She glanced down at the mail resting upon the corner of the blotter, then promptly tore into the top envelope embossed with the familiar triangular logo of the American Diabetes Association (ADA).

She read, zoning out to her surroundings and honing in on the invitation in her hands. The Red Ball Gala. Any remaining doubt cleared from her mind. She wanted to go home to where she belonged, where she was happiest. She wanted to be with Mike and all he had to offer, and she wanted to give him all the love she had in her heart to give. Although she would, reading his other emails wasn't necessary to make her decision. Elizabeth Fairchild had known all along that the spirited Lizzy Clemente in her had acted too impulsively, as evidenced by her heart and head battling since she got on that flight back to California.

Her heart rate increased so fast that she felt it against her chest wall when she cradled her mobile phone in the palm of her hand, tapping in Mike's office number.

"Hi. Is this Gwen? It's Dr. Elizabeth Fairchild. I met you in December when I visited the practice … No. Wait. It's actually you I want to speak with. I'm coming to New York and thought…"

~**~

~Twenty-Eight~
Dean Martin
(Dino Crocetti)

According to Gina, St. Valentine's Day was another one of those saintly interference days when supernatural things happened in the name of love, and, for once, Elizabeth was banking on that. She was also counting on Mike's attendance to tonight's American Diabetes Association annual fundraising event: the Red Ball Gala.

The last time she was at this grand hotel was with Salvatore Carpo during Christmas week. She smiled at the recollection of dining at the Bull and Bear and how he had tried to seduce her. That night, she couldn't remain mad at him. It was just his nature and, as she had come to realize, was the nature of so many others—specific ethnic proclivity or not. He was just a man in the end and had become someone that she could count on when it came to the professional interest of her and her sisters.

She smoothed her hand down the silk chiffon of her gown and straightened her posture to inspect each attendee in the ballroom, looking for one man in particular. Nervous was hardly a word for what she felt. As expected, she was awash with anxiety and insecurity, but came with the necessary accessory: Aunt Maria's rosary tucked in her purse for luck. A waiter walked past her and she grabbed a champagne flute from his tray, just because she needed something to do. Besides, it cooled her sweaty palms. Networking was the farthest thing from her mind tonight. There was only one partnership she wanted to make.

Her eyes continued to scan the guests, examining each back—and backside—of tuxedoed men on the dance floor if she couldn't see their face. Mike would be here; she was sure of it.

Elegantly lit by the magnificent chandelier and the balcony hanging fixtures, the Grand Ballroom looked resplendent. Decorated in varying shades of red, it expressed romance on this Valentine's Day. Garnet satin entwined with twinkling lights swagged from one opera box to the next on the balcony above the ballroom. Alternating white and scarlet colored tablecloths accented the plush carpeting and towering floral centerpieces. It felt magical and, like many of the female attendees, the color of ruby was Elizabeth's choice of evening gown. Confident that Mike's first destination would be the bar for a glass of wine, she stood waiting for him in silent prayer at the one and only bar beside the stage. Gwen had assured her of his attendance. Mike had taken the bait: hook, line and sinker and had no inkling of his assistant's mischief matchmaking when she mentioned the gala. Apparently, he was eager to attend a function to benefit diabetes, and Elizabeth wondered if he knew about her father. Perhaps their afternoon at MAA had left an impression on him.

On stage, the orchestra played a Cole Porter song, and an older gentleman approached her wearing a pleasant smile.

His British accent sounded very continental when he invited her to dance.

"Thank you, no. I'm waiting for someone."

"He's a fortunate man."

She smiled pensively, divulging more than necessary but feeling compelled. "I hope he thinks so. If he'll have me, then I know I'll be a fortunate woman."

A couple beside them laughed and the din in the ballroom seemed oppressive. She could feel the disconcerting, anxious perspiration form upon her bare back. The man leaned closer to her ear.

"If he doesn't show, *I'd* like to have you. Maybe we can get together after the gala if you don't want to go home alone. It is Valentine's Day, an evening set for romance."

Cazzo! The smile vanished from her lips. "Excuse me," she huffed, turning from him, refusing to give into her overwhelming desire to slap him. She left the jerk standing there—arms impotently hanging and mouth gaping open—most likely with a few little blue pills burning a hole in his pocket, ready to get him "up."

When the music came to a slow stop the President of the ADA walked to the podium. Through the crowd, Elizabeth navigated toward her designated seat at the banquet table. The overhead screen above the orchestra lit up and the chatter lessened as attendees found their seats. Appearing as though sentry, she fretfully stood beside her chair with her eyes locked on the set of closing double doors.

Her heart thundered in her ears.

Please come! She willed over the pounding.

The last door closed and she was the lone figure standing in the ballroom, back to the podium, facing the doors, the seat beside her still empty.

Dashed, her heart sank with her body down into the decorative dining chair and, making matters worse, she could feel the inquisitive stares of the other six guests at her table.

She meekly smiled, brushing the hair from her shoulders. "He must have hit traffic."

One sip of champagne, led to two, and then another glass, and although her vision remained fixed upon the speaker as he discussed the year's newest drug advancements, the only thing she could focus on was her disappointment that Mike was not seated beside her. Nicki was right: she had effed this up—big time! Her mind worked furiously to come up with Plan B. Perhaps tomorrow she would stop at his office. Maybe all this drama was pointless. Certainly a phone call would suffice.

The server came to stand to the right of her, filling the flute as he towered above her. She glanced up at him, mouthing "thank you," resisting the urge to ask him to leave the bottle.

The chair to her left slid out.

She stopped breathing.

Oh God! He's here!

Continuing to look away, she fought the knee jerk reaction to grin like a fool, and bit her lip as her stomach did some funky tremble inside. Unable to turn to make eye contact once he was settled into his seat, all but one of her senses came alive at Mike's presence. The familiar scent of his woodsy cologne tickled her olfactory's recollection; she couldn't help but close her eyes and inhale. His breath sounded labored as if he had run to the event. Her body could feel the heated energy expending from his. Her mouth remembered how sweet his tasted with every kiss he bestowed.

The moment had arrived. Her big reveal. How should she react? What should she say? Suddenly, the planned pretense of this "serendipitous" meeting and all that she wanted to express to him died upon her lips. She felt tongue-tied and continuing to look away, her mind scrambling for something witty—or endearing—her eyes fighting the pull to confirm her instinct that it was him and not another who sat beside her.

The ballroom darkened and the video on stage began.

A flash of an idea formed in Elizabeth's mind. Shifting her bottom in the seat, she crossed her legs then gently bumped her red stiletto into his calf, followed by a languid glide of her foot up and down.

She waited for his reaction, hoping he would remember her under-the-table flirts with him at the symposium the day of their first meeting.

No response came from him, so she again tapped her foot into his leg.

A second later, Mike's strong hand reached across her, their shoulders almost touching as he picked up her champagne glass.

Goose pimples formed on her arms, her stomach clenching within. She felt like she did that afternoon at MAA before his arrival to his office.

Slowly, she turned her head, twisting her lips into a saucy smile. Observing how he drank from the flute, their gaze locked over the rim of the crystal glass. There was an unmistakable twinkle in his eyes and it wasn't from the bubbly. She had seen this twinkle before: the night at the conservatory when they took the photograph.

Mamma Mia, he looked incredibly handsome wearing a black tux and a teasing smile when he placed the drink down on the table. His gaze never left hers.

"I know you," she quietly said, leaning toward him so the other guests would not overhear them. Unable to contain her own playful smirk, she added. "You're that plastic surgeon named Michelangelo."

"Nope. That's not me. You definitely have me mistaken for someone else," he whispered back, the playful quirk to his lips evident.

"Yes. I believe so. In fact, I'm confident that you *aren't* him. That guy's a Casanova."

He whispered in her ear. "Then it couldn't be me because I'm a one-woman man. You look familiar, too. What's your name?"

"Dr. Lizzy Clemente."

He beamed and so did she. She felt the elation grow from her heart, which was about to burst. She hadn't referred to herself with pride like that in a long time. His teasing her confirmed that he accepted her—the whole shebang. Of course he did. He was just like her: the great-grand-child of an immigrant Italian mobster!

"Haven't I seen you around Little Italy?" he quietly quipped.

"You have. I was born and raised on Arthur Avenue in the Bronx. I'm looking to relocate to the city from LA. Do you know of any podiatry positions open?"

"I may." His captivating blue eyes held her in their hypnotic spell. "Will you be staying for the duration—in the city, that is?"

"Yes, permanently. You see, I left my heart here and according to my very wise sister, home is where the heart is."

In the darkened room, he silently took her hand in his resting upon the table, his fingers smoothing hers, the tingle spreading up her arm. His sweet expression and eyes filled with love caused her own to pool with tears.

She leaned toward him, whispering in his ear. "You are my heart, Mike. I love you with every beat."

His hand cupped her cheek, their expressions one in the same. He blinked his eyes, and tilted his head searching her face. He gave her a glorious smile, and she knew then that he forgave her.

Unable to resist the breath-taking woman who had stolen his heart months earlier, Mike's fingers reveled in the softness of her face. He kissed her gently, his lips surrounding hers right there at the banquet table.

Just as Gina had said, it took time, patience and a few prayers. His Sicilian goddess had come home to the open door of his heart. Seeing her sitting there as soon as he entered the ballroom was an ecstatic shock. Those cascading waves of her dark hair were the immediate giveaway, but the planes of her bare back told him that she had definitely returned. He had resisted the urge to place his hand above the pounding cadence in his chest the moment his mind screamed "Elizabeth!" She had come—for him. No wonder Gwen was so insistent when he had tried to back out of attending the gala earlier in this afternoon.

As soon as Lizzy's foot tapped his under the table, he knew everything would be right between them. Perhaps she finally read his emails or Gina had decided to counsel her after all. Whatever it was, it was a blessing.

Their lips separated and his thumb smoothed against her cheek. "It was St. Nicholas," he whispered. "The Feast Day, our meeting at church. It all taught me to hope."

"It was Villa Fortuna—the house of good fortune, Mike. I'm so sorry for misjudging you."

"There's nothing to be sorry about. This was all destiny. I love you."

_~**~_

The video ended and the lights increased within the ballroom. The orchestra began to play again, and Mike promptly stood, not about to miss the opportunity to hold her in his arms.

He slid the chair back and held out his left hand to her. "I know it's not the moonwalk, but would you care to dance?"

A male vocalist came out onto the stage, singing his rendition of Dean Martin's romantic ballad "Kiss."

Mike's hand rested upon the small of Elizabeth's back and he pulled her closer. The scent of her hair and the feel of her body pressed against his felt like home. She was the final piece to his future and absolute happiness. All the misunderstandings seemed to have disappeared, been forgotten; they seemed so inconsequential now. They closely swayed to the music, their steps across the dance floor were unhurried, their surroundings a blur. They couldn't keep their eyes of each other.

"I'm so overjoyed that you returned, Lizzy."

"Me, too. Oh Mike, I've been such a fool. I wasn't happy either *before* or *after* I left New York. I missed you terribly in spite of all the things I assumed about you."

"I never gave up believing that you'd come back."

"It took me awhile to allow my heart to do the thinking for a change, but I'm not leaving again. I'm here to stay.

"I do have a question though …" She furrowed her brow. "Why did you think I was with other men while dating you?"

He turned her under his arm. "In a crazy scheme to acquire Villa Fortuna, my grandmother hired a private investigator to follow you. The morning after I stayed at your sisters' apartment, I found Vinnie's flowers in the closet and over lunch that day Stella showed me photographs of you with Toni, Danny, Carpo, and Vinnie. Like that Facebook page, it was circumstantial of course. There were photographs of you dining with Carpo, here at the Waldorf, and it gutted me to think you were intimate with him."

"From the moment we met there has never been anyone other than you." She touched his temple. "Only you."

Mike bent, and kissed her with smiling lips. "We *will* resume what we started that night."

"I hope so. You, um, have tormented my dreams these past miserable five weeks."

"Then I hope to make it up to you by sweetly tormenting every waking hour."

They danced in silence for a moment, both lost in their memory of the intimacies they shared on the sofa that snowy night in December.

"You may run into opposition from your grandmother," she finally blurted.

"I don't think she'll take up that argument again."

"I hope not."

"I think you'll be pleasantly surprised by all the changes taking place, especially in my own life."

"Tell me!"

"Well, you've inspired me. Your dedication to your career was the impetus for me to finally move forward. I've taken steps to re-branding my practice and dissolved the MAA corporation. Effective June 1st, I'll be focusing solely on reconstructive surgery, free and clear from my father's influence."

"I am so happy for you. Congratulations. How do you feel about that? Are you scared?"

"A little intimidated but I can't wait."

He could see the admiration in her eyes, her excitement for him evident.

"There are other changes, too…"

"Oh yes, my sisters mentioned that Ann is having puppies soon."

He laughed. "She is, and Stella is preparing Hillside Manor with housebreaking training pads, a heat lamp, even pink and blue booties. She's hired an expert to whelp the litter. So my grandmother has been super busy and out of everyone's hair, thank God. I never imagined that her taking in a stray dog would eventually make a nonna out of her. It's a real metamorphosis, now that she accepts that Villa Fortuna is out of her grasp."

"I guess all those nights sneaking out caught up with the poor pooch. But can Stella accept mixed breed puppies in her home? Who knows what kind of dog her Antoinette shacked up with? That little Lhasa Apso might well have found herself a Cirneco stud from Sicily and then what will your grandmother do?"

Mike laughed. "Well, she better deal with it because her grandson has permanently committed his heart to a feisty Sicilian-American woman."

"Uhh, there's something you should know about me, Mike: my great-grandfather was Mafioso."

"Oh yeah? So was mine. In fact, they knew each other."

"Unfathomable." Elizabeth laughed then sobered slightly, arching an eyebrow. "Did I hear you say, 'permanently', Dr. Garin?"

"Yes. Permanently, Dr. Fairchild."

"You can call me Dr. Clemente, you know."

"I'd rather call you Dr. Garin."

"I like the sound of that, but you'll have to change the embroidery on my lab coat."

**

~Twenty-Nine~
Sempre Felici e Contenti
(Happily Ever After)

The towncar carrying Lizzy and Mike pulled up in front of Messina bakery and double-parked before the lovers' mouths separated in good-bye. Heated to the core, in spite of the chill outside, they panted with flushed cheeks and swollen lips like teenagers ending a date.

"Are your sisters expecting you?"

"Not really. I think Gina hoped I'd go home with you tonight. She didn't say anything apart from reminding me to use protection."

He chuckled, and she knew he recalled the sleepover when they *almost* consummated their relationship.

"I'll walk you up," he offered, fixing her evening wrap around her shoulders.

"No, really, you don't have to. I have a key. Will you call me in the morning?"

He laughed. "Absolutely."

"What's so funny?"

"Nothing. Really, let me see you to the door."

"Fine. If you insist, but be careful not to lean against the building's exterior. They are painting after having restored the inside of the apartment building."

Mike exited the car then held out his hand to assist her, drinking in those sexy legs of hers when the slit of her gown shifted in her exit.

Before walking toward the entrance, Elizabeth stood at the curb with her arm tucked into the crook of Mike's. She recalled her arrival on December 4th when Dean Martin's voice filled the Avenue with holiday spirit. God—how she wanted to bolt at that moment. But now ... now

324

she felt entirely different. Arthur Avenue truly was a marshmallow world year round. A feeling of absolute contentment spread over her. Her sisters were overjoyed when she showed up on their doorstep this morning—and so was she. Coming home did something to her soul. After all, she'd always be a girl from the neighborhood.

Mike tilted his head, searching the expression upon her face. "Are you okay?"

"I couldn't be better."

"I'm glad. So, you're happy to be back in Belmont?"

"Yes. It's home. It always will be. My aunt Maria was right, by running from my background and my faith, I ran from who I was. Born Italiano, always Italiano. I love this place."

He smoothed a loose tendril from her temple, tucking it behind her ear. "Then you should never live anywhere else than here."

Together they walked arm-in-arm to the door concealed below metal scaffolding. Each step felt more grounded than ever before. Her true future—not the one she tried to mold herself into, in a place where she never fit in, where happiness always eluded her—was all around. Beside her was Mike, her *innamorato* who would share their destiny; just up the stairs were her sisters, whose good intentions were born out of love and family; and up and down Arthur Avenue was the community that had loved her like the daughter she was. She was where she should have been all along: Home.

"I bet it's a nice surprise to see your sisters' building under construction."

"It is. Mr. Primo sold the building and the new owner is putting on a fresh face. I'm sure that if any Cladosporium or Penicillium mold had existed in my sisters' apartment, they're gone now.

Their apartment was the third one renovated. In only five weeks, they have an entirely new place, no more stained ceiling or press and peel tiles, but they kept the tub."

He smirked and she figured it was in response to the tub and its grape juice rings.

"I'll have to stop by and see the facelift. Maybe tomorrow we can all have lunch. You can invite Mr. Gracioso with that baseball bat of his and of course, Josie, Toni, Mrs. Genovese, and Mr. Primo. I'll invite Mia up and even cook. You can bake something yummy for dessert. No doubt they'll all be so happy to see you."

They stopped in front of the apartment building entrance and Elizabeth gazed at him, silently questioning how he knew the names of the entire "Messina family."

"That sounds great." She slid the key into the door and turned the knob, feeling disappointed. "Regrettably, this is good-night, until tomorrow—"

"Well, let me walk you up."

"And you'll give me a proper goodnight kiss at the threshold of my sisters' door? Always such a gentleman," she teased desiring so much more than a kiss.

Mike grinned, threading his fingers with hers as they ascended the steps.

"I had a wonderful time tonight, Mike."

They stopped on the second floor landing and he turned to kiss her, one hand smoothing down her arm teasingly. "Me too, but the night doesn't have to be over, *bella*. I, um, had plans for you and me to pick up where we left off in December."

"But the girls …"

The bewildered expression on her face made him chuckle and he kissed her again as his other hand reached into the pocket of his tuxedo jacket. He withdrew a key.

"Don't worry about them. They won't hear us," he said, sliding the key into the apartment door next to them. "They're one flight up."

Elizabeth's jaw dropped when the door opened. "You … you … live here?"

Mike chortled. "Of course I do. Mia lives one flight below. We purchased the building."

She threw her head back, her laughter filling the hallway. Mr. Primo opened the door above them as Mike tugged her into his apartment.

They stood just inside the open door, the jubilance enveloping them tempered to playfulness then passion. "I'm looking for a new roommate. Are you interested?" he asked.

In a heartbeat, she consumed his smiling lips, and he slammed the door behind them with his foot as his arms wrapped around her body.

"Welcome home, Lizzy."

~La Fine!~
(The End!)

Italian Wedding Cookies

1 ½ cups unsalted butter softened
¾ cup powdered sugar
¼ tsp. salt
1 ½ cups finely ground almonds
1 ½ tbsp of vanilla extract
3 cups sifted all-purpose flour
1/2 cup powdered sugar for rolling

Preheat oven to 325 degrees F. Cream softened butter in a bowl, then gradually add powdered sugar and salt. Beat until smooth. Add almonds and vanilla then gradually add flour, mixing well. Onto an ungreased cookie sheet shape drop one teaspoon of dough, shape into crescent shapes.

Bake for 15-20 min. Do not brown. Cool then roll in powdered sugar.

~Taken from Gardiner family recipe

Glossary For the Italian Challenged:

A fanabala! – Americanized Italian curse meaning "Go to Naples."

Affabile = amiable

Agita = anxiety caused stomach pain

Andiamo = let's go!

Arrivederci = good-bye

Aiutami, per favore = help me, please!

Babbo Natale = Santa Claus

Balls of my ass = broke, no money

Bel-esprit = a woman of wit and intelligence

Bellisima = very beautiful woman

Benvenuta, bella = welcome, beautiful

Buona Fortuna = good luck

Buon sangue non mente = good blood doesn't lie

Buonasera = good evening

Buongiorno = good morning

Biscuit = slang, good looking woman

Cabbage =money

Ciao bella regazza = hello beautiful girl

Capisce = understand

Cazzo = di@k

CME = Continuing Medical Education, a state requirement for license renewal

Cornuto = mother fu*@er

Crostata = an Italian baked tart or pie

Croupier - someone who works the games in a casino

Dolcini = sweets

Facile = easy

Finito = final, done

Ginzaloon = loser Italian-American Man

Hair in an egg = nitpicking

Idioso = idiot

Innamorato = sweetheart

La dolce vita = the sweet life

Malocchio - the evil eye

Mammiaism = slang, too attached to the mother

Mangia = eat

Mantovani = an Italian orchestra conductor

Mi Scuzi - excuse me

Malocchio = evil eye

Molto bello = very handsome

O mio Dio! = oh my God!

Pace Nel Mondo = peace in the world

Pezzo di Merda = piece of sh@#

Pronto = quick, fast

Prozia = great-aunt

Puttana = whore

Sei pazzo! = you're crazy!

Short arms = cheap

Testa di cazzo = dickhead

Testa di merda = sh*thead

Un cucciolo = a puppy

Vivace and giocosa = vivacious and playful

Song references

"Marshmallow World" Recorded by Dean Martin, Reprise 1966

"Right as Rain" Recorded by Adele, XL 2008

Album: Mob Hits Christmas, Medalist Entertainment, 2000

"Do You Hear What I Hear?" Recorded by Bobby Vinton, Epic Records 1964

"The First Noel" Recorded by Connie Francis, MGM 1959

 "Dear Future Husband" Recorded by Meghan Trainor, Epic Records 2014

"All About That Base" Recorded by Meghan Trainor, Epic Records 2014

"Let it Snow! Let it Snow! Let it Snow!" Recorded by Ella Fitzgerald, Verve 1960

"What'Cha Gonna Do About It" Recorded by Small Faces, Decca Records1966

"Billie Jean" Recorded by Michael Jackson, Epic Records 1982

"Sleigh Ride" from *Three German Dances*, Composed by Wolfgang Amadeus Mozart, 1791

"December" Recorded by Earth, Wind & Fire, Legacy Records 2014

"Love Me" Recorded by The Little Willies, vocals Norah Jones, Blue Note 2006

"Houndog" Recorded by Elvis Presley, RCA 1956

"Kiss" Recorded by Dean Martin, Capitol Records1952

About the Author

Cat Gardiner loves to take you around the world in her novels, places you may never have been with music that maybe you've never heard. A member of National League of American Pen Women, Romance Writers of America, and her local chapter TARA, she enjoys writing across the spectrum of *Pride and Prejudice* inspired romance novels. From the comedic Christmas, Chick Lit *Lucky 13* to bad boy biker Darcy in the romantic adventure *Denial of Conscience,* these contemporary novels will appeal to many Mr. Darcy lovers.

"I love an adventure! So my storytelling uses fresh innovation to bring the reader on a multi-tiered journey. Incorporating technology with visuals and music, the reader becomes immersed with Spotify playlists, blogs, and inspirational image Pinterest boards. Books should be an escape to a time, place, or world where you can lose yourself."

Married 22 years to her best friend, they are the proud parents of the smartest honor student in the world - their orange tabby, Ollie. Although they live in Florida, they will always be proud native New Yorkers.

Connect with Cat here:
Catgardiner.blogspot.com
facebook.com/cat.t.gardiner
facebook.com/groups/1498363713738325
twitter.com/VPPressNovels

Other Austen-inspired books
published by Vanity & Pride Press

Lucky 13
by Cat Gardiner

Winner of Austenesque Reviews Favorite Modern Adaptation for 2014: "What a phenomenal read!! The attention to detail and the clever way the author immersed her audience in the story was such a terrific experience!"

A contemporary Austen-inspired, *Pride and Prejudice* novel - New York City advertising executive, Elizabeth Bennet is determined to find a respectable date to take to Christmas dinner with her insane family. So, what's a girl to do with only 26 days remaining? She and her best friend embark on a mad-cap dating blitz. Speed dating and blind dates become a source of frustration when one man continually shows up, hell-bent on either annoying her or capturing her heart. Fitzwilliam Darcy, wealthy, hunky, part-time New York City firefighter is Elizabeth's new client, one of thirteen men chosen for a fundraising, beefcake calendar. Sparks fly and ignite as misunderstandings abound. Sit back and laugh for an unforgettable, hot, holiday season in the Big Apple.

Denial of Conscience
by Cat Gardiner

"Denial of Conscience smolders with action, adventure, and romance. Darcy and Liz are hot together! I'd beat down Jane Austen herself for this Darcy!"

A fast-paced contemporary, Austen-inspired *Pride and Prejudice* novel - Fitzwilliam Darcy is steel, rock-n-roll, and Tennessee whiskey. Elizabeth Bennet is orchids, opera, and peaches with cream. Thrown together in a race against time to save her kidnapped father, they are physically and emotionally charged TNT, ready to explode!

Dearest Friends
by Pamela Lynne

"Dearest Friends is one of those rare stories that quickly grabs hold of the reader and never lets go; it is a thrilling ride filled with danger, seduction, romance and humor. I never wanted it to end."

A heartwarming, *Pride and Prejudice* Regency variation – Fitzwilliam Darcy and Elizabeth Bennet have both experienced betrayals that have caused them to reconsider many of their preconceived notions of life and love. When they see each other again in London, they bond over a shared grief and begin a courtship in spite of Mr. Bennet's insistence she marry another. They are supported by an unlikely group of friends and as they follow Darcy and Elizabeth on their road to happiness, connections are formed that will change their lives forever.

Sketching Character
by Pamela Lynne

"Such a book, the kind you don't want to stop reading until the end. It was fantastic! I must say I was pleasantly surprised. I laughed, I cried and so much more."

A *Pride and Prejudice* what-if variation - When a tragic event involving a beloved sister shatters Elizabeth Bennet's confidence in her ability to accurately judge a person's character, she leaves Longbourn for Kent. Carrying a secret that would ruin her family if exposed, she must deceive the ones closest to her to conceal the truth. Unexpectedly encountering Mr. Darcy on her journey, their daily encounters in the woods soothes her weathered conscience and she soon falls in love. Her doubts, along with the well-placed words of another, threaten to destroy the peace she finds in his company and she wonders if she has again failed to sketch his character correctly.

When the truth behind her deception is uncovered, will Darcy shun her as Elizabeth fears, or will his actions prove that he is the very best of men?

Made in the USA
Charleston, SC
27 February 2016